Quantum Mind

MD Hanley

Table of Contents

Copyright

ISBN 13: 978-1-7345-7279-7

Published by Hanley Adams Publishing

Copyright© 2022 MD Hanley

All Rights Reserved.

Acknowledgements

Edward T. Hanley

Throughout the writing of this book, my older brother Edward T. Hanley, has always encouraged me and given me just simple support in this endeavor, by urging me *"to just keep writing"*. It may seem simple, but to other writers who know the value of this, it is monumental.

John McKenna and Daniel McKenna

My uncle John is a Master Stone Mason in York, Maine. When I described the parts of this book with all the stone monuments, he regaled me with stories and photos of some of the most incredible stonework I have ever seen. Each stone specifically picked by himself and my uncle Daniel McKenna, placed into various sea walls, bridges, stone chimneys, retaining walls, and buildings. A lifetime of stone works to endure for centuries.

Like the stone monuments described in this book, his masonry is remarkable and has a signature of being perfectly flush, straight, and strong enough to withstand anything the northeast weather can throw at it. Like his stonework, he has endured with a strength and permanence as unyielding as the Earth. <u>As simple as that!</u>

Marcia Ann Firsick

My sister, Marcia, for her constant caring and support in writing this book. Her knowledge of graphic design, and always being there ready to help or offer advice.

Christine A. Adams

I also want to thank my mother, Christine A. Adams, for her endless editing and direction. Her guidance and mentoring have always helped me to see my way through to the end of the story.

---

*Anyone can have a great story,
but you need to be a good storyteller to
make it real and inspire imagination.*

Ogham Characters

A		N	
B		O	
C		P	
D		Q	
E		R	
F		S	
G		T	
H		U	
I		Y	
L		Z	
M			

* The Latin letters   J   K   V   W   X

do not have corresponding Ogham characters

Ogham Numbers

1		11	
2		12	
3		13	
4		14	
5		15	
6		16	
7		17	
8		18	
9		19	
10		20	

Quantum Stone Properties

Stone	Positive	Negative
*Blue	Gain Knowledge	Lose Ignorance
Red	Body Healing	Body Death
Green	Nature Healing	Nature Death
Yellow	Strengthen	Weaken
Pink	Speed Up	Speed Down
Grey	Time Forward	Time Back
Violet	Truth	Not Truth
Crimson	Heavier	Lighter
Brown	Jump To	Jump From
Orange	Visible	Invisible
*Olive	Compel	Comply
*Lilac	Protection	No Protection
White	Amplify	
*Black	Nullify	

* - Not in possession of

Prologue

In the Cygnus constellation, there is an orange dwarf type star called Tol. Tol has 5 planets orbiting around it. The fifth planet is called Ghia. Ghia is the home of a very advanced civilization. This race of people are very similar in physiology to humans, and they have evolved to gain complete mastery and control of everything that surrounds them. They have learned how to stop aging and can live for an eternity. They have mastered terraforming and have made their planet into a perpetual paradise of warmth and comfort. They want for almost nothing. Their only desire and their only vice is they always want to learn more. Knowledge is their power and their obsession.

Over the millennia, the population of Ghia has waxed and waned. Later in their evolution, this greed for knowledge caused them to argue and fight against each other. Whoever was more knowledgeable was always the victor. Knowledge of the sciences was critical during one phase of their evolution, but this changed to become knowledge of how to fight and kill. This now became the target to attain at any cost. Many of the most knowledgeable scientists of all different modalities became the threat to those who knew how to war.

Their society became fractured and almost to the point of extinction. One of the War scientists in the higher echelons of their regime found out that an asteroid was on its way to collide with Ghia in two years. This event would surely wipe out the entire population of Ghia unless plans were made now to survive this or try to alter its course.

Little groups of people started to learn about this. As news of this catastrophic event became more known, an underground movement started to form whatever scientists were left from the old days before the era of wars and fighting. They sought a way to save Ghia and the people living on it.

At this time in the history of Ghia, the planet started to become something more than just rocks, water and minerals. It started to become self-aware. It was in pain because the warring caused great damage to it over the years. It wanted to heal and help the people to learn to take care of it.

As Ghia became more self-aware and sentient, it found and sought out the people who wanted to help Ghia avoid the imminent destruction coming toward it. The people learned how to talk to Ghia and Ghia found out how to work with the people to prepare for the asteroid coming toward it.

It was at this time when the Quantum Guild was established. Ghia and the people depended on each other to get through this calamity. It wasn't going to be easy, but a plan was formed.

In the days leading up to the point when the asteroid was about to hit Ghia, the majority of the population in favor of war science left Ghia and never returned. The small fragment of civilization who remained went underground to survive the imminent disaster.

Many centuries later, after Ghia had revived and the population which remained were again living around the planet. The people helped Ghia to heal by using science and applying this to the areas which were very damaged. The planet and the people started to work together for many centuries.

Ghia knew the relationship it had with the population must not be unique. Ghia reached out to other planets which might be starting to undergo this process of self-awareness and sentience. It showed these planets and the people living on these planets how they could live together in a beneficial symbiosis where each helps the other to survive. Colonists were sent out to potential planets to assist in the awakening of these planets into sentience.

This is all recounted in the first book of this series called Quantum Genesis. This second book, _Quantum Mind_, describes the story of when the Quantum Guild reached out to the Earth and sent colonists 5000 years ago. It starts in modern day, and tells how a small group of people help them try to connect to the Earth and complete their vital mission.

Enjoy!

MD Hanley

Chapter 1 - Patrick Themis

Construction Site - Winthrop Center

Boston, Massachusetts

Tuesday 6:15 AM

Balance is a jealous mistress. Always on the lookout to upset your ordered life and throw you into chaos. Give it one inch in the wrong direction, or too little attention, it will upend your life ten times greater than you could ever imagine. Operating a large mobile building crane was like this. Be always on guard for a miscalculated balance of weight and counterweight. It's always at the ready to throw you from the sweet delicate point of balance where everything just clicked, and a beautiful harmony is attained. Patrick Themis knew this, and he has always kept his mistress' pleased and happy. At least, he thought this was true in his short history as a large building crane operator. Today, unfortunately for Patrick, wouldn't be a good day for balance.

Pat arrived at the construction site at 6:15 AM. It was Tuesday and a beautiful clear September day. Yesterday, was a scorcher and the heat and *cooling down* over night was very comfortable. He didn't stress out over the outside temperature since most of his day would be sitting inside a 6 foot by 4-foot enclosed cab operating a large crane with the A/C cranked up to high. He carried a large thermos full of scalding hot black coffee, a bag of two Boston crème donuts he bought in South Station MBTA train station's Dunkin Donuts, and a clipboard of notes and numbers for the schedule of materials he would be lifting with the crane today.

Pat has a tall athletic build which he earned from always staying active and not afraid of stretching himself physically in sports or working out. His trade of being on a construction site also helps him to maintain good physical condition with enumerable tasks which require a fair amount of strength and conditioning. His face was unremarkable but at a closer look you can see he has a kind face with piercing grey eyes and black hair. A former girlfriend had talked him into getting his hair bleached blond. It was a bet they made one night while watching the Patriots and she won. He cursed Tom Brady for letting him down in one of the only years he was not winning the Super Bowl. He made good on the bet. She was long gone but the hair stayed. He actually kind of liked having his hair with thick black roots which were almost always showing up soon after the full bleach was done. He kept his hair at a medium sized length. He had a sharp widow's peak he didn't want to advertise so he never went too short. He was dressed today the way he was always dressed, comfortable jeans, steel toed boots, and a large t-shirt.

The construction site was a large flat dirt lot with materials scattered all around a central area which housed the focus of all this activity. In this central area, a large new building was starting to take shape and would become just one more addition to Boston's skyline. From an outsider's perspective, the activity going on this morning would look like chaos. Everyone was walking around the site in every direction. Each person was singularly focused on an important task which they needed to get done. Pat liked all the movement. It was a carefully orchestrated dance and when you were on the ground, you only saw a small intersection of this orchestrated chaos. When he was in the crane and looking down at all the people below, he could get a broader view of this complicated activity. It helped to be able to see how each person was a bigger part of the whole operation. In one area, men were unloading the latest flatbed truck of pallets and materials to be used later in the day. The people in another section were preparing an area to receive a load of concrete tomorrow. Forklifts scurrying around moving piles of materials from one area to another area.

His path to the large crane which he was operating today took him on a direct line to walk past his boss, Jim Stickner. Jim was engaged in a conversation with two other foremen who were working on the lower levels of the building. He silently wished he had taken a different path, but he was committed, and it would look odd if he took any other way than to walk past Jim.

As usual, he got the disapproving side glance from his boss, as he arrived on the site. If anything, Jim's behavior was predictable. Jim would give a nonchalant glance at his watch and then the razor-blade side glance at Pat as he walked toward the area where the large building crane was left last night. Who wears a watch nowadays? He was certain he would hear about his tardiness at some point later today. Jim was the type of boss who expected you to clock in on a job 15 minutes early; and if it was any less than that, then you were late. Pat just gave him a nod and pointed at the crane with a brief smile. He knew it was laced with sarcasm, but he felt confident Jim wouldn't recognize the intention. Jim likened Pat's smile as an acknowledgment of his loyalty to working as hard as possible to get the job done. The smile took many years to perfect. His current boss, like many other bosses, was buying every ounce of it.

Pat didn't go directly to the crane. He walked over to an area in front of the crane where a group of people were huddled around a large square frame holding several slabs of granite. The steel rack was built to hold 10 monstrous sheets of granite. The frame of the rack was designed to hold each sheet vertically placed and evenly spaced by a steel pole between each sheet. Each sheet of granite was a reddish grey kaleidoscope of colored stone about 12 feet high and 15 feet long. With the sheets of granite placed in this steel rack it looked like a set of dishes sitting in a large dishwasher. Although, these dishes were quite heavy at about 2200 lbs. apiece. Today, Pat would have to take each one of these sheets of granite up to the 10th floor and place them around the center column of the building.

The outside framework of the building is way behind schedule so the more strength they can build around the central column core the better. The latest report he got was that the third floor was completely enclosed and was starting to support the weight of the upper floors. Still, seven floors of equipment and material is an awful lot of weight to carry. He should be pissed off with his boss wanting him to keep adding weight to the top floor. He let it slide. If he really looked at why he didn't make a ruckus about the schedule, he would surmise it is just easier than fighting people over it. I'm just following orders. Technically, it was an easy rationalization, but it was easier than the alternative which would get messy.

In the back of his mind, he knew he should be really raising hell about the schedule. The people around this large frame rack of granite sheets were his friends and people he has known for many years working on different jobsites. They trusted him and he had worked hard to earn their respect. They depend on you to keep them safe, and you depend on them to make sure they are keeping the way clear for you.

When he first started doing construction, he had a knack for being able to maneuver forklifts into places where others couldn't. He just had a natural talent for balancing a load and safely moving items around a site. He was always interested in the big cranes and how they worked. A big part of the job of operating a large crane was inspecting all the parts of the crane. Cranes come in all shapes and sizes, and it is important to inspect the hydraulics, or the lines doing a large part of the lifting and moving. He was always ready to help out doing some of those jobs.

About five years ago, he became friends with one of the large tower crane operators named Al Friedman. He was working on a job in a 40-story building. Pat was very low on the totem pole of workers on a construction site, so if someone wanted you to run around and be a gopher then that is what you did. It was more fun than working at a burger joint, so he didn't mind so much. This one day, Al was coming out of an elevator and bumped into someone coming around a corner too quickly. The coffee he was holding ended up falling out of his hand and splashed on the floor. After a couple of obscenities and apologies from the person who bumped into him, he looked up and saw Pat standing there watching the whole episode.

Pat went over to try and help clean up the coffee with some rags and Al asked Pat to run out to the *roach coach* to get him another coffee. This is how Pat started to learn how to operate the big cranes. At first it started to be, "hey kid, would you go out and grab me a large coffee?"

"Sure, no problem," he would say at the first couple of times he was asked. Then he added, "It will cost you 3 questions."

Pat would walk away and get Al his coffee and try to think of the best questions he could ask him when he got back. After a couple of weeks doing this, Pat brought a jelly donut one time and told him the donut would be worth an extra 2 questions.

Al started to show Pat how to operate the crane. Pat absorbed everything like a sponge. He understood the mechanics better than most people usually understood it even after several years of operating a crane. He gave him many different places he could go to learn more about it and what types of testing he would need to become certified. He even spoke to the site coordinator to see if they would pay for the cost of the testing. Sometimes, Al gave him a bunch of books and materials on the function and theory behind becoming a certified crane operator. He also allowed Pat to go up in the cab with him when he had any type of break or sometimes during his lunch breaks. He would just ask him dozens of questions like rapid fire. Al loved talking about the mechanics of operating a crane and he never got tired of the questions.

One time, Pat was in the cab booth with Al, and they were lifting a large pallet of sheetrock from an open area of the building which was 3 stories below them and lifting it to 14 floors above them. The crane they were using was a building tower crane. The crane itself is affixed to the side of the building. In order to accomplish this lift, the crane had to take hold of the pallet and lift it up about 5 feet and swing it out about 20 feet past the radius of the outside of the building; and then lift it straight up about 170 feet and then swing it back into the top floor. The only dangerous part of this was when the crane was swinging the load outside the radius of the building structure and when it was swinging inside the structure.

The mast of the crane went straight up vertically where it was met with a horizontal jib. The horizontal jib has two parts. A long horizontal structure which uses cables and pulleys to lift the load. The shorter horizontal jib is responsible for the opposing counterweight force of the weight lifted. The point where these horizontal structures met contained the motors and mechanisms to rotate these horizontal jib structures around the mast of the crane.

They had just lifted the pallet about 5 feet off the ground and were in the process of swinging out past the radius of the building. While the cab was rotating, Al jerked his hand abruptly to cause the rotation to stop suddenly. Pat saw a wild look on

Al's face, and he knew something was wrong. He yanked Al's hand off the joystick and continued the rotation to keep the load rotating and slowly brought it to a stop. If he hadn't countered the abrupt stop of the rotation and slowly slowed the rotation to a stop, then the load would start to swing. If he hadn't done this, the pallet would surely have hit the side of the building, or worse.

Pat looked at Al and his face was like he was watching melting chocolate. The left side of his face was sagging slightly. His eyes were fluttering and started to roll up toward the ceiling of the cab.

The walkie talkie next to Al came to life and barked, "Ok, Al. You're all clear and ready to lift straight up."

Pat grabbed it and said, "Ok guys. Give us just a minute here. We will let you know when we're ready to start the lift up."

It was only about 15 or 20 seconds, but Al started to come around. He looked confused.

"Al, what happened? Are you ok?"

"Yeah kid. I am fine, now. I feel sick to my stomach though."

"You stopped the rotation really abruptly and the load started to swing. I got it to keep rotating and slowed it down to stop the swing. The load is clear and ready to go up. Do you want to abort this load and come back later to try it?"

"No way, kid. Let's switch seats and I will have you do it. You have asked me enough questions already to be an expert at this job so let's have a little solo flight time."

"You sure? The guys watching us might not appreciate it if they see me behind the wheel here."

"Fuck 'em! I'm running this crane, not them."

They switched positions and Al took the walkie talkie and said, "Ok guys we are ready to lift to the 14th floor. Everyone clear of the load?"

The radio squawked back, "All clear here Al."

Al said, "Ok, Pat let's do this like I showed you. Easy on the joystick and start off slow and easy and take it straight up the pole."

It was the last time Pat worked with Al. He was in his mid-forties, and he really did enjoy talking and teaching people about cranes. He had hidden the fact he had a very mild form of epilepsy for years and the medication he had been taking to avoid seizures stopped working as well. Sometimes this happens. It might take a while to get the correct dosage or try a different medication to stop the seizures. Al decided to stop running the cranes and decided to get behind teaching and testing young guys or girls how to operate big cranes and become certified. It didn't have the same sense of excitement when he was teaching about it rather than doing it, but it still paid the bills.

Pat never told anyone about the seizure Al had. The next day, Al came to Pat and told him he was getting out of the business of operating the cranes. Pat told him he wasn't going to tell anyone about what happened the day before. Al surprised him by giving him a big hug and thanked him for helping him to find a new challenge. He was gonna start teaching smart ass kids like him on the correct way to operate a crane. Pat was surprised but really happy for him.

After Pat finished working on that building, he got his certification and was able to be low bid for the next opportunity to operate a small crane to offload ships and their cargo. Slowly he started to become more experienced and work on a variety of different projects.

Since then, Pat has worked extremely hard to get the jobs he did. Always trying to learn wherever he could, he imagined someday there would be a time when he would be in a similar position to teach someone just starting out in this field of work. He always kept himself open to the opportunity if he saw it.

For today's job, the three people standing by the steel frame had been waiting on him to arrive. Roger, Kristen, and Brad have been working with him for the last couple of weeks doing similar lifts like the one they were about to accomplish today. He got along well with them and they knew exactly what he needed them to do to get the job done safely.

"Did Jim give you the evil eye when you walked by him?" Brad asked.

Pat replied, "What do you think? I'm getting used to it. As long as I smile and give him the thumbs up, he's happy. Hey Kristen, how is your sister doing?"

Kristen let out a big sigh and said, "9 pounds 6 ounces! I got the call last night at midnight she gave birth to a whopping

9-pound baby boy. Takes after her father but OMG she's gonna be sore for weeks!"

"Congratulations! Why don't you and Brad stay down here rigging the load and if we get done a little early you can probably split and go see your new nephew." Pat turned to Roger and Brad and said, "You guys OK with that?"

They both nodded. Roger said he would go up top and clear the area out for the first load Pat would drop up there.

The three of them checked their walkie talkies and the channel they were going to use. Pat turned around and headed towards the side of the big crane. He climbed up the 20 rungs of the ladder built into the side of the crane to gain access to the interior of the cab. Once he got seated in the operator chair and harnessed up, he turned the power on for the crane and the different hydraulic systems.

The console in front of him was a myriad of dials and gauges which showed different hydraulic pressures, or power status of the different parts of the crane. The crane was made up of several parts. Behind the cab was the main boom which could be extended outward with a number of tubes fitted one inside the other. This particular crane would be able to extend out to 160 feet. One joystick controlled the left and right movement of the boom of the crane. The other joystick controlled the forward and aft movement. On the floor were two pedals responsible for retracting and extending the telescoping sections of the boom. They also control the amount of pressure being generated by the hydraulic pump. When the joysticks or pedals are used, it causes different hydraulics hoses to open or close which causes the load to be lifted or lowered. There is also a different hydraulic system at the rear of the crane which operates in the same way, but it controls the stabilizing and the counterweight and balance of the crane itself.

Pat got the boom into position and extended it out to 110 feet. Once the boom was extended, he lowered the hook and tackle block to the area above the steel rack holding all the granite slabs. Kristen and Brad used three different straps on the first sheet of granite to be lifted up. Each of these straps could be winched super tight around the piece of granite. They then hooked these straps onto the hook Pat dropped from the extended boom.

Once Kristen gave the OK signal, Roger came on the walkie-talkie and said he made a temporary holding area for the granite sheets. He told Pat he was all clear to load the lift up. Pat picked up the sheet of granite and lifted it above the steel rack and once it was clear, he rotated the crane to move the granite away from the steel rack. Once it was clear, he added more power to the hydraulic pumps to retract the cable attached to the block and tackle at the top of the boom. He wasn't in any hurry, so he just lifted it up to slowly. The wind started to pick up a little bit.

Pat watched the load of granite slowly climb up to the 10th floor. At the top of the boom was a camera allowing him to see the area below the top of the boom which gave him a view of the area where he would be depositing this slab of granite. This was very tricky because he couldn't see the area directly and needed to visualize it with the camera and commands from Roger. The landing spot was just like the place it was taken from. Roger had a similar steel frame like the one on the ground and had it all ready for Pat to position the granite and lower it into the frame.

Once Pat lowered the first piece of granite into the frame, Roger untied the winches and Pat raised the boom and swung it around to go down and pick up the second piece of granite. After a couple of minutes of going back down and grabbing a second piece of granite, Pat was once again rotating the base of the crane to move the piece of granite closer to the steel frame Roger was waiting at.

Pat was just about to lower the piece of granite down onto the frame and he noticed the floor in front of the steel frame looked strange. At first, he thought it was just the lens of the camera, but the floor looked like it was tilted down slightly and got worse as the floor extended out to the edge of the building.

Pat picked up the walkie-talkie and said, "Roger, what's happening up there? The floor looks like it is tilting down towards the edge of the building. I think the floor is gonna give way any second."

Roger squawked back, "Yeah it is tilting down some. Hold off on dropping it right now and let me check it out."

As if it was happening in slow motion, Pat started to see the whole section of the floor create a large crack going under the middle of the steel frame. Oh shit! The floor was going to give way.

Pat yelled into the walkie-talked, "Roger, get everyone to the stairs now!"

As he said this, he saw 4 people running to the stairs which would be the strongest part of the building. Pat also saw the outer section of the floor was tilting way down now and was going to separate from the building and cartwheel outward from the edge of the building. The only thing Pat could think of was the top floor would fall outside of the building edge and most likely crash into the building next to the dirt lot. With horror in his eyes, he looked at a possible crash site which would be directly on top of a school building next to the construction lot.

The only thing Pat could think of to counter the floor breaking off and cartwheeling outward was to drop the load of granite down hard. In the back of the crane was where the hydraulics were controlling the counterweights for the load on the boom right now. If he released some of the counterweight it would increase the load on the boom and force it to come down hard. It would also unbalance the crane and tilt it forward. He stomped on the pedal to release the counterweight and from the camera in the boom he watched the granite hit the floor really hard. The top floor broke free at this point and now was going to cartwheel inward to the stairs.

Pat knew this would be fatal if the floor flew into the stairs. In his mind, he imagined the floor breaking in half and then those pieces being broken in half. Surprisingly, yet not understanding how it was happening, he saw all the large sections of the floor being broken apart exactly as he was imagining them to break apart. All those small pieces were now dropping down onto the floor below. Pat knew the same exact thing was going to happen to the next floor below. It would break and then it would cartwheel outward into the school. The only thing Pat could think of was to do exactly the same thing he did before. He released the counterweight and let the boom drop the load of granite down hard. And surprisingly, the pieces he saw from the camera once again broke in half the way he imagined them breaking in his head.

He also did the same thing for the floor below and one more time for the floor below that one. When the slab of granite hit this last floor, it broke apart into three different pieces and was no longer being held by the crane. Now the weight on the boom decreased by one ton. This violently upset the delicate balance of the crane itself. Now the entire crane rose up and for almost one full second it felt like it was about to right itself and come back into balance. But it didn't. The entire crane was now removed of the weight on the boom and the counterweights were too great to keep the crane right side up. It flipped upside down onto its back. Luckily, the cab wasn't directly below the giant boom, or it would have crushed the cab. Pat hit his head severely on the side of the cab door and was momentarily knocked unconscious.

Luckily, it was still early in the day and most of the people were on the ground or working on the first 3 floors. The long boom landed on a fence around the dirt lot and landed on top of two cars. Thankfully, no one was injured.

Vaguely, Pat could hear people coming up to the cab of the crane. He was bleeding from his forehead where his head struck the side of the cab door. People were yelling and screaming, and one very boisterous woman was yelling at everyone to get out of her way. Slowly, Pat opened his eyes, and he could see Kristen yanking open the door to the cab.

"Careful, Pat, there's a lot of broken glass here. How are you doing buddy? You, OK?"

Pat looked around and a lot of people were coming over to the crane, albeit they were all upside down. Obviously, Pat was still in the harness of the seat in the cab, and he was the one upside down.

Pat said, "Yeah I think I am Ok. Can someone clear the glass out of roof of this before I release the harness."

Kristen and others got rid of the glass and helped Pat get out of the cab. When he got out of the cab, he immediately felt weak in the knees. He told the others to let him just sit down for a minute.

"Is Roger Ok?"

"Yeah, he and 3 of the other guys are coming down the stairs now. Nobody was up above floor 3 so we were lucky. Jim just about shit himself when he saw the big crane doing the complete flip."

"He's *friggin* lucky no one else was up higher than floor 3. Jeez what an asshole. You can't put so much weight on those floors without anything to support them. We should have never started putting those sheets up there."

As Pat said this, he looked over at the steel frame holding the remaining sheets of granite. They were pulverized right now underneath the bulk of the main boom of the crane. If the steel frame hadn't been there, it most likely would have kept falling more and come down heavily on the cab. The steel frame had most likely saved his life today.

Kristen handed him a moist towel and some paper napkins to put on his head. She said, "Take it easy. An ambulance is on the way here to get you sorted out."

"I don't feel so good right now."

About twenty minutes later he was in the back of the ambulance on its way to the hospital. The paramedics asked if someone was following the ambulance or would be able to help with the paperwork and point of contact for him. He pointed to Kristen and told the paramedic she was his sister and he asked if she could ride in the ambulance with them. They didn't want to, but they figured it was only about 5 blocks away and wouldn't really be a big deal. Pat winked at Kristen and said she was going to get to the hospital sooner rather than later to see her nephew.

Chapter 2 – Emergency Quench

"Fall if you will, but rise you must."

- James Joyce

Brigham and Women's Hospital Emergency Department

Boston, Massachusetts

Tuesday 10:00 AM

The ride over to the hospital was very fast. Pat was still getting his senses back to normal. The dominating thing he was feeling right now was the pounding headache he was having. He used to get occasional headaches when he was growing up, but he attributed them to stress or when he got really angry. Ironically, it was usually when he and his twin sister got into a huge all out fight, about the stupidest things.

The EMT's in the ambulance were well accustomed to all the jostling of abrupt starts and stops the ambulance driver was making. She did this in conjunction with the screaming sirens to notify the other drivers in a very impolite way to give way and yield to the ambulance. She chose the most expeditious way to progress through the congested traffic which often caused it to make sharp lefts or rights to get them to their destination. It's really fascinating to watch the people in the traffic pattern, to see how they respond to an oncoming ambulance. There are people who just instinctively yield the right of way. Others who can claim to be absolutely clueless and won't realize an ambulance needs them to yield. However, there is a small subset who are just infinitely stubborn and selfish who won't yield under any circumstances.

Thankfully, it was a short drive. When they brought the ambulance into the Emergency Department area, they opened the back doors of the ambulance. Everyone in the area was looking intently to see who was being unloaded in front of the emergency doors. They were looking for a gory and bloody scene, but the disappointment they were feeling was almost palpable when they saw it was only a young man being wheeled out of the ambulance with just a cut on his head.

He was quickly wheeled into the emergency department and brought into a little cubicle where he was moved onto a different bed. His mind was still in a little bit of shock, so all the questioning and the actions of the ER doctors was a blur. He saw Kristen off in the periphery of the group of hospital techs and nurses working around him. He looked at her and gave her a thumbs up signal and told her to go see her nephew. She said she would be back in a bit.

They got a blood pressure cuff on his arm, an oxygen sensor on his finger. The bed he was on was propped up at an angle, so he wasn't lying flat. The ER doctor came in and started to take charge of the situation and the people around him.

"Patrick, I'm doctor Kneeland. How did you get the cut on your forehead?"

"I'm a crane operator working on the new Winthrop Center building near the common. The crane became unbalanced and flipped upside down. The boom almost crushed me, but I was lucky it didn't fall on the cab, or you and I would not be having this conversation. I think I got knocked out for a little bit though. My head is killing me right now," Pat said.

"How does your neck feel? Can you turn your head to the left and to the right?"

Pat moved his head to the left and the right. The doctor pulled out a pen light and checked his pupils. He then asked Pat to move his eyes up, then down, then to the left and then to the right. They looked for other lacerations and checked his reflexes. The doctor felt his abdomen. He then asked if anything else was causing him pain.

"Just my head is throbbing right now,"

"That's understandable. I think your bump might have given you a concussion. I want to make sure there is no damage to your spine or other areas just to make sure. The scan shouldn't take too long, and we can talk some more after we get the results."

Pat was about to ask for something to help with the throbbing pain in his head, but the ER doctor had already gone out of the little curtained room.

Twenty minutes later, he was taken down to the Radiology department where he was given a set of hospital scrubs to change into. Pat was then taken into the MRI room where the scan was going to be done. This was the first time, he had ever been tested or scanned with an MRI machine. The ER physician thought he was doing the correct thing, bypassing the normal step of requesting a CT exam. Today, however, the CT exams were backed up for several hours. He decided it would be easier to just send Pat in for an MRI scan.

The room with the MRI machine was brightly lit with several overhead fluorescent lights. The forbidding tubular opening had attached to it a long narrow bed for the person being tested. This bed would slide the patient in and out of the giant maw of the machine with its powerful supercooled magnets.

It almost seemed to be a slightly sarcastic joke, but the person who designed the look of the room, created a rectangular section of ceiling tiles above the narrow bed painted in sky blue with several pinpoints of lights to simulate an early morning sunrise, or evening sunset. The room was quite tidy with just a few cabinets. A special shielded door allowed access into the room. There was also a large window of smoked glass giving the people operating the MRI machine a view into the room. Curiously, on one wall there was a large red button stating, "Emergency Quench". Like any big red button, it almost dared a person to press it.

The attendants asked Pat dozens of questions about his medical history. The questions were easy to answer since it was a "NO" on every question. Especially a double "NO" to being pregnant. He didn't have anything implanted or any metal in his body.

The women who led him into the room, motioned for him to get on the narrow little bed attached to the opening of the large MRI machine. She put a pillow under his head. She then put some earplugs in his ears and slid on a set of headphones programmed to some random music channel the technician had suggested. Finally, she put a cage-like apparatus over his head. Once he was all situated, the narrow little bed slid into the tube. He silently just hoped this wouldn't take too long.

A disembodied voice came to him from the headphones and said, "OK, Pat we are going to start the test. You will hear some loud knocking noises. This is normal and is just the magnets aligning themselves. Just relax and it will be over soon."

Pat didn't know any better, so he just responded with an "OK."

Slowly he heard the machine starting to initialize and go through its positioning of the magnets. The sounds of the magnets were very loud. The sound was like the grinding of something metal against metal. It also came in pulses. Grind, grind, pause grind, grind, pause. The sound was intensifying, and Pat could feel the noise coursing through his body. Something really strange was happening to him as each pulse of grinding noise was happening. His body started to vibrate. Vibrating in a really bad way. Not like a tremor of the hand but a whole-body twitching. Sort of like sneezing. It was an involuntary reaction his body was having. It felt like being attacked and someone punching you in the stomach when you least expect it. After the first couple of punches from the grinding sound, he instinctively pushed back. It wasn't a physical pushing back as if you are pushing back someone's arm, but more of a mind and whole body shoving back.

The grinding took a slightly higher octave of grinding, and this was the worse punch yet. He focused his mind on the machine and mentally pushed the internal parts of the MRI machine to move. He wasn't really pushing the internal housing of the tube away from him, it was more like using the force of the magnets to push against themselves. With all his might and focus he flipped the charge of the magnets to repel each other. If you have two magnets both pointing to north, they will be repelled if they get close to each other. This is what Pat instinctively tried to do.

Over the earphones he heard the technician say, "Pat, give us a sec here. We have to reinitialize the system. Just hold still and it will be over soon."

Sarcastically Pat thought, is this what the spider said to the bug stuck in its web? He acknowledged the technician and said, "Yeah, OK. Is the whole machine supposed to vibrate like this normally?"

"Hang on one sec. We are going to start this over."

Not really an answer to Pat's question but more of a stalling of what was happening. Pat was about to tell the technician he wanted to get out of this claustrophobic tube and just wanted something for his pounding head. The machine started to re-initialize and the knocking and grinding noise started over again. Grind, grind, pause, grind, grind. As each pulse came, he felt the physical punch of his body reacting to the magnets. He pushed back again this time a little harder. The noise changed to just a long grinding that didn't stop. Pat pushed a third time and then the noise stopped. They had given Pat an emergency ball to squeeze in case of an emergency. Pat squeezed the ball really hard. Nothing happened. It wasn't easy, but he started to slide out of the machine. It was made all the more difficult because of the cage-like apparatus around his head. He managed to push it out of his way and started to slide out of the tube little by little.

He got to be about halfway out of the tube and the bed started to slide out. He just relaxed and let the bed carry him fully out of the tube. When he was finally out of the tube looking up at the light blue faux sky, he could feel and see a lot of smoke and steam coming out of the sides of the MRI machine. Pat could see the technician was trying to open the door to the room but was unable to push it open. The pressure in the room was definitely different than it was before he went into the machine. He ripped off the earphones and sat up in the bed. The technician was pushing the door really hard, and it suddenly broke the pressure seal and flew open so hard it hit the wall with a loud thud.

The technician was yelling at him, "What did you do to the machine?"

Pat couldn't hear him because he still had the earplugs in his ear. The technician demanded again with his question, "What the hell did you do to this machine?"

Before Pat could respond, the technician ran over to the big red button saying, "Emergency Quench" and pushed it. Suddenly more steam and air came into the room. The technician went over to the door again and he tried to open it. It was once again stuck from the pressure differential in the room. With a huge effort and pull he was able to yank the door open.

Pat was left sitting on the narrow little table, not really sure what he was expected to do at this point. All he did know at this point was he had a massive headache and just wanted to find a less bright and less faux sky over his head. After about 30 seconds, the technician came back in. This time the door wasn't so difficult to open up. The technician had daggers in his eyes, though.

He rounded on Pat again, and demanded, "What did you do to the machine? You must have some metal or something in you, or on you, to make it act this way. Do you realize you have just ruined a multi-million-dollar piece of equipment?"

Pat looked at the guy as if he was speaking a different language. Pat was also getting annoyed with this person.

He yelled back at him, "I didn't do a damn thing to your machine. Your stupid machine was the thing vibrating the hell out of me in there. I was banging around inside there like a sneaker in a dryer. Check it out for yourself, I didn't do anything. How about you get in there and I will start pushing the buttons to have the stupid test be done on you. Let's see how you like to be inside the broken dryer. Where are my clothes? I want to get out of this place."

Surprisingly, this young tech was really pissed off. Actually, to the point of pushing Pat back down on the narrow table when he started to get up.

"Stay here!" he snapped.

Pat went instantly from being annoyed to pissed off. He shoved the guy back a little too hard and the guy bumped into a little plastic cart next to the MRI machine. The cart crashed into the wall and whatever it contained was now on the floor. This further frustrated the technician by falling completely on his back. He almost made a full recovery, but his weight and balance were just tipped in the wrong way. The technician stuck out his arm quickly to support himself so he wouldn't fall on the ground. He almost made it, but his hand hit the floor at an awkward angle. An awful sound came from his hand. It was the uncanny sound of a small bone being snapped. The kind of sound you might hear if you got the wishbone of the Thanksgiving turkey and someone pulling the other end until it snapped in half.

The technicians face and body shuddered. There was a funny delay in the sound of the bone snapping and his face displaying the shock of hearing this sound. It took a full second before the surprise of the sound and the pain emanating from his wrist to finally register in the pain receptors in his brain. He then let out a loud howl at Pat.

"Sounds like you broke something there, maybe you should get an MRI for that?," Pat said half chuckling, "Now where are my clothes?"

The door to the room opened up and a woman in hospital scrubs came in carrying a small key.

Pat asked, "Where are my damn clothes?"

She told him to go down the hallway to the end and take a right to where the lockers were. Pat quickly exited the room and figured it would be best to leave at this time. God, his head was killing him. In a few minutes he had changed back into his work clothes. He almost made it to the elevators to get out of the hospital, but a pair of hospital security guys came directly toward him.

"Sir, we need you to come with us. We have a complaint you assaulted one of the staff and damaged a very expensive piece of hospital equipment."

Pat was exhausted from this never-ending string of difficult situations he was going through today. The two security guards were very big boys and could probably wrap Pat into a pretzel in short order. Maybe Pat could use this to his advantage.

He exhaled slowly and said, "OK boys, I'll go with you, and I won't give you a hassle but, first you gotta get me some Tylenol. I flipped a huge crane on its back this morning, so I'm having a bad day."

They each looked at each other and exchanged some kind of informal dialogue. The bigger of the two of them reached into his pocket and pulled out a small bottle of extra-strength Tylenol pills. He gave Pat 2 large capsules. The other one pushed the "up" button for the elevator. Pat "dry swallowed" the two Tylenol and hoped it would relieve this incredible pounding of his head.

About 5 hours later, Pat was finally released from the hospital. He called his boss and told him what happened during the MRI exam, and they think I damaged it. His boss wasn't happy about this news. Jim was getting yelled at from his superiors so like any good middle manager he passed it right down the line.

"Jim, if you think I was the one who damaged the crane today you're nuts."

"What are you trying to say here, Pat?"

"It's a wonder you don't have more people hurt by your incompetence"

"My incompetence?"

"You only had 3 floors completely enclosed. These 3 floors were trying to support an additional 7 floors of material and people on top of them. The load was too much, and it is just dumb luck it had not collapsed earlier."

Jim paused, and Pat could hear him exhale. He said, "Pat give me a call me at the end of the week. I don't know when or what a new schedule is gonna look like. This crane problem is gonna mess everyone up. If I am still here at the end of the week, I'll try to give you an idea of what work is available. This is the best I can do right now."

"OK, Jim thanks. I'll give you a call on Friday. Just one last thing, OK?"

"Yeah."

"It wasn't a crane problem,"

Pat ended the call.

Chapter 3 - Katriona Themis

You know, somebody actually complimented me on my driving today. They left a little note on the windscreen, it said 'Parking Fine.'

- Tommy Cooper

Hollingsworth Farm

Leesburg, Virginia

Tuesday 4:30 AM

Katriona's cell phone was buzzing and chirping to the ringtone of the Beyoncé song, *"Put a Ring on It"*. She glanced quickly at her clock by her bedside and groaned. She knew who it was calling at such an early hour. As she picked up her cellphone, she silently prayed it would be good news.

Katriona Themis is in her mid-twenties and physically was in good shape. She had long midnight black raven hair she liked to wear in a tidy knot in the back. Her hair was very straight and contained a luster and sheen of calm water in a black bottom pool. Her deep set captivating emerald eyes commanded attention but were also kind, gentle green eyes. She wouldn't allow anyone to call her by her full name unless they were from the registry of motor vehicles or a police officer. Most people who knew her only called her Kat.

Kat had packed her med bag with supplies last night just in case this would be happening, and she needed to leave quickly. She was glad she did. Right now, she was on autopilot as her body started to slowly awake and go into full alert mode. TEVA, or Total Equine Veterinary Associates, has been working with the Hollingsworth Farm in Leesburg Virginia for the last 40 years. They were a family farming and animal ranch which has passed from generation to generation over the last 100 years.

Kat was the veterinarian on call this week. One of the mare's, Jinny, was ready to foal very soon. She had been out there yesterday, and suspected Jinny could deliver at any time. Sarah was one of the caretakers at the farm, so Kat's first thought was it would be her.

"Hi Sarah. How's Jinny doing?"

"Kat, I'm sorry to call so early but Jinny started to go into labor about 30 minutes ago. She's lying down right now, but something isn't right. She's really agitated and sweaty," Sarah replied nervously.

"Sarah don't worry honey. I'll be there in 15 minutes. Are you alone or is Teddy with you? If he is, tell him to get some blankets or towels and a big bucket of water. I'm leaving now. Call me if anything changes. This is good news, hun. Bye"

TEVA had a lot of business from many of the farms stabling and boarding animals in the area. At one point, they were very involved in the breeding of thoroughbred champion racehorses. Although, they weren't involved with the infamous Secretariat, there were a few thoroughbreds who went on to be very profitable for the owners.

Kat despises the owners and breeders who are in the business of creating giant moneymakers for fat greedy men. It's an unavoidable trait of some of the farms which exist in Virginia. Even though, she's repelled by this, she can see how this does help with the care and wellbeing of the horse population on the various farms Kat takes care of.

The sun was still well hidden in the sky, so she had to watch carefully for the turn to the long driveway to the back stables of the farm. As Kat pulled her little green Subaru into the parking area outside the stable, an automatic motion sensing light came on. She was glad for the light to help her see what she needed to get out of the back of her car to bring in with her to the stable.

Kat knew exactly where the horse would be, since she had just been there yesterday to look in on Jinny. When she came over to the stable, she could see Sarah on her knees near Jinny's head, patting her neck and crooning to Jinny in comforting and gentle sounds. In the corner was a big 5-gallon bucket of water, and on top of a bunch of hay were the blankets and towels. The farmhand, Teddy, was standing there and let out a big sigh when he saw Kat come around the corner into the stable.

Teddy was holding up a cup of coffee for her. She gladly took it and listened to Teddy bring her up to date on what had been happening. As he was talking, she took the cup of coffee and her med bag over to a table just outside of the stable stall to put them on. There was a faucet and a small sink near the stall where Jinny was. Kat quickly started to wash her hands in preparation for the birth of the foal. She took a bottle of antiseptic out of her bag and lavishly applied it to her hands.

When she went back into the stable, she knelt down next to Jinny. As she started to assess the situation, she was once again amazed at how big and strong an animal like Jinny was. The birth of a foal can usually be a quick process, lasting only a couple of hours. Since the beginning of time, horses have been able to foal totally without the help of humans. It isn't very common when the foal is turned or is in trouble during the birth and labor. If it does happen, it must be assisted very quickly. If not, then the chance of the mare or the foal or both surviving is low. Rare, but always a possibility.

Kat was able to see the placenta starting to emerge from Jinny. She was able to keep one hand on the hind quarters of the horse and use her other hand to reach into the birth canal to feel around and to make sure the front legs were coming out first. The birth of a horse is different from a human baby, whereas a normal baby is usually delivered headfirst and the arms at the sides along with the rest of the body. For a foal, it must be the front legs first. If you could imagine you're kneeling down on all fours, imagine if you had to lay down flat on your stomach. You would put your hands above your head and your legs behind you, so you're now lying flat on your stomach. It's somewhat similar, in a rudimentary way.

She was feeling around with one hand and listening to Jinny as she breathed. She could feel the heartbeat of the large horse.

Kat's breathing and her pulse started to become the same. She knew she had a special gift of being able to synchronize her body with the body of the animal she was working with. She had to concentrate and shut everything out of her mind. Kat has always been able to focus her mind to slow down and feel an animal she was in contact with. She has in the past done this without touching the animal, but it doesn't happen often. It's easier for her to use her tactile sensation to be able to focus and *feel* the animal.

This was the first foal for the mare, so naturally Jinny was afraid of what was happening to her. Sarah stayed near Jinny's neck and continued to gently comfort Jinny and not interrupt Kat. She could feel the head of the foal, but the feet weren't where they should be. Her mind was now tuned directly into what Jinny was experiencing. She felt every breath, every beat, and every muscle flexing. She needed the big horse to stop pushing the foal out. It could be dangerous if the legs came out all buckled and bent. Her sense of feeling in sync with Jinny started to make her aware that Jinny was about to go into another labor push of the foal. Now with both hands, Kat pushed in the opposite direction and was trying to push the foal back in. She focused on the birth canal and no matter how much she pushed into Jinny to keep the foal in place where it was, the force of the labor contraction would be too great. She needed another plan.

Kat had her hands inside Jinny up to her elbows. The mare was probably only going to be able to give one or two more pushes, so it had to be now. She leveraged her hands to open the birth canal wider than it was capable of being stretched. She could feel the horse and the pain which was now screaming through the mare. The birth canal started to rip slightly, and blood started to pool on the floor of the stable stall. Quickly, she reached in, and she was able to find the front legs. She didn't have any other option. She pulled on the legs as hard as she could to the front of the foal's body. By doing this she increased the ripping and stretching of the birth canal and finally, she was able to get both the front legs to the front of the foal's body.

She knew she had to forcibly cause damage to the mare. With Kat's mind still synched with Jinny, she concentrated acutely on the pain and the tissues which were damaged. She could feel each area which was in trouble and causing waves of pain. She cut off the pain where she would take the pain on herself and spare the horse from feeling it. She could just feel and sense the areas needed to be healed. Kat's life force was so mixed with the lifeforce of both Jinny and the new foal. The combination of all three forces were an energy store of vitality she could use to heal the areas damaged. There was something else she could feel in this mixture, but she wasn't exactly sure what it was. It didn't matter. Maybe, it was Sarah and her proximity to Jinny and stroking her neck. After two more pushes the new foal was out.

Normally, when the foal is finally removed, it's really important to allow the foal and the mare to rest. It may take anywhere from about a ½ hour or a couple of hours before the placenta is expelled from the mare. What happens during this time is all the life nurturing fluids and blood is being transferred through the umbilical cord to the newborn foal. Once the fluids have been transferred, the mother will normally break the connection herself, but it's usually only when she's able to stand.

However, this wasn't happening right now. Jinny was still in distress and Kat could feel something wasn't quite right. Jinny was breathing very heavily now. She was whinnying with each contraction. She reached inside Jinny again and was surprised at what she was feeling. Another set of feet! Oh my God, Jinny is going to deliver another foal. This foal was positioned correctly, and thankfully the umbilical cord wasn't entangled around its neck. Still tactilely connected with Jinny, she could feel another labor contraction and willed with her mind and energy for Jinny to push really hard now.

In her peripheral vision, she could see Sarah still kneeling next to Jinny. She could feel the worry starting to emanate from her while she was patting Jinny. It was difficult to do both staying in sync with Jinny and using her energy to assist the biological condition of the mare, but she wanted Sarah to also help with the life force she was contributing to Jinny. She looked at Sarah quickly to mouth the word, "Twins!"

The second she did this her tactile sense of Jinny and the life force she was feeling also seemed to increase. It appeared as if the mare found some new energy. She wasn't really quite sure, but it might be Sarah's bond with Jinny that buoyed her up and with the happiness Sarah felt was being transferred. Kat could feel the positive force of happiness in the mare, and she channeled the force to assist with the last and final push to release the sibling foal.

She could feel and sense the mare was getting close to exhaustion. She concentrated and focused all of her energy on Jinny and put her other hand on one of the foals. The energy of the newborn was infusing its unbound energy into the mother. She placed her hand on the other newborn and the same thing happened. The whole time she was touching the foal, the lifeforce coming from each of the foal's was so pure it allowed Jinny to heal those areas which were damaged. Kat directed as much of herself and the lifeforce surrounding her into a healing force for Jinny.

"Two foals! Wow!"

She was getting tired, but there was still more to be done. She kept patting Jinny, but she was able to take back her focus back from the mare. Kat soon felt just synched to her own body.

She looked at Sarah, and said, "I wasn't expecting Jinny was going to have two foals this morning. Can you believe it? Jinny needs to rest for a little bit. Now, we need to wait until the afterbirth is delivered and Jinny can start to nurture and get the foals to suckle."

Sarah looked at Kat, her forehead was covered in sweat, but she had a big broad smile on her face. She asked, "Are the foals, OK? Is there anything you want me to do?"

"No. You did beautifully. Jinny is really bonded to you. You're comforting her was a big help to both her and me. It helped her anxiety and kept her energy focused. You could feel Jinny during the whole process, right? I mean feel as in knowing when she was getting ready to push or if she was starting to feel pain, you bolstered her up to get her through it."

Sarah looked sheepishly at Kat because she was thinking almost exactly the same thing. During the process, it felt like she was dancing with the perfect dancer or the perfect lover who was able to anticipate every move or every sensation. It really felt exhilarating and unlike anything she has ever experienced before.

"Yes, I did feel that. Oh, God thank you so much for helping with Jinny. She really is so very special to me."

In the next couple of hours, Jinny was able to finish the delivery of all the placenta and afterbirth messiness. The two foals put on a remarkable *edge of your seat* and *nail-biter* performance of instability as they tried to stand for the first time. It was a very heart worthy and touching symbol of what was done here today. Teddy didn't want Sarah or Kat to see his *"teary eyed"* emotional joy of seeing the foals stand for the first time. He rushed out saying without facing either of them, he would rustle up some breakfast for them.

After cleaning and feeding the newborn foals and Jinny, they were moved into a cleaned-out stall with plenty of hay and blankets. Now it was time for all of them to rest. Teddy was making breakfast for them in the little kitchen off the main house of the farm. He cooked a nice plate of eggs and blueberry pancakes that he had made for all of them. Teddy and Sarah were overjoyed and beaming with happiness.

Teddy asked between bites, "Isn't it really rare to deliver 2 foals?"

"Yes, it's very rare and only happens once in maybe 1 out of every 1000 births. My fear with the first one was its front legs bent back and not out front. Jinny is strong and was able to let me correct it for her. Once it happened then nature took over and did the rest of it."

"Is there something we should be looking out for on the front legs?" Sarah asked.

"I don't think so. We'll keep an eye on them both for the next couple of weeks. What I want to know is what are you gonna name them?"

Sarah hesitated at first, but then started laughing. "I really don't know, now we have a boy and a girl foal." She giggled.

Kat absent-mindedly added, "Well twins are a lot of work. I should know. My brother and I are twins!"

Why did she say that? She really wished she hadn't said that. Very few people knew about her twin brother, Pat. It wasn't like she ever denied it, but she never went out of her way to tell anyone about her difficulties growing up in Boston.

She quickly changed the subject by saying, "How are the rest of the horses doing in the main stables? I thought for sure, Buster was going to be running around barking at everyone to get out of his barn."

Buster was the feisty Jack-Russell dog who roamed the stable at all times barking at anyone coming near his horse buddies. He could be temperamental if you weren't familiar to Buster, or if in general you were a human.

Sarah smiled and said, "No, Buster was left in the main house today. He has been a nervous Nelly since yesterday, and earlier this morning before I called you. I'm not gonna bring him into the stable until Jinny gives the OK for him to come by."

"If the foals have any sense, they will give him a little kick in the rear end to make sure he understands the social pecking order that exists," Teddy laughed a little.

After another cup of coffee, she went out to the barn to start to gather up her belongings and take a last look at the foals and Jinny. The foals were resting on the hay and Jinny lying next to them. All seemed to be in order, and she was relieved everything turned out so good.

Kat said goodbye to Sarah and Teddy and headed off to go home and get some rest. She was going to have a bunch of paperwork later, but it could wait. As she drove home, she replayed the conversation she had with Sarah and Teddy. Why did she blurt out about being a twin? This was a rule she rarely, if ever broke with herself. She hasn't thought about Pat for a couple of years. They usually exchange cards on birthdays, and it is this ridiculous test they play on each other. It's like a cruel dare. Like saying, "I dare you to not remember you have a twin that shares the same birthday."

Isn't it perverse she asked herself? Growing up is a virtual minefield of touchy memories and very few happy times. Kat grew up with her brother in the foster care world, always hoping to be adopted but no one was ready to take on a set of twins. There were two times they went into homes to prospective parents, but those poor people were totally unprepared for managing and raising twins. Eventually, they both aged out of the system at 18.

She was able to eventually break free from her environment in Boston. She was always inquisitive and read everything she could find, no matter what the topic. It was an escape for her to shield herself from the loneliness and uncertainty of each day or month in the system. Pat protected her mostly from some of the bullies, but she was always able to behave in a way, so most people didn't really notice her. She found reading books was a way to cope with many of the challenges she needed to face. Books didn't let her down or disappoint her like many of the things she came against. Books became an anchor for her so she could see past the failings of the foster care system and her circumstances. It helped to develop a strong shield around herself which was rarely breached by any type of disappointment or failure in life. The only thing she ever allowed herself to open up to was when she was near animals.

Animals comforted her in ways which nothing else in life could give to her. It gave her a strong feeling of joy when she played with animals. She had a knack of understanding exactly what an animal was feeling. This feeling of fear or anxiety wasn't foreign for her. She recognized it immediately when a dog barked, or a cat hissed. She was able to emphasize at a core level with an animal. She learned by accident when she was young, she could transfer energy into an animal to help calm its mind or ease its pain. She didn't really think about it when she did it. It was just something she felt and identified with at its instinctual level. She was only there to help or comfort and not cause hurt.

Chapter 4 – Road Trip

"A tourist is a fellow who drives thousands of miles so he can be photographed standing in front of his car."

- Emile Ganest

James Fenimore Cooper Service Plaza - Mile Marker 39

I-95 – New Jersey Turnpike - Northbound

Thursday 11:50 PM

It was around midnight when Kat pulled into the service area on the New Jersey Turnpike. Kat had been traveling for about 3 hours so far. She was also getting low on gas and needed to get some coffee to keep her alert on this crazy and farfetched trip she was taking. She trusted her intuition the last time she felt like this, and she just knew it would drive her insane if she did not take this trip to Boston.

Two days ago, she helped deliver two beautiful foals from the Hollingsworth Farm. It was a rare experience to deliver a set of twin foals. It was one of those amazing experiences she loved about her work as a veterinarian doctor. In an unguarded moment, she was talking to the caretakers she worked with after the delivery, and she shared with them she had a twin brother. This was not something she ever talked about with anyone. Nothing was wrong with being a twin, but it was just something she left behind her six years ago when she moved away from Boston.

Since that day she has had a terrible feeling, something was not right, or some unknown force told her she needed to see her brother, Pat. She let it pass at first. She felt it was just an irrational and momentary feeling. As more and more time passed, she felt it was really important to get in her car and head to Boston. Kat still didn't understand why she needed to go. It was just a feeling she couldn't shake. Kat knew and physically felt if she didn't go, then she would be sorry.

Because Kat wasn't especially close to her brother Pat, they didn't have any drama between them. They both shared a common history and there was really not much else to it. She called the last contact number she had for Pat's cell phone. This turned out to be a dead end since the last number Pat had given her was not in service. There really wasn't anyone she could call. They didn't have any family or mutual friends. Although, she knew the last address he had given her was correct.

She called the building and spoke with a person from the office in charge of the large apartment building he was supposed to be living at. Kat found out her brother, Pat Themis, was still living in the building in apartment 537B. At first, they didn't want to give her the information, but she was super polite. Kat used her sympathetic and flattering voice to say how she understood the huge responsibility to safeguard their tenant's private information. The person relented and said she had the correct information and also his rent was up to date. Kat knew she was pushing it, but she asked if he could get a message to him to call Kat on her cell phone. She promised to buy him a cup of coffee if he did. Surprisingly, he told her he would be happy to do this for her, and he added if she made it a cup of dark tea then he would take her up on it. After Kat hung up, she realized she didn't even know the other person's name. Oops!

Kat made a couple of calls to let TEVA know she would be gone for a couple of days. The foals she had helped to deliver were doing fine after she checked with Sarah and Teddy yesterday. Kat also asked one of the other vets to go and check on them over the weekend to just do a wellness check. Apparently, the foals received some attention from the local paper and Sarah said she was getting a lot of calls from people wishing the foals well.

Once she had cleared her schedule for the next couple of days, she packed up her little green Subaru. Kat put a couple of days' worth of clothing and other incidentals she might want once she arrived in Boston. Kat kept her med bag in the car just in case it might be needed. Then she got in her car and just drove northeast to jump on I-95 north toward Boston, Massachusetts.

Kat pulled off the New Jersey Turnpike to pull into the James Fenimore Cooper service plaza. She saw only two pumps were in service and there were a couple of cars ahead of her pumping gas into their fuel tanks. Apparently, the regular unleaded gas was not available, so people were lined up waiting for the hi-test which was the only gas being sold right now.

Normally, Kat didn't like to pay the outrageous price per gallon, but this was not something she was willing to risk on a long drive and with the fear of running out of gas. The big white Cadillac in front of her inched forward. When they were in front of the pump, a man wearing a brilliant safety orange colored coat, got out of the passenger side of the vehicle and put his card in the machine. Once he had locked the pump handle in the gas tank and started filling the big tank, he began talking to the driver. After a brief exchange with the man driving the Cadillac, the man went into the main service area building.

While he was gone, she heard the unmistakable click of the pump shutting off when the tank was filled. The driver of the vehicle got out of his car and put the pump handle back into the pump. He got back in and then drove away from the pump. She pulled up to the pump and got out and started the pump to fill up her gas tank. While she was watching the gallons being dispensed, the man who was in the passenger side of the vehicle previously in front of her car, came over to the pump. He looked really confused.

"Did you see where they went?" he asked her.

Assuming he meant the big Cadillac, she said, "I saw him drive away but I thought he was going to the main building like you did."

"Are you sure he went over to the parking area, or did he get back on the Pike?"

"I'm sorry. I really was not paying that close attention. I just assumed he was parking over there," as she pointed to the large parking area.

The parking area she pointed to only contained about a dozen cars at this hour. She could see very clearly the big white Cadillac was not parked among them.

"Thank you for your time."

He turned and walked back to the main Service Plaza building.

Kat didn't really know what to make of the whole situation. It sounded like the person he was traveling with decided to just leave the guy here stranded on the New Jersey Turnpike. She didn't know what the whole story was, and she was not really inclined to get involved in someone else's problems right now. She had her own issues to deal with and right now all Kat wanted to do was get to Boston.

After she finished filling the gas tank of her little green Subaru, she pulled over to the parking area she had just pointed to. Kat got out and went inside the main building of the service area. She was hoping to find a place to grab some coffee and a lite snack. It was a smorgasbord of shops like McDonald's, Subway, Cinnabon, Starbuck's and the convenience stores selling just about anything you could possibly imagine. Maps, sparkplugs, candy, dress shirts, evening gowns and just about anything else you could possibly imagine some traveler might potentially need. She knew she did not need an evening gown for her destination to Boston.

She went over to Starbuck's and treated herself to a vente Carmel Macchiato with an extra shot of espresso and a cranberry orange muffin. While Kat was waiting for her coffee, she spied the older man wearing the bright orange coat. He did look a little lost and she felt sorry for him.

"Did you find out where your friends went?"

He looked up and said, "Nope. They left me here. I was hoping to get a little further north but it's just as well. Someone will come along sooner or later."

She knew she was going to regret this but before she could stop herself, she said, "Where are you headed to?"

"Boston."

Before he answered her, Kat already knew this was what he was going to say. It was one of those strange and weird déjà vu experiences when you are sitting at home and thinking about your grandpa Pete out of the blue and then phone rings and it is Grandpa Pete. Isn't this exactly what she's currently doing right now with her brother Pat? In the back of her mind, Kat was also reasoning it might not be so bad to have someone help keep her stay awake and alert.

Cautiously she said, "I am heading north so why don't I help you get a little further north on the Turnpike and see what happens."

The way he looked at her, she could tell her face was betraying the futile battle going on in her head. She was now committed so she might as well make the best of it. She reached out her hand and said, "My name is Kat."

He shook her hand and replied, "My name is Alder Gwyndion. Nice to meet you. I really appreciate the help. I can pay for any gas you need or anything else along the way."

As he shook her hand, she got a better look at his face. His aged blue eyes were like brilliant bright stars. Very captivating and fiery with an intense penetrating gaze which missed nothing. His face showed him to be older than she first thought. She could see his face was weathered, and he was older than she first suspected. Kat would estimate he would be in his mid to late 50's. He had a kind and gentle face though. If she hadn't detected this last quality in her first impression, she knew she would have made a wrong decision. She trusted her instincts which told her she was not in peril with this man.

When they walked over to her car, Alder apparently didn't see it or wasn't paying attention, but he tripped on one of those parking blocks at the front of where she was parked. As he was struggling to get his balance, Kat was surprised to see how agile he was, and she instinctively reached out her hand to assist. When their hands touched, she felt a tingling of static electricity pass between them. She felt an incredible strength in this older man. He was not weak or frail at all, but she sensed it was more than physical strength. It felt like a vast ocean of lifeforce energy around him. It all happened in a microsecond, and she quickly dismissed it.

He smiled and said, "Sorry, I can be a klutz sometimes. Haha. No worries, I am OK."

They both got into her car and made their way north on I-95.

Kat asked, "Where are you from?"

He responded vaguely, "Well I'm originally from Ireland. I have lived in several places in Europe, though. I'm heading to Boston to meet someone. I am a teacher by trade. I got a call yesterday from a friend who asked me to help someone they know in Boston. How about you? Where are you from?"

"I used to live in Boston, and I am heading up there to see my brother," she responded and silently forced herself to make sure she did not say "twin brother" this time.

She added, "I'm a horse veterinarian."

"Really. It must be very exciting and rewarding. I just read about a farm in Virginia which just delivered two twin foals. They mentioned the mother horse was named Jinny. A really rare occurrence, right?"

"It's funny you mentioned this. I am surprised it was reported beyond the local paper. Yes, it is a very rare occurrence. I was the vet who delivered them. It was a really remarkable experience."

He was stunned. "Oh boy, I am traveling with a celebrity! How fantastic it is to deliver two newborn horses at the same time. Please, you must tell me all about it. How long did it take? Where there any problems? What is the horse Jinny like?"

Kat smiled and started to tell Alder everything about the delivery. He kept interjecting little questions about the details, or some aspect he wanted her to expand upon. He was a good listener and as she was telling him as many of the details as she could without actually mentioning the parts about her helping

Jinny heal herself. Kat neglected to elaborate on how she took on some of the pain from Jinny during the stretching and tearing of the tissue to get the first foal out. They both laughed as she described the newborn horses trying to stand up for the first time.

She could see those sparkling blue eyes twinkle and burn even more intensely as he laughed. It was surprising to Kat, but she felt comfortable and safe telling him these things. With most people she wouldn't say anything as detailed about what she felt during the delivery and how she could tune herself and mind with animals. She felt comfortable and safe telling him these parts of her story. The only other person who had any clue about this was her brother Pat.

As they talked, Alder told her a little bit of his background. He was from Europe originally, but he has been living in the United States for the last 26 years.

"Why did you move to the USA from Europe," she asked.

"Well, I have a sister and she moved here at the same time. We thought we could do some good by moving here. We were foolish and young. I have traveled all over the country, but I usually end up back in Boston for some reason. If I might ask, how did you get into being a veterinarian?"

"I read everything I could get my hands on when I was younger. We had to move around a lot, my brother and I, so the one thing I always went to was reading books on just about any topic. We never had any animals where I grew up. There was a lady who used to take her dog to a park where I was living. It was a huge Saint Bernard named Misty. Poor woman was getting pulled everywhere this dog wanted to go. I used to help her walk and train him not to pull her in every direction. She was such a sweet dog. She was just so excited to be outside and be able to interact with every single person in the park. I mean literally every single person in the park.

"One day, Misty ran out into traffic and was hurt really bad. The poor thing went to Angell Animal Hospital in Boston. I went to the hospital and helped keep Misty calm. The injuries she received from the car accident were just too great. This was when I decided I wanted to help animals like Misty. And I have never looked back."

"Oh, my what an amazing story that is. You must be very special to be able to help animals the way you do."

"Animals are so much more honest than humans. They love without really wanting anything back. I have always had a knack of connecting to animals and understanding when they were afraid or happy. The hard part for me is seeing them when they are in pain or not treated right."

It was about 3:00 in the morning and they were nearing the end of the New Jersey Turnpike. Kat decided to stop at the last Service Plaza, get some gas, bathroom break, and grab another cup of coffee. Alder insisted he pay for the gas, coffee or anything else she wanted. Kat stayed in the car while he paid for the gas. They found a table outside the plaza where they could sit for a moment.

She hesitated a second before saying it, "Alder, I have enjoyed talking with you on this road trip. I am going to Boston, so I will be happy to have you accompany me for the rest of the trip up there. Is that, OK?"

Those stunning blues eyes lit up like an exploding star and he beamed at her, "I was hoping we could continue on up to Boston and I would be honored to accompany you there. Thank you for helping me in my quest."

"I didn't say this, but I am really heading up to Boston on a hunch. I haven't talked to my brother in a couple of years. A couple of days, after I delivered the twin foals, I mentioned to the caretakers who were assisting me that I had a brother. My brother is my twin. Ever since then, I can't seem to be able to shake this feeling of impending doom. It is totally focused on my brother. It sounds irrational, but it is making me feel so strongly that I **MUST** go to see him. Having you travel with me is helping me to stop debating the decision of what has possessed me to make the decision to go to Boston. I suspect everything is fine, but it is just a strange déjà vu I can't seem to escape. Have you ever had anything like this happen to you?"

"Yes. I have experienced this before. It is somewhat scary, but I have always trusted the feeling. In the past when I got this feeling of, what did you call it? Déjà vu? I have learned to trust it and act upon it. It's not irrational. It's irrational when you don't act upon it. It usually makes sense afterwards. Doesn't it?"

"Your right. Everything usually happens for a reason. Even if I don't know what it is right now, I am sure my going to Boston is part of the plan. Shall we get back on our voyage to Boston?"

"Absolutely, my fearless navigator."

As they got back into her car, she said, "I never asked you what it is you taught?"

He smiled at her while they got back onto the highway.

"I teach many things, but mostly I teach Science and Social Studies of Sciences."

"Oh, that is interesting. I know what Social Studies is, but what are Social Study of Sciences?"

"It is similar to being a scientist, but your laboratory is what a society does as they become more evolved. Think of it, like if you were around about 150 years ago and someone mentioned climate change or carbon footprint. Many would think you were talking nonsense. People were not aware enough at the time to imagine the climate changing. They would say, 'The climate doesn't change.' It is only in the last 60 years or so when we have noticed a lot more about how the environment is changing. The equation between the earth and the humans have never been equalized and it is bound to happen. Humans need the Earth, and the Earth needs us."

"Climate change is a topic many people are really fuzzy on. I think I understand, and I see the changes in the weather patterns. Farms are where I am most often, so it doesn't really come up too much. What do you mean when you say the Earth needs us?"

"Well, if you think about the planet and all the many ways the Earthlings use the planet to exist, they plant trees and they use the soil, they build dams, they take care of the *planets*, and they multiply. The Earth really love *Earthlings*, and they do some good sometimes, but not always. It is a complex relationship the Earthlings have with the Earth. What do you think? Does your species do things to help the planet?"

It didn't go unnoticed to Kat how Alder referenced *Earthling* and his use of pronouns. She replied, "Yes, I think there are some good things we have done with regards to planting of trees, cleaning rivers and lakes, helping animals who are near extinction levels and I'm sure there are many other things we do I'm just not involved enough in it to really understand it."

For the next hour, Alder talked about the different projects he was involved with. He told her about his work with a number of well-known scientists to find some breakthroughs in Quantum energies when he was in Europe. Kat was intrigued. She had read some books about quantum mechanics, she found it interesting, but the math was just beyond her. Alder told her about the hidden energies contained in subatomic particles. He told her about how all matter exists with a certain vibration and a spin. He said it goes a lot deeper than just those two characteristics, but it is something which we can use to start to understand how it all works together. It was a fascinating topic to talk about. She didn't have any background in heavy science like this, but Alder was an expert at explaining the different concepts in easily understood ways.

It was about 4:30 AM and a car far up ahead of them was zigzagging back and forth across the highway. There was only one other car near it. The other car sped up to get in front of the zigzagging car. The car put on its hazard lights and while it slowed down it was still zigzagging but eventually it was able to pull over to the side. The rear wheels on the right side of the car found some loose dirt and grass and when it finally stopped it was stopped perpendicular to the highway. It was safely off the road as to not be a hazard to other cars. Something was wrong though. As they got closer, Kat could see the driver and passenger were in distress. Instincts told her to stop.

Alder said, "Yes I agree, we should stop. The woman is in distress."

Kat pulled off the road quickly so she could come to a safe stop in front of the car. When the car was fully stopped, she reached in the back and grabbed her medical bag. When they went over to the car to see what was happening, a man wearing a Seik turban on his head was frantic and upset. He told them his name is Bella. His wife, Shanti, is ready to give birth. They were on the way to the hospital, but the baby was coming too fast.

Alder looked at Kat and said, "I know this is different than delivering a foal, but do you feel up to delivering a baby this morning? I can see and feel this baby is stubborn and will not wait any longer."

Kat said to Bella, "OK, but we need to get her into the back seat. Do you have any blankets or towels?"

Kat turned to Alder, "Can you get me one or two of the water bottles from the back of my car? Also, we need someone to contact 911 and get an ambulance here."

Before Alder turned around to go back to her car, he reached in his pocket, and he gave her a small red stone.

"Put this in your pocket. It will help you to have a strong connection with Shanti and her baby."

This was strange, but her mind was in overdrive at the moment. Bella and Kat were able to get Shanti properly seated in the back seat lying down. She told Bella to get in the other side of the car so he could help keep her propped up.

She grabbed a few things from her medical bag. Alder returned with the water, and she was able to clean her hands as best as possible. When Kat first touched Shanti, they exchanged a similar electrostatic shock which she had experienced earlier this night with Alder when he stumbled on the parking block at the service plaza. She started to clear her mind and to try to tune herself to Shanti. She hasn't really been able to do this with another person before. She had only allowed herself to open up to animals. This time though she found she could tune into the life force energy of the woman and the baby. She was stunned at how much energy this little baby was putting out. It was also anger. It wanted out right now.

"Shanti, is this your first pregnancy? This is going to be fine. Your baby wants to come out and say hello to the world," Kat said with a reassuring smile.

When she looked underneath Shanti's dress, she could see the baby was starting to crown. She knew this was going to be a quick birth. With one hand on Shanti's stomach, she could feel the areas which were causing pain and she tried to take on those areas and let the body focus on the next part of pushing the baby into the birth canal. She didn't need to worry about a breech, or if the baby was positioned correctly, she could just feel the baby's position was correct. After the last push she could see the shoulders starting to come through. She looked at Shanti and told her to give one last final push. The baby was starting to come farther out. She could feel the lifeforce of the baby and the happiness it felt by being outside. Boy, this baby is strong. She could just feel the force of it coursing through her body combined with the baby. Kat was able to slowly pull the baby out so its little *bum* was clear, and she could easily pull the rest of the baby out.

Bella was in tears, Shanti was in tears, and suddenly the babies piercing crying made everyone laugh hysterically among the tears of joy.

Shanti said in a broken English/Hindu, "Thank you. Thank you. What is your name?"

"My name is Kat and for a select few, I'm also known as Katriona. Your baby is very happy to see its mother and father right now."

They both conversed for a minute in Telegu which was their native tongue and they finally said, "We will name our new baby girl Katriona."

"Are you sure? I would be honored. Thank you."

As she was saying this, she could hear other voices coming over to the car. The ambulance had arrived. Kat spoke with the paramedics for a little bit and told them exactly what had happened during the birth. They were a little disappointed they had not gotten there quicker to be part of it, but Shanti was in good hands right now and ready to go to the hospital. She gave them her contact information if they needed anything else from her.

Alder was smiling and his twinkling eyes just radiated joy when she went back to her car. They were just north of New York and crossing over into Connecticut. They were discussing how incredible of an adventure this has been. Kat didn't forget the part of just before they had stopped, Alder had said *"Yes I agree we should stop"* and she's positive she never said the statement out loud but was thinking about it. Kat was going to say something, but she let it pass. What she wanted to know about was what the little red stone was. When they were passing into Hartford, Connecticut, Kat took the stone out of her pocket and handed it to Alder. It was warm and it felt like it was vibrating slightly.

"Alder, what is this red stone you gave me?"

"It is an old stone, a very, very old stone. I have carried this with me for many years. It has a power and I thought it would assist you in helping to deliver the woman's baby. You must have felt its power when you connected with the woman, right?"

"Well, I did feel something. I can't usually connect to a person the way I can connect to an animal. This time, I could really feel the life force of the baby so strongly, it was almost overwhelming because it wanted to be born right then and now. When I connect with an animal, I can sometimes assist with the pain it's feeling. I can take the pain on myself or redirect energy into healing and assuaging hurt areas needing it. I didn't really feel any of the pain today, however I was ready for it and expecting it. I think the mother gave its love to the baby and it wasn't too uncomfortable for her. It just felt very natural. I don't really understand how I can connect with animals and exactly how I can feel it when they are frightened or are in pain. It's just something I have always been able to do. The stone felt warm, and I got a little static shock when I first touched it, but I also got the same shock when I reached out to you when you almost tripped back at the service plaza."

"Yes, I knew you would be able to use this particular stone to help the woman deliver the baby. It's a stone which has a lot of power if it is used in the right way. It can heal people or animals when used properly. I can also make someone ill if it's used in the wrong way. There are many stones which exist. Each one contains many different amazing powers. Maybe someday, I can show you these stones and the powers which they contain. They are truly astonishing when used in the correct way."

Kat said cautiously, "Wait a minute. You said this little red stone could make someone ill? Weren't you taking a big risk of giving me this stone and I might have accidently hurt this woman or her baby?"

Apologetically he said, "Yes, there was a risk, but I was certain you wouldn't use it in such a way. A person who is ill can make another person ill. The illness isn't so much a physical malady but more of an ill will or spirit. You don't have this, and it was why I was sure when I gave it to you it would only be used to heal or help."

Kat laughed and giggled. She said, "Alder, my new friend, you are a strange road trip pal."

They both laughed as Kat finally turned onto the Massachusetts Turnpike about 40 miles to go to Boston. It was about 5:30 AM and it was starting to have more cars on the road as the morning rush hour into Boston began. They stopped at the Natick Service Plaza to do a last fill up of gas, bathroom break, and another coffee. The service plaza wasn't too busy at this time in the morning, but it was starting to have more people pulling into the service plaza. When they got their coffee's, they found a table where they could sit for a few minutes before completing the journey.

"So where in Boston are you going to?" she asked.

He said, "I'm really not sure of the street address. I only know how to get there by subway. If you can drop me off anywhere near one of the MBTA stations it would help me out greatly."

"Well, my brother lives in the Back Bay part of Boston. There are many MBTA stops near his place. What if your friend isn't there? Where will you go? I don't want to leave you stranded in Boston if your friend isn't around."

"Oh, no it's fine. I'm booked at the Copley Plaza hotel so if my friend isn't there, I will go back to the hotel and wait for them there."

"OK, I don't want to leave you stranded. I have enjoyed our talk this morning."

"Thank you, I was really fortunate to have those people leave me at the service plaza in New Jersey, wasn't I."

An hour later, Kat pulled up to her brother's apartment building. She told Alder where the subway stop was about a block away. When he got out of the car, he looked at Kat and smiled.

"Kat, does your brother live in apartment 537B?"

"Yes, he does. How did you know that?"

"Is your brother's name Patrick Themis? I think he's the friend I'm supposed to see."

Kat just looked at him totally perplexed.

All she could say was, "OK then let's go see my brother. I hope he's here."

Chapter 5 – Queen Boudicca

What's another word for Thesaurus?"

- Steven Wright

Metropolitan Museum

New York City, New York

Thursday 10:00 AM

As an archaeologist, Harriet Chander wasn't one to get all gushy over some big rocks or some ancient historical artifacts. Harriet was sitting in front of her computer in the offices attached to the New York Metropolitan Museum on the fourth floor. She's 33, wearing a striking, deep red skirt and white half sleeve blouse ensemble. Her dark skin and with her dark hair pulled back, made her attractive and stunning good looks stand out. Harriet's brown eyes were an abyss of warmth, compassion and sensitivity. Her facial features, sometimes, betrayed what she was feeling. The trade-off, however, was she looked like she could connect with people at a deep personal level.

She was holding a picture of the inside of an ancient stone chamber in South Woodstock, Vermont, informally known as Calendar II. Her girlfriend, Ellie, had taken the picture from the entrance of the chamber and Harriet was standing in the middle of the rectangular room. It was taken at sunrise of the winter solstice on December 21st of last year. The first rays of sunlight lit up the wall behind Harriet in the picture and showed how detailed and precise each stone was placed in the back wall and the walls; on the left and the right of her.

It is believed the ancient Celts, Druids, Norsemen, or even the early Irish monks who made their way to New England around 2000 to 3000 BCE, built these large chambers. It is also believed, there are marked similarities between the stone chambers scattered around New England, with their mortar-free walls and celestial alignments, to the many other Neolithic sites in Ireland. These sites in Ireland, such as the Hill of Tara, Knowth, or Newgrange all contain the same types of intrinsic masonry, precision craftsmanship and celestial alignment.

She had camped out with her faithful companion, Ellie, and her young beagle Buck. It was bitterly cold in the predawn hours of December 21st. Harriet got dressed and Ellie grumpily started to get dressed. Buck sensing adventure was ready to go at a moment's notice. They hiked the short distance to the Calendar II stone chamber and Harriet and Ellie got the camera and equipment ready.

When the sun came over the horizon it was perfectly aligned to the opening of the chamber. They had taken many pictures of the sun coming through and lighting up the interior of the chamber. They also took many pictures of the intricate masonry of the walls where each stone was perfectly positioned without any mortar to hold them in place. Truly remarkable was the ceiling of the chamber which held huge megalithic stones 15 feet wide and at least 1 foot thick. How they managed to get those stones into place so perfectly was a mystery.

One of the pictures caught her eye. There was something on the wall of the chamber which she didn't recognize. Her first thought was she, or someone who had handled the picture, might have left some foreign matter on the surface of the picture. No, this was something on the wall of the chamber she had not noticed before. On the back wall she could see some lines were cut into the lower portion of the wall. Those markings looked like ancient Ogham letters.

Harriet has studied many of the ancient civilizations like the Celts, Druids, Norsemen, Iberian adventurers, and Irish monks. Many of these used a very crude way of communicating. For example, the Celts and the Druids carved Ogham letters in stone artifacts and cairns. The letters were written vertically from the bottom going up. The letters were a mix of vertical, horizontal, and angled lines carved into the stones.

The picture she was looking at was a printed copy. She needed to see the digital version so she could zoom in closer. Harriet got up and went over to her computer and called up the picture on the hard drive. Once she opened it, she zoomed in as far as she could without losing the resolution. Yes, it clearly was the ancient Ogham writing. It read vertically starting from the bottom:

"To find truth find mother"

Harriet was flabbergasted. "How did I miss this?" she asked herself. A more perplexing question here was what it means.

Who is mother? What truth is being sought here? The more she thought about this, the more questions she had. She thought of calling Ellie, but she hesitated. Ellie was fun to be with, but the relationship petered out soon after it got going. No drama at the end. If anything, they were both glad they could share a moment of truth and it would just be hurtful to continue under a false pretense. The hell with it. Ellie might have other pics she took on this morning.

Harriet dug into her cell phone contacts and looked up Ellie's contact information and pressed send to call her.

Ellie answered after the second ring, "Hello?"

"Hi, Ellie it's Harriet."

"How is my Nubian Queen? It's nice to hear from you. How are you?"

Nubian Queen was a pet name Ellie privately called her. Harriet told her about some of the archaeology trips she had taken to Egypt and Africa. Ellie said she was a reincarnation of a Nubian Queen.

"I'm good, thanks. Hey, I was wondering if you could help me with something?"

"Whatever the Queen desires, the Queen gets," Ellie said cheekily.

"Do you remember when we went up to Woodstock Vermont to check out the stone chamber last year in December? We froze our asses off camping there. You took a bunch of pictures that morning. I was wondering whether you had any other shots of the interior walls which you might have filtered out as not being framed correctly or not in focus. One of the pictures I have from you was a picture you took from outside the chamber and looking in at me. I noticed today on the wall behind me there are Ogham letters carved into the base of the stone wall."

"Hold on a sec let me check."

Harriet could hear Ellie booting up her laptop. She asked, "How is the little rascal Buck doing?"

"Buck is good, he's so done with listening to me. When he wants to go outside, then it is right now and not later. He wants the full bed not just part of it. He's just being a pain in my ass, but he's good. He misses your belly rubs. OK. Here we are. I got the folder open and yes there are 14 photos which did get filtered out. I'm looking at some of these now and some are semi salvageable. The others are really out of focus and not really usable. Of the fourteen I think I have about 7 of these which might be what you're looking for. Do you want me to upload them to my cloud drive? I'll put them under the folder called Woodstock and I'll send you a link."

"Thanks a lot, Ellie. I appreciate it. How's everything else with you?"

For the next 15 minutes, Ellie and Harriet got caught up on all the latest happenings and events going on in their lives. When Harriet hung up the phone, she was glad they were still able to talk sincerely and be friendly to each other. Everyone at some point gets into those relationships which are a game of avoidance. Harriet called it, "*The I love you and I hate you at the same time game!*". Ellie was a genuine and good person. The both of them were just looking for different expectations about being together and were honest enough, to admit this and not let it be hurtful.

She checked her email and she saw a new message from Ellie containing the link to the new pictures. She clicked on it and copied the photos stored on the cloud drive to her local hard drive. She started to look at the pictures and she saw another set of symbols on the left-hand wall. Part of Harriet's head was in the shot, and she could see why this was filtered out. This picture was darker than the one she looked at earlier. Makes sense since there was less sunlight on the right and left walls of the chamber. Harriet was able to clean up the picture and change the contrast and sharpness so she could make out the symbols carved into the stones. The symbols spelled out a cryptic message.

Brú na Bóinne

Harriet checked and rechecked her translation of the Ogham symbols. No, they were correct. She was sure of it. The *Brú na Bóinne* referenced the *Palace or Mansion of the River Boyne*. There are several ancient monuments just north of Dublin, Ireland in the Boyne Valley area. The largest of the sites was called *Newgrange*. This is just one of the many ancient megalithic sites in Ireland. This stone chamber in Woodstock Vermont is a long way from Ireland.

She's missing something here and she just can't wrap her brain around this. Specifically, the term, *Brú na Bóinne*, is a catch all name of a group of other stone monuments in this area around the Boyne Valley area in County Meath, Ireland. The other stone monuments are called Knowth, Dowth, Hill of Tara and the most popular site called Newgrange.

Maybe she needed another perspective on this? It was about 10 years ago when Harriet last traveled to Ireland. She went there to experience and explore several of the ancient sites like Knowth, Dowth, Hill of Tara and many more scattered around Ireland. It was at the *Newgrange* site, or it is commonly called *Brú na Bóinne*, where she spent most of her time.

She was young and fresh out of college and hungry to learn. A much older and very experienced archaeologist, Allen Westfall, sensed her eagerness and he figured he could throw her bits and scraps of his experience and knowledge, if she would be his helper lackey. She didn't mind being his personal gopher. He told her a lot of the history of the Newgrange site and also the many more he has studied which are scattered around Ireland. It was fascinating hearing him talk about some of the conclusions archaeologists made about these different sites and also and why they were built.

Unfortunately, Allen died a few years ago from cancer. They had briefly kept in touch over the years, but this would be a great question to get his ideas on this riddle. He always credited a large amount of his insight and source of information from a women named Aren Mulloi. Allen had mentioned Aren offhandedly, because he was doing exactly what Harriet was doing. Fresh out of school and eager to explore, he also visited different archaeological sites around the world. Aren was the old timer full of experience and Allen was her student.

Harriet wondered if Aren Mulloi was still doing further archaeological research on other sites. When Allen spoke of Aren, he had suspected she was long since retired and most likely dead and buried. If she were still alive today it would put her age to be at least 130 or so. If she wasn't alive, she surely must have some published works or maybe she taught in a school somewhere. This was an intriguing mystery now for Harriet.

She started to search on the name for Aren Mulloi. Of course, when she *googled* it, she got back a meaningless amount of hits on the name. How about "Aren Mulloi archaeological". Again, too many hits returned back to being of any use. Now, let's try, "Aren Mulloi archaeological Newgrange". This trimmed the result set considerably. There were two hits which came back. One was "*Arwen Mulloy awarded teacher of the year award.*" The second hit was for a genealogy site where you could trace back your ancestors who came to Ellis Island in the late 1800's and early 1900's. Just for the heck of it, she clicked on the Ellis Island site.

After clicking around and navigating the site, she was able to determine there was a person with a similar name who arrived at Ellis Island. The person named on the ship manifest was from a ship out of Ireland in 1890 carrying an Arwen Mulloy. The name was slightly different, but it was close. This would also support the comment from Allen when he ever spoke of her. He had suspected she would be long gone and couldn't possibly still be alive. This was most likely the person who was being referenced.

Just for the hell of it, she went back and clicked on the other link which was about the teacher from Plymouth Massachusetts who received the Teacher of the Year award. The webpage brought up a local Plymouth newspaper which carried a story of Aren Mulloy. There was a small, grainy black and white picture of a woman receiving a framed award certificate for the teacher of the year. Harriet's jaw *fell on the floor* when she saw the picture. The woman depicted was the exact same likeness of an old Celtic Warrior, called Queen Boudicca, who fought the Romans viciously and ruthlessly about 2000 years ago. This woman was the exact likeness of her.

As the story goes, Boudicca's husband, Prasutagus, ruled as a nominally independent ally of Rome, and left his kingdom jointly to his daughters and to the Roman emperor, Nero, in his will. However, when he died, his will was ignored, and the kingdom was annexed, and his property taken. Legend says Boudica was flogged, and her daughters raped. In a revolt which included the Iceni, the Trinovantes, and other ethnic groups who would join her army, she led them into a fierce battle campaign. Her growing army destroyed or burned several major Roman occupied cities and settlements. The body count for both Roman and Britons is estimated to be 70,000 to 80,000 dead. When Harriet was studying and learning about these ancient civilizations, she always admired Queen Boudicca and considered her as a total bad ass! She didn't sound anything like a *Teacher of the Year*, yet the likeness in the picture is uncanny.

Quantum Mind

Her mind was spinning right now. Dozens of questions and possible scenarios of what she should do next. Should I try contacting this Arwen Mulloy? Do I just come out and say something like, "Hey, are you Queen Boudicca?" Or how about, "Hi, have you ever been to Ireland and gone to the Newgrange site in the Boyne Valley?" Still worse yet was, "I translated an Ogham inscription which read *'to find truth find mother'*. Are you mother?"

With a long sigh, Harriet needed to stop her mind racing. She got up from her desk and decided it was a nice time for a break. She went into the little cafeteria to get a snack to distract herself. She went to the vending machine and felt today was going to be a *Reese's Pieces* Day. There were very few people in the cafeteria, so she was able to find a small empty table. There is no possibility this woman was the same person who Allen told her about so many years ago. Physically, this was just an impossibility. Harriet knew if she didn't derail her thinking, she was going to go slightly insane until she resolved this.

The average lifespan of a human is roughly about 80 to 100 years. What if this woman, Arwen Mulloy, had children? Maybe, she passed on some of her knowledge or maybe some of her journals or notebooks are contained in some forgotten box. Hopefully, there was some clue, or some detail which might help her understand this mystery which was gathering momentum running amok in her head.

Reluctantly, Harriet knew she was fighting a losing battle here. She would have to call this teacher and ask her the questions spinning around in her head, even at the prospect of making herself sound like a deluded psycho. Well, she should at least formulate what questions she would ask, if and only if, she was able to speak with her.

Harriet got up and went back to her office closing the door. At least she could only look foolish to just one person and not the whole office. She went back to the webpage where she saw the article. The teacher was from Plymouth East Middle School. There was also a link to a website for the school. She called the main number of the school. The person she spoke with was very nice but had the no-nonsense attitude of an office administrator. Harriet asked if she could speak to or leave a message for Arwen Mulloy. The administrator said Ms. Mulloy was in a class right now, but they would break for lunch in about a half an hour. She told Harriet she could leave a message and a call back number, and she would put this into Ms. Mulloy's message box. She gave the woman her name and cell number.

When Harriet hung up the phone, she felt a little deflated. She was all set to blabber on a rant asking, or rather accusing, this women of being an ancient Celtic Warrior Queen incarnate all because she saw a picture of her being awarded a teacher of the year award. This was crazy but maybe this could be something worth playing out.

What if she told this woman she was doing a research or thesis on Queen Boudicca and the ancient history of civilizations like the Celts, Druids and Norsemen. Maybe she could spin this into something a little more believable. Tell her about her mentor Allen. The more she started to think about this, it really was starting to sound a little more credible than she first thought.

Precisely 33 minutes later her cell phone rang, and the caller ID said Plymouth East Middle High School. Harriet answered and said, "Hello. This is Harriet Chander."

"This is Arwen Mulloy. I received a message that you called asking to speak with me."

"Thank you so much for calling me back. Is this a good time to call? I can call back later if you don't have the time to speak with me today."

"No, this is fine. How can I help you?"

So far so good Harriet thought. She replied, "Ms. Mulloy, I'm an archaeologist in New York City and I have been doing research on ancient civilizations like the Celts, Druids and Norsemen. Many of these ancient civilizations left different artifacts and monuments that have puzzled archaeologists for centuries. About 10 years ago I was in Ireland in the Boyne Valley area which is north of Dublin. I was working at an archaeological site called Newgrange. Have you ever heard of this particular site? Sometimes it might be also called *Brú na Bóinne* using the old Irish language name."

Arwen replied, "I don't know if I have, but I'm curious now."

"OK. Great. Well, about 10 years ago, I met another archaeologist named Allen Westfall. He was an expert in the monuments around Ireland. Allen spoke of a woman, named Aren Mulloi, whom he told me was the most knowledgeable expert in ancient Celt, Druidic and Northern tribes regarding these monuments. I recently uncovered a new clue which might be related to these Irish monuments."

"Really? Now I'm even more curious. What did you find?"

"OK. There are several sites scattered around New England which closely resemble some larger monuments and different ancient sites found in Ireland. I found a clue at one of these New England sites, specifically a stone chamber site in South Woodstock, Vt. The clue I found accidentally today was some writing on the back wall of the stone chamber. It was in an ancient alphabet called Ogham. The clue said 2 things. The first was a reference to the Newgrange site in Ireland and written in Irish as *'Brú na Bóinne'*. The second clue was really strange. It was written in Ogham also, and it said, *'To Find Truth Find Mother'*."

Surprisingly, Harriet heard giggling on the other end of the call. She said, "Ms. Mulloy, are you still there.?"

"Yes, I'm still here. I'm sorry. It just sounded like a fortune cookie saying." Arwen continued, "Do you think I'm the *mother*?"

"No, certainly not. I'm not sure yet what to make of this. The link to the different Irish monuments isn't a new theory, but the cryptic message baffles me. I contacted you because of the similarity of your name to the person my old mentor told me. I also saw a picture of you when you won a teacher of the year award. I have to say, I would agree how absurd it is, but you are the spitting image of an Irish Celtic Warrior Queen named Boudicca. Have you ever heard of this name before?"

Silence. Harriet asked, "Ms. Mulloy are you still there.?"

More silence. Harriet thought for sure Ms. Mulloy had hung up on her. She was about to end the call and she heard, "Harriet, I haven't heard that name in a very, very long time. I do know who Queen Boudicca was or used to be. Your cryptic message isn't really so cryptic. First, you have to find out what it actually is that the other needs in order to survive. Answer this question and you will know who *mother* is. Harriet, I'll be in Boston this weekend at the Copley Plaza hotel. If you're around the Boston area, come to me with your answer, we will have a very long talk about these monuments. If not this weekend, I'm usually in Plymouth and we could continue this discussion there. Give me your email address and I'll send you all my contact details."

Harriet gave her information to Arwen and said, "Thank you, it was nice talking to you."

When Harriet ended the call, she was stunned. That didn't go exactly the way she thought it would have gone. Still reeling from the phone call, Harriet realized she. wasn't any closer to figuring out this perplexing riddle. On the other side of the coin, she would have a nice 4-hour drive to Boston to figure this riddle out. Maybe, Ellie and Buck would like to make a weekend out of it?

Chapter 6 – Burned

Some days you're the fire hydrant, and some days you're the dog.

- Parker Conrad

Brian Keefe

Plymouth, Massachusetts

Thursday 1:30 PM

"Make it bigger, Brian. Make it bigger and hotter," the little boy crowed.

"Are you sure?" the other older boy said.

"Yes, I'm sure. Come on do it," the little boy said impatiently.

"OK, Jerry. Stand back and will you please be quiet. I gotta think really, really hard on this. Besides, I don't want mom to hear you squealing like a little girl, OK?"

Both boys were standing in their backyard next to a BBQ grill their father had used earlier. There was a small above ground pool off to the right. The older boy pressed the ignition button on the grill. The propane ignited and the sound of gas hissing was what they both wanted to hear.

"Get your marsh mellow ready," ordered the older boy.

"Roger dodger, marsh mellow all set."

"OK, put the marsh mellow in there when I tell you."

"Rodger dodger, check."

The older boy stared intensely at the flame burning through one of the vents in the burner tube. The flames got bigger and bigger. He reached with his finger over to the flame and it appeared as though he took a tiny flame from the grill. A small flame was attached to his finger. He then took his hand and touched Jerry's marsh mellow. The marsh mellow lit on fire. Brian stared at the flame, and it burned brighter and brighter.

Jerry said, "OK, that's good. Now just let it burn."

Jerry reached up to push Brian's hand away from his stick that was holding the marsh mellow. He didn't realize when he pushed Brian's hand away, he was pushing Brian's finger toward his t-shirt. Jerry's t-shirt started to catch fire. Jerry didn't realize it at first.

The flames were burning hotter than normal since this was the original flame Brian had deliberately tried to make hotter with his mind. The shirt was quickly burning away and then it started to burn the flesh. Jerry's eyes were wild and panicked with fear. He started to scream. Brian froze. He couldn't move. He tried to move and couldn't.

He screamed at his little brother, "Jerry, jump in the pool! Jump in the pool!"

He couldn't figure out why he couldn't move. He tried to move with everything in him, but he was frozen in place like a statue. Off to the side, he could hear the back door opening and his mother yelling, "Get down and roll Brian! Get down and roll"

Why were they telling him to roll when Jerry was the one burning? While he was asking himself this question, he felt as if someone was body slamming him into the ground. He could feel someone throwing towels and blankets over him and patting him down vigorously. He started to feel like his own skin was burning. It got more and more intense. Now, Brian was feeling the excruciating, intense, and almost heart stopping pain emanating from his burning skin. He blacked out.

The man on the bed woke up with a start. He was the only person in the big bed. Brian had been tossing and turning and the sheets and bedclothes were strewn all over the bed in a pile. He slowly came to his senses as the shadows of the familiar nightmare receded. This nightmare was familiar to him. Brian has been having this same dream for the past 15 years. He looked down at the scars on his shoulder and arm and they were the same scars he had received from long ago. He got them one night when he and his younger brother, Jerry, were playing with fire. He was trying to light Jerry's marsh mellow on fire and just like in his dream he tried to make it go hotter and bigger. It wasn't Jerry who was burned. He was the one who got 2nd degree burns on his arm and shoulder when he accidentally touched his own t-shirt and it caught on fire. He was trying to show off to his younger brother.

He glanced at the clock by the bed, and it read 1:30 PM. He wished he had slept longer but he was wide awake now. He was a firefighter for the town of Plymouth Massachusetts. He came home this morning after a 24-hour shift at firehouse 5.

It was a relatively quiet shift. There was only one call dispatched last night at about 1:00 AM. They had to go out to a house and take care of a small fire located in the kitchen. Apparently, the husband and wife were celebrating something, and they had the bright idea of making a flambé desert of bananas foster. One of the kids was fascinated by it. The little boy wanted to recreate it when he woke up later in the night and wanted a snack. He had been too close to the refrigerator. Like most kitchen refrigerators, it is a common place for people to stick or clip papers to the outside of it. Some of the papers caught fire. Nothing major, just small flames which created a lot of smoke. The wife had woken up to the smoke detector alarm and she tried to put the small fire out using a small kitchen fire extinguisher. She had taken care of most of the papers burning but she panicked and got everyone out. The little bit she left burning, just went out on its own.

Shift change was at 7:30 AM so when he was finished at the firehouse he came home and crashed. His wife, Julie, works in Boston for an engineering firm, so she had left shortly after he came home. His 10-year-old son, Malcolm, was at school and he had left with Julie to drop him off. Mal had baseball practice at 3 today, so he was supposed to meet Julie and Mal at his school tonight at 5:30 for a parent and teacher conference.

He knew why he had the dream. The call he was dispatched to last night was caused by their son Joey. Joey was about the same age as Mal. It also wasn't surprising his brother Jerry was also about the same age as both kids. God, your mind is really creative in the ways it decides to torture you. He's almost certain his son Malcolm hasn't inherited his quirky ability to be able to strengthen or weaken a fire just by thinking about it.

He can't start a fire, nor can he totally extinguish one. When he looks at a flame and it is dancing around, he's able to see beyond the flames and see how everything is vibrating. He can make it go bigger and brighter by forcing it to vibrate faster. The way he envisions it in his head is like stirring up a cup of coffee and how it changes when you add cream to it. It starts out as being like a mirror and all black. When you add cream or milk to it, the colors all swirl with many different colors. When you stir it up, all the colors blend and become one solid color. When he thinks about it in this way and concentrates on the fire, then it will become hotter and grow in size.

To get the opposite to happen, he needs to slow the vibrations down. When he concentrates on making the vibration slowing down. He concentrates on the fire being like the sound of a string vibrating like a guitar string being strummed. If you place your hand on the string it will stop vibrating. When he concentrates on the fire, he doesn't need to touch the fire, but he needs to be close to it.

His fellow firefighters don't know he has this ability, and he would never admit it to them. They do know he is usually the first one who goes into the flaming building or structure. He knows when he goes into a building all of his other firefighters are looking at him saying, "Don't make us have to go in there and save your ass also." So far, he has not let any of them down. So far at least, knock on wood!

His wife Julie knew about his ability. She didn't understand it, but she also knew it was something he couldn't ignore. It was also the reason why he was a fire fighter. Fire was something he wasn't afraid of. He knew it took a lot of strength to run headfirst into a fire, but if it was to save someone, he would do whatever he could to save them.

His dreams always came to him when he was least suspecting. When the dreams first started, they always played out exactly as his earlier dream happened. There was really no rhyme or reason as to why or when these would happen. He was pretty sure the call they were dispatched to last night was probably due to the parent's son, Joey. Joey was about the same age as his son Malcolm. Joey got up in the middle of the night and he wanted to have bananas foster and the magical flambé part as a late-night snack. Every parent probably goes through some period of time while a child is growing up to be fascinated by fire. The best thing to do in most cases is show them how to be safe around a fire. Show them how to put a fire out. Each fire isn't the same, so in the case of a grease fire show them how to put it out safely versus an electrical fire where they could electrocute themselves.

He got out of bed, showered and got dressed. He went around doing his normal routine of cleaning up the dishes from breakfast and putting a load of laundry into the washing machine. When he had finished tidying up to house he got into his pickup and headed to the bank. He was hoping he could run a couple of quick errands before he met Mal at the baseball field to watch the tail end of his practice.

Tonight, there was a *parent-teacher conference* both he and Julie were expecting to go to tonight. He hoped it wouldn't bring any surprises. Mal was a good kid. He had a couple of friends who were like him. It was very rare when Mal acted out or was disrespectful. Today's kids have it so much harder than when he was in school. In the latter part of the nineties, you could still survive without having a massive social media pedigree and presence on the internet.

Now in Mal's generation of kids, social media was what made you or broke you in the social structure of adolescents. It was a lot of work to follow it nevertheless be a part of it. You had to make all the appropriate likes of people in your social circle. Only post the appropriate number of posts. Too many was a nuisance, and none were like you were alone on an island. Brian made the mistake once of posting a "WAY TO GO BUDDY!!!!" response to a post Malcolm put up on twitter of a picture showing him hitting a home run in a recent game they won. The responses Mal got back were, "Mal tell your dad we can hear him across town" or "isn't it cute when adults use twitter?"

Julie, however, was a Jedi master in the internet social media force. She checks into his social media accounts once in a while, but she tries to be as hands-off with Malcolm's social media accounts as much as she can. She knows if Malcolm wants to have a social media presence, he could have multiple social media accounts if he wanted to. One account he used only for his parents with just the safe stuff and another account just for his friends for what is really going on. She can access their internet feed into the house, and she can see exactly what internet domains he was spending his time on.

Brian never really understood the internet and all its inner workings. He was surprised, when Julie asked him one day about a site he had recently gone to. It was a Victoria secrets kind of website, and he only heard about this site from a suggestion of another fireman. His friend mentioned this site was having a special Valentine's Day promo he had used. He suggested checking out if he was stumped on what to get Julie for Valentine's Day. He was looking for a special body lotion Julie mentioned she liked once. She ruined his surprise, so he went with his other choice of giving her tickets for a new play in Boston she wanted to see. It was the better choice. At least he hoped it was. He knew if he did anything with respect to Mal's social media accounts, he would consult with her first.

When he pulled into the parking lot for the baseball field, he saw several cars in the lot he recognized. When he got to the fence on the edge of the baseball field, a few other parents and kids were watching the practice. He saw Mal at third base. A baseball was being thrown around the bases. First base to second base, then to third base, and finally thrown to home plate.

It was just reaching 5:30 PM so the practice was almost over. Over his left shoulder he noticed Julie's familiar Chevy Malibu pulled into the parking lot. He kissed her hello when she came over to him.

"How was your day?"

Julie replied, "Not bad, just the usual. Sometimes I feel like the firefighter putting out all of these different fires in order to keep our schedule not crashing to a standstill. I might borrow your helmet sometime when I go into the office."

"Well, my helmet is all yours, but it might smell like burnt rubber."

She smiled at him, and said, "So what do you think we are going to hear tonight from Mal's teacher? He seemed nervous to me when I dropped him off this morning."

"I don't have a clue. I think if there was something wrong with his schoolwork, we would've seen some sign of it. But then again, I could be totally wrong. I just don't see Mal being able to pull off a near perfect subterfuge. You know how when you look at something and it looks almost perfect or at least perfectly normal, you might think it is too perfect. We see the whole gamut from him. Some grades are good, and they aren't a surprise. Some areas he struggles with, but again it isn't a surprise. I'm going to just wait and see what the teacher has to say. I'm hoping to not be surprised but if we are then we can figure out the best way to help. Right?"

"Yes, that is exactly what I was thinking."

About 45 minutes later they were both sitting down with Mal's teacher, Ms. Arwen Mulloy. She was explaining how Malcolm was doing in his classes. She went over each of the classes he was currently taking. On the whole, she praised Malcolm for being a wonderful student. He was attentive to homework and more importantly asking questions when he didn't understand something. She also mentioned numerous times when Malcolm has helped other students to understand a task or subject. He's very good at math and excels in his peer group. He's also keenly interested in science.

Brian and Julie listened intently to Ms. Mulloy's progress about Malcolm. It was not a surprise to either of them, but at the same time it confirms your perception. Brian noticed her eyes were a brilliant grey with flakes of blue near the center. Her eyes reminded Brian of his grandmother. This was his first thought when he was introduced to her. His grandmother was the only other person whose eyes had a similar color and intensity. He also could see her face was kind and patient. Ironically, Brian thought you would have to have the patience of a saint teaching middle school children.

A tug at his elbow by Julie told him he wasn't paying attention and missed the question directed at him by Malcolm's teacher. Oh shit.

"I'm sorry, I got distracted by your positive report on Malcom and I was just thinking how it confirms the impression Julie and I have of how Malcolm is doing. I mean, as a parent you would tend to not be very objective, and it is nice to have someone else confirm it. I'm sorry what was the question?"

Out of the corner of his eye, he could see Julie giving him the "*nice recovery*" look. He was going to hear about this later tonight, he was sure of it.

"I was asking about your job as a firefighter here in Plymouth. Malcolm isn't one to boast like some kids do about the work their parents do, but he has confided in me how proud he is to have his father saving lives. I was wondering if your fire department has done any fire safety outreach programs?"

"Well, I know once in a while we go to different schools in the area to do a fire safety talk. You might want to ask the Fire Chief about this as to what the town itself does in regard to this. What did you have in mind?"

"This weekend, there is an outreach program for teachers and a few parents which is being held in Boston. It is being conducted at the Copley Plaza hotel. I asked the principal, about who would be a good person to send to this event. He recommended I ask you if you were interested. I know this is very last minute, but it could be a really nice get away for Malcolm, Julie and yourself to attend. They have many different topics on anything from science, chemistry, education, engineering, law enforcement, fire safety and so many more. There really is something for everyone."

She handed Julie and Brian a list of the various seminars and the schedule of when they were being held.

She added, "This event company has been doing this for the last several years and they usually allow a few schools in the area to invite some teachers and some guests to go with them to the conference. Everything is paid for. Hotel, food, and they are also offering tickets to go to Blue Man Group at the Charles Playhouse."

Brian was stunned and not expecting this. His first inclination was to look for the *gotcha* which always accompanies these *"too good to be true"* schemes. After Ms. Mulloy explained all the details, one quick look at Julie and he knew she was already packing her overnight bag in her head. He still knew there was some underlying motive here. These types of things don't happen like this. Eventually you will always find the reason why it is free.

Still not sure if everything was legit, he and Julie agreed to go. If anything, it would get them out of the house for the weekend and just have some fun.

Ms. Mulloy, who now insisted they call her Arwen, gave them all the details of the seminar. The event company and her contact information. Julie asked if she needed to be part of the Fire Safety seminar or could she visit other ones. Arwen said it was totally up to her to go to any of the seminars she wanted to go to.

Arwen could see the skepticism in Brian's face. She said, "There is one small *gotcha* on this event though."

Brian's inner voice was screaming, *"see I told you it was a scam."*

Before he could voice his thought, she said, "There is one requirement of attending these seminars. The sponsors and the event company ask you to fill out a short questionnaire about the quality of the seminar and the person conducting the seminar. They are very keen on using feedback to improve future seminars on different topics. This feedback is essentially the currency you are using to pay for the hotel and the food. The event company really wants the feedback, and each questionnaire is anonymous and only takes less than 5 minutes to fill out."

Well, if all they want is the feedback then this was something he could easily do. He was *in* and looking at Julie he could tell she was *in* too. Brian started packing his overnight bag in his head now.

Chapter 7 – Rolling Stones

Iceley Tower Apartments 537B

Boston Massachusetts

Friday 8:30 AM

Kat and Alder were standing in the hallway outside of apartment 537B. Kat had just knocked on the door of the apartment. After a moment, they both heard the door unlock and a security chain being taking off the door. Pat opened the door and didn't really seem too surprised to see Kat. However, in just a fraction of a second, Kat saw Pat lock his gaze on Alder. Pat wasn't expecting another person to be accompanied with Kat and he snapped his guard up almost instantaneously.

Dispensing all usual pleasantries, Pat looked at Alder and demanded, "Who are you?"

Alder replied, "Good morning to you. I'm Alder Gwyndion. I was told you had an accident earlier this week. I'm a scientist of sorts. I was hoping I could talk to you about this accident. I think I can help you understand exactly how you were able to stop the collapsing floors from landing on the roof of the school below. I also know about the issue with the MRI machine, also. You were lucky to not get hurt inside the machine."

Kat was standing there, and he still hadn't said a word to her yet. Annoyed, she said, "Hi Pat! You know, the sister from Virginia who you haven't seen in 3 years?

Pat finally looked at Kat and said, "Hi Katriona. Sorry. Come in. Place is a little messy. How are you doing down in Virginia with the horses?"

Both Alder and Kat sat down on opposite ends of a grey leather sofa with a glass coffee table in front of it. Pat sat down on a chair opposite to them.

Kat ignored his question. She said, "Alder you didn't tell me who this person was you're supposed to be helping. I would like to know more about this help you're proposing here. Did you know my brother and I are twins? I can't help but feel you're being a little less than honest here."

Alder looked at Kat, and his remarkable eyes burned intensely blue. He said, "Kat, I didn't realize you were Pat's sister until I gave you the red stone. Also, when I tripped in the parking lot, I got a little electrostatic shock when you reached out to help me. Both of these things told me you have a similar gift to the person in Boston who I'm supposed to help. It is truly providence you're brother and sister. The Earth is in desperate need of help. It is slowly dying and needs our help now. I'm here to talk to you to inquire if you might be able to help. Your help is needed but only if you're inclined to do so."

Pat said, "Kat seriously? You just met this whack job a couple of hours ago? Wow, that takes the cake! Holy crap."

Kat spat back at him, "So what accident did you cause?"

"I didn't cause it! Get your facts straight. It was just pure dumb luck it didn't end up on top of the high school next door to the construction site. And yeah, I ruined the freaking MRI machine but the 'tard who put me in there just lct mc bounce around the inside of the machine like it was a new ride at Canobie Lake Park or Six Flags."

They both turned their heads to Alder and glared. Kat said, "Alder this is the time you need to tell us everything about your mission to Boston."

"Yes! Yes, you're right. There is more information I should tell you. May I get a glass of water? It will give me a moment to collect my thoughts so I can explain this to you."

Pat didn't say anything or make a move to get up to get a glass of water. Kat just reflexively got up and went into Pats kitchen. She found a cabinet which held glasses and filled one up with water.

She returned and handed it to Alder, and she sat back down on the couch.

"Thank you, Kat."

Alder reached into his pocket, and he brought out two small stones. One was a deep crimson color, and the other was bright yellow. They both looked like colored types of quartz. Kat sensed they were similar to the red stone Alder gave her just a few hours ago.

He quickly tossed the crimson stone to Pat. Without even thinking about it and just reacting to it, Pat easily caught it in his left hand. Alder tossed the yellow-colored stone to Kat. She also just reacted to it and reached up with her right hand and easily caught it. It happened so quickly and unexpectedly, they both looked stunned and surprised.

Alder smiled and said, "Sorry about the surprise toss, but it tells me a couple of things which would help me to get a better understanding. You both just instinctively did what felt natural and didn't have to think about it. Specifically, Pat you chose to catch the stone with your left hand. It is also not surprising to see Kat using her right hand to catch the stone. I'm also a twin and have a sister who is similar to me but like you two, she would react naturally using her left hand to catch something tossed to her. She also thinks she is smarter than me because she does things differently than I do."

"Welcome to the club," Pat said and was looking at Kat.

"Pat, what do you feel when you hold the stone in your hand?"

Pat thought about it for a second and said, "I can feel it is a little warm. I know this sounds crazy, but it feels like it is squirming around and trying to get out of my hand. Weird, right? It feels heavier than I would normally think it would feel."

"Pat, you said you weren't at fault in the crane crashing, is this the way you still feel?"

Pat's eyes flashed, "Yes I DO!"

"Think about it carefully, did you cause the building floors to break."

Pat hesitated before answering him. It looked like he was struggling and trying to figure out the question. Pat said, "Well yes and no. This is weird. I feel really angry about the floor breaking and the damage done, but I also feel OK about it. I kept the floors from cartwheeling out onto the school, but the 7th floor was breaking, and I had to force the other floors to break so they wouldn't land on top of the school. As a result, the crane had no other way to react than to just flip over. This is how I got the cut over my left eye. Wow, that is weird. I feel angry and calm at the same time. What the hell is this stone?"

Alder looked at Kat and said, "How do you feel, Kat?"

Kat was also trying to figure out exactly how she felt with this new stone. After a second, she said, "It feels differently from the way the red stone felt. It doesn't feel warm it feels cool, like I just took something out of the freezer. I should feel tired right now from all the driving up here to Boston. I don't feel tired. I feel energized like I'm about to start a long day of work. What are these stones?"

"There are 14 different colored stones, and each stone contains a very specific set of properties. Kat as I told you earlier about the red stone, it can be a very powerful stone in assisting with healing. Pat the stone I gave to you is a complex one with powerful abilities. It can focus your mind with a single-minded intent, or it can bring a wave of a calming influence to the person holding it or to another person who is connected or touched by you. Is this what you felt Pat?"

"Yes. At first, I felt really angry and upset about the crane and the damage to the building. Yet, I know it wasn't my fault. The work on the floors below were way behind schedule. When I think about it, I can't come up with a better scenario of how to solve the problem when I saw the 7th floor breaking apart. I can't imagine how horrible it could've been had I let the huge sections of the floor fall onto the roof of the school. It gives me the chills thinking about it. Also, yeah what the hell happened in the MRI machine? Why did it react the way it did with the massive vibrations?"

Alder said, "I can see the bruise and the cut you got over your left eye, is it bothering you or causing you to be in pain? I can help you with this, if you want me to."

"No, I think I'm alright. It hurts a little but not so bad. You didn't really answer my question about the MRI machine and the vibrations," Pat replied.

Alder stood up and reached in his pocket and pulled out the red stone he had given to Kat earlier. He asked Pat to give him back the crimson-colored stone. Pat handed the stone back to him.

"The answer to your question is complicated and requires a long-complicated explanation. If you will allow me, I would like to heal the cut above your left eye. I can explain it better to show you how the vibrations of the world around us are all combined and how they make up our very existence. Would this be, OK?"

"Sure, I suppose, I guess. Is it going to hurt or is it going to vibrate the hell out of me like the stupid MRI machine? I'm sure I can mimic the sound the magnets make."

Alder didn't understand the pun Pat was making and he seemed baffled by the statement. He said, "I don't know of any noises magnets make. What do they sound like?"

Belatedly, Alder said, "Oh, yes I get it. Sorry I didn't understand what you meant. No, this will be done without the magnets making noise."

Alder stood next to Pat and put his hand on his shoulder. Kat was watching intently, and she still wasn't 100% on board with what Alder was doing. Interestingly, Pats skin around his left eye started to get brighter and glow. It was as if someone took a bright red magic marker out and started to color in the gash Pat had over his left eye. At first the red color was very bright, and slowly it started to become less bright and intense. Alder had his eyes closed and just stood next to Pat. After about 20 seconds, the glow was gone, and Alder took his hand away from Pat's shoulder.

Kat was astounded. If she hadn't seen it, she wouldn't have believed it. The cut above Pat's left eye was gone. It was replaced by healthy tissue which showed no sign of damage or a cut.

Pat saw the reaction Kat was having and the feeling of the dull ache went away. For just a second, Kat looked at Alder and it seemed like he was older looking. Alder never mentioned his age, but she guessed it was a lot older than he looked. Alder took his seat back on the grey couch. He also picked up the glass of water and drank almost half of it.

"Water is an amazing resource, isn't it? It sustains us when we need it."

"Alder, when we were in the car you mentioned '*how the Earthlings use the planet to exist*'. A human born of Earth would never refer to people or humans as '*Earthlings*'. It is like going to a Zoo and calling the inhabitants '*Zoolings*'. It wouldn't be correct. We are human and they are animals in the zoo. I don't think I have ever heard someone refer to humans as '*Earthlings*' unless they aren't born on the planet Earth."

Alder smiled and said, "Kat you are so very observant. I have so much I need to explain to you both. If you both can be patient, I would like to explain all of the this and dispel with the intrigue I'm sure you are both feeling. My friend who told me about Pat's accident with the crane and the MRI machine is actually my twin sister. Her name is Arwen and I think it would help if both of you to hear about the very long journey my sister and I have taken to get here. I can promise you both you will want to hear what we have to say. I also think it will help answer questions you both have had regarding your inner voices that intuitively know how to survive against adversity."

"Dude, how old are you exactly?" Pat asked.

Alder chuckled and smiled. Kat looked at her brother and it looked like she was going to scold him for asking such a rude question, but she hesitated. It was also a question she wanted to know the answer to.

"How old do you think I am?"

"Alder you do know when you are asked a question, your answer is actually another question. OK, I would guess your age is older than you look so I would say maybe 50 to 60."

"Kat, how about you?"

"I'll go along with Pat's answer."

"Well thank you both for being so kind, but I'm much older than that. I have seen and experienced things you would be very interested in hearing. Pat, I have worked with some of the most incredible people who were truly advanced beyond imagination. These masters knew and utilized the mechanics of using cranes to build some of the most incredible buildings and huge monuments."

He took another long drink of water and looked at them both.

"Kat you must be tired from driving all night. Can I tempt you both into coming to the Copley Plaza and introduce you to my sister? She should be arriving in Boston in a few hours. I'm a little tired and would like to recharge a little. I can provide a couple of rooms in the penthouse floor if you decide to hear us out. Kat I'm sure you need to catch up with Pat and if you would like to come into the city a little later, I would be most pleased."

Alder stood up and put his orange coat back on. Pat looked at Kat and just shrugged. Alder started to walk to the door but stopped and said, "I would really be happy to work with you both. The situation is very dire and I'm sure you will understand. I really hope you're able to meet us later. I'm certain it will answer all your questions. When you get to the hotel you can either call me from the front desk or Arwen and I will be waiting for you in the lobby."

"What time?"

"Whatever time is best for you. We will know when you're in the lobby."

Alder turned to Kat and said, "Kat, I'm sorry if you feel I have misled you, but I really enjoyed our discussion in the car on the way up here. I'm also grateful for the assistance to get up here to Boston. I hope you both can make it today. Both my sister and I are going to be in the hotel all weekend. Thank you."

Before he opened the door, Kat handed Alder back the yellow stone he had tossed to her earlier. Pat reached out to shake his hand before he left. Pat seemed surprised at the strength of the handshake and the electrostatic shock he got.

After he left, Kat returned to her seat on the couch. She told Pat about the ride going north with Alder. She told him about how she met him. He was traveling with someone, and they took off on him when he went into the service plaza to go to the bathroom.

Pat said, "Why on Earth did you decide to trust him riding with you up to Boston? He could be a serial killer who picks up people and murders them. You and your lost puppy thing."

Testily, Kat shot back, "Don't start with me. I'm exhausted and I only came up here because I thought you were in trouble. What happened with the crane? And the MRI machine?"

"It was nothing. The foreman kept stacking up floors and it becomes this huge *Jenga* puzzle. The floor I was dropping sheets of granite on started to break off. I could see it happening, but it was like watching a replay in slow motion. I knew the floor would break and it would hit the floor below and then bounce out and land on the school. I caused the crane to drop the sheet of granite on the floor below so it would break the momentum of the upper floor cartwheeling out to the school. I did this to 2 additional floors and then the granite broke off and the crane flipped on its back."

"What did you hit your head on?"

"Yeah, I nearly got killed but the boom landed on the frame we were using to hold the granite slabs. I hit my head on the side door of the crane cab. Lucky, it wasn't worse. I got sent to the hospital anyways."

Pat asked, "Now your turn. What happened with a baby you delivered on the way up here? Is the red stone he mentioned the one he used to heal me?"

"Yes. It really is so strange. If I hadn't seen it myself, I wouldn't have believed it. The whole thing was really strange. A car ahead of us started zigzagging all over the place. The husband was driving the car and he was freaking out because his baby wasn't going to wait until he got to the hospital. Alder said to me, '*I agree we should stop*'. The thing is, I *never* said anything to him about stopping. It was just something I was thinking at exactly that moment. Seriously, I have thought about this a bunch on the rest of the ride up here. I'm positive I never said anything out loud."

"And the red stone? Did you use the stone in a way similar to the way he used it on me?" Pat asked.

"No. I just put it in my pocket. When I was helping the women delivering the baby, I could feel the energy or the life force of the infant. It's like eating raw sugar. Infinite and just pure energy. This baby was pissed too. It wanted out and wasn't going to wait for anything as pedantic as a hospital."

Kat got up and went into the kitchen area to get herself a glass of water. When she returned, she continued, "He gave me the stone and I put it in my pocket when all this was going on. You know how I have this quirky ability to connect closely with an animal."

"Yes, I know how you love animals more than people," Pat said sarcastically.

"And this is coming from the person who flips a crane as a hobby," Kat retorted and said, "Do you want to hear the rest of this or not?"

"Sorry. Yes, please continue."

"When I do this, I can feel the pain, the strength, and the energy an animal has. I can help it lessen the pain by taking on the pain myself. I need to be careful when I do this because sometimes it can be overwhelming. So, this is the weird part. The mother and the baby were all connected to me, and I felt everything. It felt a lot easier than the way I did this in the past. It felt like I was the director and just channeling the mothers love and energy into the baby and to temper the baby's anger slightly. The baby felt the mother and incredibly it just directed its energy from anger to love of the mother. Nature took over at this point and the baby was born a few minutes later. It was one of the weirdest connections I have ever felt."

Kat yawned and said, "So what happened at the hospital?"

Pat also yawned as a reflex to her yawning. He said, "How about you take a nap for a little while and I'll tell you the MRI story later. What do you think about meeting this guy and his sister later this afternoon?"

"I know it is strange and goes against any real logic, but I trust him. I can't explain it any better than that. It's about 10 AM now, let me sleep for a couple of hours and if you are OK with it, then I say let's go to the Copley about 3 PM. How does this sound?"

"Yeah. I'm curious about what his angle is. I just hope they aren't whackos or terrorists enlisting us into some cult. My radar is on, but I'm willing to go and meet them."

"OK. I'm going to get some sleep. Can I use the couch in your game room?"

"Sure. I'll wake you about 2:30. I'll get you some food from *Gino's* and have it for you when you wake up."

Kat got up and walked into his second bedroom he used as a gaming room for XBOX and other game consoles. She was asleep as soon as she lied down.

Chapter 8 – Magnet Pop Tarts

Don't get mad, smile and creep them out instead.

-Unknown

Clarks Restaurant

Boston, Massachusetts

Friday 12:00

Alder got off the subway and made his way up through the various elevators and escalators to arrive in the lobby of the Copley Plaza Hotel. He looked around the lobby briefly, and saw his sister, Arwen, sitting in a comfortable chair reading a newspaper. He walked over to her and sat down in a chair opposite to her. Putting down the newspaper, she stood up to hug her brother.

She was first to speak, "You have more grey hair than I remember since the last time we saw each other. It looks more distinguished. Women in this century are wary of changing or letting their hair go grey. I don't really understand the reasons for it, but I have changed my hair color so many times, I have forgotten what the original hair color was."

"Red and fiery as I remember it. How have you been? Are you still teaching?"

"Yes, I'm still teaching and enjoy the little minds a lot. Otherwise, I'm doing well.

Alder asked, "Are you hungry? It would be nice to eat something real rather than coffee and donuts."

"Sure, we can get something. There is a little restaurant here called *Clark's*. I ate there once a long time ago. I'm surprised it still exists. Apparently, Clark isn't a person but was the owner's pet dog. There are many different places to eat in the area we can go to, if you're looking for something specific."

"No, Clark's would be fine. Let's go. You lead the way."

The restaurant was about a couple of blocks from the Copley Hotel, but it was cool inside and wasn't terribly busy. The entrance to Clark's was split into 2 sections. On the left there was a long bar with a bartender serving several people out on their lunch hour. To the right was a section with many tables and along the wall some padded green booths. The restaurant was about half filled. They asked the host if they could sit in a booth in the corner.

After they ordered and were waiting for the food to be brought out, Arwen said, "I had a real shock yesterday. A woman from the New York Metropolitan Museum called me out of the blue. She asked me if I was Queen Boudicca. I almost dropped the phone. It has been so long since I have heard someone say my old name. She found our clue in the South Woodstock chamber. She also knew the young upstart, Allen Westfall. I asked her to come to Boston if she wanted to discuss the clue she found in more detail. She may show up, but I'm not 100% sure of it. I told her if she was in the area then to call me. How many years has it been since we first carved those stones? I would have thought someone would have found it sooner. How are Katriona and Patrick? I assume you connected with Katriona, and she gave you a lift up here to Boston."

Alder said, "You are correct. Kat is very interesting, and she is very powerful. I haven't met someone with the raw power like hers in a long, long, time. I just came from Patrick's home. He's a *leftie* spin like you. I'm not really sure how he will react with the reunification of the stones. He might hinder us. I gave him the crimson stone. He said he felt both angry and calm when I asked him about the accident with the crane. I'm not really sure which side he will end up on. I think he could be very powerful. I just hope the power is used to help us and won't go in the direction as some of our former compatriots went."

Arwen said, "Did you have any problems with the stones? Did you bring all the stones with you from New Jersey?"

"Yes, I brought all the stones with me. With your 4 stones, it still leaves us with 4 of them missing. It's a shame we don't have those. They would really help. Mordag and Kobin can't use them, but it still makes me angry if I think about it."

"Alder, I'm angry at them also. We came here with thousands of our brothers and sisters. They all lost their way and forgot our beautiful homeland and our mission. Earth is our homeland now and we are the last few of the original explorers. Mordag and Kobin abandoning our mission wasn't your fault. We must withstand this final attempt to contact and connect with the Earth. I think Patrick and Kat may be the ones we have sought for so long."

The waitress came back with the two sandwiches and French fries. The food was very good, but the portions were enough for 3 people. After they had finished their sandwiches, the waitress came over and asked if they wanted desert and left a menu for them to look at. After the waitress left, Arwen said, "Have you ever tried a thing called *chocolate lava cake*? Order it for desert and I guarantee it will make you very happy."

After lunch they both walked back to the hotel and Alder checked in. Arwen told him about Brian Keefe and how she hoped her ruse of the technology conference would bring Brian to Boston. They agreed it was risky and could blow up in their faces, but he smiled and thought it wasn't really a bad idea. It may get a little dicey if it doesn't go as planned.

He went upstairs with Arwen and each of them went off to their different rooms. They agreed to meet in the lobby in a few hours around 3:00 PM. Alder went inside his room and was asleep in a few minutes.

Massachusetts Bay Transportation Authority – MBTA

Copley Plaza Green Line Station

Boston, Massachusetts

Friday 3:15 PM

The subway car Pat and Kat were traveling on was part of the different routes of subway stops referred to as the *"Green Line"*. The MBTA transportation system of Boston, or colloquially called the *"T"*, has a number of different subway routes denoted by color, the green line, the red line, the orange line and the blue line. They jumped off for the stop serving the Copley area of Boston.

As they made their way out to the street, Pat continued his story about the MRI machine, "I remember them asking me dozens of questions about metal in me or on me. I didn't have anything I could answer yes to. Then they put me into this huge machine. When the noises started, it felt like I was being punched in the stomach. Have you ever had any animals get an MRI?"

"No, I don't think I did. I know we have some animals who sometimes need to get them. I know a little bit about the mechanics of it. It uses huge magnets which are energized, and it creates a magnetic field which is supposed to force the molecules to point to the north pole of the giant magnets. They are able to get a difference from which molecules turn to the north pole on the magnet and the types of different tissue density inside your body. Metal is very bad though. It sounds like you were very lucky. Did you really ruin the machine?"

"First of all, you kind of lost me after you said *molecules*. I don't know how I could ruin the machine. My brain was killing me at the time and all I wanted at the moment was a couple of Tylenol to get rid of the headache. The noises the machine made were really loud and then it felt like I was being punched. I just kind of tried to push back on the machine or the magnets or whatever it was."

"Did you tell the tech this?"

"What do you think? Yes, I told him, but he ignored me. The tech restarted the program to reinitialize or something. Whatever he did, it felt like the machine was punching harder. I was pissed, so I just pushed back, like mentally pushed back really hard. Then the noises in the machine stopped. Then the tech came in and hit the *Emergency Quench* button."

Pat held the door for Kat, and they walked into the lobby area of the hotel.

She said, "You were lucky you didn't have any metal on you or in you."

Pat looked around the lobby and there appeared to be many people milling around the lobby. He suggested they sit on one of the couches or chairs where they could be visible to see Alder or his sister, Arwen.

In a few minutes, they saw Alder and a woman with auburn brown hair walking over to them. Alder introduced Arwen to the both of them. It wasn't expected, but when they touched Arwen to shake hands, they both got a small electrostatic shock. It was similar to the zap both Kat and Pat had received from Alder.

"Is this a universal way of saying hello where you both come from?" Pat said with a smirk.

Arwen seemed to take it in stride and said, "Yes, it is."

Pat was speechless and didn't know what to say. "Sorry, I just wasn't expecting it is all I meant," Pat said apologetically.

Kat smiled when Arwen sarcastically replied to Pat. It's about time that someone gave it back to Pat in equal measure.

Thankfully, Alder broke the awkwardness, suggesting they go into one of the conference rooms to talk to Pat and Kat.

They walked over to the elevators and took it to the 4th floor. They got off the elevator and walked down a short hallway to a set of doors which opened up to a large atrium. In this atrium was a large central staircase which went up 2 floors above them which circling around this open atrium. Each floor had a walkway which took people to the many different conference rooms or large meeting rooms accessible from the walkway. The walkway overlooked the large atrium and large central staircase. On the level they were currently on, it also contained many meeting rooms. Apparently, there was supposed to be a large conference going on this weekend so there were a couple of people walking around who looked like they were part of the multimedia or service staff of the hotel.

Alder walked across the atrium area and down another hallway and opened one of the meeting room doors. Inside the room there was a large conference room table set up with multiple comfortable chairs. At the head of the table was a large whiteboard and several markers. At the front of the table Arwen and Alder took a seat on one side of the table and Pat and Kat sat opposite to them. In the back of the room there was a water dispenser. Arwen went over to it and got a cup of water before she sat down.

When they were all seated, Alder said, "I'm so happy both of you could join us today. I know earlier today, it probably left you with more questions than I provided answers to. Hopefully, we can clear up some of those tonight. Ok, well to start off with,

Arwen and myself have been given a mission a very long time ago to see if we could bring about a balance between this planet and the people who live here. You see, humans need the Earth to thrive, and the Earth needs humans equally as much. The destiny of the Earth and the humans are intricately linked. It is a symbiotic relationship where each must take care of the other, or they won't be able to exist separately."

Alder paused and Pat injected, "OK, I agree it might be a symbiotic kind of thing. Kind of like bumble bees and plants, right? But if this is the case what the heck can Kat or I do? We are just 2 people out of the other 7 billion people who live here."

"It won't be easy to accomplish but we must start. You both are very special people. Brother and sister twins are linked in unbelievable ways. Earlier today, I showed you some of the stones which are magnifiers of quantum properties. I also mentioned there are 14 of these stones. I have 6 of them and Arwen has 4. There are still 4 stones we are hoping to find, and we have a suspicion of where they might be, but it may also turn out we might not need them. Would you like to see these stones?"

Pat was almost panting with anticipation when Alder said this. Kat just nonchalantly nodded affirmative.

From inside Alder's bright orange coat, he reached into a pocket, and he pulled out 6 small colored leather pouches. Each pouch had a drawstring at the top to close the opening so the contents would stay securely inside the pouch. He didn't make a move to open any of the small pouches.

Alder said, "Now earlier today, I showed you both the yellow stone and the crimson stone. Pat, you held the crimson stone. Now I would like to see how the yellow stone feels to you."

He opened the yellow bag, took out the yellow stone, and gave this to Pat.

After a moment of holding the stone, Pat said, "Wow this is strange. It is similar to earlier today when I held the crimson stone. I feel both refreshed and tired at the same time. Like Kat said earlier, she felt refreshed and strong. I feel the same way, refreshed and strong. But at the same time, I also feel like I could take a nap right now. Is this the way I'm supposed to feel?"

Alder looked at Arwen and she smiled.

Arwen said, "Pat, there is no real correct way to feel. These stones are just tools to enhance some of the quantum properties and the quantum forces we interact with in our everyday reality. Each quantum property vibrates and spins in a certain direction and at a certain speed. It's interesting you're feeling both energized and tired at the same time. Alder told me you felt angry and calm when you held the crimson stone. This is similar to how I used to feel when I held the crimson stone. Now I have learned how to channel these feelings, or quantum properties, into a directed path. The balance between the two are tricky, but they are really wonderful tools. The one important thing you must understand is, it is your responsibility for the power and projection of the particular quantum properties. Does this make sense?"

"Nope. Not one word of it. I really don't understand quantum gibberish, but I'm sure what you're saying is what you believe though."

Arwen smiled and said, "It is a complicated subject. Let's try a different method."

She reached into her pocket and produced two square black magnets. Each of them was about an inch thick. The two magnets were stuck to each through the magnetic bond of the magnetic poles. She placed it on the table in front of Pat.

"Now I would like you to hold the yellow stone in one hand and then place the other hand above these magnets. Don't touch them just put your hand above them."

Pat was holding the yellow stone in his right hand, and he placed his left above the magnet. When his left hand was only about an inch above the magnet, they separated quickly. One magnet flew to the other end of the long conference room table the other flew to the front of the room and flew into the whiteboard. Everyone was stunned.

"Well done, Pat!" both Alder and Arwen exclaimed.

Pat looked at Kat and said, "Holy shit! I didn't mean to do that."

Alder asked, "What did you feel like when you put your hand near the coupled magnets?"

"It's funny. I felt a little bit like I did when I was in the MRI machine. I remember the awful feeling I had inside it and I sort of automatically tensed up to not let it punch me. When I did this, it's like I'm pushing something away from me. Separating these magnets is what you were looking for right?"

"To be honest, I wasn't quite sure how your reaction to the magnets would be. It was a way to show you an example of the unbelievable power you both possess. The yellow stone contains a power to help create a strong bond between two objects. It can also weaken the bond or force between objects. Let's try this again if you don't mind."

Alder got up and picked up the magnet which had flown to the other end of the room. On his way back to his chair, he stopped and picked up the other magnet at the front of the room. He placed these on the table in front of Pat. This time the magnets were separated by about six inches.

Alder said, "Now Pat, this time see if you can increase the attraction each magnet has to each other. Try to see if you can bring these two magnets together, like they were before you separated them a few minutes ago."

"OK, any instructions on how to do this? Or do you want me to just *wing it?*"

"No just '*winging it*' is fine."

Pat had the yellow stone in his right hand before. He put the stone in his left hand and placed both hands on the table with both magnets in the space between his left and right hand. When he put his hands on the table even before he got within a foot of the two magnets they snapped together quickly. As magnets are supposed to do, each magnet will be strongly attracted to its opposite pole. If the poles are the same, they are strongly repelled by each other.

Pat exclaimed, "Wow. This is very cool."

Kat had been sitting there watching all of this, not saying anything. She then asked, "So separating magnets is supposed to save the world? Nice trick, but I don't get what it is you want from either of us."

"Chill Kat! This is kind of fun."

Alder said, "Kat, I know you're hesitant to believe the nature of what we're saying, but you will understand soon. Would you like to see how the crimson stone feels to you?"

"Yes, I suppose. Is it the one where you feel angry and calm at the same time?"

"It really depends on the person. These stones link with how a person is made up of different particles with each one vibrating and spinning at the atomic level. You can cause the vibrations and spins to increase or decrease. Pat felt angry and calm at the same time because it was something he is troubled about. You may have a totally different reaction when you hold the stone in your hand. Additionally, you might not feel or see anything happen. If this is the case, then it might mean there is a balance between the vibrations and the spins of the particles or in this case the magnets."

Unconvinced, Kat thought, well let's just get it over with. Alder gave her the crimson stone and she placed it in her non-dominant hand, which was her left hand. She placed her right hand over the two magnets. As her hand got closer nothing seemed to happen. She could feel the magnet even though her hand wasn't touching them yet. She tried to become in tune with it in the same way she did with animals. She closed her eyes and tried to slow her breathing down and feel the magnet and sense its particles.

Even though her brain was saying this was a colossal waste of time, she could very slightly feel the particles of the magnet. She could feel it vibrating. The magnet on the table wasn't moving or vibrating it was just sitting there. In her mind, she felt the vibrations and then she felt she could slow these vibrations down. As she felt these vibrations slow down, now she could see the source of the vibrations. It was the magnetic poles which were causing them to vibrate. She focused her mind on each pole and when she did this the vibrations slowed. She felt she couldn't completely stop them, but she could make the vibrations dramatically slower. When the vibrations slowed down enough, she opened her eyes and looked at the magnets. The magnets were stuck together like they were before, but each magnet was the size of a large wafer about the size of an envelope.

Alder and Arwen were beaming. Pat sat there with his mouth open trying to think of what to say.

"Well done, Kat! Well, done!"

"Sorry I didn't mean to ruin these magnets; I just slowed them down at the source of where they were attracted to each other."

Alder asked, "Kat do you think you could restore the magnets to their original size and shape?"

"I'm not sure how to do that. I just saw the magnets were vibrating and I just slowed them down at the poles. I wouldn't have thought about the magnets having different poles until I felt them buzzing around. I just slowed down the particles which seemed to be buzzing back and forth all around the edges of the magnets. How do I make them speed up? If I do this, will it make them go back to the same shape?"

Pat said, "Try putting the stone in your right hand this time. This is what I did when I tried to bring the magnets together. Then again you really flattened these suckers like a steam roller just went over it. Remind me to not piss you off in the future."

Arwen agreed and said, "Yes, your brother is correct, sometimes using a different hand changes the way it reacts, but not always. This particular stone has a way to deflate and slow down the quantum particles, but it can also help if your mind is very focused to speed them up. Give it a try."

Kat put the stone in her right hand this time and when she put her hand above the magnets, she could only feel a little bit of the motion and activity in them. She then imagined making those particles go faster. At first, it seemed like nothing was changing. She still felt only a minimum of activity. If she focused on the north pole and then the south pole of the magnet and went back and forth, the activity and buzzing of particles started to increase. It took several seconds before Kat could feel enough activity so she could purpose them into a swarming cloud of particles. She imagined the magnet was like a foldable table, and she was allowing and forcing the legs to unfold and the magnets to regain their original state. When she opened her eyes, the magnets looked almost exactly like the shape it was before when Alder placed it in front of her. The rectangular shape and thickness of the magnets were the same, but the corners were not sharp edges and were slightly rounded.

Kat looked at her brother. If he was stunned before, he was even more stunned now. It wasn't often, but she kind of liked the fact of pushing her brother to the point of being speechless. Arwen and Alder were smiling.

Pat finally found his voice and said, "This is just crazy. What is this? Do you guys work for the government or something?"

Arwen smiled and said, "No, we don't work for the government, but we do have a mission of trying to help the planet."

Kat asked, "Alder I saw the red, yellow and the crimson stones. What do these other colored stones do? You said there are 14 of them, right?"

"Yes, there are 14 stones, and each contain properties which can influence the different forces all around this. Let me write down the properties of each of them."

Alder turned around and he picked up an erasable magic marker and started to write on the white board at the front of the room.

Quantum Mind

For the next thirty minutes, Alder started to list out the different colored stones and their properties. The list looked like this.

Stone	Positive	Negative
***Blue**	Knowledge	Ignorance
Red	Body Healing	Body Death
Green	Nature Healing	Nature Death
Yellow	Strength	Weakness
Pink	Speed Up	Speed Down
Grey	Time Forward	Time Back
Violet	Truth	Not Truth
Crimson	Heavier	Lighter
Brown	Jump To	Jump From
Orange	Visible	Invisible
***Olive**	Courage	Fear
***Lilac**	Protection	No Protection
White	Magnify	
***Black**	Nullify	

"As I said there are 14 stones. Each one contains positive and negative opposing properties. For example, Kat, I told you about the red stone and how it can assist in healing. It can also make someone feel ill or if the intention is strong enough, it can kill."

"The stones I marked with the asterisk are stones which are missing. We think we know where they might be or who might have them. As you can see, each of these stones have a different power which can help in a positive way or in a negative way. The negative way isn't always a bad thing. As you both showed today, the yellow stone was used as a strong force and a weakening force. Also, with the crimson stone it can be a calming or willful force. Everything around us is vibrating and spinning. We don't usually notice this because it's happening at a level beyond what we can see.

Now if you were to use a powerful microscope and look at each of these particles close up, you would be able to see more of what is happening to them and how they operate. Each of these particles have a nucleus, with even tinier particles spinning around this central nucleus. All these particles are bouncing around with other particles doing the same thing. There are so many it is hard to even imagine or quantify. Let's just say there are a lot of them. When you pour sugar into your coffee, it might not really taste any sweeter, but if you stirred it up then the sugar particles, are spread all throughout the coffee you will taste the difference."

Alder stopped talking for a moment to look at both Kat and Pat. They both nodded for him to continue.

"When I hold one of these stones, I can feel the vibrations of the particles around it and around me. Each of these vibrations are also spinning in a certain direction. The interesting part of it is, if I'm able to focus on feeling these vibrations I can control them in a way which is unique for the different stone I'm touching or holding. Sometimes, it takes a lot of practice, but I can control the spin and the vibration. I can make either of them go faster or slower. I can actually make them even disappear in one place and show up in another. Let me show you."

Alder picked up the brown pouch and took a smooth brown oval shaped stone out. It had a shininess to it as if it was freshly waxed. Alder put the stone in his right hand and then touched the water cup in front of Arwen. He closed his eyes and the cup vibrated subtly causing very small ripples in the water. Then amazingly, the water cup and the water it contained just disappeared. Kat and Pat looked incredibly surprised. Alder pointed to the other end of the table. To their amazement, the cup of water was sitting there.

They looked at Alder and were speechless. Arwen just said, "Show off!"

Pat couldn't get over his amazement. Again, Kat smiled to herself as she saw her brother was speechless once again. Pat blurted out, "This is like Star Trek stuff. 'Beam me up Scottie!' If I hadn't seen this, I wouldn't have believed it. Can you make it come back to the front? Or do you have to be touching it or located nearer to it?"

Alder was silent for a moment and then said, "It helps to be closer to it, but as you saw with the magnets you have to focus very hard on the object and then move it. Let me ask you a question. When you were in the crane and you saw the 7th floor was starting to break, did you try to break it more so it would arrest and counter the momentum of the floor debris flying off the construction site?"

Pat thought for a second before answering, "Yes, I suppose I did. I knew when I brought the load of granite down to slam into the floor, then it would cause it to fall inside the central core of the building. I just assumed it broke because of the granite, but I think it was more than just the slab of granite. I think I did see it in my mind. I wanted the floor to break and when it did, I used the weight of the granite to slam into the floor below. If I hadn't, I think the debris would have fallen outside the perimeter of the job site."

Alder smiled and nodded.

Pat asked if he could try to bring the cup of water back to the front of the table. Alder hesitated for a second and then Arwen said, "It took me a long time to get this correct. We talked about how there are all these particles around us, and the tiny particles are spinning in different locations. If you were to actually look at them and watch them in like slow motion, you would see these particles are spinning and they periodically blink out and then blink in. When these tiny particles blink out, they disappear and normally they show back up in the same place as expected. As you said earlier when you were in the MRI machine you pushed against it. This is the opposite thing here. You must focus on it and *will* it here. The *willing* of it means to the landing zone of where you want to put it. This stone can allow you to force the object you are focused on to blink back in a different spot. Also, only focus on the cup and the water. If your focus also includes the table around the cup of water, it will move a section of the table and be brought back here."

Alder gave Pat the stone. Pat stood up, closed his eyes and put his hand out with the brown stone in his left hand.

He looked at all of them and said, "Shazam!!"

Nothing happened. He could see Kat wasn't impressed and was quickly losing her patience.

"OK. This time for real."

Pat focused on the cup. He tried to imagine how he had pushed against the big magnets in the MRI and then he focused on how he could move the magnets together. After a second or two he could feel the vibrations around the cup of water, he thought he could do it if he made the vibrating bits spin in a counterclockwise or left spin and *will* them to blink out and blink back into the area in front of him. When he did this, he felt a snap. Almost like wearing an elastic around your wrist and snapping it. There was a momentary sting but like an elastic it was forgotten almost as soon as you felt it. When he looked down at the table in front of him there was the cup but no water. When he looked down at the end of the table where the cup was just a second ago, he saw the water wasn't moved with it and was now all over the table.

Arwen, Alder and Kat were amazed. "Nice going Pat! Wow I can't believe you just did this. A little messy, but very impressive."

"Pat, this is really incredible. It took me many tries to accomplish this. The focus you have on the cup must also be focused on what is inside of the cup. Next time should be a piece of cake."

Arwen's cell phone rang. She answered it and went to the back of the room to talk privately. When she came back to the front of the room, she asked if any of them were hungry.

Pat nodded and said, "I know I don't need room service or take out anymore because of this beautiful brown stone. I just have to imagine a Big Mac and then presto it's in front of me."

She looked at Alder and said, "That was my new friend from New York. She just checked into the hotel, and I asked if she would like to meet us for dinner."

"Any place special either of you want to go to? Our treat. You both deserve it after meeting with us today."

Chapter 9 – The Band of Five

If there is no struggle, there is no progress.

- Frederick Douglass

OAK Long Bar and Kitchen

Boston Massachusetts

Friday 7:00 PM

Boston has a distinct pulse to it. Wherever you're in Boston, you can feel the pulse beating. The sounds and noises of the city encompass you. It becomes part of you. The air you breathe; the smells of everything being so tangible; and the feeling of just being one little piece of a large sprawling puzzle. You could hear the cars from 3 blocks away, honking their horns or just car engines speeding up to race to the next stop light. In nice weather, the number of people outside is usually doubled.

In Boston, Thursdays are the new Friday, so if you are out and about on Friday then you are a day late to the start of the party. The beat of the city is felt as you walk past restaurants or bars. Normally, people were in the restaurants filling every seat, or a select few of the customers would be sitting in the premium seating in the outside tables.

Quantum Mind

The restaurant was very busy this evening. Alder, Arwen, Katriona and Patrick were nestled in the corner of the restaurant sitting at a large table. The hostess came over to them with a tall and very smartly dressed woman of color with an attractive pixie haircut dressed in grey pinstriped pants and light blue shirt.

Arwen stood up to introduce herself, "Harriet? I'm Arwen and we spoke on the phone. Please have a seat. This is my brother Alder, and my friends Patrick and Katriona."

Harriet went around and shook everyone's hand. It didn't go unnoticed to Pat when Harriet received a slight zap when she shook Alder and Arwen's hand. Harriet took a seat, and the waitress came over with a menu for her.

Arwen started the conversation by asking Harriet, "You mentioned on the phone you worked with Allen Westfall at the *Brú na Bóinne* sites. How is he doing?"

Harriet said, "I'm sorry but Allen died a few years ago from cancer. I kept in touch with him periodically, but his health got the best of him. He talked about you a lot. He credited you for helping him and other archaeologists furthering the knowledge and answers to many of the mysteries surrounding the ancient monuments in those parts of the world. You can understand my curiosity, when I found out by accident that the ancient Ogham symbols carved into the stones in Woodstock Vermont. I'm still having a hard time understanding how the site in Vermont is linked to the *Newgrange* site in Ireland."

Kat said, "Ogham. I think I have heard or read that word before. Is it linked to Viking's runes or letters?"

Alder smiled and said, "The Ogham letters are different than the Viking runes. The Ogham names of each of these letters were meant to represent different kinds of trees or shrubs. They were usually found on the borders of a property to mark the land with the owners name."

"There are approximately 500 stones with different Ogham letters on them, scattered around Ireland." Harriet said.

Arwen said, "Harriet how was your drive up to Boston today?"

"Oh, it was fine, I thought it would be a lot more congested, but it went very smoothly. Arwen, I really have to say this, I have looked at dozens and dozens of historical data sources. It's uncanny how similar you look to the Celtic Warrior Queen Boudicca."

She reached in her pocket and produced 2 pieces of paper. One piece showed a woman who without a doubt was Arwen receiving the teacher of the year award. The second page, showed a picture of a statue of a woman standing up on a chariot pulled by two horses, carrying a spear and wearing a crown as she goes into battle. When Alder saw the picture, he chuckled. When he did this, Arwen gave him a steely glare. He quickly stopped and tried to cover his chuckle as a cough. Kat was sitting next to Alder, and she saw the look from Arwen. It was the look you knew instantly to be wary of, you were treading on dangerous ground.

Alder broke the silence and said, "When did you visit the stone chamber in Vermont.

Before Harriet could answer, the waitress came over to take their orders.

After they ordered their food, Harriet continued, "Last winter on the morning of December 21, I was trying to catch the first rays of sunlight. As others have speculated, the opening to the chamber is aligned with the winter solstice. I have great respect for the builders of this monument and the precision of each stone placed there. It's a beautiful work of craftsmanship. I took pictures of the interior as the sun lit up the inner chamber. It wasn't until yesterday, when I noticed the Ogham markings on the walls. I have asked myself many times on the trip up here what the meaning of the riddle *'To Find Truth Find Mother'*. Sadly, I don't think I'm any closer to an answer."

Arwen said, "Harriet, I'm sorry for being so vague about this clue. The reference to mother goes back to some of the earliest explorers and clans originating from northern parts of Europe. These people held a great reverence for nature and the changing cycle of the year. They would have festivals at the Winter and Summer solstice to recognize the shortest and longest days of sunlight. Additionally, they would have special festivals for the spring or fall equinoxes. It was always in reverence to ***mother nature***. and the Earth. They needed the Earth to provide food and sustenance. The Earth also needed to have life growing on it. All life, which mean all trees, animals, fish or anything else living."

Harriet interjected, "Yes, now it makes sense. You were right it's so very simple. I was looking for something more arcane. Talk about missing the obvious! I can guess the meaning of *truth* is the balance between the settlers and *mother nature*?"

"Yes. It was also a call to stop an evil corruption which was becoming more common at the time. You see, many of the leaders and elders became very powerful among the clans and tribes. They were the ones who were called to settle disputes, or how the land was farmed. If a fall harvest wasn't fruitful enough to feed the people through a long winter, then something ill or dark exists in the clans or tribes. They used to sacrifice people in the hope it would appease *mother nature* and give them enough to survive the winter. It was barbaric, and it was wrong. Many of these elders and leaders became corrupt. The *truth*, as the carving indicated, was the need to stop this practice and go back to the old ways where they could have predictable harvests."

"It sounds more like graffiti sprayed on a stone wall, to me," Pat piped in, as he was devouring the breadsticks on the table and inbetween bites added, "Why be so cryptic? Just say, 'the earth is pissed off and stop killing people'."

Arwen's face softened when she heard Pat's comment. She gave Pat a deadpan look and said, "Too many letters to carve!"

They all laughed, and it broke the tension which was beginning to rise when Arwen explained the earlier Druidic customs. Kat noticed something which she hadn't really felt before when she was with her brother. She felt envious of the way Pat's crude interpretation of the riddle in the stone chamber caused Arwen to look at her brother the way a mother would look at her son. She was guessing this, since the both of them didn't really have a mother role model to experience. It was a momentary feeling as the waitress came back and delivered their food.

During dinner, they discussed more of the nature of their mission. They told Harriet the Earth was in danger and needed help. Pat explained his experience with the MRI machine and Kat told Harriet of her experience delivering the twin foals. They didn't mention anything about the different stones. Alder or Arwen didn't say anything about them, so they just didn't bring them up.

Harriet looked at Kat who was sitting closest to her and said, "So, Alder and Arwen are twin brother and sister. Are you and your brother, Pat also twins?"

"Yes, we are, as much as Pat wishes it wasn't true."

Harriet said, "I had a twin brother also. He died in a car accident when we were teenagers. I send a birthday card to my parents every year on our birthday. His name was Barry, as in *Barry and Harry*. He had a knack for instruments. He could pick up just about any musical instrument and in just a few minutes he could be playing as if he had been playing for years. I, on the other hand, am tone deaf and couldn't play a small ditty on a piano if my life depended on it."

"Allen Westfall must have seen something in you though. I know Allen wouldn't have even given you the time of day if he didn't see someone who was at least near his intellect."

"I was just out of school when I met him at the Newgrange site. I was eager to learn about the history of Newgrange and the different archaeological sites located in that part of Ireland. He needed a gopher and I happily obliged, but I gained a lot of knowledge and experience from him. I have you to thank for this as well."

Alder, who had been silent during much of the conversation over the meal was looking intently at the vase in the middle of the table. This vase contained a pink rose as a centerpiece. When they first sat down, the rose looked exactly what you would expect a rose to look like. It wasn't wilted and was still vibrant, since it had probably been cut fresh earlier in the day. When Harriet talked about her twin brother Barry, Alder noticed the flower became even more vibrant and fresh. He looked at Arwen and she immediately understood what he was looking at and why.

Alder asked, "Harriet, this might seem to be an odd question, but do you have any house plants or do any gardening?"

Harriet's eyes lit up. She said, "As a matter of fact I do. My apartment in the city has a nice balcony to grow plants on and the roof of my building is a co-op for farming fresh foods. I love taking care of plants and growing vegetables. It really is a passion for me. My grandmama use to take me out to tend her plants and gardens. She could grow tomatoes and corn anywhere, even if there was no soil. I suppose some this came from her."

Harriet become very conscious of everyone looking at her right now. "Did I say something wrong?"

Alder took the cue and asked, "Would you be so kind to do me a favor. I have a green stone which I would like you to hold, and I would like to see what would happen to this beautiful rose in front of us, if you held it. This green stone has been with me for many years, and as I have seen in the past; it can connect people with growing things, like this rose in front of us."

"Sure, I suppose. It won't hurt me, right?"

"No, nothing of the sort. I promise it's safe. I just saw this flower change slightly when you were talking about your brother Barry."

"Sure, I don't mind. Don't be shocked if I hum a little. It's what I normally do when I tend to my plants. I think they grow bigger, so I'll leave them alone and they won't have to suffer my humming."

Harriet took the stone Alder gave her. She held the stone in her left hand and touched the stem of the rose in the vase with her right hand. Harriet started humming very lightly. Nothing seemed to happen at first. Slowly one of the petals of the rose fell into the water of the vase. The petals of the rose started to open up more and more. A new bud was forming in the place where the petal of the rose just had been. The bulb became larger and larger. It was very slow to happen, but it truly was happening. The new bud started to open up, and now the rose was made of two flowering bulbs. It was still much smaller than the original bulb, but it was definitely on its way to becoming as big as the other flowering bulb. As the bulb grew and the petals started to open you could see this new bud wasn't the same color as the original pink one. It was a bright yellow rose. Miraculous.

Harriet looked as stunned as everyone else around the table. Harriet quickly looked around the restaurant to see if anyone had noticed the flower and thankfully no one was paying any attention. Harriet opened her left hand and looked more carefully at the stone. The stone was a perfect oval shape and had rounded edges. Other than the green color it looked like a normal flat oval stone.

Harriet handed the stone back to Alder and asked, "What a strange feeling. What kind of stone is this? When I first saw it, I immediately thought it might be a piece of jade stone, but jade has a slightly lighter color green. I could feel the stone become warm in my hand. When I touched the stem of the rose and started humming, I could feel something strange passing through me. It's hard to explain. The first thing I thought of was the feeling when you wake up in the morning. The first stretch and yawn when you wake to shake out the sleepiness. I don't think I'm explaining this correctly, but it just felt like that. I could do a lot of good with this stone in our co-op, I'm certain of it."

Alder asked, "Harriet when you first touched the rose, you started humming. Was the humming coming from you or was the humming coming from the rose and you were just humming along with it?"

"Hmm… I never really thought about it. My grandmama always hummed when I was with her, so I just hummed along with her. If I think about it, I think you're right. The humming was coming from the rose, and I was just humming along with it."

Pat said, "Harriet, your humming was very nice. Actually, it was great. Your brother may have had a knack for musical instruments, but I think you got the voice. You should go on American Idol."

If *eye rolling* had a sound, then it would drown out all the noise in the restaurant when Kat rolled her eyes at Pat.

The waitress came back with coffee and cleared their plates.

Alder said, "Well, this has been an exciting day and I'm so glad to have connected with all of you. I'm sure you have been having questions about what it is Arwen and I are trying to accomplish. Our mission started a very long time ago. If we told you how long ago you would think we are crazy, but suffice it say, let's just say a very long time ago. Our mission had one objective, to bring the Earth out of hibernation and isolation into the full sentience entity it is meant to be. You see, the Earth is a living and sentient force. It loves the Earthlings who live and populate the planet. It has a mutual beneficial symbiotic relationship with Earthlings. The Earth needs life living on the planet. Earthlings needs the resources of the planet to live. It is still a young planet and has a long way to go but it needs our help to make the Earth wake up. It also needs the inhabitants of Earth to take better care of the resources of the planet."

Total silence from everyone around the table. Pat said, "Earthlings, really? So, when you say Earthlings, I get the feeling you and Arwen are not from Earth. Where exactly are you both from? Please, for the love of God, don't say Roswell, New Mexico."

Alder looked at Arwen. Arwen said, "We are from a planet called Ghia. It's similar to the Earth in its climate and gravity. The gravity is slightly more but not really noticeable. It has two moons instead of one. On our planet, we have an organization of sentient planets which are in a symbiotic relationship with the dominant race on many different planets throughout the universe. This organization is called the *Quantum Guild*. It is something which has been around for eons, and it has over 40 thousand planets in its membership. The Earth was scouted about 100,000 years ago and it was thought if the planet was able to gain sentience, the Guild could help nurture it along to gain the full symbiosis with the dominant species and help the planet to attain its full potential in the universe." Arwen paused to take a drink of her coffee.

Alder continued for her and said, "When Arwen and I arrived here, we came with 5,000 of our brothers and sisters to start the mission. Our first goal was to build a shelter for ourselves, farm the land, and create a functioning and self-sufficient colony. After this initial project was completed, we started to build a powerful instrument for the leaders of our colony to connect and communicate with the young planet. We built several of these instruments. You might guess the monuments, and the ancient symbols scattered around the Earth were made to help us connect with the Earth. We tried many times. We built the monuments in the Boyne Valley, Stonehenge, the Pyramids, the Aztec temples and many more. Every time we thought we were making progress, it ultimately failed."

Quantum Mind

"There was a great dissention and struggle within our people. As a unified colony of explorers, several factions insisted on moving to warmer climates. Many groups within our colony, sought to break off and go to Egypt, some went to the Mediterranean areas, and others went to the South Pacific and colonized Asia. In all this time, we never once connected with the Earth. Some of our brothers and sisters came back to the northern climate and become members of our colony in Ireland again. Then about that time Mount Vesuvius erupted over Pompei. When it erupted, we knew the Earth had woken up. We felt it. We think something happened which caused the eruption. We have studied this very carefully and we think the Earth was angry for some reason."

"Where is your spaceship? It must be a cool spaceship if your people traveled to 40,000 different planets. How long did it take for you to travel from Ghia to Earth?" Pat asked.

Again, Arwen and Alder looked at each other before answering. Arwen said, "Pat you remember earlier today what you did with the brown stone. It's similar to how we traveled from Ghia. It's more complicated than it sounds. We were teleporting 5,000 people across a great distance. Shorter trips are much easier and less painful."

"That's so frickin' cool! Harriet you should see these stones they have. They will blow your mind. I popped a cup from one end of a table to right in front of me while holding one of these stones. Kat pancaked a magnet right in front of us and then brought it back to its original shape. Really far out sci-fi stuff.

It's exactly like the rose you just made grow. I'm still in shock over it."

Kat looked at Alder and asked, "I have one question I have been holding off on all day. Now we know more about your mission, the one thing I'm still unclear about is what exactly are you asking us to do to help?"

"There is another person we hope to arrive tomorrow who also might help us. He has an amazing ability similar to the three of you. What we are asking you is to combine your unique talents to become a unified force to do one of two things. Help us try to contact the Earth and communicate with it. If we fail to do this, then we might need your help to contact our home world. They may know what it is we are doing wrong. There is also one additional stone we might regain from one of our former compatriots. There is no reason for you to help us other than just your honest desire to help. It won't work if you feel compelled to cooperate. We learned this the hard way so long ago. Your intention to help us must be pure and of your own volition. If you choose not to help us, then we will say goodbye and wish you the best of luck in your future travels. We have enjoyed meeting all three of you."

Without hesitating for a heartbeat, Pat said, "Count me in!"

Harriet said, "I'll go where the Queen wishes me to go," and winked at Arwen.

Kat said, "I'll go along. I need to clear this with work before I can say yes."

Alder and Arwen smiled, and they could really see how grateful they were. Alder said, "I have lived a long time and I haven't been happier than I'm right now. We can provide hotel rooms for you at the hotel if you want, it's up to you. Whatever you want, or need, don't hesitate to charge it to the room. Everything is on us!"

"Don't be surprised if I take you up on the offer for charging to the room. I have always wondered what $25 macadamia nuts taste like. I want to test if they are really 5 times better than the 4.99 ones."

All five of them arrived back at the hotel a short while later. They all agreed to meet for breakfast at 8:00 AM."

Alder couldn't stop smiling all the way back until he got into his room.

Chapter 10 – True Colors

Everyone gets the experience. Some get the lesson.

- TS Elliott

Boston Copley Plaza Hotel - At The Fair Restaurant

Boston Massachusetts

Saturday 8:00 AM

The Copley was very busy this morning. The technical conference was a big draw from many areas around the country. The lobby was filled with people wearing blue lanyards around their necks, carrying laptops or knapsacks with their essential *stuff*. The hotel laid out a large breakfast buffet in the restaurant on the first floor. It was busy and just about every last seat was taken. People could come in, get what they wanted, and then move on to the conference meeting rooms. It was easy and efficient for the wait staff, since the majority of their work this morning was maintaining a steady beverage service and cleaning away plates or clearing tables to flip it for the next customers waiting to be seated.

Alder, Arwen, Harriet, Pat and Kat were just coming back from their first trip to the buffet. Pat needed to get at least one of everything, so he went back up for a second trip to get every breakfast item he didn't get on his first trip.

Pat viewed buffets like an explorer to a new country. He needed to sample at least one of everything being offered. He likened his behavior as being a guest in someone's home; he didn't want to insult the host. His second plate gave him the 100% percent of food sampling coverage he was seeking.

Alder said, "Today, I would like to continue our discussion about the different stones and some of the properties they contain. Maybe even see if we can try using them a little bit. Also, I would like to discuss what our next steps might be. Would this be OK with all of you?"

Arwen's cell phone rang. Arwen got her phone out and got up and left the table to continue her conversation in private. While she was gone, Alder said, "Arwen is expecting to meet a person who might join us. If he agrees, she will meet up with us shortly after."

Arwen came back to the table and said she needed to leave for a little bit and meet with someone in the lobby. She would meet up with everyone in about an hour. Alder looked around the table and asked if everyone was ready to go upstairs to the conference room. They all nodded yes.

As a group, they all headed over to the elevator to go to the 4th floor where the conference was being held. When they reached the elevator, Arwen split off from the group and went over to the lobby of the hotel.

The lobby seemed to be even more crowded than before. Despite the crowds and the noise Arwen was able to spot Brian and his wife, Julie, and their son, Malcolm.

Arwen said, "Thank you for coming to this event today. Julie, were you able to find some interesting presentations today you might want to go to?"

"As a matter of fact, I have found several. I really find Fire Safety a fascinating discussion, but Brian has allowed me to skip those sessions."

Arwen reached into her pocket and produced three blue conference lanyards with conference passes attached. She looked at Malcolm and said, "Malcolm, there's a game development presentation also going on here today. I'm told, on good authority, this is a presentation geared for experienced gamers. There will be other gamers around your age playing each other also. There will be challenges set up and prizes for the best scores and such. They are going to be showing some of the most popular games and will be discussing some of the tricks to become better gamers. If this is something you aren't interested in, there are a lot of other interesting places to visit, provided this is OK with your parents."

"Heck no! I would rather go to the gaming session," Malcolm looked at his parents.

They both nodded an affirmative.

Arwen continued, "The gaming session is a long one, but it's mostly attended by other children around Malcolm's age. I think it might be fun. I was tempted to go myself. Knowing and understanding these games can give a teacher a slightly higher ability to teach different concepts which are more practical and relevant to what the kids are doing nowadays. To be honest, I really like playing some of these games, provided they are not too negative and bloody."

"Brian if you want, I can show you where the presentation for fire safety is being held."

Brian nodded to Arwen and looked at Julie and Malcolm and said, "Julie how about we meet back in the main conference pavilion where lunch is being served at 12:00?"

"OK, sounds good. Have fun."

Arwen and Brian went over to the elevators to go to the main atrium of the conference.

On the way up in the elevator, Arwen said, "Brian, I need to talk to you about something before we go to this meeting."

"Sure, not a problem."

They walked down the hall and Arwen went into a conference room which was half the size of the conference room they used yesterday. Arwen and Brian sat down at a small table.

"Brian, I need to be honest with you. There is a *fire safety* session being presented here today in one of these conference rooms. However, I asked you here to this conference for a different reason. I have a brother named Alder. I would like you to meet and talk to him, but first I need to talk to you for about 10 minutes. There is a very difficult problem which you might be able to help us solve. He's in a room down the hall from us, teaching some amazingly gifted people how to use some very special stones we brought with us. Alder is my twin brother. Do you have a twin brother or sister?"

Brian was visibly surprised by this question and replied, "Yes. I did. His name was Ryan. He didn't live for very long. My parents told me my twin brother only survived for just a couple of weeks. It was extremely tragic for them. My dad said it changed my mother after the baby died and she was never the same. Why?"

"Sometimes twins have a connection which is more than what is normally visible. My brother and I can sometimes sense or read what the other is thinking or is about to do. He has special abilities which I can't possibly imagine and likewise there are things I can do which he cannot do. I think you have some abilities which only you can do. I think it's one of the reasons you are a firefighter. Have you ever been able to influence fires to lessen them or make them burn hotter or faster?"

Brian hesitated before answering. Something else was going on in his mind. Arwen added, "Brian, I understand if your hesitant to say anything. This conversation won't leave this room. Let me demonstrate something first."

Arwen reached in her pocket and took out a small round pink colored stone. She went to the back of the room and got a small glass of water similar to the glass of water she had gotten from the other conference room yesterday.

When she sat back down, she placed her right hand over the cup of water. Her left hand was holding the pink stone. When she did this, the water in the cup started to become colder until it was one solid cup of ice. She asked Brian to touch it or feel if it really was solid ice.

She could see the look of surprise on his face and said, "Now, I can change it back to how it was before I manipulated it."

She changed the rock from her left hand and put the stone in her right hand. This time, she placed her right hand over the cup of water. Faster than any microwave Brian ever saw, the cup of water was now at room temperature.

Arwen looked at Brian with her piercing grey eyes and said, "My brother and I have several other stones which have similar but unique abilities. This stone lets me change the speed of the atomic particles which make up a drop of water. I can spin them up faster to make the water start boiling. It can also let me slow the particles down to the point where the water turns into ice. I think you can do this in a similar way with fire. Am I correct?"

Still hesitant, Brian said, "Yes, I can do a similar thing with fire. I can make a fire slow down to almost the point of where it goes out, or I can make a fire burn hotter and bigger. At times, it has helped me, and also many of the other firefighters working next to me, to assist in getting a fire put out. No one at the firehouse knows I can do this. The only other person who does know about this is my wife and my younger brother." Brian sighed and took a deep breath before continuing. He said testily, "Is this the reason you wanted us to come up here from Plymouth today? To show you my little trick with fire?"

"Brian, this isn't a little trick. It's much bigger than this. Please, allow me to tell you the whole story and the reason why you were asked to come here today. Will you allow me to do this? If you do, I promise you can go and do whatever else you want to do here today. The conference and the hotel are all paid for. There are no strings attached, I sincerely promise you that."

"OK, I'll let you say your piece."

For the next 15 minutes, Arwen explained to Brian the mission she and Alder were on. She told him about the other people they met for dinner last night and how each of them reacted differently for each type of stone. She spoke of the Quantum Guild, and all the other planets who were members of it. She spoke of the different groups of original settlers and how they had failed to connect with the Earth. Finally, she told Brian about how they were trying to make one last attempt to connect with the Earth. If the plan failed, then the new plan would change to try and contact their home world to request help.

"So, you're not from this planet? This is going to take me a little bit to wrap my brain around. Wow! When did you and your brother come here? I have about a million questions right now which are floating to the surface in my head. Wow!"

"Brian let's try something else with your permission of course. I also have another stone which I would like to show to you. Would this be, OK?"

"Sure."

From her pocket, Arwen took out a violet-colored stone. She placed this stone in her right hand and said, "Brian, this stone has an ability to detect if something is true or not true. It's actually a little more complicated than that, but you get the gist of what I'm saying here. Now what I would like you to do is to think of a number, any number, and also to think of a color. When you are ready let me know."

"OK. I'm thinking of a number and a color."

Arwen touched Brian's hand. She said, "The number is 99 and the color is red. This was from the song you heard this morning."

Arwen could see the surprised look on his face, and she knew she was right.

"OK, now your turn. I'm going to think of a number and a color. Focus on those two things. You are going to see very strongly in your mind, a number and a color. Sometimes it comes with other stuff associated with it, but the most prominent is the number and the color. Whenever you are ready just touch my hand and you will know what I'm thinking of."

Brian put the stone in his left hand and then he touched Arwen's wrist."

He said, "The number is 31 and the color is blue, I think. It is definitely a shade of blue. It's weird though on the color. It's like some numbers are green and some are yellow, but the number 31 is blue. Am I right?"

"Yes, you are correct. I have 31 children, and they are all very dear to me over my long life. I see certain numbers as colors. I see prime numbers as blue; I see odd numbers as green; and I see even numbers as red. I seem to be the only one in my family who does this. The reason I showed you this was so you could see the truthfulness of what I have just told you about the Earth and the relationship it has with life living on this planet. This is why it's so vital to connect to the Earth to help nurture it and develop a mutually beneficial symbiosis. So, you can ask me any question you want, and you will know if I'm telling the truth or being false."

"I'm still trying to take this all in. It might take me a little bit to digest all this information. One thing which sticks out for me is the fact your mission started so long ago, thousands and thousands of years ago. Why haven't you aged? Do you have to be reborn or rejuvenated to stay the same physically throughout all these years?"

"An excellent question. My brother and I, and all the rest of the explorers were born with genes which slow down the aging process. If we're hurt in a way which is deadly, we will die as any other human would die. We are not prone to disease and have a strong life force inside of us which is supplemented by the Earth's sun, and the radiation it transmits. The energy of the Earth and the life on this planet sustains us. Would you like to meet my brother and the rest of the people we've been working with to help us accomplish this mission? They are in a conference room only a couple of doors down from this room."

"Sure. I doubt they could show or say anything to me which would surprise me any more than I am right now."

"You may not want to bet on this," Arwen smiled back.

Conference Room B - 10:00 AM

Arwen and Brian walked down the hallway and went into the conference room where Alder was working with Harriet, Kat, and Pat.

She introduced Brian to everyone. Brian shook hands with everyone and sat down. Pat sat there and smiled when he saw Brian getting a little zap when he shook hands with Alder. After introductions were made, Arwen said, "Brian is a firefighter in Plymouth, MA and is here to possibly work with us establishing a connection to the Earth."

Pat, always not the shy one, asked, "Did Arwen show you one of the stones they have? What color is it and what can it do?"

Brian, not really surprised by the question, said, "The stones Ms. Mulloy, sorry I mean Arwen, showed me were pink and violet colored. With the pink stone she made a glass of water turn to ice in a second. She could also bring it back to room temperature just as quickly. The violet stone let me guess a color and a number she was thinking of. It was pretty amazing. How about everyone else? How are you connected on this quest?"

Since Pat had spoken first to Brian, he offered, "Well I can beat the shit out of an MRI machine! Yesterday, I teleported a cup from one end of the table to the other. I forgot about the water in it when I teleported it, so it was a little messy."

Harriet said, "I was able to make a rose grow another rose bulb."

Kat said dryly, "My superpower is I can take a magnet and flatten it like a pancake. Oh boy, isn't that incredibly helpful!"

Arwen looked at Alder. Alder said, "These stones are really just a magnification of what each of us already have. Harriet, you mentioned the way you can interact with plants and how you help them grow. You can do so many more things with these stones. Let me demonstrate."

Alder reached into his pocket and produced a small oval shaped stone, similar to the other stones, but this one was orange in color. He said, "This is an interesting stone. Let me demonstrate it for you."

Alder placed the stone in his right hand, and simply just disappeared. Everyone in the room, except Arwen, was surprised.

After a few seconds, Pat looked at Arwen and asked, "Did he teleport somewhere or did he become invisible."

"You tell me."

"I think he teleported somewhere. If I had known, he was going out I would have asked him to buy me a lottery ticket."

After about 20 seconds had past, the shock and surprise had worn off. Now they were looking to Arwen to say something. She didn't look worried about any of it.

Suddenly, Alder appeared almost in the same place he was before. He was holding a small piece of paper and handed it to Pat. It was a Powerball ticket for tonight's lottery.

"I knew it! You teleported to the lobby and got me a ticket from the little store in the lobby, right?"

Alder just nodded his head and said, "This stone is similar to the brown stone I showed you yesterday. The brown stone won't teleport anything organic or living. This stone will allow you to teleport something which is living. A plant, animal, fish, etc. In order to do this, you have to feel all the particles of the space you occupy and speed them up to the point where you can feel the particles blinking in and out. You have to force yourself to blink out and then blink back into another space. I forced myself to appear down in the store in the lobby. Or, if you want to disappear then you can just force the particles around you to move very fast. When this happens, your eyes can't see you because the particles are moving so fast."

Alder looked at Brian and said, "Brian when you focus on a flame you try to make it vibrate faster or vibrate slower, right?"

"Yes, that is the best way I can understand it. I usually imagine a fire being like a guitar string which I can control the vibration of."

Alder continued, "We keep talking about vibrations of particles. The particles are made up of the different elements on the periodic table. Water is made up of two different elements, hydrogen and oxygen. Each element particle normally contains electrons, protons, and neutrons. There is an even smaller level than just these elemental particles. This is when the vibrations and spins of the various elemental parts are what we're changing with the stones. Each of you is unique, because you also have the ability to influence them without the stones."

"Wish you had a time machine so we could jump ahead and get the numbers for the lottery. Jump back and play them today, Ka-Ching!!"

Arwen looked at Pat, "We do."

"Wait, seriously? You have a time-machine, or a stone that you can jump around time?"

Alder answered this time, "We have a stone which can track the history of the particles around us. The history of where a particle has been allows us to go back to the specific time where the particle was. It's a very difficult stone to manipulate. There are some real problems using this stone."

Alder looked at Brian and said, "Brian, I'm sorry we are throwing so much at you all at once. Do you have any questions?"

"Arwen told me about how you and the rest of your group got to the Earth and your mission to help connect humans with the Earth in a symbiotic relationship. That part I get, but she mentioned 14 stones you have. My first question is, did you bring them from your planet, and my second question is what does each stone do?"

Alder stood up and went back to the whiteboard and rewrote the same table he put on the board yesterday.

When he finished writing the table of stones, he said, "The stones were brought from Ghia. These stones are manipulating things at a level which is at such a fundamental level, it's the level of the building blocks of what the whole universe is made of. The Earth could easily make these Quantum stones, but the Earth doesn't know how to make them, yet. It needs to be shown or given a stone for it to copy."

He also explained they currently have 10 stones. There are 3 stones they don't have control of which are the black, olive, and lilac colored stones. There is also a blue stone which is missing. The black stone has the ability to nullify any of the other quantum stones. The lilac stone has the ability to shield you, or to break a shield. The olive colored stone allows you to manipulate or compel someone to obey your command. It can also make you become released of your own will and in turn be the one who is compelled. The blue stone allows you to be able to process knowledge in a unique way. It can let you add knowledge very quickly or it can make you lose knowledge you already know."

"You mentioned the other settlers with you and how you broke apart from them a long time ago. Are they still alive? Where are they? Are they a danger to us by going on your mission to help Earth?"

Alder said, "We came to Earth with thousands of our kinsmen, our brothers, and sisters. After many years of not being successful trying to communicate with the Earth, groups in our settlements started to want to move to warmer climates; and try to make a connection to the Earth in those parts of the world. We spent many decades in other parts of the world, building ways to communicate with the Earth. Most of us grew tired of doing it. About half of us moved back to the northwestern parts of Europe. We continued to try to reach the Earth. It was a very frustrating endeavor for all of us."

Harriet was bursting and exclaimed, "Alder are you saying the people who emigrated to the Mediterranean were your people. Do you mean to tell me your people were the founders of the Roman Empire? The pharaohs of Egypt? The Aztecs? Your people who inhabited the cradle of Earth's civilization were not from the Earth. It all makes sense, now! The time frame and the monuments, right? The Pyramids? The Aztecs? Stonehenge? Unbelievable!"

Alder replied, "Yes, sadly they were. The groups which stayed in the Mediterranean part of the world became very different people. The native inhabitants of Earth treated them like gods. They became very powerful rulers of many of the civilizations in those parts of the Earth. They could manipulate the stones properties and to the people at the time, they were gods. Our people just lost their way and became obsessed with gaining power and wealth. They raised armies to invade other areas and claim it for themselves. This lust for power and their greed also led these people to lose their ability to stay healthy. They were starting to die from sicknesses, diseases and just old age. It was a very dark period for both Arwen and I, but also for the thousands of our people we came to the Earth with."

Arwen said, "This was a lot of information for right now. Is anyone hungry? It might be a good time to take a little break for lunch. We can meet back here at 1:30. Is this OK with everyone?"

Brian said, "I have to meet my wife and son in the lobby. Arwen or Alder, is it OK to tell her about this revelation today? She is the only other person who knows what I do with fire. I'm sure she will keep this information private. I can't keep secrets from her. She knows me too well."

"I understand that Brian, in more ways than you can imagine!" Pat said looking at Kat and smiling at her.

Arwen asked Brian to stay for a minute. Everyone else filed out of the room with Alder to get some lunch.

She said, "Brian, I know you have to tell your wife. To do anything other than this would be dishonest. She can handle this information in much the same way you have. If you want to share this information with Julie, then by all means go right ahead. The one caveat on this is Malcolm. He's a young boy who may have no problem understanding this, but I would appreciate it if he doesn't know about this right now. My only concern are the possible repercussions for Malcolm if other kids knew about this information. It could potentially backfire and be problematic for Malcolm. He's a smart boy, and he seems to have found a way to navigate the social discourse of young kids. I would hate to jeopardize it for him."

"Yes, you're totally right. Malcolm wouldn't have a problem with knowing about this. Actually, he would be very excited about this. However, I wouldn't want this to make his life difficult by other kids. It's tough enough for kids these days."

"I agree with you completely."

Chapter 11 – Ready, Set, Go

There's no crying in Twitter,

that's why you have a Facebook account.

-Anonymous

Copley Plaza

Boston Massachusetts

Saturday - 12:05 PM

Arwen and Brian walked out to the main atrium of the conference. Many of the conference guests were streaming out of the various session rooms. They were being directed to a large ballroom where a buffet lunch was being served. Brian saw his wife Julie off to the side waiting for him.

When Julie came over to them, Arwen asked, "Julie, did you find some interesting sessions to go to?"

"As a matter of fact, I found several of them which looked promising, but the two sessions I went to were extremely interesting." She looked at Brian, and said, "I think Mal is hooked on the gaming session he went to. They were demonstrating how you can write a few lines of software code and create a new object in the game. He never really took an interest in the software programming aspects of the games he plays on XBOX. Who knows, it could change and there could be something totally different next month. They even have their own lunch buffet so the serious gamers wouldn't lose time by eating lunch. How were the Fire Safety meetings?"

Before Brian could answer, Arwen excused herself and said she was going to meet up with Alder and the rest of the group. She told Brian if he wanted to continue the meeting, they would start up again at 1:30 PM in the same conference room.

"Arwen, thank you for inviting us to this conference," Julie said to Arwen before she departed to the main luncheon area. Julie knew her husband well, and she sensed something was bothering him. She said, "Hey, why don't you and I head over to *Jake's Grill*? It's about a block from here?"

"Sure, let's go."

Jake's Grill was a small little deli down a narrow side street, just about a block from the Copley Plaza. Come rain or shine, this little deli and burger joint was a secret only the locals knew about. During the week, most of the customers coming to Jake's worked in one of the many financial towers crowded around the Copley Plaza. Since today was Saturday, it wasn't as busy, but it still had a line of people trying to place an order for takeout.

The plaza is normally busy with many people getting outside into the fresh air while they could eat lunch. For some people, it was just a place to hang out. Once Brian and Julie got their food, they found a bench in the middle of the plaza to sit and talk. Julie said, "How did the Fire Safety thing go?"

For the next 20 minutes, Brian told Julie everything about his meeting with Arwen and the rest of the people in the conference room. He ended up telling her about Alder disappearing for a minute and then showing back up with a lotto ticket from the lobby. He also told Julie about how Arwen knew about the stuff he could do with fire.

Julie said, "How could they know about your ability to control fires. You told me the only people who knew about your being able to do this was your brother Jerry, your mother, and me. I never said anything, and I know Malcolm doesn't know about it. Do you think Jerry would've said anything?"

"It was my first thought too, but I know Jerry wouldn't say anything about it. I doubt he even remembers I can do this. My mom wouldn't even tell my dad about this, and she's no longer around. I know you wouldn't say anything, Malcolm, I'm pretty sure, doesn't know. Even the guys in the firehouse don't know. They just think I'm a little too overly anxious to run into the burning buildings and trying to score some *Hero* points."

"When was the last time you remember using your fire ability?"

"Maybe about 8 or 9 months ago. The fire was at the nursing home on Lexington Drive. Some of the older folks wanted to have a special surprise birthday for Edna's 100th birthday. They all gathered in the nursery garden in the back of the hospital. Well, the fire from the 100 candles on top of the cake which caught on fire to something. When we got there, it was still just a small fire. They were lucky it didn't take down the whole place. It was starting to head toward the main part of the building. I was able to slow it down a bunch and I was able to get the rest of it extinguished. I'm certain no one saw me doing it. If they did, they would just think the fire was going out on its own."

Julie thought for a minute before saying, "If I didn't know you better, I would think you were crazy. You said Arwen and Alder are twins and they are from a different planet? What's that all about?"

Brian said, "Oh yeah. This is really strange. She told me her brother, Alder, is actually her twin brother. No big deal, right? It gets weirder. Arwen knew about my twin brother, Ryan. I don't know how anyone could know this. I didn't even know about it myself until I was 7. It was painful for my parents to talk about it, so we never really did."

Brian continued, "This thing, Arwen did with the cup of water. I saw her do it and I can't explain how she was able to make a cup of water at room temperature turn into solid ice and then have it almost instantly change back to room temperature."

Brian could tell Julie was trying to think of how this was a trick, and she would have some scientific explanation of this. Brian continued, "The other thing, which was really strange, was she pulled out a violet-colored stone and she asked me to think of a number and a color. I couldn't help it, but I thought of the song we heard this morning. You know the old song with the '99 Red Balloons'. She held one of these stones and then touched my wrist and she knew I was thinking of the number 99 and the color of red. Then she did the same with me. I held the stone and when I touched her wrist. I could see these numbers in my head, but they were all different colors. The one which was strongest was the number 31 and it was blue. She told me she sees numbers in her head as different colors. Some colors are for *odd* or *even* numbers and others are for prime numbers. It's really weird."

"I have heard about people having the ability to see numbers or sounds with different colors associated to them. I think it's called synesthesia. Maybe this is what she has. It's kind of spooky though. So, what now? Do you want to continue with the rest of their meeting, or do you want to just *bag it* and do something different?"

"I'm actually still curious about this. When does Mal's session get done?" Brian asked.

"I spoke with the guy who's running it and he told me they would wrap up at about 6. They will be doing the same thing tomorrow and picking up where they leave it tonight. I'm fine attending a few of the other sessions this afternoon. If you want to continue with Arwen and Alder. I'm fine with that," Julie said.

"OK. If Mal still wants to continue with the gaming session it doesn't seem fair to yank him out of it if he likes it."

"Absolutely! Maybe they will show you their spaceship if you are lucky," Julie teased.

"Not funny. Let's head back over to the conference. It will be starting back up in a few minutes."

Conference Room B - Copley Plaza Conference Center
Boston Massachusetts
Saturday – 1:30 PM

For the next couple of hours, Alder and Arwen discussed more about the nature of the Quantum Guild of sentient planets. Alder explained how the Guild started and the history of working with the many planets which maintain a unique balance between the inhabitants of a planet and the planets themselves. He talked about the life on Ghia and how it has been a center for the many planets spanning across large areas of the galaxy. Each planet is different and unique in the way it maintains a symbiotic relationship with its people.

There are a couple of different types of symbiotic relationships. One is called mutualism and the other is parasitism. Mutualism is beneficial for both parties in the association. With the help of everyone in the room assisting us to accomplish this we might be able to establish a connection with the Earth. The Earth can help life on this planet grow and thrive. Ghia's long history tells us of a time when the relationship between Ghia and its ancient descendants were ignorant of how the planet was sentient. The people who lived during this period of time, were causing the planet Ghia great harm. It was a time when our technology was becoming very advanced. Ultimately, it was on the verge of destroying Ghia. This was a parasitic type of symbiotic relationship, which thankfully, transformed into a more mutualistic relationship. Our people and our planet could exist together and give benefit to each party in the relationship. Without it, we would have never known about the sentient life of the many planets in the galaxy.

Pat asked, "How do the stones factor into all of this?"

Alder said, "This is a very good question. It is not easy to answer though. The stones act like a lens for an individual or a group of people connected together. Each of us, are born with different genes. Therefore, your DNA and my DNA are very different. Arwen's DNA is different than mine, but the differences between us isn't as vast as the differences between you and me. These stones allow us to focus and interact with the particles around us and make subtle changes of the vibrations and the spinning of these particles. We can influence the speed of the vibrations in them. The particles are all vibrating, and we can increase these vibrations, or we can slow them down. Another aspect we can influence is the direction of the spin of these particles. We can make the particles spin faster or slower, clockwise, or counterclockwise."

Alder continued, "Earlier today, I used the *orange* stone, and I created a cocoon like bubble around my whole body. I then made the particles in this cocoon like bubble vibrate and speed up and go faster. I was able to vibrate them and speed them up to a point where I would effectively be invisible. Think of it like the blades of a fan moving so fast you wouldn't be able to see each fan blade. Then I changed the spin of those particles while they are vibrating around me, the spin of each particle is *winking in* and *winking out*. This is a grossly simple way of explaining it, but what I'm trying to get across is these particles disappear or *wink out* in one place, and then *wink in* a different location. It's a crude way of explaining it."

Pat said, "Wicked!"

Everyone around the table laughed and agreed it was really amazing. Alder anticipated the next thing Pat would want to do is to try it for himself. So, he beat him to the punch and asked Pat, "Do you want to give it a try?"

Alder said, "Pat, this is somewhat similar to the brown stone. With the brown stone you pushed the cup from one place and forced it to show up in a different place. If you can concentrate on making a cocoon around your body and then try to make the particles move faster and faster. Try to focus on doing that."

Pat took the orange stone and held it in his left hand. He clenched his right hand into a fist. His left hand squeezed the stone. At first nothing happened. Everyone was staring at Pat, expecting something to happen. For the briefest moment, his body seemed to shimmer slightly. It looked like his image flickered. Pat's forehead broke into a sweat. It seemed like he was trying desperately to do what Alder had done, but it didn't happen.

Alder said, "Pat put the stone in your right hand to slow the particles down."

Pat shook his head no and his brows squinted even more. His image flickered again and then miraculously it went out. Pat was truly invisible. After a couple of seconds, Pat's image re-appeared, and he was holding the stone in his right hand.

Everyone in the room was stupefied. Pat had a big smile on his face as he looked at the reaction from everyone.

Arwen said, "When the bubble surrounded you, were you able to see the different particles winking in and winking out?"

"You know, it's funny. I started to feel like something was enveloping me, but the harder I tried to have it surround me, the harder it became to increase the size of the bubble. It felt counterintuitive to just relax, and not force it. I kept the thought of a large bubble surrounding me and when I relaxed, then it began to grow and fully surround me. I didn't see anything winking in or winking out, but I really was just trying to keep the bubble around me. One thing, I did notice was once the bubble was completely around me, everything outside of the bubble seemed to glow. The only way I can explain it, is it seemed like I was wearing one of those old style red and blue 3D glasses and everything looked like it was a double image. Is this expected to happen?"

Arwen said, "In a way, yes. The thing you have to realize is this envelope, or bubble you surrounded yourself with, is moving extremely fast. Remember how we said it is like looking through a fan and the blades are moving so fast you can't really focus on one blade. It's similar to that. You're on one side of the fan looking out at all of us. We are not moving, so you can see us through the fan blades. The image is a little distorted because you're looking through the layer of particles around you. We are on the other side of the fan, and we are only able to see the cocoon around you. We can't see you, because you're in the bubble around you. So, you're in effect invisible to us. Does this make sense?"

"Sure, I think I get it. Can I try it again?"

Something unspoken went between Arwen and Alder. Alder nodded and Pat smiled his goofy grin. Putting the stone back into his left hand, Pat closed his eyes and focused on trying to create a bubble around himself. His appearance started to change and shimmer a little bit. It looked like he was vacillating between being visible and invisible. All at once he just disappeared. The others in the conference room heard a very high-pitched sound. It sounded like someone laughing, but the high pitch of the sound made it seem like *"Alvin and the Chipmunks"* laughing.

Everyone was surprised to hear a knock on the conference room door. Before anyone had time to react, the person knocking on the door came into the room. It was Pat and he was beaming with excitement written all over his face.

Alder asked, "How did it feel when you made the jump to arrive outside the conference room?"

"Actually, it didn't feel strange. I just thought of the name plaque which is outside the room here. The plaque says, *Conference Room B*. I saw these little blank spaces in the bubble, and they would pop in and pop out of view. I concentrated really hard on the plaque outside the room here and the next time one of these blank spaces showed up, I just leaned into the bubble and all at once I was outside the room looking at the little room plaque. I didn't touch the bubble, but I figured it would be bad to touch it. Would I lose my hand or something if I touched the bubble?"

Alder replied, "Not necessarily. This bubble around you changes as you move. It can also grow larger if you concentrate on it becoming larger. For example, if you were holding someone's hand the bubble would surround you and also the other person. This would make both of you invisible. Just making yourself invisible and transporting outside of the room here is quite an achievement."

Kat asked, "You mentioned to Pat he could be invisible if he held the stone in his left hand. If he wanted to become visible, he should put the stone in his right hand. Can you explain how using the stones in different hands changes the behavior of the stones?"

Harriet chimed in, "Also what if you're ambidextrous? How does it work if you can you use a stone in either hand?"

Alder's face lit up and he smiled. "All very good questions. The dominant hand does play a role in how the stones react. Arwen is dominant in her left hand, and she can do anything I can do with the orange stone. There are some things she is able to do more easily than I can do. It takes practice though. This is where it gets a little complicated. I have been using the term *particle,* but a more accurate term is atom. An atom is made up of even smaller elements. Imagine an atom is like an egg. When we crack an egg and cook it, the yellow yoke is like the nucleus of the atom. It's made up of some yummy goodness, but in this case let's just say the yoke is made up of two things, neutrons and protons. Now picture the egg being cooked. The yoke will become more solid the longer you cook it. The egg whites go from being a clear liquid like substance to a more visible white part of the egg. The white part of our egg which is surrounding the yoke, or the nucleus of the atom contains a bunch of electrons. These electrons fly around the nucleus in different orbits. Some orbits are closer to the nucleus and others are farther away. Each one of these electrons is also spinning and rotating in a clockwise or a counterclockwise direction. Clockwise direction is spinning to the right and counterclockwise is spinning to the left. OK, here is where the question about holding the stone in your left or right hand comes into play. The electron can be influenced to spin in a clockwise direction or a counterclockwise direction. Does this make a little more sense?"

Kat said, "I think so. I don't think I understand how I can influence the spin of the electron though."

"All of you have a very special gift. You are able to interact with the earth and the universe in a way most people can't. The stones are a way to filter or aim your focus, or will, to a task. Many of the people who came with us so long ago to Earth, could interact with the matter all around us. We used the stones to make accomplishing certain tasks much easier. After a while, many of our people forgot how to interact with the matter around us. They forgot how to use the stones. Arwen and I are able to survive because we still remember how we can interact with the matter around us. It's been a long and difficult road for us. There have been several times we haven't wanted to continue but we must fulfill our obligation to the Guild."

Harriet asked, "So what are our next steps in this endeavor?"

Arwen said, "The next thing we should talk about is how can we activate the device to communicate with the Earth. As you might have guessed we have many sites around the world, but our best chance of contacting the Earth is at Newgrange. We also think there is another stone we might find. Alder and I think the *blue* stone might be located there. One of you could be the one which unlocks the real power of the *blue* stone. Once activated it would help us to find the correct way to contact the Earth."

Harriet said, "Arwen, the Newgrange site is usually restricted from allowing people to gain access to the physical site. I have some friends over there who might be able to sneak us onto the site."

"That would be very helpful. I think we should practice a little more on the stones, but I think by tomorrow afternoon we should have a better idea on the when and how we could travel there. It's probably a good point for us to break now. I think some other sessions are ending in a few minutes. Can we all meet back here tomorrow morning at about 9:00 AM?"

Everyone nodded and started to get up from the table. Pat went over to Alder and picked up the orange pouch which was on the table and put the stone back inside it.

Pat said, "Thanks for the lotto ticket earlier. Now you had to become visible to get the ticket, right? You couldn't just take the ticket while you were in the bubble and invisible?"

"Yes, I did this because I didn't know how to operate the machine. Using the brown stone in conjunction with the orange stone would allow me to teleport an inorganic object to me while I was invisible with the orange stone."

"Wow! I still can't believe this is possible. Thanks for teaching us today. It's definitely been the highlight of my week."

"I'm happy to do it. You and Kat are very special. The both of you are so strong in your natural ability. Together, you will be able to help us connect to the Earth and help it grow and evolve to be the planet it is supposed to be in this universe."

"I'm excited about this and I'll be here tomorrow morning at 9:00 AM sharp."

A few minutes later, Pat was getting off the elevator for the floor where his room was located. Once he opened the door of his hotel room, he walked over to the little hotel room table. He reached into his pocket and pulled an orange-colored stone out of his pocket and placed it on the table. This was the stone which he'd *supposedly* given back to Alder.

He said to the stone, "I think you and I are going to take a little trip tonight to Las Vegas. We're going to have a lot of fun tonight!" Pat went into the bathroom to shower and get cleaned up to get ready for his trip to Vegas.

Pat felt a little guilty for the deceit to Alder, but he just couldn't resist. He's always been a master at palming something and handing it off to someone else, or make it appear he was putting something away. Alder would most likely find out the orange stone was really just a couple of *Starburst* pieces he had put in the little pouch.

Pat learned this from one of the kids he had to room with in one of the many foster care group homes he was shuffled around to. His roommate, Tony, showed him how to expertly pick someone's pocket. They used to get the staff badges they wore around their belts. Those badges gave them freedom to go to places which were not allowed. Sometimes when they were outside at a park, or around crowds in the city, they would be able to lift a person's wallet or phone or whatever they wanted.

He never really got in trouble for it and the excitement wore off eventually. He was pretty good at it, but he had his wallet stolen once and he was really pissed about it. He vowed he wouldn't do it anymore. He just knew at the time; karma was letting him know, enough is enough. He never did it again, until today.

Alder's Room 1343 Copley Plaza Hotel

Boston Massachusetts

Thursday – 10:00 PM

In a room down the hall from Pat's room, a phone was ringing. Alder picked up the receiver and said, "Hi Arwen."

"Did he take the stone?"

"Yes, he did. and he left me two pieces of *Starburst* candy. They were very delicious."

"Are you sure we should be letting him do this? If he goes to Las Vegas, you know he will run into Kobin. That will make this adventure end on a pretty sour note."

"I agree, but I'm sure Kobin will do what Kobin has always done. He will try to get the rest of the stones and destroy them like he has always tried to do. I know you have your doubts, but I'm pretty certain about this. I feel like this time, we will contact the sentience of Earth. I think this will be the last attempt, so take heart in this. It will end our long, long journey. Have faith, Arwen. We will be through this soon."

"OK, but just so we are clear. Repeating the same pattern time after time and getting the same result is still just insanity wrapped in a different package. Good night brother."

Chapter 12 – Newgrange

"Never confuse movement with action."

— Ernest Hemingway

Copley Plaza Conference Room B

Boston Massachusetts

Sunday 9:00 AM

The next morning everyone assembled into the conference room with a noticeable person missing. Kat asked if anyone had seen Pat this morning. Alder told Kat that her brother would most likely not be joining the group today. Kat was furious. She was barely able to control her anger and frustration.

"I knew it. I just knew it. I drive 500 miles from Virginia, and my shithead brother bails out. This is so typical of his crap," Kat said. She realized everyone was looking at her venting her anger and apologized saying, "Aargh! Sorry everyone. It's just that I have seen this movie too many times to count."

Arwen calmly said, "Kat, I know this is an unfortunate change of plans, but Alder and I still think it's worthwhile to continue. What do the rest of you want to do?"

"I'm still curious about this, so I would like to continue," Brian said.

"I would like to continue also. I'm not sure how much my *little hum and grow* thing will help, but you can count me in," Harriet added.

"I also want to help with this, even if Pat is just being a jerk. I'm in as well," Kat said in a more even and less frustrated voice.

"Great! I'm so glad you all want to continue." Alder reached into his pocket and pulled out a grey colored pouch. He opened the pouch and produced a small oval shaped grey stone. It was similar in size as the other stones they used yesterday. The color of the stone was a light grey. It was really indistinguishable from any other stone you might find at a beach or anywhere else. "This stone is a very special one, but it's a bugger to use and requires a lot of patience to gain mastery of," Alder said.

"This stone allows you to view past events or to view future probabilities. It can also let you physically move backward or forward in time. Let's just focus on the viewing part of this right now. I can use this stone to view past events of an object or person. Let's say, I can't remember if I left a tip for the waitress who served me breakfast this morning. I could use this stone to actually see myself signing the bill for the breakfast. I would be able to see whether I left a tip or not. If Arwen paid for breakfast this morning and she signed the bill, then I could also see whether she left a tip or not. These events have happened in the past and they are immutable."

Brian raised his hand like he was a student in a classroom. After Alder nodded to him, Brian said, "Isn't there supposedly a law of time where you can't go back in time because it would create a paradox or something?"

Everyone looked at Brian quizzically. He replied, "What can I say? I was brought up watching every episode of Dr. Who."

"No, Brian is right about what Dr. Who said, but Dr. Who was wrong. Viewing of the past is a non-changeable event. There is a certainty of what has happened in the past and just viewing it won't change our present or our past. Going forward in time and viewing the events are different than viewing events of the past. Looking into the future will give us some of the *probable* events which might happen. The events are not a *certainty* like the past events. They are a factor of *maybe* events. Yesterday, Pat asked me to get a lottery ticket for the Powerball drawing last night. When I got the ticket, the lottery had not happened, so I didn't know what the winning numbers were. Now remember, this is only to view the past events which have happened or to view the future possibilities of events."

Harriet asked, "When you say future possibilities, then you mean the events you are seeing in the future are only a *probability* of an event and not the certainty of the event. This means the *viewing* of a future event could change, right?"

"Yes, you're correct. If Pat had rephrased his request to ask me to look into the future before I purchased the ticket, there would have been a high probability the numbers I saw in the future lottery drawing were the winning numbers. However, there are many different possible scenarios which may have happened. The time difference isn't enormous so the number of different scenarios of events which *might* have happened isn't incredibly large. Let me give you an example. Maybe, when I looked at the numbers drawn, I thought one of the numbers was an 8 or a 0. The actual number could have been a 3 and I misread it. Granted, this is a big deviation, but it's also a possible outcome. Now, let's say I went forward in time to a longer time period. Maybe, I would look into the future to one month from now. You would probably agree with me, there is an enormous number of different probable events which *may* happen between now and one month from now."

Kat asked, "Going back to what Brian asked. Isn't there a thing called the grandfather paradox? If I went back in time and killed my grandfather, then I wouldn't be born. Isn't this a paradox?" Kat asked and looking at Brian, said, "I'm also a big Dr. Who fan."

"There are a couple of rules that apply to time travel. Anything you do in the past can't be changed. If I went back in time to purchase a Powerball ticket from the past, it doesn't change the past. From everyone's perspective I purchased a Powerball ticket. If I gave the winning ticket to Pat yesterday or sometime before the Powerball lottery happened, I would have changed one of the possible probabilities of the future. I know this gets incredibly complicated and doesn't seem to make sense, but let's try and look at this in a different way. We all like to go to the movies, right?"

Everyone nodded in agreement. "Which movie are we going to watch?" Harriet playfully asked.

Alder looked flustered when she asked him this question. Then, all of a sudden, he understood what Harriet meant by her question and replied, "Well how about a long movie with a lot of drama and action and also just a good story. Has anyone seen the movie 'Titanic' which came out many years ago? I was a passenger on the Titanic the night it hit the iceberg and sank. It really was a beautiful boat to be on. It's a shame it sank. OK, sorry for the little digression there. Maybe I can use the whiteboard to demonstrate this in a better way."

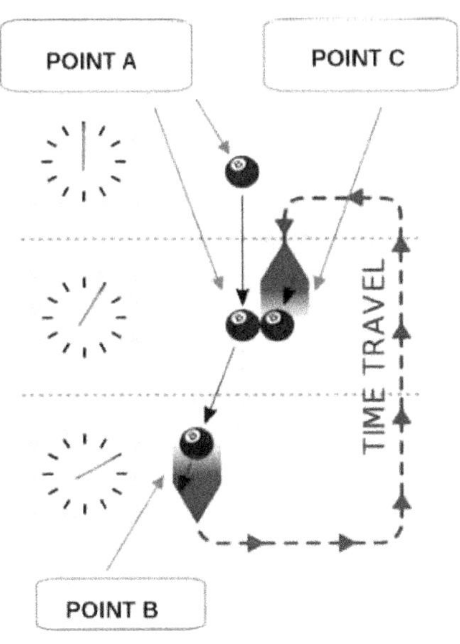

Alder continued, "Now I'm sitting in my seat for the movie which starts at exactly 8:00 PM. At 8:05 PM, I realize I forgot to get my popcorn. At 8:05, I get up from my seat and go out to the concession stand to get my large bag of popcorn with extra butter. I get back to my seat and it's 8:10. I have missed 5 minutes of the movie. I use the grey stone to jump back in time to the point when I got up from my seat to go out to the concession stand at 8:05 plus one second. Now I continue to watch the movie to see the 5 minutes of the movie I missed.

"It's important to remember one thing. Time happens along a singular line and the order of the events are important. The first event happens at 8:05. I get up to get popcorn. The second event is me waiting in line for the popcorn. The third event is when I sit back down in my seat at 8:10. It's at this time when I used the grey stone to jump back in time to 8:05 plus one second to watch the rest of the movie. If I jump back to exactly 8:05 it will become a loop and will keep repeating itself. This is why I jumped back to one second after I left my seat to get the popcorn.

"Everyone sees me get up at 8:05 and walk out to the concession stand. At 8:10 plus one second, everyone around me sees me with popcorn. Their point of view is watching me with the popcorn. Those 5 minutes of time between 8:05 and 8:10, I'm catching up to everyone else's timeframe. The others around me will see me at 8:10, with a bag of popcorn. So even though they see the order of events differently than I do, it's still happening in a singular line of time events."

Kat asked, "Wouldn't this appear odd to people watching you sit down and then all of a sudden have a bag of popcorn in front of you?"

"My perspective is still the same and to everyone else there is no conflict or confluence. I'm still seeing the 5 minutes of the movie I missed. There is also one golden rule which applies when you are traveling backwards in time. When I traveled back in time for 5 minutes, I couldn't travel forward in time until after the point of where I first initiated the time travel to go back 5 minutes. I used the grey stone at precisely 8:10, so this means the 5 minutes between 8:05 and 8:10 are locked out. Those 5 minutes of time happen only once. My point of view is different in the order of events, but they are consistent with having a single track of time which events happen only once. Makes perfect sense, right?"

"What happens when you use the stone to move forward in time?" Kat asked.

Arwen jumped in and said, "Moving forward in time is also complicated to answer. I'll give Alder a little rest on trying to explain this properly. It's unfortunate the Titanic sank on that night, but it really was a spectacular boat."

Arwen paused a second to gather her thoughts and said, "A long time ago when all of us arrived from Ghia, our first priority was to build a self-contained settlement here on this planet. It took us about a year to get us all settled and adjusted to the Earth. We started to build stone monuments which we believed would be a way for us to make a connection to the young planet. Some of these took decades to build. The first couple of times when we tried to make a connection, we failed. We thought we could find the answer by using the grey stone.

"Some of our people did try this. We mistakenly thought we could jump into the future, take a look at the results and then jump back and report what was working and what wasn't. It never worked. The timeline is like a singular track of events. When you jump forward in time, you leave the current time period and travel to a future time period. We always reconnected with anyone who ventured forward in time, and they all stated only a moment had passed for them. For the rest of the people who didn't travel forward in time, years or months had passed."

Harriet said, "That must have been so frustrating to you and your fellow colonists."

Arwen replied, "Yes, it was very difficult to stay motivated after having so many failures. Failures can also be a path to learning. The grey stone would let you travel forward or backward in time, but we learned there was one rule about manipulating the timeline. The time period between where you **jumped from** and where you **jumped to** in time, was blocked from any attempt to jump forward or backward into those time periods. It wasn't until later, when we realized the grey stone was unfolding time along a singular timeline. This meant everything had to have a one common definitive **start** and one common definitive **end**. In other words, if you wake up on Monday and you want to skip Tuesday and go to a point when you wake up on Wednesday, you can do this. However, you cannot jump back to any part of Tuesday or jump forward to Tuesday if it has been skipped. It's a crazy puzzle to figure out."

Brian said, "Um, physics wasn't really my strongest subject in school, but I can try to understand this. I think my cable company has a DVR option to pause, rewind, or fast forward what I'm watching on TV. Isn't this similar? I mean, if I'm watching a game or something and when a commercial comes on, then I can fast forward past the commercials. I can do this with a DVR, but it sounds like what you are saying is I can fast forward, but if I go too far forward, then I cannot rewind it back over the part I skipped? I guess the same is true for rewinding. If I rewind too far then I can't fast forward until I get to the point where I rewound it from. Is this correct?"

"Yes, Brian. This is exactly what it's like," Arwen said, and looked at everyone else and asked, "Does this make sense to everyone?"

Kat and Harriet nodded yes. Kat said, "I mean no disrespect here, but how is attempting to connect with the Earth any different with us helping?"

Alder answered, "Arwen and I have used the grey stone to move forward and backward in time to view or even to visit many different time periods. We have tried so many times to find a way to make the connection to the Earth. Each and every time, we failed in the end. This time, we are trying to establish a connection to the Earth with people who have been born on Earth and are genetically from the Earth. The reason we have failed in the past could just be as simple as the Earth not recognizing us because we were born on Ghia. Any of our children, who also possessed the ability to use the stones were still genetically not purely from Earth. You are all so special, because it has taken us almost 5 millennia to find people who possess this quantum connection with the stones and their magical properties."

"Wow!" Harriet stated the obvious.

"I'll second that," Kat said and then asked, "you said the first place to go was to this place called Newgrange, right? When did you want to do this?"

Arwen answered, "Well as soon as it's feasible for the rest of you. We know this is very unexpected and you also have work and home to think about. It depends on when you would like to go. It may take a day or two once we are over there, but it shouldn't be longer than that."

"I need to get my passport if we are traveling out of the US. Unless you are planning to teleport us there." Brian smiled as if he was just told something very funny. "I can't believe I just used the term *teleport* in a normal way, like it's an everyday thing. Sheesh!" Brian said.

Kat added, "Same here for me. I would need to arrange it with work to get another doctor to look after the animals I'm taking care of."

"I need to get my passport also. As for work, I can just tell them it's an archaeological trip. They will be fine with it."

Arwen said, "I also have to arrange for a substitute teacher to cover my classes. This shouldn't be a problem though. This is just too important to not go."

Brian belatedly added, "I also need to talk to my wife about this. I think she should be fine with it."

Alder was smiling and said, "Thank you all for this. It makes me so happy to have you help us with this task. Now, is probably a good time to break for lunch and make whatever arrangements you need to. Let's meet back here at 2:00 and we can see where we end up on the planning. Harriet, you said you have friends at Newgrange who might be able to give us access to the some of the different monuments in the Boyne Valley area. Any help from your friends would be most helpful. I think Arwen and I have friends there also who might give us some additional help. Also, one last thing, we won't be flying commercial to Ireland. We have a private charter plane which can take us anywhere we want to go and at any time we need to. Kat, if you need to fly to Virginia to get your passport then we can do that. The same is true also for you Harriet."

As everyone got up from their seats, Brian waited until Harriet and Kat had left the conference room and he asked Alder and Arwen if he could speak with him. "Do either of you mind eating lunch with me and my wife Julie? It would help reinforce what I told her about the meeting we had yesterday."

They both nodded their heads yes. The three of them walked out to the main Atrium of the conference where they were going to meet Julie.

Copley Plaza Conference Room B

Boston Massachusetts

Sunday 2:00 PM

After lunch, they all assembled back in the conference room. Getting people to cover for you at the last minute is usually a difficult thing. Luckily, it appeared they were able to accomplish this without too much difficulty. The next thing they needed to worry about was that any international travel would require passports.

Brian told everyone he was available all of next week. His wife Julie was heading back to Plymouth to get his passport and bring it back to him here at the conference.

Harriet was able to rearrange her schedule to also be able to be absent from work for the next week. She asked her friend Ellie, go to her apartment and get her passport and meet her in Connecticut at 6:00 PM tonight. She had also called her friends at Newgrange, and they were excited about helping to give them access to the Newgrange site and many of the other monuments in the area.

Kat called her friend who was covering for her this weekend. They were more than happy to cover for Kat next week. All of her animals were doing well; and she could take as much time as she needed. Kat also called Sarah and Teddy at the Hollingsworth Farm. They were still over the moon about how Jinny and the foals were doing. They were in perfect health, and everything was just fine. The only thing holding Kat back at this point was getting her passport.

Alder asked her if she wanted to try an experiment with the brown stone. He felt confident she could be able to teleport her passport from Virginia. He told her it was important for her to know the **_exact_** place where her passport was located in her house. He asked her if she wanted to practice on a cup of water like he did with Pat yesterday. She agreed and thought it would be best to do a trial run through first.

Alder got up and placed a cup of water at the far end of the table.

Kat closed her eyes and focused on the cup and the water inside it. She could feel the cup. She imagined holding the cup and the weight of the water inside it. She could feel the delicateness of the paper cup. She could see and feel the tiny particles moving around the cup and the water within. Kat imagined in her mind a swarm of particles flying all around the cup of water. She started to see many of the particles disappearing and reappearing. Her senses began to be in tune and synced with the cup and the water. When the particles disappeared, she pushed all the particles of the cup and the water to disappear and direct the particle swarm to reappear in front of her. She could feel a tiny snap, like an elastic band. She knew the cup was in front of her before she opened her eyes. When her eyes opened, she looked down at the cup and the water was right in front of her.

Harriet clapped and said, "If I didn't see it happen myself, I wouldn't have believed it. Wow!"

"Great job Kat! Very impressive," Arwen said with Alder next to her smiling as well.

"Do you feel up to trying to get your passport?"

"Sure. Can I do it from being so far away?"

"Yes. The particles disappearing and reappearing don't know or care about the distance. It's just popping out from one space time to a different space time. However, you have to be very exact on where your passport is. You need to have a mental picture in your head of where your passport is and taking just the passport and nothing else."

"Ok, I know exactly where it is. I can try to do it."

Kat closed her eyes. She focused on only the passport and the place where it's stored. She kept it in a desk drawer and her passport is inside a leather passport holder. She could feel the leather of the passport holder. As she did with the cup and the water, she could feel the particles swarming around the entire leather holder and when she could see the particles appear and disappear, she pushed and forced them to disappear and then reappear in front of her. She got the same snap she did last time, although it felt like a harder snap than it was before. She opened her eyes, and in front of her was the familiar leather document holder with her passport tucked inside. She wasn't sure it would work, but surprisingly it did.

Harriet and Brian were very amazed at this display of what could only be described as magic and not science. At least not of the science Brian or Harriet knew about.

Chapter 13 – Viva Las Vegas

When we lose the right to be different,

we lose the privilege to be free.

- Charles Evans Hughes

Bellagio Hotel and Casino

Las Vegas, Nevada

Sunday 10:00 AM PST (1:00 PM EST)

Victor Santyrous, or Vic as most people called him, was a forty-year-old man, with obsidian black hair. He kept his hair short, lest any strands of hair start a mutiny encouraging others to go grey. He was a tall man with powerful shoulders and a serious face. His penetrating brown eyes were like a lighthouse with a sweeping gaze and his pupils were flecked with gold, like beach pebbles. He exuded an aura of immense strength. People who knew him well, saw him as someone who is very adept at defending himself in all situations. It was rare when he took an offensive stance, but if he did, then it would be to the death, and no mercy. This last quality was fortunately, or unfortunately, inherited from his father.

Vic has been around gambling his entire life. His father taught him how to play poker when he was just seven years old. His father showed him how to bet and wager. His father changed roles when he was teaching Vic how to play poker. The person, whom he called *Pop,* now became a ruthless task master who punished Vic every time they played. In the beginning, his father won almost every hand. Vic was playing with his weekly allowance, so any time he lost a quarter, it was one less candy he could buy. His mother gave him what little extra she had to help him out. One night, he started to win a couple of hands from his father. His father, in the end, still took away all of his allowance, but he could feel a sense of excitement. He kept getting better at playing against his father.

One night, they had been playing for several hours, and Vic was winning a lot more of the hands than his father. It finally came down to one last hand of play. This last hand was an *all-in* bet. His father had a *tell*. A tell is a subtle unconscious signal of your behavior or demeanor, it might give a clue as to what kind of hand a player holds. His father wasn't someone to go *all-in* on a hand, unless he was certain he would win. His father's hand was a *full house* and Vic's hand beat a full house with four of a kind. This was the last hand of poker he ever played with his father. It was also the last time Victor did any gambling. He lost the taste for it. His father was an above average player. He didn't realize it at the time, but his father did teach him a lot about the casino games and the importance of factoring into consideration every single detail, whether small or large.

Vic normally took a walk around the casino floor at least once or twice a day. He enjoyed seeing the people having fun and a good time. It put him in tune with the overall *feeling* of the casino. He usually did this when he came onto the property, but his schedule wasn't predictable. He liked the fact, no one could predict when he would do his *walkabout's*. He felt it was good to let the pit bosses and the other casino staff know he was there. His presence wasn't meant to be punitive, but to help or to assist. He also wanted to see if the players were enjoying themselves. The more they enjoyed themselves, the more money the casino made.

If there was a problem with the staff not doing something correctly, or wasn't acting professionally, he would handle it at a time when it was appropriate. The same was true for the players. It was important to make sure the players were acting in accordance with the code of conduct expected on the casino property. If a player was disrespectful of any of the casino staff, then Vic would insert himself into the situation and resolve it immediately. It was just common sense.

There were always two sides of a coin. It wouldn't serve either the casino or the person involved, unless all the details of a particular situation were known. This was helpful for the casino. Sometimes, the rules of a casino lacked the imagination of a particular type of problem. If this was the case, then the rules and procedures needed to be updated. It didn't happen often, but Vic needed to make sure he could be objective. As a result, the casino would insure the loyalty of the staff and a low attrition rate. The customers and the players are also under scrutiny. They might mistakenly think the customer is always right. In a store or restaurant, this was the deciding factor. In a casino, the law of the land was just the opposite and money ruled supreme.

However, once the details were identified, a judgement would be decided by Vic. Any behavior which caused harm to the reputation of the casino, such as fraud, theft, or lying, were handled quickly and the decision was final. He was still surprised when dealers, players, or staff, tried to participate in fraud or theft. It was common knowledge there were about 3000 cameras stationed all around the casino. It was impossible to deceive or to commit something wrong without any of these cameras covering every possible angle.

Vic had a rare knack for patterns. He took in every detail of his surrounding at all times. He would pick up the most minuscule detail and factor it into his overall situational awareness. Any detail alone could be nothing. The orange juice you poured out this morning just didn't seem as cold as it should. Or there were no ice cubes in the freezer for your ice coffee this morning. If you start to associate the small details with the larger picture it becomes fairly easy to intuit your refrigerator might need to be serviced.

These patterns are not as simple as just a cause and effect. The softer details also need to be included and given a forum to mix into this detail soup. Why would the person put their job on the line to steal a couple of hundred dollars? The answer was sometimes obvious. The person crossed the line into an area of bad conduct and criminality and any casino around the globe would act swiftly, and decisively. Other times, if you did take in all the variables, there might be a mitigating factor which could change the outcome.

As he walked by the craps table, one of the pit bosses, Wayne, called him over. He told Vic he was seeing some unusual play by one of the players. Wayne said he was certain the kid was yanking chips off the table. It wasn't just house chips it was player chips also. He wasn't able to actually see him do it, but he felt sure there was something more going on with this kid playing. This wasn't an unusual event. Wayne was like most of the people at the casino. They were hardnosed players, and they could smell when something isn't right. Vic asked Wayne what his bankroll was at. Wayne said he was about $150K ahead, but this was the reason why he thought something odd was happening. The kid came with only a couple of hundred when he sat down earlier, and he couldn't correlate his play to the chips in front of him. Vic thanked Wayne for alerting him. He would get some of the people monitoring the *eye in the sky* cameras to review the last couple of hours of play. In the meantime, he asked Wayne to give him a *cool down* in one of the suites on the upper floors. He also told him to call him on his cell if he ran into any additional problems.

Vic continued his walk around the play floor before he went up to his office. When he got to his office, he sat down at his desk and booted up his computer. Once he logged in, he pulled up his email and calendar to check the things he needed to attend to today. He was only there for a couple of minutes before his cell phone buzzed.

His phone told him it was Wayne. He answered it and said, "Hey, Wayne, what's going on?"

"Yeah Vic, I tried to cool the guy down, but he wasn't having any of it. He left the craps table but he's over at pit 9 playing on table 3. I can't put my finger on it, but something with this guy just ain't adding up. Let me know if you want me to do anything with this guy."

"OK, thanks for the heads up. I'll let you know if we uncover anything more about this guy."

Vic pulled up the main security program they used as their *eye in the sky*. He navigated to pit 9 and looked at table 3. All the tables down on the floor were deliberately setup like a maze around the casino floor. This maze is broken up into many different clusters of different game tables all positioned around a central area called a *pit*. Each pit might be surrounded by anywhere from 4 to 6 different craps tables. It's the same setup for the roulette and blackjack tables. This gave the casino the means to have the many different tables sprawled all around the casino floor.

Each pit was managed by one or more pit bosses. They are there to help manage all the games being played around the pit. The pit bosses managed the money coming into or coming out of each table's *bank*. They managed any cash money the players were exchanging for chips, and also what the dealers are paying to the winning players for the different bets. They are a jack of all trades normally. The most important thing is to make sure if the proper procedures have been followed or not, and most importantly, they make sure if the guests are treated well.

Vic had two monitors on his desk. He called up the player at pit 9 table 3. He left the video playing real time. From watching him for a few minutes, he couldn't see anything obvious about his play not being normal. Vic absently counted the chips in front of him. He had about $24K in front of him and he was playing modestly with a range of bets from one thousand to two thousand for each point the shooter was trying to get.

While keeping the real time video on one screen he called up the video of 2 hours ago when he was playing at Wayne's pit. He put this on his second monitor. He fast forwarded the video every couple of minutes to see how his chip stack increased. He slowed it down a couple of times to look at the players chip count. He was at about an hour into the video when he saw something strange happen.

It was just a habit for him. Most people in the casino or gambling business could look at a stack of chips and without even thinking about it, could tell you how much money you had in chips. What Vic saw was a big jump up in the value of the chips in front of the person Wayne told him about. The number of chips strangely didn't increase, but the value of the chips changed by a lot. This guy had 40 chips in front of him totaling to $20,625. They were 5 green $25 chips, 15 black $100 chips, 18 blue $500 chips, and 2 pink $5000 chips.

The player to the right of him also had 40 chips in front of him in total $91,000. This player had 15 pink $5000 chips and 15 yellow $1000 chips and 10 black $100 chips. While everyone's attention was focused on the dice rolling at the opposite end of the table, the high dollar chips in front of this player were replaced with $100 and $500 chips. His total amount of chips dropped by $66,700 in chips.

Quantum Mind

Vic couldn't see where the switch happened. One of the *special* owners of the Bellagio had specifically told him about this particular circumstance. On one of his rare visits to the Bellagio, he was asked to have lunch with one of the owners, Kobin Dylan. He told him he had plans in the works to building another casino in Italy. Vic's father was a second-generation Italian, but it wasn't really much more than that. Kobin talked about many things that day. On the whole it appeared to go smoothly and Kobin took a liking to Vic and the work he was doing.

Kobin had an ulterior motive for asking Vic to have lunch with him. He wanted him to be on the lookout for a special kind of cheat. It was so special, there were only a few people who knew about it. Kobin had several additional tools in place to scan the casino with a special set of cameras. He put Vic in front of a computer and guided him on how to use the software and the special login he had created for exactly this type of cheat. It would scan the casino with special thermal imaging and some extra filters which could show a different type of overlay for the video. Kobin had mentioned something about quantum imaging. At the time it went over his head, but he felt confident he could operate the tool to scan the casino for this type of cheat.

He logged out of the system and logged in again using the credentials Kobin had given him. Vic cued up the video to the spot he thought was the place right before the video he had looked at a few minutes ago. He then used the new software tool to scan the casino using the new filters and imaging settings.

Sure enough, when he replayed the video, he could spot it as clear as day. The thermal image of the suspicious player showed him reach over to the other players chips and make a bunch of them disappear and be replaced with new ones. These new chips were thermally hotter than the ones he took.

OK, first thing to do is replay the tape and copy the section he just saw. Next, he needed to contact Kobin to let him know about this. He called Kobin and he picked up on the first ring. Vic said, "Kobin sorry to disturb you, but I came against a player who was trying to do exactly what you told me to be on the lookup for when we first met."

"Good man, Vic. I get an alert when anyone logs into the software. I was hoping it was just a cursory kind of checking for the status quo. I knew you had the knack for spotting this. So, what are the damages?"

He replied, "He took a little over $66 thousand from another player. I'll have to go over all the time period to see if it's just this one time, but I suspect it was more. Also, I gotta hand a lot of credit to the pit boss who alerted me onto this. He has some really keen senses for this kind of stuff."

"What's his name?"

"Wayne Harshall."

Kobin said, "I'll take care of Wayne. Now Vic, here's the important thing. First, I need you to get him off the casino floor and take him to an empty sweat room. I want you to take everything he has on him, wallets, phone, chips, keys, or anything he has on him. I don't care if you have to strip him naked. He's probably carrying something on him which I want very badly. Also, last thing, get two strong security guys to hold his arms at all times. This is important Vic. I want someone to be physically in contact with this guy. Even if you have to strip him naked, make sure the security guys don't let him go for a second."

Vic knew better than to question the motives of Kobin. It was important for him to make sure he understood exactly what was expected of him. He purposely slowed his breathing down a little and then said, "Kobin, let me repeat this so I make sure I understand what you want. Get two security guys to physically lay hands on him and take him off the casino floor and put him into one of the sweat rooms. Get everything he has on his person. Also make sure the guards never break contact with him even when we get his clothes off of him. I'll give him some scrubs to wear in the meantime. Now once we get everything from him, do you want the security guys to keep holding him or is it safe for them to not stay in contact with him? Does this sound about right?"

Kobin replied, "Yes this is exactly what I want. Get the stuff he has on him away from him. Make sure the guards don't release him while they are getting his clothes. Once you get all of his belongings off of him, then the guards don't need to be in physical contact with him. Great job on this! I'm going to get on a plane in an hour and I'll probably be at the Bellagio about 5 PM. If there is any change call me. I'll let you know when I'm on the ground. Thanks again."

Cashier Cage North - Bellagio Hotel and Casino
Las Vegas, Nevada
Sunday 12:00 PM PST (3:00 PM EST)

After Vic ended his call with Kobin, he called Wayne. He asked Wayne to get Teddie and Pete to meet him at the cashier cage. A few minutes later he met all of them waiting for him. Vic said, "Wayne I checked out the tapes and I saw him switch and replace some chips of the player next him at position four. Do you have any info on this player?"

"Yeah, it was Mr. Lombardi, and he's a regular here about every month."

"What's the name of the player who you alerted to me earlier? Did you get any info on him?"

"At first, he didn't want to give me his name, but I sweetened the offer with a nice, comped room. He told me his name is Patrick Themis. I looked him up and he isn't on any database in any of the casinos, so he isn't a player, as far as I could tell. I did *google* him and the only thing I got was a person in Boston with the same name and age. He does have a little bit of an accent, so it might be him."

Vic looked at Teddie and Pete and said, "I want both of you to stay a little back from the table. Wayne and I are going to see if we can get him away from the table for us to talk to him. Once we get him away from the table, I want each of you to take hold of one of his arms. We are going to be taking him to the holding room, 1A. I want you both to keep your hands on him, even if he isn't struggling. Don't let go of him and just steer him to the holding room. Once we get into the holding room, don't let him go. We are going to have to remove everything he has in his possession, including clothes. We'll give him some scrubs to wear after we have collected everything he's wearing or carrying in his pockets etc. It can be a little awkward to have both of you keeping contact with this person. Just coordinate together to do this a little at a time if you have to. I don't think he will cause a problem, but it's important to not let go of him even if he resists. Once we have collected everything and he has the scrubs on, then you can release him. These are the directions coming from one of the owners of the Bellagio, so I hope this doesn't get messy and this person cooperates. If he doesn't cooperate, then it is important to do everything we can to get the situation contained as quickly as possible. Any questions?"

Pete asked, "Underwear, shoes and socks off too?"

"Yes, this is the way I understood it, but yes. Good question. Hopefully, we can accomplish this and not make it not too uncomfortable for everyone."

Pit 9, Craps Table 3 - Bellagio Hotel and Casino
Las Vegas, Nevada
Sunday 12:30 PM PST

Victor walked over to the craps table where Pat was playing craps. The person who was currently rolling dice had rolled a seven and *sevened out*. All the players around the craps table who had won any money for their bets were being paid out. After this was done, the players losing the bet, had their chips taken off the table and collected into the table's bank. Once this was accomplished then the dice was passed over to the next player to the left of the previous shooter. Victor walked over to Pat and asked him if he could talk to him privately away from the active gambling at the table. Pat seemed surprised, but he knew if he disagreed it would make a scene. He told Vic the only way he would talk to him was only after he cashed his chips out. Vic agreed and notified the dealer to *color up* or consolidate his chips into higher denominations. Pat had about 50 or 60 chips in front of him and the dealer was able to consolidate this to about 13 chips. Two of the chips were $100 chips. He passed these off to the stickman as a tip. Once Pat had gotten his chips, he put these in his pocket with the other chips he had collected earlier. Pat stepped away from the craps table. Vic asked him how his night was going so far. Pat told him it was going well, and he was getting ready to end his streak. Vic mentioned he could escort him to the cashier's cage, and he could skip the line at the cashier's cage and get his winnings paid out. Pat was hoping this would happen.

At this point, Wayne came over to Pat and shook his hand on an amazing run at the craps tables. As he shook hands with Pat, Teddie and Pete came up from behind him and placed their iron steel grip on Pat's arms. Pat was surprised and struggled at first, but it was only a temporary struggle. The two hands placed on each of arms were steel and unyielding. He looked at Vic for an explanation.

Vic said, "Pat we need to talk to you. It will be easier if you coopcrate. The two men on each side of you have been given instructions to hold onto you no matter how hard you struggle. I suggest you don't test the strength of my friends here." Vic looked at Teddie and asked, "Teddie how much can you bench press?"

Teddie said, "325 this morning."

This seemed to register with Pat. Pat was relatively strong himself, but he knew Teddie could outpower him. Pat said, "OK let's go where you want me to go. I go on my own power."

Vic smiled and said, "Pat thank you for agreeing to comply with this. Teddie and Pete will still hold on to you until we get to a little conference room where we can talk privately. The sooner we get this over with, the sooner you can relax and do whatever you want to do."

Teddie and Pete maintained their steely grip on Pat's arms and steered Pat from the craps table area to a nondescript door which Vic opened with a special key card. It opened to a long wide hallway which was a system of corridors and walkways to various parts of the casino and the hotel. These hallways were a shortcut most of the staff used to navigate around the different areas of the inner workings of the hotel and casino. Cocktail hostesses used this sometimes as a shortcut to get drinks to customers or high rollers as soon as possible. It wasn't uncommon to see various people in uniforms or wearing expensive suits in this hidden area.

They arrived at the holding room for Pat. Wayne used a special key to open the door to the room. Inside, it was essentially a non-descript rectangular room with three chairs and a single table in the middle of it. On top of the table was a set of pants, shirt, underwear and socks. Teddie and Pete steered Pat into the room and didn't release their grip on Pat.

Vic said, "Pat, this next part can go easily if you cooperate, but if you don't, it will be uncomfortable. We need to take everything you currently have on you and place them in this bag sitting on the table. My friends have been instructed to not let you go until we get everything you have on you right now. We will give you some clothes to wear in the meantime." Vic pointed to the clothes on the table. Vic continued, "Your items will be kept secure and under my control. They will be given back to you once we are done. Will you comply with this request, or will this be uncomfortable for all of us?"

"Seriously? Tell me why first."

Victor gave Patrick a big smile and looked at Wayne and then back to Pat. He simply said, "No. Wayne let's get this over with."

Wayne nodded to Vic and looked at Pete and Teddie who tensed up for what was coming next. Wayne walked over in front of Pat, reached out and undid the belt on Pat's jeans. He continued to unbutton his jeans and commenced taking them off. He took off each shoe and got Pat's pants totally off. He then continued to take off Pat's underwear while at the same time putting on the new underwear from the table. Next, he put on the scrub pants from the table. Finally, with the help of Teddie and Pete coordinating the arms of Pat, Wayne was able to remove this shirt and place a new shirt on him. All of Pat's clothes and belongings were put inside a bag neatly folded and anything inside the pockets were enclosed in a clear ziplock bag.

Once everything was removed from Pat, and he was dressed in new clothes, Vic nodded to Teddie and Pete to release Patrick. He now turned his attention to Pat and said, "Mr. Themis you can relax now. My friends here were given explicit instructions to separate you from anything you had on your person. Your belongings will be returned to you once we are done conducting this discussion. I apologize for the show of force, but it was necessary. There is someone associated with the Bellagio, who is very interested in talking to you. In fact, he's on his way here right now. In the meantime, you'll have to sit here and wait for him. When was the last time you ate? The Bellagio has some great dining facilities available. If you're hungry, we can have some food delivered here if you would like."

Pat didn't answer right away. He was furious. He knew when he was this angry, he needed to be careful. If he let his emotions take control it would explode in a very self-destructive way. He knew better than to drink when he was this angry, but maybe it could give an illusion of his defenses being dropped. He still hadn't said anything, and Victor was waiting for him to respond. Finally, he said, "How about a double Rum and Coke? Don't water it down like the floor drinks."

"Very well. We can have it delivered here in a few minutes. Anything to eat?"

"Nope!"

"Very well. Teddie and Pete thank you for your help. If you don't mind, I would like you both to wait outside for right now. Wayne thank you for your assistance here, I'll follow up with you in a little bit. Thank you."

Once Wayne, Teddie and Pete left the room, Vic called a number to place the order for Pat and instructions for where it was to be delivered. The only thing left to do was to wait until Kobin arrived. It was about 1:30 PM. For Pat it would be about 4:30 PM Sunday evening. Pat must be running on just reserve energy at this point. He had been playing craps all night and a good part of the day. Vic now understood why Pat didn't resist any more than he did. Getting stripped naked isn't comfortable for anyone involved. Vic was grateful it had not gotten messy.

Once everyone left, and Vic and Pat were alone in the room, Pat asked, "What exactly is this all about? I didn't resist so hopefully this can buy me a few points here."

"To be honest with you, I'm really not 100% sure myself. There is someone who I report to who is very interested in talking to you. I don't have any other details than what I told you. It sounds like you have a little bit of a Boston accent. Are you from Boston? My wife is from Billerica. We usually go there around the spring to visit her family," Vic said this to deliberately try and change the topic. Vic's wife was from Arizona and had nothing to do with Massachusetts. Victor has been there twice. Once for an international trip for a layover and the other time to visit a friend from New Hampshire.

"Your wife is from Billerica, huh? Yeah, OK, I seriously doubt it, but you get points for pronouncing it exactly the way someone would pronounce it who has never been there before. So again, what is this all about?"

"Again, I have as much information as you do. So, we'll have to wait until this person arrives. In the meantime, you'll have to wait here until your meeting is finished."

There was a knock on the door. Vic went over and opened it. Teddie was holding a tray with a small bucket of ice, a Styrofoam cup, a bottle of Coca Cola and 2 Bacardi nips plastic bottles. Vic took the tray and placed it on the table. Pat got up from his chair and made a drink using one of the Bacardi nips, half of the bottle of Coca-Cola, and several ice cubes in the Styrofoam cup.

Once Pat prepared his drink and sat down, Vic sat down on a chair opposite him. He asked, "What do you do in Boston, if I might ask?"

"Construction of big buildings. What do you do?" Pat asked flipping it back over to Vic.

Fair question he thought, but a smart-ass answer. This deserved the same type of response. Vic said, "I catch people who cheat."

Pat chuckled at this. "Well, you and I have a few things in common. A lot of buildings going up across the world are cheating in one way or another. They are always trying to bend the rules or blur the line between what is safe and what is dangerous. There isn't much difference."

"Hmm. That is an interesting point of view. You are correct. Cheating a gambling casino is very dangerous. If you play by the rules of the casino then you are free to play and try to win. If you don't want to gamble, then there are many different ways to entertain yourself or your friends. To most people, this would be considered a safe activity. Wouldn't you consider stealing from the Bellagio or any of its customers is bending the rules or blurring the line?"

Pat didn't answer Vic's question and instead asked, "So when is your buddy going to get here?"

Vic laughed, "He will be here soon enough. Do you have any other advice for me about things we might have in common?"

Pat just stared and said, "Nope."

Chapter 14 – The Color of Anger

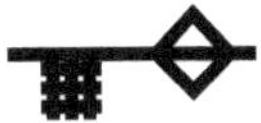

"He who angers you conquers you."

- Elizabeth Kenny

Bellagio Hotel and Casino

Las Vegas, Nevada

Sunday 5:00 PM PST (8:00 PM EST)

The Gulfstream G700 Jet carved through the night sky like a viper, soundlessly leaving higher altitudes before waiting for the sound to catch up. Plunging from 44,000 feet and seizing on its prey of Las Vegas' McCarran International Airport. It was almost too easy, since it was the brightest of any other lights on the ground for miles. The Gulfstream sensing its prey, screamed silently from 44,000 feet to land.

Kobin Dylan was looking out the window of the jet, when the co-pilot came out from the cockpit to let him know they would be landing in 15 minutes. Since it was just Kobin and the two pilots, flying with less weight allowed the jet to fly at maximum airspeed and higher altitudes. This helped to shave off an hour of the normal flying time.

Kobin was wearing a dark navy-blue suit with a white shirt. His jacket and red tie were draped over the back of the luxury recliner seat in front of him. Kobin was a tall man with powerful shoulders, a fierce dark face with a closely cropped beard, and eyes which seemed to flash and glitter with savage laughter. It was a face to be dominated by, or to fight. It was never a face to patronize or pity. All his movements were large and perfectly balanced, like those of a wild animal. Even though the cabin of the aircraft was roomy enough for him, he seemed like a wild animal held in a cage too small for it.

Kobin was deeply involved in the financial markets on Wall Street. He has connections all over the world investing money into a cacophony of different markets and currencies. He has made numerous connections over the last 100 years of shepherding these different worldwide markets. Some connections were beneficial and helped to increase his reign over those markets. Sadly, many of those connections were just the opposite. These were the ones who lost either money or reputation as a result of his actions or investments. These are just the rules of commerce. It's always a case of a win, or a loss. Nothing more and nothing less.

A good example of this was his flying out to Las Vegas at a moment's notice. He owned this jet, and also two other planes in hangars at different airports. The company he used to manage these planes, leased them out as timeshares for many different executives, companies, or the jet set crowd, who needed some extra privacy or flying on a moment's notice. This company was responsible for the upkeep of the aircraft and all the other trivial details to make a profit. The profit Kobin received from this was minimal. It was at times like this, it was very useful and justified the expense to have a jet on standby and be able to be able to drop everything and get on a plane 30 minutes later.

His assistant was tasked with making all the arrangements, while he was flying from New York. She had his normal room he stayed in at the Bellagio cleaned and stocked. When they landed, she had a town car waiting for him when he stepped off the jet to drive him to the Bellagio. It was the typical congestion of traffic clogging up Las Vegas Boulevard, or as most called it, *the Strip*, on a Sunday evening. His driver knew several *cut throughs* to get him to the Bellagio without too much delay. He also called Vic on his way over to alert him he had landed and was on his way to meet him in the holding room. For the briefest moment, he felt a feeling of satisfaction he hadn't felt in a long time. He didn't want to get his hopes up, but if Vic has indeed caught someone with his special cameras, then this person must have one of the quantum stones, or Q-Stones as he called them.

The unfortunate history of the Q-Stones was a deep disappointment for Kobin. At one time, he and his sister, Mordag, had physical control of most of the different colored Q-Stones. They lost control of all but 3 of the stones about 2000 years ago. It was at a time of great upheaval among the many different human civilizations. At this period of time in human history, wars raged all around the globe. The fighting was always about control of land, wealth, and power. It was back at a time when Arwen was known as Boudicca, the Celtic Warrior Queen. The bloodshed and battles in Ireland and England were devastating and brutal.

At the height of the blood lust, his son Creyn, betrayed him. Creyn blamed him for the loss of his wife and two sons. She was killed by one of Arwen's warriors. He was forced to watch her being killed along with his two sons. Creyn felt there was nothing left for him to continue living. Before, he committed suicide, he gave almost all the stones to Alder and Arwen to get back at him. When the war finally ended in the siege of London, or Londinium as it was called back then, Kobin was restored to power and took control of the Roman armies. Arwen and Alder just disappeared.

He searched for Alder and Arwen for a long time, but he never was able to find any clues of where they might have gone. Alder was very adept at using the grey stone to control time. There was no trace of either of them. Kobin suspected Alder used the time stone to jump forward in time. Once he and Arwen jumped forward, they wouldn't be able to go back to a time just before the war raged. It would make sense if you were to go back in time, it would only allow you to go back to a point when you had control of the grey stone. If you didn't have control of the stone, then you wouldn't be able to go to this point in time. Alder and Arwen had lost control of the grey stone about 1000 years prior to these huge battles. This would be the only point in time which they could jump back to. It's one of those riddles. Which one came first, the chicken or the egg? At least this is what he understood about it. The results could be very unpredictable if you change something in the past.

His driver pulled into the *service* entrance for the Bellagio. Kobin didn't want to go into the main lobby area, ironically it was because of all the cameras watching. Vic told him he would have someone waiting for him at the service entrance. Kobin got out of the town car and followed the man into the bowels of the back hallways and entrances to the many different parts of the hotel. They stopped in front of a door, and Kobin walked in to meet the person Vic had tagged from the casino floor a couple of hours ago.

Pat was sitting on the other side of the table. He didn't stand up. Kobin shook hands with Vic. Kobin turned to Pat still sitting at the table and he offered his hand to shake with him. Just out of pure reflex, Pat shook hands with Kobin. When his hand touched Kobin's, he got a static electricity zap as he had previously gotten from both Alder and Arwen. Pat exclaimed literally being shocked out of his surliness with Vic, "Damn it! What is it with you people? Is this some sort of custom on your planet where you zap people when you first meet them?"

"Yes, it is. Now try to imagine what we do about the people we don't like," Kobin said mysteriously.

Pat normally would've responded with some sarcastic come back. He decided it would be better to go back to his sullenness he had adopted when he was talking to Vic. The new guy seemed to be running the show tonight.

"Kobin, do you want to look at the video I copied earlier?" Vic asked as he pulled up a tablet with the video all cued up for Kobin.

Kobin and Vic watched the video and made no offer to let Pat see it. It wasn't very long, maybe 20 seconds or so. Kobin was smiling. He knew the extra expense for the cameras would be worth it, someday. Sooner or later, someone would think they wouldn't be able to be caught. It was always a long shot, but investing was similar to gambling. It was always good advice to cover a variety of different profitable scenarios. Alder or Arwen would certainly be suspicious of using one of the stones to pull off a stunt like the person in front of him did. He also knew beyond a shadow of a doubt, money wasn't something either of them cared about.

He was also pretty sure any of the original settlers who were still alive, most likely carried a lot of wealth through the generations. It was hard for him to remember the last time he met someone from his native planet. It's probably been at least 50 or 60 years since he was last contacted by someone he knew from the early days of the settlement. There are fewer and fewer of them who are still alive today. His guess would be about only a couple of dozens of them were still alive.

He rarely talks to his twin sister, Mordag. She has almost completely isolated herself, living in a large, secluded compound on Nantucket Island off the coast of Massachusetts. The only thing she cares about now are the animals she takes care of. About every 5 or 10 years they meet for dinner or go on one of her safari's she sponsors. She maintains a secret trust for many of her animal shelters and endangered species habitats around the world. Kobin set up the trust for her, and it has always been able to be profitable in attracting many different donors and sponsors. It gives her some meaning to living. He can understand this. Once in a while, there is some new novelty, something fresh, or a new quest he encounters, which helps to sustain him. It might be a relationship, or a project like the Bellagio, or any of a number of things he has found to keep him from just giving up on life, like his son, Creyn.

All of the children he has had throughout the centuries, have all lacked one important factor. They were not born on Ghia. It didn't matter whether he mated with someone who was from Ghia or not, there was some missing ingredient they all lacked. Most of his children in the beginning had very good and long lifespans. One of his first children was born a couple of hundred years after they arrived on the planet. He's still the only one to have lived the longest. He died when he was approximately a little over 800 years old.

This was in the beginning years when they first arrived on Earth and established many different settlements around the globe. Every child he fathered, kept living shorter and shorter lives. Any descendants of those children rarely outgrew their parents. His last child, a daughter, lived to be 103. She died about 300 years ago. He gradually drifted away from his children, and they all eventually died. Every time he encountered the grief of losing a child, it becomes just too much for him to endure. He decided he didn't want to have children anymore, because in the end they die, and he's always left a little broken.

This is a maudlin soup of negatives bubbling up in his mind, but this isn't the reason why he's here today. The person in front of him was using a stone and he wanted to see which one it was. Kobin pulled everything out of the bag where Vic had put all of Pat's clothes into. He took out the separate ziplock bag and placed the contents which consisted of the Bellagio chips, his wallet, cell phone and the orange stone. Kobin laid all of the items on the table in front of Pat.

When Kobin saw the orange stone it was hard to keep his excitement registering on his face. He looked at the stack of the chips and said, "Vic, do we know who the player was who owned these chips?"

"Yes, we do. It's a regular player here at the property and he usually comes in once or twice a month. He has also been known to bring some of his *whale* friends with him at different events we have going on here. I have asked Wayne to reimburse Mr. Lombardi in a discreet way so as not to alert him his chips were taken."

"Good, I was about to suggest the same thing. Now Patrick, you and I have a problem in front of us. You were trying to cheat the Bellagio out of a steady stream of income. You do realize, we are not going to allow this. However, we have recovered the chips taken. This puts me into a little bit of a bind. One item, I'm curious about, is this orange-colored stone. I saw the video of you using the stone and I'm impressed you were able to accomplish this. I have been searching for this particular stone and several others for a very long time. Who gave this stone to you? Alder? Arwen?"

"I have no idea who those people are. This stone was given to me by my niece. She found this on a beach up in York, Maine," Pat bluffed.

"I highly doubt that. It must be either Alder or Arwen who gave this stone to you and showed you how to use this. I would also be willing to bet you took this stone without either of them knowing. How am I doing so far?"

Pat looked at Vic and said, "This is who you work for Vic? Can I get another rum and coke?"

Vic looked at Pat and half growled, and half laughed and said, "Pat, I think you should be more concerned about Mr. Dylan's questions than asking for another drink."

Pat's face looked perplexed. He looked like he was furiously thinking, trying to figure out a riddle, or some complicated math problem. Pat responded, "Now I get it. You are Kobin. You came to Earth with Alder and Arwen from some planet. What was it called? Something like Chia-pet. No, that isn't it. Those are those magic growing plants. Have either of you had one of those? They are amazing. I love those suckers. Wait, no that isn't it. OK, your planet's name was Ghia, right?"

Apparently, Vic wasn't in the loop knowing that Kobin was an alien from a different planet. Pat enjoyed seeing the surprise on Vic's face. Kobin briefly looked at Vic and recognized the surprised look on his face. Some kind of non-verbal exchange happened between them. Vic nodded to Kobin. Kobin then turned to look at Pat and he just smiled.

Pat smiled back, knowing he had scored a point in his favor of this high stakes game. Pat knew he was starting to run out of time before things would really blow up. He had an intuitive sense to not say anything further and just let the tension build.

After about 30 seconds of silence, Kobin asked, "What else did my friend, Alder, tell you about the early days of coming to the Earth?"

"Not much really. Getting information from him is like pulling teeth. He will only tell you what you need to know and nothing more. So, I probably know about as much as your friend, Vic knows about your past. I do know, however, you're one of the bad guys who has been a screw up for all these years since you arrived. I also know you lost many of the stones you once had possession of. I also know that your mission to wake up the Earth has largely failed. How am I doing so far?"

"Well, I would say you're not really doing so well. Everything you just said is incorrect. The only correct thing you did mention, is Alder is someone who is very reluctant to share information. He left me and all the others who came here on this mission, without any of the information we needed to accomplish it. Alder isn't the good guy as you are portraying him. He's jealous of anyone knowing the full plan of our mission. Vic mentioned to me you're someone from Boston who is involved in constructing large buildings and skyscrapers. Now imagine, if you're told to build a very large building and you're only given a set of plans for just one room in the building. It seems straightforward, but you know as well as I do, it's an impossible task to complete without knowing all of the details about the building. Which floor is this room going to be built on? How many floors are there in the building? What is the building footprint?"

"Right now, I trust him a hell of a lot more than I trust you," Pat added.

"Is he trying to get you to help him contact Ghia and the Quantum Guild? Pat, listen to me. We have been here for eons, and we still don't know of all the details he has kept privately to himself and Arwen. Did Arwen mention the hundreds of thousands of people she and Alder killed in their war against their fellow kinsmen? She killed my son, his wife and their 2 boys who were identical twins. Those two boys were both 10 years old. Don't underestimate her ability for ruthlessness. Those two boys, even at the age of 10, were more adept at using the stones than both Alder and Arwen together. Those two children probably could have completed our mission here on Earth. Alder and Arwen were afraid they would surpass them and become more powerful than they were."

Pat looked down at the table, picked up the Styrofoam cup, and finished whatever liquid courage was left in it. He giggled the cup a little to get whatever ice was left in the bottom of the cup. Before he placed the cup back on the table, something inside him clicked and he knew what his next moves would be. Directly in front of Pat was his cell phone and his wallet and between both of those was the orange stone. He tried to relax and focus his mind as he was placing the Styrofoam cup on the table, he focused on the vibrations in the wallet and the cell phone. The cell phone has a bunch of magnets inside the little case of the cell phone circuitry. It was easy to separate the vibrations and force them to exponentially increase and start buzzing like crazy. In one fluid motion as he brought his hand down on the table holding the cup, he pushed the cell phone away from him using his mind similar to the way he had done this with the magnets on the table in the conference room in Boston. It was the same feeling he had when he was in the MRI tube. He pushed hard and the cell phone jumped off the table as a projectile. It bounced off Vic's shoulder and then flew into the wall, smashing it to pieces.

This caught both Kobin and Vic by surprise. Without any delay, Pat scooped up the orange stone and his wallet. In Pat's next breath, he relaxed and spun the atoms around his body and became invisible. It was easier for him to do this now. He had a lot of practice when he was on the casino floor. Once Pat's vision became the weird double image, he felt confident he was invisible. It didn't last, however. His vision started to become clearer and more normal. He looked at Kobin and he was holding a smooth black colored stone. Something was going wrong here. Kobin laughed at Pat because he knew the black stone was nullifying any power of the orange stone.

Pat knew if he panicked right now it would be all over. He suspected Kobin was nullifying the orange stones powers, but did this also mean it would nullify all of the quantum stones equally at the same time? Pat figured, what the hell. He had nothing to lose other than just trying to surprise Kobin again. The memory of being in the crane and punching the floors to break in a certain way might seem like a long shot, but he had nothing to lose. He repeated the same thing he did with the granite sheets on the building crane. He brought his hand down quickly and smashed the conference table. When his fist made contact with the table, he pushed the table with his mind. He wanted to break the table in half in a similar way he broke the floors of the building to force them to break in a certain way. He was using granite sheets to do this on the building. His fist was the only mechanism he had available so he hoped it would be enough. It was. The table broke into two large pieces and fell to the floor. This surprised Kobin again.

Pat repeated what he did before, and he quickly became invisible again. Now he focused as hard as he could on the same room plaque of the conference room he had teleported in front of yesterday. He started to see the particles blinking in and out. He got the picture of the name plaque of the conference room firmly in his mind. The next time the particles blinked out, he just leaned into them. Once again Pat was in front of the conference room door.

"Wow. Holy shit! It worked!"

Pat looked around him to see if anyone was following him, or if someone saw him just pop into the hallway like this. It was probably about 8 PM right now. He just wanted to go back home. It has been a long couple of days, and he was tired both physically and mentally.

He was bummed about losing his cell phone, but it saved his ass tonight, so it was a small price to pay. In hindsight, it was foolish for him to go to Las Vegas. He was certain Kat was going to be very pissed off at him for quite a long time about his excursion to Las Vegas. He did also feel guilty about swindling Alder and everyone else by jumping ship. Kobin raised some serious questions about Alder and Arwen, and if they were being sincere or not. He usually had a good internal sense about people. With Alder and Arwen, he didn't feel like they were being disingenuous with him. Hell, he even liked the old coot! Kobin did bring up a good point about what this whole plan is about or not.

At the moment, all Pat wanted to do right now was to go home and relax. Using the orange stone again, he focused on an image of what he would see if he was standing right in front of his refrigerator door. When the picture of his refrigerator door was firmly in his mind, he used the orange stone to teleport himself there. In the time it took to blink, Pat vanished from the hallway with the conference room, and he was now in front of his refrigerator in his apartment.

Pat was so grateful to be home right now. It has been a long couple of days for him. Looking at his answering machine, he saw there was a message waiting for him. It was a message from Kat, and she was asking him to call her right away. The timestamp of the message was from one hour ago. He's still one of the few people in the world who still has a landline.

He called Kat. She answered almost immediately. He knew she was pissed. She told him they were leaving for Dublin in two hours at 10:00 PM. If he still wanted to help Alder and Arwen with their mission, then he needed to meet them all at Logan Terminal E. Pat could sense she was trying to be nice to him and not start an argument. He asked if he could sleep on the flight, and she said yes. She told him to bring his passport and clothes for a few days for the trip.

When he hung up, he got himself ready to go onto the next part of the adventure. He really hoped he would be able to catch up on his sleep to recharge.

Bellagio Hotel and Casino

Las Vegas, Nevada

Sunday 5:30 PM

Kobin was surprised by Pat breaking the table. He was angry at himself for allowing the kid to gain the advantage. Now what? He looked over in the corner of the room and the kid's cell phone was on the floor. The force of it being thrown at the wall damaged the phone, but how badly damaged was it? There might be some data on the phone which he could retrieve.

Kobin walked over and picked up the cell phone. The back casing and the front screen were broken and cracked. Some of the corners of the phone had broken totally off. The cell phone had left a large divot in the wall. He pressed a button to see if the phone was able to power on. It did but the screen was partially working. This wasn't a total loss.

Vic said, "Let's give this phone to one of our security techs to see if they can extract any information on the phone."

Kobin nodded and said, "Why don't we go up to your office and wait. How is your shoulder? It looked like it took a good hit from his phone."

"Yeah, he got me pretty good with the phone. If my shoulder hadn't slowed it down a little, it would've probably gone right through the wall."

"Vic, I'm sure you're wondering right now about what happened with the kid and how he disappeared, right?"

"Honestly, I'm a little pissed we didn't put a stronger table in this room. I saw the video earlier of him spontaneously disappearing earlier, so seeing him do it again wasn't very surprising. You pay me to take care of the hotel and the players best interests. The player was reimbursed so to it sounds like everything is as it should be, right?"

Kobin smiled as he opened the door and said, "Let's get this phone to the tech and go wait in your office."

Both men left the room with the two pieces of the table oddly laying on the floor as if they were bowing to each other. They stopped at the security office to drop off the broken cell phone. Vic gave them instructions to have someone dissect the data on the phone and get the call logs and the GPS data of where the calls were made and who called him. He asked them to make this a high priority task and to bring the report and the data extract to him in his office. The person he spoke to said he would probably need about 30 to 45 minutes to get this to him.

The Bellagio has some of the sharpest technical minds in electronics and cyber security. Every day there is some new exploit someone is trying to use to cheat the casino. Smartphones are just one of a dozen gimmicks people use to either count cards playing Blackjack, forecast the roulette wheel, or predict the spins of the slots. Dumping cell phone data of just about any phone available is an easy request and it can be done very quickly.

After about 30 minutes, one of the Bellagio's tech specialists, came into Vic's office with a folder of papers and a thumb drive. The first page was a report of what was found on the phone. It had a list of the numbers coming in or going out of the phone. It also had a list of contacts and addresses. There were a couple of other pieces of information such as text messages and a handful of email messages. On the thumb drive was a copy of the images, music and other bits of miscellaneous information. The tech who handed the report to Vic said there was very little information on the phone. He also said the phone was either brand new or was just rarely used. Most people he said, usually contain normal data about a hundred times this size.

Vic thanked him for getting this done so quickly. He turned to Kobin and gave him the folder.

Kobin looked at the information and after a few minutes it appeared he had found what he was looking for. He said to Vic, "Do me a favor? Look up the Boston Copley Plaza and see if there are any events happening there this weekend. Some of his recent calls are showing what looks like Pat's phone made a call to another person with the same last name of Themis. He has a contact in his contact list for a person named Katriona Themis. She lives in Virginia, but she received the call from a Boston cell tower near the Copley Plaza. Sister maybe? He wasn't wearing a wedding ring so not his wife, I suspect."

"OK. I might have found something here. There is a conference this weekend at the Copley which is a technical conference. It ends on Tuesday afternoon. It looks like the conference is a hodgepodge of everything from games, software, physics, and a lot more."

"That must be where the son of a bitch is!"

Vic asked, "I know this is probably none of my business, but when you say 'son of bitch' you mean this person *Alder*, right? Or are you referring to Pat?

"Actually, I suppose I mean both. There is a lot of history between me and this person Alder. Pat alluded to this earlier, but it's a long story. I know today has been full of a lot of fantastical stories and information. At some point we can have some drinks and laughs, and I can tell you the whole story. Please do me a favor and just keep this between you and I, OK? Your handling of this situation was perfect today and when I get back to my office in New York, I am going to ask my assistant to draw up papers to grant you a big chunk of stock options in some of my best performing assets. You will probably be able to sock this away for a nice nest egg to use however you want to."

"Kobin, really thank you very much. It is incredibly appreciated, but I was just doing my job."

"Don't be silly. This is the least of what I can do. Wayne's last name was Harshall right?"

"Yes, that is correct."

"I'll also cut a nice bonus check for Wayne also. I am going to head off back to the airport and get back east. You did great work today. Thanks."

Kobin got up and left Vic's office. An hour later, he was flying at 39,000 feet on his way to Boston.

Chapter 15 – Almost

☷ ॰

"All things truly wicked start from innocence."

— Ernest Hemingway

Shannucke Habitat Compound

Nantucket, Massachusetts

Sunday 11:00 PM

Nantucket Island is located off the coast of Massachusetts. The Cape Cod peninsula jealously guards the Boston Bay, with its distinctive hook to the west. Farther east, off the coast of Cape Cod lie two distinctive islands, Martha's Vineyard and Nantucket. Nantucket is the eastern most of the two islands. These islands are the fabled getaway spots for the rich and powerful, but it is much more diverse. Many people flock to Nantucket who are looking for the slower pace and reclusiveness of being on the island. Included in this group are also people who just beat to their own drum and dedicate themselves to creative talents or who are avid nature enthusiasts.

The Shannucke Habitat Compound is a mixture of being exclusive and also reclusive. The name Shannucke is a Wampanoag Indian name for squirrel. It is a nearly self-sufficient, and sprawling section of land, located on the northern part of the island. The compound is a sanctuary for many different animal species, who are on the edge of extinction and dedicated to help them come back to levels where they flourish. The person who founded this compound ran it, so it was a well-oiled machine, capable of almost no interaction.

The founder of this compound was Mordag Donovoni. She was swimming laps in her heated pool hidden in the rear of the main residence building. She grabbed a plush light blue, terry cloth robe draped over a chair next to a small bamboo table. She also grabbed her cell phone which was lying on the top of the table.

Mordag is a powerful woman, who walks with an athletic and calculated, gracefulness and agility. Her hair was a long, satiny, bright copper with dark and light auburn highlights. There is a curious style, and a great sense of high voltage about her. She doesn't stop the party when she walks in, but you'd like to get to know her. Her vulnerable qualities mask, the strength of a warrior. Her face is defiant and intense. Her dull grey eyes are constantly scanning and evaluating the nearest escape routes. Fight or flight.

Those days were long gone now. She has been stuck on the Earth for almost 5000 years. Very little can hold her interest these days. Her advocacy for animals has given her life a purpose and given her the determination to crusade for the benefit of all animals. Her mission and reason for coming to the Earth was to help the planet. The animals are part of the Earth's ecosystem. She was responsible for helping many different animal species who were on the edge of extinction and helped them to come back to levels where they flourished.

Her life is much different now from days past. She rarely ventures away from her Shannucke compound. Everything is predictable and safe, and there is very little reason to look for a fight or flight moment. This instinct is so ingrained in her, it's hard to not automatically be constantly looking and evaluating each situation. She knows she has let her keen senses, be a little diminished, and not as sharp as they were a few centuries ago. She has a bad habit of holding herself and others, to impossible standards. At one time, she was in perfect physical conditioning and her mental sharpness was unlike any one on the planet. There was very little she could not do, once she set her mind to it.

Mordag went inside and got ready for bed. She had a funny feeling her brother was going to be calling her at some point soon. She decided she should wait a little bit before going to bed. She went downstairs to brew a pot of lemon decaffeinated tea. She got her cup of tea and sat at her little kitchenette table with her laptop in front of her. She was reading up on some of the daily reports she receives regarding how her different habitats and sanctuaries all over the world are doing. Apparently, one of her elephant sanctuaries in India increased their population by 2 with two elephants being born earlier in the day. This cheered her up a little bit. Unfortunately, it was short lived since her cell phone started ringing.

"Hi Kobin. I had a feeling you were going to call me. What's going on?"

"I'm flying from Las Vegas to New York City. I have some business to attend to at the office in New York, but I'm going to be heading out to Boston tomorrow afternoon. It has been an interesting day. A young man was using the orange stone to steal chips from the casino and the players. That was a good idea to install those filters on the cameras. I almost had the stone before he jumped away. He's from Boston, and I think he jumped back there. Can you meet me in Boston at the Copley Hotel tomorrow afternoon let's say about 4:30 PM? I doubt Alder knew this kid was going to Vegas with the stone, but I'm positive Alder or Arwen or both are involved in this."

"Just like old times, eh?" Mordag said.

"This kid, Patrick Themis, is special. I think he's a lefty like you, and he can emulate the powers of the stones without holding them. He broke a table in two and did this without the power of the yellow stone. I don't think he realizes it yet, but he does have this rare ability. How many people back on Ghia could do this? It was very rare."

"Did you get any other information from him? If he has a cell phone, I can track it and find out where he is."

"I don't think his cell phone is of any use. He flung it into a wall, and it got smashed to pieces. I was able to retrieve some information from the phone though. I have his address and some of the recent calls he made or retrieved on the phone. One of the recent calls he made were to another person with the same last name of Themis. Both the call going out and calls being received were in the Boston Copley area. There is a technical conference going on there this weekend," Kobin said.

"Kobin, give me the cell number of the sister also. I can track her phone and see where it is now if it is turned on."

"OK. I had one of the techs at the Bellagio give me a small thumb drive of the info on his phone. I'll upload it to your cloud drive."

Silence. "Mordag? You still there?"

Silence and then Mordag said, "Kobin, why are we still doing this? I'll always help you in whatever you want to do, but I'm getting really tired of searching for something we never seem to be any closer to. The only time we have ever felt the Earth even slightly realize itself as an entity, or even recognize life was living on the planet, was when Vesuvius erupted. There has been nothing in 2000 years since then, and yet, we keep going down the same path. If we can't get back home, I can be satisfied with living out my last days here on this feeble planet. Don't you feel like this sometimes?"

"Yes, I suppose you're right. I just feel like we are very close now. Alder is a bumbling fool, but Arwen, that bitch, killed Creyn. I can't and I won't let that go."

Mordag silently exhaled and just resigned herself to submission and said, "I understand brother, I really do. I'll meet you at the Copley Plaza hotel in the lobby at 4:30 PM tomorrow."

"Thanks, Mordag, see you soon."

Mordag hung up the phone.

Copley Plaza Hotel Lobby

Boston Massachusetts

Monday 4:30 PM

Mordag walked into the lobby of the hotel, and she spotted Kobin off to the right of her, sitting on a brown suede sofa reading a newspaper. She walked over to him and sat in a similar suede chair next to the couch. He appeared not to notice her.

Mordag knew better about this. He was aware of her even before she walked into the lobby. His sense of her was equal to her sense of him. There was a background noise of tension like a string vibrating. The pitch gets higher and higher the closer you come to where the other is located until it becomes inaudible. This sense was only really useful in a range of about a mile. Once beyond this distance, sounds become less echoic and more directional.

Alder said, "You look well, sister."

Mordag responded equally, "And you do as well."

In her pocketbook, she pulled out some pictures and papers regarding some preliminary research she did on the information Kobin had sent to her last night. She printed out pictures of Katriona Themis. She also had pictures for Brian, his wife Julie, and their son, Malcolm.

Kobin was delighted by this. He asked, "Did you sneak into the Copley Hotels guest lists and security footage?"

"Of course. Doing anything less would have been an insult. There is one picture which showed a young black girl with them. I could not find out any information about this girl."

She handed a picture she pulled off of the security cameras of the whole group of them walking down the corridor where they went into a conference room. Mordag pointed to the tall woman standing next to Alder. Kobin looked at it and something looked familiar about this woman.

"I have seen this woman before. It was a few years back, but I think I have seen her before. It might have been at one of those stone monuments in Ireland we left so long ago. Why the hell are these fools at this conference? I don't understand what Alder's or Arwen's plan is here."

Mordag sighed and said, "I should have called you this morning. They all checked out of the hotel yesterday. There were 11 flights traveling from Boston to Europe. Five of those eleven were noncommercial flights. Wanna guess where three of those flights are going?"

"This cursed and blasted piece of this planet I just cannot seem to escape!" Alder said something in their native Ghian language. He took a long sigh and said, "Do you still have the olive stone kept at the bank in Dublin?"

"Yes, I do. I have already called them and told them to expect me there tomorrow afternoon."

"Ahh, you're so on top of things. OK, let's get out of here and I'll get the pilot to provision up something delicious on the flight over there. Did you bring your chess board?" The corners of Kobin lips rose.

"Silly question, brother. I never leave my compound without it. If memory serves me correctly, I have won the last 6 games, I hope you have been practicing?"

Kobin smirked and said, "Yes I practice my 'I lost' face and my 'I won' faces just for you."

Chapter 16 – Slane

What you see isn't what you get.

Frank Wilczek, 2006

Dublin International Airport

Dublin County, Ireland

Monday 9:00 AM

The morning sky was slightly overcast and windy, but at this time of year it was pleasantly warm with just a hint of winter on its way. Once they cleared customs, all six of them went over to the rental car area and rented two SUV's, one navy blue and the other a charcoal grey. Harriet was the expert in driving on the left having clocked in many hours driving around Ireland on her past archaeological trips. Arwen and Kat jumped into the navy blue vehicle. Brian offered to drive the other SUV with Pat and Alder.

The Boyne Valley area where the Newgrange monument was located, was about an hour north of Dublin. Arwen mentioned she knew of a place they could stay for the next couple of days. It was in a little village called Slane, in County Meath, and only a couple of kilometers from Newgrange. They could rest up and relax for a couple of days, if needed. She also had made arrangements for them to have a nice home cooked meal later.

She said something to Alder in a different language, and he reacted with a huge grin. His blue eyes sparkled with laughter and joy. Looking at the group, Alder told them they were about to have some of the greatest food they have ever eaten. It was becoming clear to many in their little group, Alder was a definite *foodie*.

Driving on the left was new to Brian. For most people trying this for the first time, it will take a few minutes to orient yourself and get used to it. Thankfully, it wasn't really busy at this time of day, and all he had to do was just follow the same path the other SUV was going. About 10 kilometers outside of the airport, the traffic became much lighter and easier for Brian.

Alder was sitting next to Brian in the passenger seat. Pat was in the back sleeping and snoring slightly. Some people have an ability to just sleep anywhere they are. Brian asked, "Alder, can you tell me a little more about how I fit into this plan to connect to the Earth? I'm still not sure how my ability with fire can help any of you in this situation."

"Brian, I'm not surprised by your questions. If anything, it reinforces your value to this mission to connect with the Earth. These stones are just tools which help us to focus our individual talents to interact with the different properties of the universe which are all around us. You have a unique ability to change the strength of a fire. You can make it burn slower or faster. This is only the tip of the iceberg, my son."

"Brian, you also have an ability to either take power from an energy source, or to give energy to something as simple as a battery. I know in this day and age, many people walk around with their cell phone, as if it were an extra appendage." Alder paused for a second before continuing and said, "Have you ever had your cell phone run out of power? For most people, they just acknowledge it's a device with a limited amount of power and must be recharged. Because of your abilities, you really don't have to do that. I believe if you didn't charge your phone for days or months, it would most likely stay fully charged. You do it now naturally, and you're not even aware of it," Alder said.

Brian asked, "It seems like we are in a race with someone or something to get this done. I have been in many situations, where I had to act decisively, and complete an action where the consequences were dire. In all of those experiences, the amount of information I had going into those situations, could literally mean the difference between life and death."

Alder looked at the back seat to check if Pat was still sleeping, and continued, "There is a possibility one of our former colonists might be trying to stop us from connecting to the Earth. Our friend in the back seat here, just met him in Las Vegas, and he's most probably, very angry about being thwarted from getting his hands on the orange stone. His name is Kobin, and he was my best friend for many centuries. He's tired of living out his existence here on Earth and wants to go back to Ghia. He may try and cause problems for us. I think we are still about 3 days ahead of him. However, Kobin will most likely go to Stonehenge first."

"Wait, Stonehenge? You guys built Stonehenge?"

"Twice!" Alder replied.

"That's amazing! How in the world could you get those humongous stones to be raised up, and sitting on top of each other with such precision? Even with the machines we have in this day and age, it would be a tough job to accomplish."

"Well, some of those took decades to build, and we also did this many, many, times over the course of decades and centuries. Brian, your abilities are very rare. I have only heard of one planet where it was mentioned of a rare occurrence of the people on this planet who have the abilities like you. It's a sister world to Ghia. The race who lived there are sadly long gone, but it's the only occurrence I have heard about other people, who have the same unique abilities you possess. It's said these people could take a sunbeam of light from their sun and cause this beam of light to burn or cut through almost any material, like it was butter and a hot knife."

"You mean Brian can shoot laser's out of his eyes like superman?" Pat chortled in the back.

Alder looked at Brian, and laughed, "Look who is wide awake now. Actually, sending lasers out of your eyes would be really bad for you, so don't try and do this. I think if you tried to do this it might make you go blind, wouldn't it? The way I was told was these people with this ability could take any object and intensify the light energy passing though the object to form I guess you would call it a laser. Yes, that is the more the correct term. We used to call them light spears, but yes, I think *laser* is the more correct term. We can try to explore these abilities of yours more if we have time to practice this."

"Alder?" Patrick asked from the backseat. "I'm sorry I took the orange stone from you. Do you think Kobin is going to come after us?"

"Thank you, Pat, for saying this. Yes, I do think Kobin will be coming after us. I hope we don't cross paths though."

"Why is he so pissed at you? He almost stopped me escaping from the holding room in Vegas. I know I was invisible and on the verge of jumping back to Boston. When Kobin pulled out the black stone, I could feel whatever particles were swirling around me had started to slow down. If I hadn't broken the table in a similar way, to the way I caused those building floors to break apart, I think I would be in one of those unmarked graves in the desert, just outside of Las Vegas. I get a feeling from him that when he plays, he plays for keeps, and losing is deadly with him."

Alder sadly replied, "Sadly Pat, what you're saying is correct. His weakness is he plays to win it all. He isn't satisfied with little incremental gains; it's all or nothing. His signature signal is when you win against him, make sure you're winning by your own merit. He's sly and will fail a couple of times or just a little bit. When he thinks you're overconfident, and you let your guard down for just one second, is when he will strike, and strike very hard."

Alder glanced at Brian and then Pat. Both were listening intently to him, waiting for him to continue.

Alder went on, "I have known him for so long, I can sense this tactic with him. I'm not infallible, and he may surprise me, but to both of you, question any gain you get with him. Pat, I think you have done something which I haven't seen happen in a long time. You surprised him. I think he put the orange stone in front of you as a dare to try and take it and use it. You did exactly what he wanted, but you countered him with something he didn't expect. You broke the table in two. I wish I had been there to see the look on his face. I'm glad you got back to Boston safely though. You're correct, your life to him is a trivial matter and nothing more."

Brian was following Harriet's blue SUV, and she got off the main road following a sign for a little village called Slane. Before entering the little town, Harriet turned off onto a private driveway. Both sides of the single lane driveway were wide empty fields with dozens of sheep of all sizes. The driveway was on a slight grade up and when they crested the top of the driveway, they saw an impressive 17th century castle. They had arrived at Slane Castle. Brian just followed Harriet as she drove through the high stone gateway. That led to a large central courtyard with a fountain in the middle for them to park their cars.

Pat was absolutely speechless. A tractor was going around the fountain and Brian had to make a concerted effort to focus on his driving so he would stay on the correct side of the road, and yield for the tractor. The person driving the tractor was an older man, but he nodded to Brian in a friendly manner. In the center of this courtyard, there was a large fountain with two sculptured salmon side by side, with water coming out of their mouths.

An older man and a woman came outside through a large set of doors to meet them. There really wasn't much for luggage, since everyone came with a backpack with just enough items for a couple of days. Arwen and Alder told them they could provide them with anything they needed while they were on this trip. Alder picked up several adapters for any electronics they needed. Arwen and Alder walked over to the man and the woman and gave each of them a warm long hug. The four of them were speaking in a different language, but even though the others couldn't understand what was being said, it was clearly evident these two people were very close to Arwen and Alder.

Alder introduced Cathal and Kayleigh Doogan as the caretakers of Slane Castle. Alder announced to everyone, "Arwen and I have known Cathal and Kayleigh for many years. They are our dearest friends and family. Without them, this place would have fallen into ruin centuries ago." Alder looked at Cathal who was sheepishly looking down at his feet and continued, "Well, here I go blubbering around. Sorry Cath, I didn't mean to put you on the spot. I'm just so happy to see my friends again. Kayleigh is one of the world's best cooks you could ever want. I swear she puts something magical in her meals to leave you extraordinarily happy."

Cathal looked at Kat and asked, "Alder told me about your recent experience with delivering twin foals. I would be very interested in hearing your story on this later, if that is, OK?"

Kat replied, "Sure I'd be happy to tell you all about it. It still isn't quite registering with me yet; how rare such an event is for a mare to give birth to twin foals."

Pat piped in, "So how many bedrooms are in this castle?"

Kayleigh said, "Too many! There are 15 bedrooms and 15 bathrooms. Some of the bedrooms are used as office space for some businesses outside of the village. During the summertime, we rent out a portion of the rooms as a bed and breakfast. The Boyne Valley tourism is on the rise, so we are able to profit a little bit from this. It also allows us to have a portion of the estate used as a working farm, a whiskey distillery, and we have been fortunate to hosting some extremely large musical events. We have had everyone from U2, Madonna and last year Metallica played here. We didn't think the village would survive it, but everyone had a grand time."

Cathal said, "If you want to follow us, we can show you where your rooms are, and you can relax. I didn't know if you would be hungry or not, but I put out a little buffet of some light refreshment if you care for it."

Drawing Room

Monday 12:00 PM

Once everyone got settled into their rooms, they slowly came downstairs to all meet up in a large drawing room. It was a big room with several comfortable chairs and couches, all spread around the room for people to sit and relax. Two of the walls were entirely covered with built in bookcases, from floor to the ceiling, holding thousands of books. Each bookcase had a six step ladder affixed to a rail at the top of the bookcase. These ladders could slide around the different bookcases so you could reach the top shelves. At the front of the room, there was a large 5 foot high fireplace if you ducked a little you could almost walk into the hearth. Above the mantle, was a large painting of a younger Alder with Arwen next to him and several other people in the background. They were all dressed up like they were ready to go on a fox hunt. It was one of those paintings you saw, where the size of it required it to be hung in a room which was equally as large, in order for it to look right. It would overwhelm a smaller room than this. It was a huge painting, but it just seemed to fit in a room this size.

Pat exclaimed, "It's the guy with the black stone!"

Alder had a pained expression on his face as he addressed Pat's outburst. He agreed, "Yes you're correct Patrick. That is my friend Kobin and some of our fellow colonists. I haven't seen this picture in a number of years. I forgot this was still hanging in this room. It was a very different time back then."

Harriet said apologetically, "I'm sorry you and Kobin are not friends anymore. I'm sure it was painful parting with him. At times, I have lost friends for one reason or another, but I know deep in my heart, I have always learned from each of those relationships. Whether it was a positive experience or negative experience, I have always gained something from them. I know it sounds a little corny, but it's just the way I process life."

Alder replied, "Yes, Harriet, it was difficult at that time. Thank you for saying that. And it's not corny at all, but very wise insight."

Harriet said, "I have been meaning to ask you something. Earlier, when we first arrived and met Cathal and Kayleigh, you were speaking to each other in a different language. I know Gaelic is a misused term since it's a language family which has very different tones and accents between Ireland and Scotland. Is it a hybrid of the two or something different?"

"You have a good ear for languages. It's a close variation of Irish and Ghian. You have to understand, thousands of years ago, the human population was just starting out. When we came here from Ghia, we taught the people who lived on the Earth our language. It has morphed several times, as many languages do, with more people and different localities using it. Word origins and meanings change. New words are introduced as time goes on. If you traced English back to its origins, it's a bastardization of the west Germanic language family with a large percentage of additional words from French and Latin. Arwen and I have known Cathal and Kayleigh for a very long time. Kayleigh is the great, great, great, granddaughter of one of Arwen's sons. We have known them for almost 200 years. The man on the tractor, who Brian almost bumped into when we arrived, is their son Callum."

"This is amazing. I'd love to learn more about this language at some point. Also, when we arrived, I spoke to my friend who is the Historical Director for the Newgrange site. He said he could give us access to the underground passageway anytime we want this week. He asked if we could give him about an hour notice to make sure the coast is clear for us to enter the site."

Alder perked up and said, "This underground passageway you mentioned. I'm not familiar with this. Does this lead to the internal chamber rooms, or does it take us to other rooms people don't know about?"

Harriet had discovered this underground passage from one of her past archaeological trips to Newgrange. She knew it wasn't largely broadcast but it also wasn't a secret. Many people in her field and also people who have been heavily involved with some of the tourism for all the ancient monuments which were scattered around the western part of Europe.

Harriet went on, "Hmm, I'm surprised you're not familiar with this. It's a tunnel which goes underneath the main passageway which most people are familiar with. This tunnel also gives us access to the main pillars of stones, which hold the rest of Newgrange in place. This is a good time for us to be here. We have just passed the Autumn Equinox and they are making preparations for the Samhain Festival next month. There shouldn't be too many visitors here during this time."

Alder listened intently to what Harriet was saying and replied, "Well, I'll be most interested in seeing this underground tunnel. This may be the key we have been searching for so long to make us successful in reaching the Earth. Harriet, you're a great academic scholar and I'm sure learning the facts of events from years long past is very important to you. What would you say, if I told you historians have gotten some of the facts wrong about many events of long ago?

"I would say, hearing this firsthand from someone who was alive at the time of these events, would be a monumentally huge event. This would probably shock every historian into a drooling stupor." Harriet said transfixed, and she asked very sweetly, "Please, you must tell me?"

"OK, well since you asked me so nicely," Alder said with a mischievous grin on his face, "The Autumn Festival and the Samhain Festival were always just one festival which would happen in a few days' time, on September 30th. You have to understand the climate was very different then. The autumn equinox and Samhain was for the very last harvest of the year and preparation for winter. Throughout the summer we would harvest many times. It was a celebration of the previous year ending and the new year starting. The Earth was colder during this time. After September, we carefully stored enough food and sustenance to make it through till the next year. The equinox marked a time when the Earth had an equal number of hours of day and night. This astrological event marked the halfway point of the winter months. Also, don't forget many of our people were able to harness and use the powers of the green stone. So, when it came time to harvest our fields, they were very, very bountiful."

Harriet's eyes were quickly darting back and force as her cognitive processing was taking over complete control. She finally said, "Why didn't we see this? Yes, I understand it, now. It makes perfect sense. Do you realize how many archaeologists and historians are going to be so mad when they find this out? My goodness! Every scientist I have ever talked to, has always described the world during those time periods, was very harsh to live in. If you're saying many people were able to grow and have many bountiful harvests, then this would have made life a little easier for these people, especially during the winter months."

Everyone in the room could hear some feverish activity just outside of the room. The noises got louder and around the corner came two dogs, a medium sized, black and grey spotted border collie who was accompanied with a large steel grey, thick coated, Irish wolfhound.

The border collie was very excited to meet everyone. It went over to each person, stopped and sniffed and then sat down between Alder and Arwen. The Irish wolfhound was also very excited and went around the room from person to person to make a formal meeting. Everyone gave a pat on their head or scratched behind his ears. The dog stopped at Kat and just sat down. It was as if to say, I found the one I want to sit next to. Kat reached out to pat her new friend.

Arwen said, "These little rascals are called Nico the 14th," and she pointed to the Irish wolfhound in front of Kat. She then pointed to border collie sitting in front of them and said, "This rambunctious guy in front of us is called Báisteach which in English means *rain*."

Cathal came in shortly after the two dogs entered. He told everyone there was light snack in the other room, if anyone was hungry."

Alder was the first to get up as he winked at Harriet and said, "This is my favorite time of the day."

Everyone followed him into a different room, with a large simple wooden table with 10 chairs spaced evenly around it.

There was a table at the rear of the room setup with a varied selection of breads, meats, cheeses, crackers and other condiments. Everyone grabbed a plate and started to make a simple lunch for themselves. On the other side of the table was a large pitcher of homemade lemonade or a choice of different bottles of popular soda.

Pat exclaimed, "No way! Orangina! I haven't had this since I was like seven. Kat, do you remember how the Greenley's loved this stuff?" Pat grabbed 2 bottles of the 3 bottles of Orangina available, and he turned to go back and sit down.

Since Kat was the person behind Pat, she took one of the bottles Pat was holding and put it back on the table. "Pat! You're not the only person here today. We are polite and we **share,**" she scolded him.

Pat quickly turned to his sister, and it looked like he was going to scream something at her, but he hesitated as he realized where he was. Instead, he apologized, "You're right, Kat. My bad," and he looked up at everyone else waiting in line, and said in a low voice, "sorry about that."

Arwen secretly smiled and looked at Alder. He also caught the gist of what she was thinking. "Arwen it only happened once, and it was a long time ago, but you're right, as usual," Alder said.

No one else heard this exchange, but Alder did understand the meaning Arwen was trying to impart to him. Alder was very much like Pat in so many ways. Conversely, Arwen was also like Kat in many ways. The ebb and flow of sibling tides are always there. Sometimes, it's like you're looking into an inescapable mirror of a lifetime of experiences. This mirror was always there to echo back, when times were good, and also when times were bad.

Once everyone had sat down to eat, Brian asked, "When do you think we might want to go to Newgrange?"

Alder announced to everyone, "Harriet told me her friend at the Newgrange site needs about an hour's notice to make sure they can sneak us into the site without drawing any attention. It depends on how you're all feeling. Going tomorrow might be a better idea. Kayleigh has spent a lot of time cooking for us tonight, so why don't we just relax and enjoy the day and rest up for our visit tomorrow. How does this sound to everyone?"

Pat in his typical *straight to the point* way interjected, "I was hoping to stay in the Castle tonight. I have never slept in a castle before."

Arwen smiled, and she knew Brian and Harriet were also thinking the same thing. She winked at Kat and said, "Pat you can stay as long as you like. How are you at mucking out stables? I'm sure Cath or Callum could use some help with their many chores that they do around the castle."

Kat smiled. She was glad someone else was calling out her brother, rather than her having to do it all the time.

Alder said, "There is one thing which we must do however, before we get to Newgrange. I have shown you how you can individually connect with each of the quantum stones. What I would like to try and do before we go to Newgrange, is to have everyone join together and connect to the quantum stones as a group. It's not too difficult to do this, but we should try to do this at least once before we go to Newgrange. Connecting us as a group will enhance the powers of the quantum stones greatly."

Alder looked at everyone before taking a drink of water to see if there were any questions. No one spoke, so he resumed explaining his plan for tomorrow.

Alder continued, "Harriet has told me about a secret tunnel, which I didn't know was there, but it sounds like this tunnel allows us to interact with the Earth at the foundation of Newgrange. This will be an even closer connection between the Earth and Newgrange. This might be the key for us to be able to finally be successful in establishing a connection with the Earth."

Kat asked, "I think I understand about connecting with the stones, but how are we supposed to tune into the Earth? This doesn't make sense to me. I understand how I connect with animals, but I'm having a hard time to grasp connecting with the whole planet."

"Arwen and I will be guiding the energy and the connection we make to the Earth. All you need to do is just open up and focus on the Earth. Each of you around this table have a specific ability to connect with the Earth. The Earth is huge and unapproachable if you think of it on such a wide and impossible scope and magnitude. Focus on the Earth as a single sentient entity, almost like a newborn. Kat, you can feel an animal or another sentient entity. You can sense and feel the anxiety or the fear of an animal, and also feel when they are very excited and happy. When you helped the women with the baby, you said you could feel the overwhelming lifeforce of the baby. Treat the Earth in the same way."

Alder turned to Pat and Brian, and said, "Pat you're connected to the Earth because of how powerful the forces on Earth are. Think of the power you had when you pushed the magnets away. This is the same thing. You can tap into the power that the Earth has. You can show the Earth how to use this power. Brian, your power with fire is sensing and feeling the power of the Earth's inner core. We all know at the center of the Earth there are oceans of molten lava and fire. You can help the Earth connect to this unharnessed power. The Earth doesn't know how to control those fires. You can help it and show it how to slow them down or speed them up."

Lastly, he turned to Harriet and said, "Harriet your power with nurturing life in the Earth, is critical in determining how the Earth can hear its own song. The Earth sings this song, and it helps plants and life to bloom and thrive. It doesn't know its singing while assisting plants and nature to grow. You can show it how it can listen for its own song. You might even be able to teach it some new songs."

Cathal and Kayleigh came into the room and asked if they could join them. Everyone enthusiastically said yes almost at the same time. Both Kayleigh and Cathal got a plate of some of the food, that was left on the back table, and they sat down to join them. Kat gave Pat a look when she saw both Cathal and Kayleigh both had a bottle of Orangina soda in front of them.

Kat asked Kayleigh, "How long have you and Cathal lived here at the castle?"

"I was born here. This is the only place I have ever known. We had a devastating fire back in the 1990's, and it took about 10 years to restore the castle back to the level it was before the fire. The folks in Slane village are like a family to us. We've all known each other for so long. It's nice when we have new people in the area to see or stay at the castle. Even though, we have watched everyone in the village be born and die in the village, it's always nice when we can meet new people and can interact with them."

For the next several hours, they all talked about their recent experiences back in Boston, and how they all got to come together as group after meeting in Boston. Cathal was especially interested in Pat retelling what happened to him in Las Vegas. Since Pat had come back to Boston, and while they were on the flight to Ireland, many of the others in their rag-tag group were unaware of what had actually happened. Pat embellished a bit as he told his story. He also downplayed his thievery of the stone, rationalizing it as just *practice* for the big event. Everyone let it pass, but it was clear he was avoiding admitting to everyone he stole the stone from Alder for his own reasons.

Kat changed the subject because she knew her brother felt bad about disappointing Alder and Arwen. She asked, "Kayleigh, is there anything we can help you with in the kitchen?"

Kayleigh got up and said, "No, thank you for offering. I should be getting back into the kitchen now. We'll probably be eating at about 7:30 PM if that is OK with everyone?"

Harriet said, "I don't know about the rest of you, but I think I'm going to take a nap before dinner." She looked at Alder and Arwen to see if this was, OK?

They both said it was a great idea. Arwen said she was going to be doing the same.

Brian asked, "Cathal, this castle is beautiful and amazing. I would love to see more of it if you could point out some areas we could look at."

"Absolutely, I was just about to ask if anyone wanted a little tour of the castle. It really is an amazing place. I sometimes have to remember how fortunate I'm to live here. We have a whiskey distillery here, which is partnered with a company in the US. The distillery is quite the site to see if anyone is interested.

"Did someone say Whiskey?" Pat interjected.

For the rest of the day, the whole group toured the castle, or some took naps to catch up on sleep. Later at 7:30, they were all back together in a larger dining room to dine on the magnificent meal Kayleigh had created. Everybody enjoyed the meal giving great praise to Kayleigh for such a terrific meal at the end of a long day. As Alder had promised, the meal was fantastic, and everyone was very happy and content. They decided they would get back together after breakfast and practice connecting with the quantum stones. If they felt comfortable with the results of this, then they would head over to the Newgrange site.

Chapter 17 – Lost and Found

The first time I sang in the church choir;
two hundred people changed their religion.

- Fred Allen

Slane Castle

Slane, County Meath, Ireland

Tuesday, 10:00 AM

The next morning everyone had a nice easy breakfast. The group was eager to try to continue the mission to awaken the Earth. After breakfast, they gathered outside in one of the many empty fields around the castle. They gathered in a circle and were waiting for Alder to give them some guidance on how to proceed.

Alder brought out a lonely pumpkin seed and he placed it in the middle of the group circled together. He asked everyone to focus on the pumpkin seed. To imagine feeling the pumpkin seed in your hand. He spoke to each one of them in turn.

To Pat, Alder gave him the yellow stone. He asked him to try to push the Earth away for a nice spot where the pumpkin seed can grow roots. He then gave Brian the pink stone. Alder asked Brian to feel the vibration of the ground and the air and sense the water in and around us. Try to draw any water out for the pumpkin seed to use for its growth. Next, Alder turned to Kat and gave her the red stone.

Alder asked her, "Try to tune into the life force of everything around us. Feel this energy and try to apply it to the Earth. Tune into it the same way you can feel and tune into animals."

He then looked at Harriet and gave her the green stone. He told her, "If everyone is working together as a group, you can apply this energy towards the pumpkin seed. To listen for the Earth's song and sing with it. Cajole the Earth into singing the song louder and louder. Let the pumpkin seed hear it."

Both Alder and Arwen held onto the other stones. Arwen was holding the violet and brown stone. Alder was holding the crimson and orange stone. He then said, "Be patient if you don't feel or see anything. This is more about us acting collectively as a group. OK, let's begin."

Everyone slowed down there breathing and tried to just focus on being in tune with the particular stone. In the middle of the ground where the pumpkin seed was resting, it looked like something was moving underneath the ground. Very slowly and carefully the ground parted slightly. It looked like being at the beach and grabbing a scoop of sand to build a sandcastle. The pumpkin seed disappeared into the ground. Water started to pool around the little clump of dirt where the seed had vanished.

Everyone had their eyes closed and the concentration of everyone at this moment was on the area in front of them. Kat looked like she was trying to feel something or just feel anything, but her face was betraying her frustration.

No one else heard it but Arwen whispered, "It's OK child, be patient, you're doing this perfectly. Keep trying to focus on the energy and the lifeforce around you. Trust yourself."

As if a switch turned on, Harriet started to hum. The air around them was full of random ions and electrostatic energy. This feeling was like being next to a Van de Graaff generator and a feeling of palpable electricity arcing in the air. Everyone started to hum, very lightly, almost like a whisper.

Another sound could be heard. All around them, it sounded like little wind chimes of different sizes and sounds could be heard. Sounds of several smaller wind chimes were making little tinkling sounds. In addition, you could hear a large booming sound coming out of a much bigger and louder wind chime. You could feel and hear the deeply plangent sounds. It was almost hypnotic.

Everyone opened there eyes and they saw in front of them there was a small vine with a small flower blossom. This vine would eventually grow, and a pumpkin would grow where the flower was now. The sounds had been coming louder and louder and now the sound was slowly starting to recede into the background. Everyone opened their eyes and could see and appreciate what they had all done together.

It appeared they were ready to go to Newgrange to finally try and make contact with the Earth.

Newgrange Historical Site
County Meath, Ireland
Tuesday, 11:00 AM

When they all arrived at the Newgrange site, they drove down an unmarked road, and at the end of this was a large fence preventing anyone passing closer to the site. On the side of the road was a small car where Harriet's friend from the Newgrange Historical Organization was waiting inside. When they stopped, Harriet jumped out and almost tackled him.

Pat said sarcastically, "I guess Harriet knows this person more than just as a friend." He emphasized the word *friend* using air quotes.

No one else noticed it, but Kat spotted something she had only seen once before in Pat. He was jealous. Like any full red blooded male, Pat had a variety of relationships he would be interested in at one time or another. There was one girl who hurt him a lot. He found her cheating with his roommate one day. It sent him into a chaotic spiral, but in the end, Kat and other friends had convinced him it was better to know now rather than later on.

Seeing the way Pat reacted with Harriet, signaled he might be very interested in Harriet. She suspected it was probably more than either Harriet or anyone else in the group knew. For Pat's sake, she hoped he didn't get hurt. Kat also knew better than to interfere in Pat's life. However, she would just add this to the *be on the lookout* list, in case things were going in a wrong or hurtful way. As much as Pat frustrated her at times, he was still her twin brother, and this trumps just about anything else.

After Harriet's friend had unlocked and opened the gate, he got into his car and headed back down the road they had just come from. Harriet got into the car and both cars proceeded to another unmarked dirt road which took them to the opposite end of the Newgrange site. The ground was higher on the back portion of the site. This was a portion of Newgrange which was opposite to the front passageway where the winter solstice sun greeted the first rays of sunshine.

Harriet got out and led them down a short hill, where the backside of the Newgrange site had a more moderate slope than the front. The hill had 3 terraces which allowed the slope to be less steep. They walked down to the first terrace

There was a large stone rock about 5 feet tall which was pushed up next to the terracing of the hill, to help it maintain the support of the hill. Upon closer inspection, there was an opening just wide enough for a person to slide in behind the stone. There were a lot of overgrown brambles and brush growing all around the slight opening between the rock and the Earth. Harriet moved some of the brush away as best she could. Pat jumped in to help her remove even more of it. In a minute or two they had removed enough of it for Harriet to slide in behind the rock. Alder and Arwen supplied everyone with powerful flashlights and helmets with lights to help them see.

After Harriet slid herself into the opening, she called back to everyone to come in and join her. Alder and Arwen seemed surprised this opening even existed. Once everyone got through the opening, the additional headlights illuminated the corridor more. It was a long tunnel about 6 feet high and about wide enough for two people to walk abreast.

They walked down the corridor, and at several spots Ogham symbols and spiral whirls were carved into the stones. Arwen placed her hand on each of the spirals and the carvings. She touched them as if they were like delicate silk or embroidery. Neither Alder nor Arwen showed any emotion and remained neutral. After a minute or so, Alder took out several of the quantum stones and placed them on the floor next to each of the carvings and spirals.

Arwen went to the far end of the corridor. Alder then asked each person to stand next to the particular stone he had placed on the floor. When everyone was in position, he took a spot at the opposite end of the corridor from Arwen.

Alder said, "This time, we will not be physically touching any of the stones. What I would like everyone to do is to place your hands on the wall when we get started. All I want you to do is to focus on the Earth. Think of the Earth like it's a newborn. It might not want to wake up. Try to think about the power which is stored in the Earth. Feel this power and let the Earth see its own power. Assure the Earth, it's OK to wake up. We want it to feel us, and we want to help it. Pat and Brian, you both are the power sources, let the Earth know it has its own power and force. Harriet and Kat, you're both the healers and sources of life energy, let it know you're here to help it understand its own healing ability. Is everyone OK on this?"

"Yes"

"OK, let's begin."

Everyone relaxed and tried to let their minds clear and focus on what Alder just suggested. Even though Alder was very sure this was going to work, there was still a lot of doubt amongst them in those initial seconds. None of them wanted this to fail. They all tried to focus and give it their best in spite of the odds of this being successful or not. For almost 2 minutes of silence, no one had said anything.

Pat couldn't resist and smirked, "Come on Earth, don't be a big meathead. Wake up!"

It was hard to resist laughing from Pat's little tension breaking banter. Harriet couldn't help herself and laughed and giggled at what he said.

"Sorry. Too much tension. OK, I'm focused."

Harriet, however, kept laughing. Her laughter seemed to be coming from everywhere and not just from Harriet. Now she was giggling, and it kept echoing and reverberating from every direction. She was laughing and giggling at the same time.

Arwen asked, "Harriet, are you OK?"

Harriet didn't turn to Arwen, and she kept laughing. Arwen reached out and touched Harriet's shoulder and her laughing and giggling stopped. Or had it?

They could all hear the same giggling and laughing coming from every direction. It continued and Harriet wasn't the source of it anymore. The echoing should have stopped shortly after Harriet stopped, but the echoing hung on for at least an additional 30 seconds. Eventually it stopped. When the echoing finally stopped, there was a slight rumbling of everything around them. It wasn't quite like an earthquake or a tremor of an earthquake, it felt like living near a train station and the train was storming though town. Or even a jet airplane flying low over you. Finally, all the noises stopped.

Everyone looked at Alder for any insight of what had just happened. His expression was neutral, but they could all tell he was thinking very hard to try and understand what just happened.

Finally, he said, "Now this has never happened before. Harriet what happened when you were laughing? It seemed like you were overtaken by something."

"It felt familiar to me like when I tend my plants. I hum from what I hear in the background. What I heard in the background, was like a child laughing, so my humming sounded like laughing. It was really strange. I mean when I tend my plants, I'm just repeating what I hear or think I am hearing what my plants are singing. This was different. It was definitely laughing and giggling in a singsongy way.

"Alder come and take a look at this spiral. I think this could answer something we have been missing." Arwen was looking at one of the spirals carved into the wall. It was actually two spirals next to each other.

"Yes, I think you're right. Let's give it a try, OK?"

Alder placed his index finger on the outermost line of the spiral on the left and Arwen did the same for the spiral on the right. They both, at the same time, traced the lines of the spiral around and around to finally end up in the center of the spiral.

When they both reached the center of the spiral, they both pushed the center like it was a button. The stone where the spirals were etched on reacted by popping out a small little piece of the stone wall. Arwen pulled the stone all the way out from the little section which had popped open. Alder took his flashlight to see what was inside. He reached in and retrieved a blue pouch, which was similar to the other colored pouches where he kept all the other quantum stones. He opened the pouch and pulled out an oval blue stone.

Alder closed his eyes and was holding the stone. After several seconds, he opened his eyes and smiled at Arwen. He gave her the blue stone. She repeated the same thing Alder did. She closed her eyes for a brief period and when she opened them, she smiled in a mischievous way.

"Alder, how could we have been so misled. This is incredibly frustrating. Why would Kobin or Mordag refuse to share this information? I just don't understand it."

"He's just acting true to his nature. He seeks power and nothing else. Mordag, I think just followed him, but she participated as much as he did. This is why."

Kat said, "What does all of this mean?"

Alder took a deep breath and said, "This stone allows you to gain knowledge and understanding. Intelligence is really based on how we learn about new things we didn't know or understand before. It involves taking knowledge you already have and adding to this store of facts. This stone also can inhibit learning. It can also allow you to block knowledge you have of certain events, or make you react opposite to the way you would normally act. The real power of this stone is you can make yourself or someone else to forget information, or if used in a different way, it can give information to a person. Apparently, Kobin inhibited our knowledge of a very important stone. The white stone."

Arwen implored, "Brother, how could we have allowed him to block this knowledge from us? Every time I thought about this stone, I always thought we lost it so long ago. Why didn't others of our kind tell us the white stone wasn't lost? We have had it all the time. It's in a safe deposit box in Dublin. Alder can you give me the brown stone?"

Arwen walked over to the spot where they had placed the brown stone and held this in her right hand and closed her hand around it. She looked like she was deeply concentrating. She held her left hand open and in a few seconds a leather pouch, similar to the other pouches, appeared in her hand. Inside the pouch she retrieved a long weirdly shaped bronze and steel key.

"Well done, Arwen. Where was it?"

"Inside my desk at my school. Can you believe it? I have probably looked at this almost every day and I never even thought to ask myself what it was for. I feel like such a fool."

Brian asked, "Do you need to go to Dublin, or can you just gin the stone out of the deposit box from here using this stone?"

"No, unfortunately this is the drawback of the brown stone, I don't know which safety box is mine. I know the number of the safety box I have it in, but I don't remember where it is exactly. I'll have to go to Dublin to retrieve it."

Alder said, "Why don't we head back to the castle and discuss this further. I don't want to impose on Harriet's friend any longer than we have to."

Everyone left the tunnel, got in the cars, and went back to the castle. It was only noontime, and Arwen was anxious to get back and go to Dublin. Arwen left the castle, and said she would be back later tonight, and would call Alder to update him on the status.

The rest of the day, they all relaxed. Kat asked if Cathal would show her some of the animals they have here at the castle. He took her down to the stables where Callum was tending some of the sheep. Harriet and Brian were in the large drawing room perusing some of the books in the huge library. Pat asked Alder to tell him more about how the quantum stones worked. It ended up being a discussion of Alder's home planet Ghia. Pat was insatiable. Every answer Alder that told him, he came up with 5 more questions.

Chapter 18 – Dublin Showdown

'If you would like to know the value of money, try to borrow some.'

– Benjamin Franklin

Merrion Vault

Dublin Ireland

Tuesday, 4:45 PM GMT

When Kobin and Mordag arrived in Ireland they were able to quickly clear customs and get a black midsize rental car to take them to the Merrion Vault storage facility located in the heart of Dublin's city center. Mordag was a vicious driver. She treated the road with a ruthlessness which Kobin had forgotten about when he agreed to let her drive. Kobin knew she drove this ferociously, but more than once during the chaotic trip through Dublin, Kobin had to stifle his instinctual reaction of bracing for impact. The whole time Kobin was trying to stay calm and relaxed, he noticed in his peripheral vision, Mordag was smiling.

When the car finally stopped, he looked at her and he couldn't help himself from laughing about how smug and coy she was looking at him.

"I haven't driven in 30 years, and driving a car is so much fun. I had forgotten how exhilarating it can be. This is the most fun I have felt in years."

"Mordag, you do realize that even though we're able to live for as long as we care to; it's still possible for us to die. Please, for my benefit, let's live a little longer to see this through. There may come a time when this changes, but please let me decide on the *when*, OK?"

Mordag smiled and nodded contritely. "I'll go in and get the stone. I don't think I'll have an issue doing this. It's been a long time since I have seen the olive colored quantum stone. I hope I can still remember how to use it. I should be back in a few minutes. If I have an issue, I'll call you, OK?" Mordag said as she jumped out of the car.

Kobin sat in the car for about 15 minutes, and he decided to get out to stretch a little. The last 48 hours he'd been on a plane jumping from point to point. Mordag parked in the little lot that Merrion Vault storage provided for its customers. When they arrived 15 minutes ago there were only a few spots available. Mordag was still in her zeal of driving, and she narrowly missed clipping another car's side door as she shoe-horned the car into a spot barely big enough for the mid-sized sedan.

It was just a little after 5:30 PM, and several cars were moving in and out of the small lot. A navy blue SUV pulled in and picked a spot to park. When the person got out of the car, Kobin could see her face for a brief second. He quickly ducked to make sure the person didn't see him. It was Arwen. She was still the same huntress and queen she was in the early Roman and Londinium times. It took an inordinate amount of energy to calm his emotions to not just jump out and attack her. Quickly, he realized what needed to be done.

He reached in his pocket and grabbed his cell phone and furiously dialed Mordag's cell phone. In what seemed like an eternity, the cell towers linked and clicked and finally started to ring. On the second ring, Mordag answered his call.

"Mordag, where are you exactly right now? Arwen just showed up here and is heading into the building that you're in right now."

"She's here?" Mordag paused for a second quickly going into warrior mode and said, "OK, I'm in a private room right now and I'm alone. I have the stone in my hand. Are you thinking what I'm thinking? Hold on a second, let me take a look outside this room."

The silence was agonizing for Kobin. Finally, Mordag came back to the phone. "I just saw her go into a room across the hall from where I'm at right now. She will probably take the box to a private room for her to retrieve whatever is in her box. I'm going to use the olive stone, so I can force her to give us the other stones. Give me two minutes. I'll be out shortly. If she comes out and I don't, then you will have to take care of her. You have the black stone, and the power of the lilac stone to shield you."

Mordag saw Arwen walk out into the hallway with her box where the security staff showed her to a private viewing area two rooms down the hall from where Mordag was. The security person opened the door and then left her alone. He walked down the hall to where the elevator was and waited.

Mordag exited her viewing room and walked to where her box was to be sealed up again. The security guard came over to help her. As he neared Mordag, she read his name tag and it said *David*. Using the stone, she whispered his name. David became instantly slack faced, docile, awaiting for instructions. She gave him the empty box and told him to put it back where it was supposed to go. She told him to stay here for the next hour and then forget everything about taking her to the safe deposit box.

Still with the olive stone clenched in her left hand, she walked to the viewing room she thought Arwen was in. She knocked on the door waiting for Arwen to open it. Nothing happened. She knew this was the right room. She slowly opened the door just a little bit to peek inside. Arwen was nowhere in sight. Mordag started to open the door a little more. She was still being cautious, but her senses were highly focused to be ready for anything.

The door flew open and hit Mordag in the face hard. Hard enough to cause her nose to start bleeding. She almost lost possession of the stone. The door opened so fast and pushed Mordag into the opposite wall causing her to lose her balance. She landed awkwardly on the floor, and this would be the moment Arwen would try to kick her head completely off. She knew the next 2 seconds would decide the fate of Arwen or Mordag. Focusing all of her mind and body, to force the will of Arwen to bend, she whispered in a deep guttural and growling sound, "A – R – W – E – N – (pause)- H – O – L- D," The last letter D was held onto and stretched another second or two

Arwen grimaced as if in extreme physical pain but without a sound and her face slowly and completed just relaxed to a blank emotionless visage. The cameras were everywhere in this building, so she needed to make it look like an accident. She hugged Arwen and when she got close to her ear, she used the stone to clearly say, "FFOOOLLLOOOWWW MMMEEEE"

Both Mordag and Arwen walked to the end of the hall and were met by a security guard to take them up to the main level of the Merrion Vault storage facility. In the elevator, she also checked to make sure Arwen had the white stone.

Mordag said, "GIVE ME THE WHITE STONE."

Arwen had no choice but to give her the white stone.

Mordag commanded, "GIVE ME ANY OTHER STONES YOU HAVE."

Arwen didn't move. Mordag interpreted this as a *no*.

Mordag and Arwen walked out of the building. Mordag was quite pleased with herself and even more happy when she saw the shock on Kobin's face. Mordag was uncertain of how Kobin was going to react near Arwen. She also knew time was of the essence and everything they did now needed to attract no attention. When she got closer to Kobin, she handed him the keys to the rental they were driving. She said, "Kobin take the car to the farm south of Drogheda. We will follow you."

Kobin knew Mordag was deliberately keeping him from interacting with Arwen. She was probably right. He's still so angry about her involvement with the death of his son, Creyn. He very well could do something rash.

Mordag looked at Arwen and said, "GET IN YOUR CAR AND FOLLOW KOBIN NOW"

They both got into the SUV and followed Kobin out of Dublin to head north to a town called Drogheda in county Louth. Drogheda is in the Boyne Valley area and is east of Newgrange. Once they got out of the city and traffic thinned out, it became easier to control Arwen.

The nature of the olive stone is that it allows you to control a person by taking control over the mind of the person. In essence, you're the puppet master. You can make a person physically do whatever you tell them to do. It's a little tricky to learn which way you voice the command.

In many ways, it's like an MRI machine. In an MRI machine, the energized magnets are able to force all particles within the magnetic field to point north. In a normal MRI scan, any particles of matter inside this magnetic field, is forced to point north. The composition of the matter inside this magnetic field is a determining factor of how far north the particles will point. The composition of the materials which make up this matter is important because it will show the particles pointing less north on denser matter than it will with less dense matter. This is how it's able to create **M**agnetic **R**esonance **I**maging pictures. Normally an MRI machine will have a person inside the magnetic field and the MRI is able to detect some materials such as bone to be denser than perhaps muscles, organs, tissues or veins.

The olive stone is acting as the signal, to force different particles in a person's brain, specifically the primary motor cortex, to activate. It connects voice to the actions and fires the neurons to execute signals to send to the spinal cord. Once you established a connection and have established very clear directions, it was easier. The person holding the olive stone can become the puppet master of whoever they choose to.

As with all of the quantum stones, with the exception of the black and the white quantum stones, there is an opposite property of the stone's power. The counter property of the olive stone is if you try to control someone, it can be blocked by the violet stone. The violet stone can determine truth or untruth. The violet stone can block the olive stone and it will rebound on the person using the olive stone, or the puppet master, such that they are they are now the puppet being controlled by someone else.

The combination of all the different stones can be complicated when viewing them all together versus individually. Each stone has a power to control a duality aspect of quantum properties. The stones can affect the vibration, the spin, both the spin and the vibration, or leave the spin or vibration alone for the quantum particles. It's the yin and the yang, the left and the right, the north or the south, the weak or the strong, or finally the positive or the negative aspect of each quantum particle. It can quickly become a very large matrix of properties on the quantum spectrum.

Once they were out of the city, Mordag started to probe Arwen for information. This was a little more difficult. The brain had to access the part which contains memory storage. The olive stone could not force her to disclose something in her memory, but it could force her mouth to start talking, or to stop talking. It's too bad she didn't have the violet stone so she could verify is she was telling the truth or not. The violet stone would be extremely helpful today.

However, Arwen and Mordag share a very long history. They were good and trusted friends for 2000 of the 5000 years they have been on the Earth. Arwen is very strong willed, but she may inadvertently reveal a reaction by a hesitation to answer something.

Mordag said while tightly holding the olive stone, "ARWEN. YOU MAY TALK," and then followed up with saying, "if you want to."

Arwen sat there and didn't make a move to talk or say anything.

"Arwen it's been a long time since we have seen each other. I'm curious of your travels since you left Londinium, or should I say *London*. I did come across a reference to you involved in the World Wildlife Fund operating in Africa and Australia where you contributed a considerable amount of money to help them."

Arwen still didn't say anything. Mordag added, "Well, I personally want to thank you for your contribution. Did you know who it was who started the World Wildlife Fund?"

"No, and I don't care," Arwen said through gritted teeth.

"Come now. Didn't it remind you of the earlier days, when we spent so much time working with the animals and helping them thrive? What was the name of the *woolly mammoth* you cared for when it broke its two legs? Hebnatia?"

"Hikitia."

"Well, they were very helpful when we were building all those ridiculous stone monuments. If it were not for them, we would have never been able to pull, or lift, those massive stones into the exact position we were trying to place them. I remembered the way you cared for Hikitia, and I wanted to help the Earth maintain the balance of life living on this planet."

Continuing Mordag said, "Why did you come to Dublin to retrieve the white stone? I know you don't want to tell me, but I suspect you have met some people who can use the stones to try once again to connect with the Earth. Is Pat Themis part of your group?"

Arwen did exactly what Mordag was hoping to catch. She made just the slightest twitch in her face. It was a miniscule muscle twitch. Probably about 99% of the people in the world wouldn't pick it up. Most people automatically do this without even thinking of it. If you look very closely, you can spot what the mind is thinking by the facial muscles or signals we all do autonomously. Mordag has known Arwen for 5000 years, so she can track her face and read her expression better than anyone else.

"Arwen, is Alder here in Ireland with you?"

Arwen twitched. Mordag continued, "Is he waiting for you back in Slane?"

Arwen twitched again. Mordag sighed and said, "Once we get to Drogheda, we will have you call him. I'm not sure what Kobin is thinking, but he wants to get whatever stones you have. If Alder still acts the way he did in the past, he's probably zealously guarding the stones keeping each one in its own little, sacred, colored, leather pouches. Also, what is it with his passion about wearing the color orange? I never understood this, do you know why he always gravitates to that particular color?"

For one moment, Arwen looked like she was going to say something and then chose not to. Mordag prompted, "Go ahead you can tell me. I'm pretty sure he's with you. Your face told me the second I mentioned it."

"You really don't understand what the color orange means?" Arwen asked.

"Well, obviously I don't. So please, enlighten me," Mordag shot back

Arwen took a deep breath and exhaled slowly to calm her emotions and the tone of her voice before saying, "Orange is the color which honors Ode Tillamook. The first to join with Ghia in a sentient symbiotic relationship. Didn't you learn about how he and Ghia helped our species survive when they were forced to live underground? The planet was bombarded with meteorites for almost 200 years. We were cut off from the life giving rays of our sun. Od used the color orange to help the plants photosynthesize and we grew food underground by only using the orange light. That has always been the only reason for loving the color orange. It's a sign of respect for the elders of our planet.

I don't understand how you couldn't have learned this while you were in school?"

Mordag immediately felt the sting of Arwen's words and it angered her. It angered her a lot! Her first instinct was to lash out at Arwen, but right now wasn't the time or the place. Evenly, she said, "I don't remember learning this as student. Remember, I wasn't part of a class in our society who were as privileged as yours was. Don't assume I had the same education as you."

Arwen responded quickly, "Mordag, I'm sorry. I didn't mean to say it in such a horrible way."

"It's OK. I understand."

She did understand, but it still didn't change the plan right now as Arwen followed Kobin. He pulled off the road to head down the long driveway to the old yellow farmhouse on a long sloping hill just on the outskirts of Drogheda.

Mordag pulled out the olive stone and carefully phrased her actions to tell Arwen to stop the car and exit the vehicle. She also told her to follow her and not to talk until she was told to. It was important to be extremely specific when you're using the olive stone.

Mordag has maintained this house for many years. It's a farm which produces a variety of cheeses and butters. She thought of selling it about 20 years ago, but she decided almost at the last minute to keep it. She has invested money and animals on the lands around the farmhouse. At the most it probably just about breaks even. She doesn't really care so much about the profit or lack of profit, but she has always liked to have a house in Ireland just in case. Today, was the perfect *just in case.*

The staff and the caretakers of the farm live in the large farmhouse and there is a separate building in the rear which is a place reserved for her when she visits here. Kobin has stayed here many times and he's familiar with the people who maintain it and prepare it for when people are coming to visit. He told Mordag he called them on the ride over.

The three of them walked to the rear of the house where the door was unlocked for them. Mordag told Arwen to sit in the chair by the kitchen table. She tugged on Kobin's coat and asked him to talk to her in another room.

The room was a small study with a couple of chairs and a red couch. After she closed the door, she took a seat on the red couch. Kobin sat in one of the chairs. "Kobin if you try to hurt Arwen, I'll use the olive stone to stop you. I know this is the first thing on your mind right now. We need Arwen alive if we are to get the remaining stones from Alder. Promise me, you won't hurt her before this happens?" Mordag said.

"Yes, I promise. I will avenge my son's death at some point, but I promise you I won't do this until we have gotten the stones from Alder."

"OK, good. She didn't tell me, but I'm almost certain Alder is waiting for her back in Slane at the castle. I'm also pretty sure the rest of the people we saw in the security footage are there also. It makes sense. They probably want to try something at

Newgrange. It's the only thing which makes sense. I'm surprised they chose Newgrange and not Stonehenge, aren't you?"

"No. It does make sense to go to Newgrange. Stonehenge is where Ghia felt it could talk to the Earth. I don't think the sentience of the Earth is located at Stonehenge. I know the sentience is really not in just one location, but it spans the entire planet. The actual heart of, or the actual essence of the Earth's sentience, is located at Newgrange. If we want to go back home to Ghia, we need to try this at Stonehenge. I also think the people Alder and Arwen have recruited into this crazy crusade are able to tap into the quantum properties of the stones without actually using the stones to do this. I have never heard of anyone being able to do this before, have you?"

"Well, no not really. However, Arwen decided to educate me on the history of Ghia and Ode Tillamook. I have never heard of this person before. Apparently, this is the reason why Alder is always wearing something orange. It's his way of showing reverence or respect for this person from so long ago. I still don't understand it, but Arwen told me this ancient person saved our species by using orange light to help plants grow food underground without any sunlight."

Kobin said, "If I ever did learn this in school, it's long forgotten."

Mordag said, "OK, now that we have Arwen here, how do you want to proceed on this? I was thinking if Alder is here, then we should ransom Arwen for the stones. What do you think?"

"Yes, I agree with you. The lilac stone can protect us from any nasty stuff he might try to do using the stones. Plus, we have the white stone to amplify the stone powers or use the black stone to nullify them. You got the white stone from her, right?"

"Yes." Mordag pulled the white stone out of her pocket.

"Wonderful, Let's call Alder and have them meet us at Dowth."

Mordag nodded her head affirmatively. She thought for a second before answering and then said, "We need to write down exactly what we want Arwen to say on the phone to Alder. This will force Arwen to say only what we write down. She might change a word if I give her permission to talk out loud. She might use a word which might give Alder some hidden clue or code. If I tell her to only read what we write down, then I think this will be the best way to have her comply and only read the words on the paper. Nothing else, just the words on the message. Does this sound, OK?"

"Sounds like *check and mate,*" As Kobin said this, he brought his hand up to make a motion like knocking over his king on a chessboard to simulate the final move in a game of chess.

An hour later, Mordag reread the full message which they agreed would be the exact words Arwen would read over the phone to Alder. It said:

Alder — Please don't interrupt me and listen carefully. This is a one way message and is not open to discussion. Mordag and Kobin captured me when I went to the bank in Dublin. They have the olive stone and they forced me to give them the white stone. They will kill me if you don't give them all the quantum stones you possess. They will meet you at the Dowth South Passage entrance tomorrow morning at 9:00 AM. The only response you're allowed to say here is, either a yes or a no. Give me your response now.

Both Kobin and Mordag smiled when they were done and read it out loud. Mordag said, "Let's call him now and then let's get something to eat."

Both of them went back into the kitchen. Mordag holding the olive stone in her hand said, "ARWEN. Take you cell phone out and call your brother Alder. When you're connected to him, put it on speakerphone, and then read the message written on this piece of paper. Only read what is on this paper and nothing else."

Arwen reached into her pocket of the coat she was wearing and retrieved her cell phone. She dialed the number for her brother Alder, and she put the call on speakerphone. It rang two times before Alder picked it up.

"Hi, Arwen. Did you have any problems in Dubin?"

Arwen read the message which Mordag had given her. She read it exactly as it was written and her voice was in a normal monotone, absent of any emotion or urgency. When she stopped reading, there was a pause.

The next thing they all heard was Alder saying, "Yes. I'll meet you at Dowth south tomorrow morning at 9:00 AM."

Mordag took the phone from Arwen and ended the call. Both Kobin and Mordag looked at each other as if a great weight had been lifted from them. Mordag said, "I'll get Arwen situated in the other room and make sure she has all the proper instructions for her to stay here and go to sleep. We don't have to worry about her, if I give her the proper instructions. I had forgotten how incredibly precise you need to be with this stone. I'm quite enjoying this."

Mordag said, "OK. Let's get something to eat."

Chapter 19 – Dowth

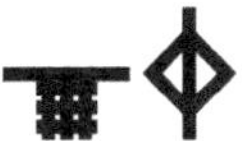

Expecting the world to treat you fairly because you are a good person is a little like expecting the bull not to attack you because you are a vegetarian.

- Dennis Wholey

Slane Castle

County Meath, Slane, Ireland

Tuesday 8:00 PM

Later in the evening, everyone was sitting in the drawing room with a massive fire burning. Everyone was talking and telling stories of the history around the Boyne Valley area and some of the remarkable history and battles which have happened in this particular region of Ireland. Kayleigh, Cathal, and Callum were telling stories about the history of the castle and some of the very bloody battles which have taken place in the Boyne valley area. Everyone was really caught up in listening to these stories.

Arwen still had not returned from Dublin yet. Alder was getting a little worried, but it could really be simply anything which might have delayed her. Alder received a call on his cell phone. He got up, exited the room, so he could talk privately and not disturb everyone else. When he came back into the room he tried to act as if nothing had happened. Harriet was the first to say something. Alder, was visibly upset by something when he came back into the room and sat down next to Harriet.

She leaned over to Alder asked him quietly, "Alder, was that a call from Arwen? Is she all right? You look troubled."

Although, he was feeling distraught by the call, he smiled at Harriet and said, "You know, you have an uncanny ability of perception and intuitiveness. Arwen is fine for now, but she has been captured by Kobin and his sister Mordag. They have the olive stone, and they are controlling Arwen with this stone. They want us to meet them at Dowth South Passage tomorrow morning at 9:00 AM. I'm told to bring them all the quantum stones we have with us and give them to Kobin and Mordag. If we don't do this, then they will kill Arwen."

Not realizing it, everyone in the room was completely silent and listening to everything Alder was saying. He looked at them and said, "I don't think I have a choice on this. I'll go tomorrow and give Kobin the stones. I may hold back on the blue stone, since this is new for us. Kobin and Mordag both know the blue stone was lost thousands of years ago. They probably have forgotten it even exists. They have the white stone in their possession. The only counterforce to the white stone is the black stone and vice versa. It's unfortunate this quest has to end so early, but it has been worth it to have met all of you. And also, to see my niece and nephews." He fondly looked at Cathal, Callum, and Kayleigh.

"Wait! So, do we just give up? Can't we trace where the phone was making the call and then I'll just pop in there and grab Arwen and like teleport back with her?" Pat exploded, venting with his apparent frustration on display.

"Kobin has the black stone, and he can nullify your power with the orange stone. This would be a problem. I'm sure he's on guard for anyone to get near her with the orange stone."

Again, Pat said angrily, "No! I can't let this go without at least trying to get her back. What about everyone else here? We have until 9:00 AM to figure out how to get this maniac from harming Arwen."

Kat looked at Pat. At first, she could see him making his, *please spare me the lecture face*. Then Kat smiled, and looked at everyone in the group said, "I agree with Pat. I don't want to let this go either, unless we try to at least get her back. There is probably danger here and we might get hurt, but I'm willing to take the risk." When she looked at Pat again, he was pleased and nodded a thank you to her for the support.

Brian also said, "I agree with Pat and Kat. I jump into fires so this is something I would feel badly about if I didn't at least try. One other thing too. My wife, Julie, is a genius with technology. If she wanted to track and trace Arwen's cell phone, she could probably do this without any problem. All she needs is Arwen's phone number and Alder's phone number. She could tell us where she's right now and where her phone is tomorrow morning. I say, let's give it a try."

Harriet looked at Pat and then said to everyone else, "You had me at *teleport*. I'm definitely in."

Cathal, Kayleigh, and Callum also agreed they should at least give it a try. Kayleigh said, "Alder, I doubt Cath or Callum would be recognized by Kobin or Mordag. I might be recognized, but it doesn't matter. Don't forget this is Slane Castle. For centuries, this castle has been the last stronghold of this area against insurmountable odds. The entire village of Slane would do anything they could do to help with this. They have known and loved you and Arwen for centuries and they don't forget the many times you have helped this village. They are with you in this too!"

They expected Alder to be pleased by this, but his face betrayed the internal struggle going on in his head. After a second or two, he said, "Your support is greatly appreciated. It really is. I can't risk this and put anyone else in danger. I suspect Kobin will kill Arwen regardless of whether I give him the stones or not. He has the olive stone, and he can give her a command to kill herself. He still blames Arwen for his son, Creyn, committing suicide. I'll go alone to Dowth tomorrow. Alone!" he plaintively looks at everyone and added, "please I can't bear the pain if anyone gets hurt."

"Bullshit! That ain't happening, no way, no how! Get over it, old man. We are going there tomorrow with you." Everyone looking at Alder nodded their heads in unison.

Harriet was totally caught up in the emotion everyone was feeling and said, "Alder, didn't you say Kobin was using the olive stone. Does the olive stone also work if you can't hear the person giving the command?"

"No, actually it doesn't. We had a problem once when the instructions were given to someone who was deaf. Why, what are you proposing?"

Harriet looked at Pat and he could see where she was going with this. Pat said, "Complete genius! Absolutely! Yes, this will work. Do you want to tell him, or do you want me too? It's your idea so why don't you tell him."

"OK. Kayleigh, do you have any kind of earplugs or earphones? The more soundproof the better. I suspect some people in the village didn't really care for the sounds of Metallica when they performed here a couple of years ago. Alder, when Pat told us about his experience with Kobin in Las Vegas, there was one key detail I think we are overlooking here. Kobin nullified the power of the orange stone because he saw Pat grabbing it when his cell phone went flying into the wall. Kobin knew this stone was being actively used. He nullified the orange stone, but he didn't expect Pat to use the power of the yellow stone. Pat did this naturally without even having the yellow stone in his hand. Pat used the power to break the table into two pieces, just like he did with the floors at the construction site. Luckily, this surprised Kobin, and then Pat was able to teleport back to Boston."

Pat looked at Harriet and said, "I couldn't have said it any better. Perfect plan. Tomorrow, I'll be invisible, and I'll put the earphones on Arwen.

"Pat, if you can take me with you, I'll put the headphones on Arwen, and you can teleport her and me back to the others who are waiting. If we keep distracting him, we can confuse him to not be able to use any of the stones at all. He'll be too busy figuring out what to do next," Harriet firmly said.

Pat looked at Alder and asked, "What other stones do they have?"

Alder replied skeptically, but not really ready to stop the discussion of a plan starting to form, "I believe he has the black, lilac, olive, and now with the latest edition he also has the white stone. The black stone nullifies any of the quantum stones. It can only nullify one stone at a time. The same is true with the white stone. The two other stones are the lilac stone, which acts like a shield against powers, and the olive stone, which will compel anyone to do what you tell them."

Pat said, "Alder you told us each power has an opposite side to it. Is there a way we can take advantage of this?"

"Yes, Pat. Yes, I think I see now. The olive stone has a negative effect in the way it can compel a person to do something. The violet stone tells you if something is true or not true. The olive stone power is such that it overrides the brains primary cortex of motor skill to do whatever it is being told to do. The violet stone resets the primary cortex so it can truly see the command coming from someone as false. It also has the effect of rebounding back onto the person who initiated the command. It makes that person lose control of their own primary cortex motor skills. Assuming Kobin is holding the stone, if we can distract him, then he might use the olive stone to control someone other than Arwen. This will give us a chance to have it rebound on him."

They all nodded at once.

Alder hesitantly continued, "Cath or Callum, I'm so hesitant to bring anyone else into this, but you both have used the Violet stone before. If we get a few people linked together as a whole group, it will rebound heavily on Kobin if he uses the olive stone."

Alder was silent for a moment and a small spark of something different was formulating in his mind. Alder stood up and looked at Brian, and said, "Brian can we take a little walk?"

"Sure."

Alder and Brian left the room and Alder said, "We will be back in a little bit."

Kayleigh said, "I'll make a couple of calls to find as many headphones as possible. Even if we have to put beeswax in people's ears. I'll also call a few people I know who can help us. They know about the quantum stones and won't be surprised. I think we can use this in our favor."

Cathal said, "I'm going to get some tea, would anyone else like some?"

"Cathal, do you have any more of the Orangina I saw on the table yesterday?" Pat asked.

Cathal smiled and said, "Yes, I'll bring some out. It's one of the favorite drinks here in Slane Castle, so we keep a lot of it on hand."

The rest of the night, everyone brainstormed about things they could do in preparation for a confrontation with Kobin and Mordag tomorrow morning. Alder came back with Brian a little later. Brian called his wife, Julie, and she was able to track and find Arwen's phone location. She tracked it to Drogheda, Ireland. Julie gave Brian software which he could access this information at any time. Kat started to practice with the violet stone to see how she could use it to make it rebound back on Kobin. She found she really had a knack for being able to see when someone said the truth or when someone told a lie. Pat felt sure he could palm some of the stones the same way he did this on Alder. Harriet was his assistant in this. After several hours they were very tired and decided it would be best for everyone to get a good night sleep.

Dowth South Passage Tomb

County Meath, Dowth Site

Wednesday 8:00 AM

Dowth is the least well known of the three great tombs of Brú na Bóinne. Although not as large as Newgrange and Knowth it has not been excavated in recent times. Like the other monuments it was built over 5,000 years ago. The mound of Dowth appears quite overgrown and neglected in comparison to the well-tended appearance of the other monuments. The mound was subjected to a very unprofessional excavation in 1847, two passage tombs were discovered but the mound was severely damaged in the process. The passage tombs are much less spectacular than Newgrange or Knowth sites, which have shorter passages and lower roofs. Both are on the western side of the mound; they are referred to as Dowth North and Dowth South. Dowth South is aligned to the setting sun of the winter solstice; the setting sun illuminates the passage and chamber about 3pm on the days around the winter solstice.

Unlike the Newgrange and Knowth sites, the Dowth site can be directly driven to without having to go through the Brú na Bóinne tourism center. The south entrance to Dowth was located in a small crater of an area where the roof had collapsed. The crater around the entrance to Dowth was dug out and used as a quarry.

The next morning everyone was in position, well before the time Kobin told Alder to be there. Kat was in a wooded area on the edge of the site. The area was quite exposed and difficult to hide your presence, but they were able to find a stand of trees which could be used as cover for Kat and the 6 strong burly men from Slane whom Kayleigh had called last night to help. In addition, Cathal and Callum were with them as well.

At exactly 9:00 AM, Kobin appeared with Mordag and Arwen. Alder walked from the opposite side to meet them. In his right hand he held a violet colored stone and in his left hand he held a grey bag which contained all of the other quantum stones. Kobin was holding the lilac stone in his left hand, and he held the white stone in his right hand. Mordag held the olive stone in her left hand.

Unbeknownst to Kobin or Mordag, Pat, Harriet, and Brian were waiting on the opposite side of the crater and were behind Kobin and Mordag. As soon as Pat saw Kobin, Arwen, and Mordag, walking toward Alder, he teleported all three of them to just behind Arwen. Harriet put a large set of headphones onto Arwen's head covering her ears. When Harriet grabbed Arwen's shoulder, she became invisible.

Mordag sensed this and growled, "HOLD!"

Nothing happened. Mordag said this again to empty air. Pat, Brian, Arwen, and Harriet didn't hear anything since they were equipped with headphones and wax to hear just silence. Mordag screamed again, and nothing happened. Alder held up his hand with the purple stone. This made Mordag hesitate before her next order was going to be directed to Alder.

The raised hand from Alder was the signal to Kat and the rest of the villagers to come running out of the trees as a group yelling for Mordag to stop what she was doing. One of the villagers who Kayleigh had specifically reached out to is a man named Crispin McGuinea. He knew Mordag from another time long ago. They had been lovers at a time when life wasn't as tortuous as it has been in the last hundred years of boredom. The relationship ended badly and painfully.

This person made Mordag hesitate for just one second, but it didn't deter her in any way. In fact, this was exactly why the person was with Kayleigh, Cathal, Callum and Kat. The resurgence of painful memories made her want to retaliate even more so she yelled at the group of people running to her and directed her command to the entire group, "STOP! COME NO CLOSER! STOP!"

This was the magic ingredient they were looking for. Mordag's compulsion was aimed at Kat and her group, so this didn't affect anyone else except the group charging her with Kat leading the group of people. Alder didn't hold the violet stone in his hand, but he unwrapped the purple grape Starburst candy he was holding.

Mordag's command rebounded on herself. All expression from her face drained. She just stayed there doing nothing as her command had told the others to do. But since everyone, except Kat, was wearing thick headphones. Kat was the only person who heard the command from Mordag, and she was holding the violet stone in her left hand.

In his peripheral vision, Kobin could sense this happening. He quickly reached into his pocket and pulled out the black stone. He cast his senses to a large area around him looking for the orange stone and its power of invisibility. He wanted to nullify this. After a second or two Pat, Harriet, Arwen, and Brian became visible again.

Brian held a zippo lighter and the pink stone in one hand, and some small balloons filled with gasoline. He threw several of the balloons at the ground between Kobin and himself. He ignited the zippo lighter to create a flame. He used the pink stone to push the flame from the lighter to the balloons and ignite the fuel. The balloons broke open and a wall of fire almost 8 feet high rose up between Kobin and the people behind Brian. Kobin was completely cut off between him and the group of people who were now forming a circle around Kobin.

Brian was too busy to acknowledge it, but he was pretty sure he heard Pat say something to the effect of, "Wicked!"

Kobin wasn't sure whether he could see Brian holding the pink stone or not, but he used the black stone to nullify it. Kat at this point had reached the group of people who were now surrounding Kobin and Mordag. Mordag did nothing and just stood there, thankfully one less threat to be part of this. The moment Kat had gained control of Mordag, her previous compulsion of Arwen was released. As Kat and the rest of the group arrived, they formed a circle around Kobin. The wall of fire was diminished almost to nothing from Kobin nullifying the wall of fire Brian had made.

Arwen was the closest to Kobin.

In a last ditch effort, he pulled a gun from his other pocket and aimed this at Arwen. If he could not get the stones, then no one could. He pointed the gun at Arwen's chest and fired the gun. Harriet saw this happening as if in slow motion. On purely instinct she lunged at Arwen to get her out of the way of the fatal bullet. She wasn't quick enough. The bullet hit Harriet in the chest. Harriet awkwardly landed on the ground with a dull thud.

Arwen roared, "NO! You silly child. NO! NOOO! Why did you do this? Oh, Harriet, please no."

Arwen's agony intensified when she knew Harriet was dead, the red stone at this point could not help her. Everyone was stunned and still tried to understand what had just happened.

In the background, the sound of wind chimes started to sound. Louder and louder, it got. The bass notes kept reverberating louder and louder. Lightning was seen and heard in the background. A massive bolt of lightning struck the ground in front of everyone. The intensity of the shock of blinding light and the palpable feeling of electricity of charged ions swirled in the air. A second bolt of searing white lightening hit the ground again. This time the lightning bolt pierced through Kobin, and he was instantly killed. His body was completely burned and seared from head to toe, and his body just crumbled into dust and ash.

The sounds of the wind chimes continued in long baleful notes. Looking for solace in the air from anyone hearing the sad dirge. The dirge became louder and louder. It changed slightly. It wasn't just an echoing of long noted sounds, but it started to gain a quicker tempo and pacing. It now started to sound like the pleasant sounds you would usually think of when you were to hear or listen to a wind chime. It had a familiar rhythm to it.

Everyone took off the earphones and the earplugs they were wearing a minute ago, they all looked at each other, confused, and distraught over what just happened. It soon became apparent the sounds were familiar but placing them was hard to vocalize. Alder was the first to recognize it. It was the sound of Harriet, when she hummed her song with the green stone. Alder reached into the bag of different stone pouches and grabbed the green stone. He knelt down and put the stone in Harriet's left hand.

The sounds and the songs continued. Everyone as a group started to hum the music. It was infectious and they were all humming and thinking of Harriet. The only person who wasn't humming was Mordag. The humming continued louder and louder. Everyone was fully involved in the music chords and sounds. Alder and Arwen stopped singing.

Harriet's eyes slowly opened. She looked around and sat up. Harriet's humming and her voice was singing the loudest now. Arwen was crying and sobbing when she saw Harriet alive. The jubilance of seeing Harriet alive was infecting everyone. The sounds of the wind chimes and the humming of everyone as one, started to slowly diminish.

Once everyone was quiet, Harriet spoke, but her voice was altered in a way similar to the way a small child would talk. Infantile and giddy. Harriet said, "I'm talking through the person called Harriet," and the face seemed a little confused and asked, "Harriet? Am I saying this correctly? Why did the other hurt her? I like *Harriet*, she made me laugh and gave me love. Harriet, Harriet, Harriet. Her name is hard to say. Harriet is better now. I don't like the other. He tried to hurt my Harriet. He tried to take life. I won't allow it. What are you called? Are you also called Harriet?"

Alder smiled as he spoke, "No we each have a name by which we are called. My name is Alder."

Harriet repeated the name, "Alder. It feels easier to say this name."

Each person standing around Harriet, told the Earth what their name was. After each person said their name, Harriet repeated the name once or twice to test it. After everyone had introduced themselves, Earth talking through Harriet asked, "What am I called?"

Alder answered, "You are called Earth. You're the most important and special thing in this galaxy. We are honored to talk with you. We are here to only help or support you and the rest of the planet."

Harriet said, "I also wish the same. You look familiar to me. You're old and have been here for longer than everyone here, except Arwen. I can't remember when you were born on me. Are you older than me?"

Alder laughed and said, "Yes you're right. I'm an old man and my sister and I have been here for 5000 years. We were not born on Earth, but we were born on a different planet called Ghia. We came to you, to introduce and welcome you into a guild of many other planets very much like you. It is called the Quantum Guild. We wanted to see if you would like to be part of our guild of planets, which work together with the different people living on the different worlds. You don't have to join our guild, but we are here to help or support you in anyway we can."

"Ghia, hmm. I think I recognize the name. I don't remember when it was, but it seems familiar to me. Can I talk to *Ghia*?"

"Yes, you can. We don't know exactly how to do this right now, but we could work together on this so we can connect with Ghia. I know Ghia would very much like to connect and talk with you. It can help you a great deal. Ghia is where the Quantum Guild was started. They have connected with many different planets and have helped them to grow and evolve. Does this sound like something you would like?"

Harriet started to giggle again. In between giggling fits, Harriet said, "There are many more like me? Yes, I'd like to meet them. They won't hurt me, right?" Harriet started to giggle again even more now. It was hard for the others to see whether the giggling was real or not. The Earth added, "What is Harriet doing right now? I like it a lot."

"Harriet is doing what we call *giggling*. It means happy and enjoyable. Giggling is a lot of fun, and we all like doing it. Ghia and the other planets like yourself would be very happy to meet you. They like to giggle also."

Harriet said, "What are those color stones you have. I can feel them, but I'd like to touch and look at them in my own way. Would you let me do this?"

Alder looked at Arwen and she nodded yes. Alder took the green stone and all of the rest of the stones from the bag or the others who were holding them in the last go around with Kobin. He gave the olive stone to Arwen.

Arwen took the olive stone and looked at Mordag and said, "Mordag, you're released from compulsion." She turned and gave Alder the olive stone.

Alder took all of the stones and placed them on the ground near the entrance to Dowth. Almost immediately, the area of ground underneath the stones was turned upward and swallowed all of the stones.

Harriet said, "Hmm, these are very strange. They are not part of me. I can feel they come from somewhere else. but they are interesting. Let me leave you now for a little time. I'll give Harriet a location where I can talk to you all again. I'll meet you there in a few days. We can then contact Ghia. I'm going to release Harriet now. I'll contact you through Harriet again in a few days."

Harriet was still sitting on the ground, but her eyes closed, and she fell back lying down on the ground. After a second or two, her eyes opened, and she took a deep breath like she had been underwater for about as long as she could and broke through with a great big inhale of air. Everyone was standing around her. She looked confused by everyone looking at her. Her eyes saw Arwen, and her eyes sparkled with happiness.

Arwen started to cry and released tears of joy. She said softly, "Child, I couldn't bear it if you died here today because of me. I'm going to relinquish my title of Queen Boudicca and I'm going to give this to the bravest, and the most fearless warrior I have ever encountered. All hail, the new Queen Harriet."

Everyone as a group said, "Hail Queen Harriet! Hail Queen Harriet!"

Ironically, Kat noticed the loudest voice was her brother Pat.

Mordag had been standing outside the group around Harriet. She was shocked when she saw what happened to her brother. It felt like a piece of her body was just sliced off. She was devastated and the last place she wanted to be right now was here at Dowth with these people. She walked away as quickly as possible. Once she was about 50 feet away, she started to run and sprinted to her car. Tears were streaming down her face. When she got the car started, she saw Alder and Arwen running toward her. They were the last people she wanted to talk to right now.

As she sped away, she could here Arwen yelling, "Mordag, please stay. Please!"

Mordag just made the car go faster. She wasn't exactly sure of where she was going to go, but as long as it was away from the group at Dowth.

Chapter 20 – Redemption

'Sometimes the best part of my job is that the chair swivels'

-Unknown

Farmhouse

Drogheda, County Loath, Ireland

Wednesday 11:00 AM

"It's too much. It's just too much. Mordag was driving away from Dowth. Her eyes were filled with tears. She felt as if she was standing on a razor edge, each thought she had was on the verge of slicing her in two. She was in shock. Nothing was making any sense right now.

The searing pain of her past relationship with Crispin McGuinea coming out of the group of people just ripped her apart. Seeing him, old wounds were savagely ripped apart rushing in the deep painful feelings of her past. It also reminded her of the incredible happiness she experienced with him. Seeing Crispin shocked her. She had thought she had completely erased the love and the hurt she had felt when she was with Crispin. In 5000 years, Crispin was the only one who gave her the most joy and in the cruel irony of fate, Crispin was also the one who had hurt her the most.

Through all of her emotional distress, she still drove the car back to Drogheda and the farmhouse. She didn't know where else to go. She needed to run away as fast as she could and allow her mind to process the events of today.

Arwen didn't need to release her from the rebound effect of the violet stone. Why did she do that? It didn't matter she thought. She felt certain Arwen knew where Mordag was headed. Either Arwen or Alder would come for her sooner or later. Of all the things racing through her mind, this one made the most sense. She really didn't have the energy to fight with Arwen or Alder today. If they came for her today, she wouldn't run. If they didn't show up, then she would head back to Nantucket and her compound. Mordag missed her animals back home. The farmhouse had a number of animals living on it. They might be able to help her just get through the day.

She pulled into the driveway for the farmhouse and parked in the back. She made herself busy by brewing some tea. Her chocolate Labrador dog named Brogan, sensing someone was in the kitchen, came in to check things out. Slowly her mind started to simmer down, and the chaos of the day was pushed out of the forefront of her mind. She let the events of the day wash over her and allow her mind to start to process of the dark storm of feelings running through her mind.

Later in the afternoon, she felt calm enough to make herself some dinner. If was just a simple sandwich with some fresh tomatoes and ham left over from last night. Brogan wasn't willing to wait until she was finished, and he nudged her until she eventually gave in to him and gave him a couple of slices of ham and cheese. For her overall steadfastness and ability to endure so much in her life, the animals knew she had a weakness when it came to them. Animals were honest and didn't worry about navigating the twists and turns of life and the social rules of interactions between humans.

When she was finished, she went over to the couch near the crackling fire and just relaxed. Her four footed friend came over and picked a spot right next to her feet. The stress of confronting Alder and the others started to dissipate letting her mind quiet down enough to realize what exactly happened today. It was a kind of miracle, aside from Crispin and Kobin. The Earth was awake. Her mind couldn't make the connection until right now. For 5000 years they have been trying to contact the Earth. Today was a major achievement.

It has been so long since she has had any glimmer of hope of achieving this. In the beginning, when they had first arrived from Ghia, she gave and put everything into the effort to commune with the Earth. The last time she has ever felt like they might actually achieve a connection with the Earth, was back when Mount Vesuvius erupted. Everyone in the Roman Empire felt this, and they knew something big was happening. They tried even harder to connect with the Earth.

At the time, the Roman Empire was expanding across Europe conquering and taking over the Celtic regions. Kobin was so angry at Alder. He blamed Alder and Arwen for not succeeding in advancing their mission from Ghia. Mordag was angry also. She didn't harbor the same bloodlust Kobin felt. At the time, she was more interested in going back to Ghia than staying on this planet. She was ready to just give up and let it go. When Mount Vesuvius erupted it changed everything. It was clear that the Earth was waking up and was responsible for creating the horrific destruction of Pompeii. It was one of the few times Mordag was afraid. Many of the original settlers also felt this. This unfortunately drove Kobin to go mad with killing and battling anyone who stood in the way.

Kobin felt like he had achieved victory when he raided the lands around Arwen and Alder. At this time, Arwen was known as Boudicca. The warrior who killed Creyn's family gave him an ultimatum, turn over the stones, or he would kill his family right in front of him. It was at a time when Kobin and his army were nearby. Creyn refused to hand over the quantum stones, expecting his father to break in at any time and save him and his family. Kobin knew Creyn and his family were being held captive and didn't try to save him, but instead he kept his army in search of Boudicca. Creyn was forced to watch his wife and children being killed in front of him. He blamed his father for this abandonment and not rescuing him and his family.

To Creyn, his father committed the ultimate betrayal to his son and his family. He was totally distraught. He convinced the warrior, who had just killed his family that he would make a deal. Creyn demanded he meet with Boudicca face to face. It was an unusual request, but the warrior agreed, and he called for Boudicca.

Boudicca met with Creyn. He asked her to grant him 2 requests. The first request was to allow him to take his own life. His second request was to deliver a message to his father, Kobin, telling him the reason why he was committing suicide. He desperately wanted his father to know how he had absolutely failed him in his time of need. In return, he would give Boudicca the secret location of where all the quantum stones were being kept. This location was only known by Kobin, Mordag, and himself. She agreed.

Since this time, Kobin has always kept a fire burning for his hatred and contempt of Boudicca, or Arwen as she is known today. Nothing has ever been the same with Kobin. In all of his day to day experiences, whether it was in business, social groups, or relationships, he could just flip a switch to a ruthless vengeful person.

When he did this, he would metaphorically take out his insatiable revenge on anyone who was in his way and decimate them mercilessly. This fire was never extinguished and was always kept burning inside. Kobin used this anger and cruelness on anyone whom he felt wouldn't be able to handle the depth of hatred and cruelty smoldering and burning deep within his soul. Everyday a little piece of himself was burned and lost. Mordag just wasn't able to think in those nihilistic way. It seemed pointless.

Mordag must have drifted off for a little bit. She was awakened by a big tongue licking her hand and tugging at the sleeve of her sweater. As she awoke, she thought Brogan wanted to go outside. Getting up and putting on her coat, she thought it wouldn't be a bad idea to take a walk. She went outside and took a path which circled many of the fields on the farm.

As she walked, she felt a little better. Most people try to avoid the cloudy days and the persistent rain which is always on the horizon. She had forgotten how much she really did love this part of Ireland. Brogan was in front of her and came over to her and nudged her hand. She absently, just reached down to stroke his forehead and his back.

Something very strange happened. As she made physical contact with the dog's body, inside her mind she could hear a voice. The voice was almost imperceptible, but it was there. In her head she heard the voice say, "keep in physical contact with this animal."

She knelt down and kept her hand on the Brogan's back. Usually, a dog would be looking every which way scouring what was around it, looking for the scents of everything. Dogs never just looked at you straight in the eye. This could be interpreted as a challenge or threat moment. Just normal dog behavior and mannerisms. The dog wasn't doing anything but keeping its focus on Mordag's face.

In her thoughts she heard the dog say, "I'm Earth. I have known you for a long time. I have watched you give love to the animals who live on me. You seem to be similar to the *other* person I saw earlier today. I had to stop him. He tried to hurt Harriet. I can't allow this. You show love to my animals, and I like this. You're also made up like *other person*, but you don't take life. Why is this? How are you related to *other*?"

Mordag was surprised, but it also made sense because of her connection with animals as a whole. She said, "I'm pleased to meet you. The *other* you're referring to is named *Kobin*. He is related to me because we are brother and sister who were born at the same time. This is the only way we are connected. He lost his child many years ago and he has never really gotten over it. He blames the loss of his child on Arwen. I didn't know the girl's name was Harriet. Kobin tried to take the life of Arwen and not Harriet. However, he did fatally hurt Harriet and I understand the action you took against my brother, Kobin. I'm sad this had to happen today. Kobin wasn't always like this. There was a time when we were much younger, he was a very good person. We all came here from my planet, Ghia, to try to connect with you and help you grow and be welcomed into a great guild of planets, called the Quantum Guild. You're very special in the universe."

"I learned how to *giggle* today. It makes me want to giggle all the time. The animal you're touching doesn't know how to giggle. Can you teach it to giggle?"

At this point Mordag couldn't help herself. She started to giggle herself. The dog looked at her doing this and it tried to imitate the sounds coming from Mordag. It wasn't the same thing, the dog was snorting and snorting to simulate giggling. It didn't officially really giggle but something even better happened for the dog. Mordag started to scratch behind its ears and scratched the big belly of Brogan. This did the trick. The Earth said through the connection with Mordag, said, "YES! I like that. It feels so wonderful."

The dog was really enjoying this. Mordag kept doing this for a few more minutes until the Earth said it couldn't take any more of this, it was just enjoying this so much. Mordag stopped the belly and ear scratching.

The Earth asked, "Will Ghia hurt me? I'm a little afraid of meeting it. I can protect myself but all life with be erased. What should I do?"

Mordag was surprised by the question. She answered, "Ghia is a beautiful world. Ghia is a world where all living things are working toward producing the best environment for the people and the planet. We follow a code of adherence to prohibit anything which can hurt the planet. It just isn't allowed. Our ancestors were very interested in creating technology for manipulating various types of environmental conditions and situations. Every part of Ghia was controlled to have the same environment all across the planet. This was harmful to Ghia since, it relies on the life and death cycles for plants and different organisms. There was a terrible war, and the people left our planet and went to a far off galaxy where they could continue their quest for more technology."

"If I met those people, would they hurt me, or would they just hurt Ghia?" the Earth asked.

Mordag was a little surprised by the child-like honesty of the question. She said, "This is an interesting question. Those original ancestors who were killing Ghia, decided they would leave Ghia in ruin and find another planet that they could continue to explore their technology. The people who were left on Ghia, barely survived. This was also at a time when Ghia was just waking up and trying to understand itself better. It didn't know it was starting to achieve a sense of sentience. It was curious and wanted to know more."

"I'm curious and I want to know more. Does this mean I'm sentient?"

Mordag chuckled a little bit and said, "Hold on there, *big fella*. Let's do this one step at a time. The people you saw earlier today, Alder and Arwen, are from Ghia and not born on the Earth."

"Ahh yeah, duh? I knew that already. Thank you for saying the obvious."

Now Mordag was really laughing at what she heard. The Earth sensed her surprise and said, "I was trying to think about how one of the others in their group would talk. His name is Pat, and he says things slightly different from the others. He makes me laugh."

Mordag continued, "It sounds like he can be very blunt. Or *cheeky* is a word we use for this type of comment. If you don't mind me saying, you need to find out how **you** talk about things or think about things in your own way and your own style. This is important. It is one of the key factors in gaining sentience. You will have a personality which is your own with all its positives and its negatives."

"Can you tell me more about Ghia?"

"Yes certainly, but before we continue, how about we head back to the farmhouse?"

"Yes, this would be good. We can go sit in front of the fire again."

When they got back to the farmhouse, Mordag reheated some of the water for her tea and brought a couple of jelly scones to share with Brogan.

Ghia put her hand on the dog's back and continued, "You see this is what Alder, Arwen and all the original settlers have been trying to do for a very long time, over 5000 years. We waited and tried many times to connect with you, but we failed. When Ghia first attained sentience, it started to explore other galaxies and look for other planets like itself. It found several planets who were just starting to wake up. Ghia helped them go through this process. It also allowed the sentient planets to work with the life living on the planet to form a symbiotic relationship. The symbiosis of the native species and the planet is truly a wonderful thing. All life on the Earth, depends on you. They can't live without the resources you provide for them, like the trees, the air, the oceans, and all the elements of the Earth. The Earth can't survive unless the people take care of the planet.

"I'm afraid of meeting Ghia. Will it like me? Will it hurt me? I have so many questions. What would you do if you were confronted with a decision like this? Would you meet and connect with Ghia?"

"Myself? Personally, I would be willing to meet Ghia. I'm a little biased because I was born on Ghia, but I think if you meet Ghia, you will learn from it. It can help you answer all those questions. I don't think the people on the Earth now will do what the original ancestors did to Ghia and go around blowing up sections of the planet. I think the people who live on the Earth, or living on *you,* are starting to realize they need to protect the Earth for the next generation of people to inhabit it. They need to take care of it in a better way than it has in the past. They are the future, and they will inherit any mistakes of the earlier generations. They will, and they have started to create initiatives which would allow the planet to be taken care of better than the previous generation. At the very least, you could also learn from the thousands of planets who are part of the Quantum Guild. They can show you things they have done to take care of themselves better."

"Alder and Arwen gave all the quantum stones to me to look at and try to understand. I feel I have a good understanding of them now and how they work. In a couple of days, I'm going to ask Alder and the rest of the group who was there today, to connect with Ghia. Do you want to be part of this group?"

"Yes, I really would like to be part of this effort. I don't think Alder or Arwen will want me to be part of this, though."

"You have taken care of the animals on me, and I think you should be allowed to choose. I'm kind of the feature attraction, right?"

"Now you get it! Yes, you're the big cheese in this operation. I'll talk to Arwen and Alder. I'm sure they will listen to me, and I don't think they will prevent me helping."

"Well, I'll be on your side if they want to ask me. I'll insist on it. Can I have one more belly rub? I really like that."

Slane Castle

Meath County, Slane, Ireland

Wednesday 7:00 PM

Later that evening, after the Earth left, Mordag got into the little rental car and headed to Slane. She was hoping to establish a truce of sorts and talk with Alder and Arwen. When Mordag arrived at the castle, Arwen and Alder met her in the castle courtyard. Alder's face was totally neutral and deliberately not showing any emotion toward her. Arwen's face looked more open to a discussion.

"I'm coming here to talk to you both. I'm not here to fight over what happened today. I'd like to talk to you about an encounter I had earlier today. I had a long discussion with the Earth today. It's hard to imagine, after so many years, we have finally made the initial connection with the Earth. We have all tried so hard to reach this point. Will you let me talk to you?"

Arwen was the first to speak and said, "Mordag let's take a walk to one of the fields in the back of the castle. We can talk privately there. Alder is this, OK?"

"Yes, certainly." Alder, Arwen and Mordag started to walk over to the large field which was shaped like a large bowl and was the perfect arena to hold a crowd to be entertained. Alder continued, "I'm very interested in what the young planet had to say to you. Mordag, I would like to move past all of the long history between you and any of the other colonists. Any differences we had before are now irrelevant. You are always our beloved sister. You have always worked as hard as any of us to help us accomplish our mission. I know you and Kobin have always worked as hard, if not even harder, than some of our group trying to realize our mission here on Earth."

They had reached the arena area of the field for people to sit around and look down to a central point. He asked, "Who was your favorite music performance here at Slane Castle. My favorites were the *Madonna* and the *Queen* concerts."

Both Arwen and Mordag couldn't stop from laughing. They were both thinking the same thing. Arwen said to Mordag, "I'll never be able to get the image of Alder singing to Madonna's 'Material Girl' ever from my memory. That is too funny."

Alder looked surprised at them laughing and didn't understand the joke. He changed subjects quickly and asked, "How did the Earth talk to you today?"

"It spoke to me through one of my dog's and spoke to me telepathically while I was in physical contact with my dog, Brogan. It explained to me the reason why it took Kobin's life today. It wouldn't let anyone hurt Harriet. She is the girl, I assume, who Kobin shot today."

"Yes, it is. The Earth healed her, and she is fine right now. She has the power of the green stone. She can hear the Earth's song. She hums the song while she is taking care of her plants back in New York City."

Mordag continued, "I'm glad she's doing OK. I had no idea, Kobin brought a gun with him. He must have picked this up from his office in New York before he met me in Boston. I wouldn't have let him bring it there if I had known. Arwen, I'm sorry for what happened back in the time when Kobin was leading the war against the Celtic tribes. I don't think Kobin ever really admitted to himself the real reason why he lost Creyn. He was angry at himself for not helping Creyn. It was much easier to blame you. I think he was never able to forgive himself."

Arwen said, "I begged Creyn to not follow through with his plan to kill himself. I told him I would give him and his family safe passage away from the battle. The warrior who captured him swore he wouldn't kill him or his wife and family. The warrior got mad at him when Creyn attacked him and he, in turn, killed his family. The warrior gave Creyn poison to kill himself. It was a bad day for all sides in those bloody battles from so long ago."

Mordag could see Alder was very keen to hear more of the discussion she had with the Earth. She continued, "The conversation I was having with the Earth was telepathically through my dog, so it was hard to understand whether the things it said were dog thoughts, or Earth's thoughts. I know the Earth really likes to giggle and really likes to have its belly rubbed or ears scratched."

Arwen said, "I'm happy the Earth spoke to you. It has been so long for us to be able to finally connect with the Earth."

"Primarily, the Earth came to me because it is afraid to meet Ghia. It's afraid of Ghia and the other planets. It thinks it might be hurt by Ghia or the other Guild planets. I insisted the Earth wouldn't be hurt by Ghia or any of the other planets. I also explained it had so much to gain by communicating with Ghia. The Earth has so many questions and it's extremely curious. It wants to meet Ghia, but I think it needs our help to bolster its confidence about how a meeting with Ghia and the other worlds can be very beneficial to it. The Quantum Guild and the other planets can help Earth and show it how to slowly evolve and become the special kind of planet it is supposed to be. I also stressed how wonderful it is to develop a strong symbiotic relationship with the native people of this planet. Has Harriet or any of the others mentioned anything about earlier today?"

"No not really. They just know what we know, and the Earth said it would contact us again in a few days. It would talk to Harriet to give her a location where we can contact Ghia. I'm really longing to talk to our home world," Arwen said.

"I'll help you with anything you want me to do." Mordag offered and then said, "If you would want me to assist in this, I'll do whatever I can. I would really like to contact Ghia also. If you wish me to not be part of this, then I'll go back home to Massachusetts. I'll do whatever you ask."

Alder sighed. A look of sadness appeared on his face soon replaced with warmth and the kind gentleness they all knew. He responded, "Mordag, the past is the past. I think it's only natural for you to be part of this. You have earned your place to be with us. Of course, we want you to be part of this. We don't know when the Earth will contact us and ask us to meet somewhere together to contact Ghia. I suspect it will be Stonehenge, but I'm not sure of this yet."

Arwen said, "Mordag, I agree with Alder. We should be celebrating. Also, we should celebrate Kobin. He's been with us since all this started. I think the rest of our talented little

Earthlings would like to meet you. Let's go back to the castle and have a nice evening of relaxing and celebrating what was accomplished here today."

"I would like that." Mordag said as she stood up with Alder and Arwen and headed back to the castle.

Chapter 21 – Inbetween

'Never interrupt your enemy when he is making a mistake.'

– Napoleon Bonaparte

Slane Castle

Slane, County Meath, Ireland

Thursday 8:00 AM

Harriet never really liked being the center of attention. She would rather enjoy just being quietly in the background of the crowd. It wasn't a lack of esteem or a sense of isolation or any such nonsense. She just felt more able to communicate and participate when in a smaller group. Some people, like Pat, were really good at being the center of attention. He could defuse a stressful situation with his class clown antics, but it didn't mean he wasn't serious. It was just something he was better at doing and it just naturally came to him.

Since yesterday, after the incident with Kobin, everyone now called her Queen Harriet. At first it was funny and flattering and she went along with the joke. It was meant as a way of affection or in a complimentary gesture. She understood this. The only problem was she has no memory after the point when she jumped in front of Arwen. She was acting purely on instinct, and her goal was to just get Arwen out of the way of Kobin's gun. Then she woke up on the ground with a big blood stain on her shirt. She didn't ask anyone whose blood was on her shirt. She knew it was hers. The problem was she couldn't remember getting shot or feeling any pain or anything after the moment when she jumped in front of Arwen.

Everyone calling her Queen Harriet was in good fun. She did this with her ex-girlfriend Ellie. It was a private joke, and no offense was intended. This was the same thing, but for some reason, it was just really irritating her. Why? She just couldn't shake this irritableness she was feeling whenever she heard it. After everyone ate breakfast, Harriet asked Arwen if she could go for a walk with her.

They set out to walk over to one of the large fields where they were getting ready to harvest one of the fields of grains. These grains would be used in the production of the Slane Castle Whiskey. While they walked, the border collie, called Báisteach, decided to join them. Harriet decided there was no way to slowly ease into the conversation about what she was feeling, so she just blurted it out.

"I have been a little out of sorts since yesterday. I can't really put my finger on it, but yesterday when I woke up with the blood stain on my shirt, it scared me. I don't remember anything inbetween jumping to push you out of the way and then waking up on the ground with blood all over my shirt. I remember what you said after I woke up, and everyone is calling me Queen Harriet. I don't know why, but it bothers me. I know everyone's meaning toward me is absolutely pure and not malicious. I just wish I could understand what happened. Can you tell me more about what exactly happened?"

Arwen put her arms around Harriet and gave her a big hug. She looked at Harriet and said, "I think I understand what is happening. Many years ago, I had a daughter named Róisín. She was so beloved by all. She would be the first one out in the morning and be the last one back from a day of hunting or gathering food for the families in our village. She was a fierce warrior and could never be surpassed.

"She was captured by another tribe. The leader of this tribe had a son who wanted to marry Róisín and take her away to his village very far away. She didn't want to marry him. You see Róisín was in love with another man in our village. The son found out about this and killed Róisín's lover.

"Our clan and several others went to war with these people. It was very bloody, and many lives were lost on both sides. Róisín was rescued and brought back home. She was overwhelmed with sorrow. She grieved for all the lives who were lost. It hurt her deeply and she felt responsible for all of the death. It took her some time, but she did understand why the people fought for her. Slowly, her bright spark did burn again. You see she blamed herself for being captured. She was the person who always reached out to help people. She felt if she had been less conspicuous of helping people, she wouldn't have been captured in the first place. It took some time, but she did realize the love of the people fighting for her, was because of the love she gave them."

Arwen could see in Harriet's face a glimmer of understanding. "You see Harriet, when you jumped in front of Kobin to protect me, something miraculous happened. The Earth woke up. The Earth saw you being hurt, and it stepped in and wouldn't allow this to happen. The Earth loves you so much, and you in return have given the Earth so much love. This is why it wouldn't let Kobin hurt you."

Harriet was listening to every word Arwen was saying and she understood things a little bit more. She was still bothered a little bit and said, "Thank you Arwen. It helps to understand it a little better. I don't think I'm 100% there yet, but it's a start. To me though you will still always be Queen Boudicca."

"OK. Fair enough, but you will still always be Queen Harriet to me," Arwen smirked playfully.

"Arwen, so what happens now the Earth is awake? Kat told me the Earth is going to contact us in a few days. Are we supposed to do anything while we wait?"

"Actually, the Earth said it would contact *you* with a location it wants all of us to meet with the Earth, so we can contact Ghia. We don't know the location of where we are supposed to be, but we suspect it will be at Stonehenge."

"Yes, it does seem to make sense going to Stonehenge. I haven't been contacted or felt anything about this. I'll let everyone know if I hear anything from Earth. It still seems very strange to say that."

"Yes, I can understand how it can be strange. I guess, I have just grown up with Ghia being a physical entity, it never really entered my thinking of the planet not being sentient. I can understand how it may be a difficult thing to get used to, especially if you have never known it before."

"Yes, it feels a little intimidating. Hard to imagine interacting with the Earth on such a big scale is hard to grasp."

"I have an idea. Mordag is driving back to her farmhouse in Drogheda this morning. She's going to get her dog, Brogan, to bring him back here. The Earth communicated with her through Brogan. Ask her if you can go along with her. It might be helpful for both of you to talk and understand what happened yesterday."

"Yes. I think you might be right. I didn't really get a chance to talk to her much yesterday. Do you think she will be mad the Earth chose me to live versus her brother Kobin? Won't she be upset with me?"

Arwen smiled at Harriet. It was a smile which radiated wave after wave of warmth. Harriet suspected Arwen didn't realize this, but Harriet was wrapped up and engulfed in the warmth, like a warm cup of soup slowly warming you from the inside.

Arwen said, "I know she's still trying to process what happened yesterday with Kobin, and she also wants to understand your connection to all of this. You see, Mordag is a caretaker of the Earth just like you. She helps the animals on Earth, and you help the plants and trees. You and Mordag are more alike than you might think.

Later that morning, Mordag and Harriet drove over to her farmhouse in Drogheda. Mordag went back to her ferocious style of driving. Harriet was smiling while she did this.

Mordag asked, "My driving doesn't bother you?"

"No, this is normal driving for me. I live in New York City and the driving is very much like this. There are a lot more pedestrian you need to dodge, though."

Mordag smiled, "I had forgotten what driving in New York City was like. Harriet, I'm sorry for what my brother did to you yesterday. I didn't know he was going to try to shoot Arwen. I wouldn't have let him do this. I'm really glad you were able to be healed by the Earth."

Harriet explained, "I'm sorry about Kobin also. I lost my brother a long time ago and it still hurts, even today. I still don't understand this whole thing with the Earth. Can you tell me a little bit about what happened yesterday? Arwen said you talked to the Earth through your dog Brogan.? I'm just curious and trying to understand it all."

"Sure. Well, the Earth is fascinated with giggling. It made Brogan try to giggle, but anatomically it can't. Kind of a snort more than a giggle. The Earth is still trying to understand where it fits in as a sentient being. It wants to learn more about it. We are supposed to try to contact Ghia and the Guild at some point. The Earth is intimidated by Ghia and the other planets. Its afraid Ghia will hurt it."

"I can understand this. It must be frightening, if you have never known anything or anyone different," Harriet said.

"I've tried to convey to the Earth that Ghia wants only to help it and help it understand. It can learn from Ghia, and it can learn from all the other member worlds in the Guild. The Earth is just learning about itself, and it acts in many ways as an infant would act. We need to help guide the Earth. I think the Earth trusts the both of us because we care for other life on the planet which are not human."

"Can you tell me a little more of what your home world is like?"

It took Mordag a second or two before she responded, and said, "Ghia is a beautiful planet. It's similar to Earth in many ways. The gravity is slightly stronger, but not by much. The days are about 6 hours longer. We have two moons, they are called Noth and Druna. The Noth moon is a thriving metropolis. It's mostly urban, and it keeps a second headquarters for the Guild. It's also where most of the major health and education schools are. The other moon, Druna, is where we have enormous farms and natural resources. It's an interesting kind of relationship Ghia has with the two moons. The moons aren't sentient, but Ghia believes they are. It nourishes Druna with vital resources and in return it let us utilize these resources for Ghia, for ourselves and also for other worlds. We also grow and cultivate the quantum stones on Druna. Both of these moons are a really fun places to go to, but native Ghia is where we feel the most connected to it. Ghia has so many areas which are so beautiful, it's hard to describe. Our people have been searching and reaching out to many different species for so long, we have adamantly tried to preserve our native and historical culture centers on Ghia. The universe is so big and vast, we wisely made a decision to protect the origin of our people, and not let it be changed by increased exposure to other worlds. It might seem to be xenophobic, but it's just one last part of Ghia which we wanted to preserve for ourselves as a race. Most other worlds also do a similar kind of thing. We encourage the diversity of the communications we have with other worlds, but we always want to remember where we came from. I think the Earth will want to do a similar type of thing if it decides to join the Guild. What do you think?"

"I think the people will want to preserve the heritage of it's past, but I wonder if the Earth might have a different opinion of this. Do you think the Earth might think our moon is sentient? That would be interesting for all of our scholars and astrophysicists to basically just short-circuit trying to understand that fact alone. Never mind the Earth being sentient. This is going to be an interesting phenomenon to watch in the coming months or years."

They were just pulling into the driveway for the farmhouse, and as Mordag stopped, Brogan came out of the side door to greet Mordag and Harriet.

Mordag said quietly, "I sense this isn't Brogan right now."

Both Harriet and Mordag went inside the back door of the farmhouse. Brogan followed them in. Mordag motioned for Harriet to sit on the couch in the other room while she brewed a cup of tea.

Harriet went in and sat on the couch. Brogan came over to Harriet and waited for Harriet to initiate physical contact. When she touched Brogan's head, Harriet could hear in her mind, Brogan/Earth talking to her.

"Hi, I'm Earth. We met yesterday when the other, or rather the person named Kobin, hurt you. Are you feeling better?"

"Yes, I'm much better right now. Thank you for healing me. I'm sorry Mordag's brother was killed, but I understand it better now. How are you feeling, today?"

"Well, I know two things. I like to giggle, and I love belly rubs," and as Harriet heard this in her mind, she could detect the simpleness of the need. It, the Earth, desired attention and affection. It was so basic and just so simple. It was a little surprising to just see it this way.

Harriet reached down to scratch the belly of Brogan and the Earth just went into overload. Instant joy. Mordag came in with two cups of tea for them both. Mordag smiled as she saw Harriet giving Brogan, or rather the Earth, the belly rub. She also connected to Brogan, or the Earth, by scratching his ears. Both Harriet and Mordag were just laughing out loud at the reaction of the Earth.

Finally, the Earth said, "Stop, stop, it's just too much."

Harriet asked, "Have you tried to communicate in another way instead of through Brogan?"

Both Mordag and Harriet heard Brogan say, "I just never thought of that. What do you suggest I try?"

"Well, when we were underneath Newgrange and outside of the castle we heard sounds like chimes. Do you know what chimes are?"

"Yes, I do, but I don't know whether I can vibrate the air enough to make intelligible sounds or vocalizations. Wait a minute, I think I know what to do. Mordag, can you open the door and let me go outside for a minute?"

"Certainly," she answered aloud, and she got off the couch and opened the door by the kitchen.

Brogan got up and went outside. Mordag came back and sat on the couch with Harriet. She looked a little confused and whispered, "I'm not sure if it needs to go do its business or what have you. Strange, I have never had a dog ask me this before."

Brogan came back into the little farmhouse a few minutes later. He was carrying two round oval blue stones in his mouth. They both resembled the blue stone Alder had left on the ground at Dowth. Both Harriet and Mordag picked up the stones and held them in their left hands.

In each of their minds, the Earth spoke to them, "How about now? Can you hear me, OK?"

Harriet and Mordag could hear the Earth and it said to them excitedly, "Yes, much better."

The Earth said, "I wasn't sure it was going to work, but I'm glad it is. Those stones Alder gave to me were very strange, but in a weird way I understand them pretty well. Mordag did you tell the others at Slane Castle what we talked about yesterday?"

"Yes, I did. I came here today to bring Brogan there. I'm sure they all have a lot of questions for you."

"I thought they might. I have been thinking about what we talked about yesterday. You mentioned, I should develop my own style and my own voice of who I am. This doesn't make sense to me. I don't know what other planets like me act like or what they think about."

Mordag said, "I think this is why it can be so helpful to talk to Ghia. I can understand your feeling of being hesitant to contact Ghia, but I think it can help you out so much in this. When Harriet and I were born, we didn't understand or even know how we were supposed to act or think. It was our parents who helped us understand the difference between right and wrong. They helped us to be able to understand ourselves in a very important way. We learned how to think and act with billions and billions of other people just like us. This is where Ghia and some of the other member planets are really helpful."

"I think I understand what you're saying. I'm still a little afraid to meet the other planets. It just seems to be too many for me to digest at one time. Maybe, if all of us could talk to just Ghia at the same time? Is this possible?"

Without waiting for an answer, the Earth spoke and said, "See, here is the other thing? What does '*digest*' mean for a planet? What happens when you feel your insides burning? It makes me want to do the opposite of '*digest*'. Is the correct word '*puke*'? It makes me spit up red liquid on different mountaintops?"

Mordag and Harriet were in hysterics at this point. In their mind they heard the Earth start to giggle. It made Harriet and Mordag laugh even harder. It took a solid 5 minutes before they could contain themselves.

Harriet said, "You giggled!"

The Earth said, "I did? Oh yes. You're right I did. Wow it's such a nice feeling."

Mordag said in Irish, "*Táimid tar éis fanacht chomh fada chun bualadh leat.*"

Harriet said, "Wait, you just said, '*We have waited so long to meet you*' and you said it in Irish. Wow, how is it I understand this being said in Irish."

The Earth said, "I know all the languages which have been spoken on me. Do you want to know what Whales say?"

Harriet and Mordag looked at each and frantically blurted out, "Yes, please."

In their minds they could hear the moaning and clicks and bleeps of how whales sound. Now Mordag, looked at Harriet and smiled. She said, "You know the Earth is playing a trick on us. Nice try Earth, but I don't buy it."

They both heard the Earth giggling again. Which also made Harriet and Mordag start to laugh and giggle.

Finally, Mordag said, "Let go back to Slane Castle. I know everyone is dying to meet you. As you said yesterday, you're the main attraction here, so let's not keep them in suspense."

The Earth said, "Yes, I agree. I can contact you when you arrive. I don't want to disturb your driving ability on the way to Slane. Bye for now."

Chapter 22 – Contact

"If a turtle doesn't have a shell, is he homeless or naked?"

- George Carlin

Slane Castle, County Meath, Ireland

Thursday, 2:00 PM

Once Mordag and Harriet arrived back at the castle, everyone was eager to communicate with the Earth. Brogan was so happy to meet everyone. Brogan became even more excited when he saw Kayleigh and Cathal. He also recognized a familiar scent of Nico the 14th and Báisteach on them. The other two dogs, Nico the 14th and Báisteach, were closely behind Kayleigh and Cathal. Mordag gave each of them a warm hug. They all went into the castle. Kayleigh gave a quick look at Cathal, and then she guided them into a different room from where Alder and Arwen first came to Slane Castle a couple of days ago.

Cathal split off from the group and headed in a different direction. Cathal picked up a subliminal anxiousness, from Kayleigh, and he immediately knew exactly what she was thinking. He suspected Kayleigh thought it might be a little too soon for Mordag to see the huge picture of her brother, who was part of the painting hanging over the fireplace in the drawing room. He knew he needed some help to get this large picture out of the drawing room and do it discreetly. He stopped by the kitchen to get one of the staff to help him wrangle the picture down from the wall. Thankfully, this wasn't really such an unusual of a request. They frequently changed pictures hanging in different rooms throughout the years. There were thousands of paintings in the castle, so this was something which happened pretty regularly.

As the group paired off from the front entrance of the castle, Kayleigh guided them into a different room with many pictures all over the walls. This large room had hundreds of different sized paintings occupying every square inch of each wall. Harriet was stunned when she saw all the pictures. Some of these pictures were done by famous painters. Harriet also thought she had seen some of these in the Smithsonian.

Kayleigh saw the surprised look and said, "We regularly swap pictures with various museums throughout the world. Most of these are unique and owned by the castle, but a few are from the Smithsonian Museum."

"Yes, there are a few I recognize. I was always too busy spending my time on archaeological sites and never really took in all the art which the Smithsonian has in their registry. They look great by the way. I could spend hours in here looking at each one of these. There are so many."

Mordag was also admiring some of the paintings in the room. Once everyone got settled, Harriet gave the blue stone to Alder. She explained how the Earth communicated with her and

Mordag back at the farmhouse. Alder closed his eyes and when he opened them, he said, "The Earth has asked us to initiate a conversation with each one of us, except Harriet and Mordag, using one of the blue stones. It wants to do this so it can learn each person's unique signature. If it knows this, then it can communicate with all of us as a group or individually, without having to use the blue stone."

Pat predictably said, "Can I go first?"

Arwen smiled and she looked at Kat. She could see by her face and body language; she was expecting Pat to say exactly this. The stone was passed to Pat. After about 30 seconds, Pat passed the stone to Brian who was on his left. Mordag in turn gave her stone to Arwen. After a few minutes, everyone had a turn of holding the blue stone.

The Earth said to everyone, "Hello. I'm so glad to meet all of you. I'm still new at this, so forgive me if I say something wrong. Mordag said, 'I need to develop my own personality'. I'm trying to do this, but I have so many questions. I'm told there are nine planets that rotate around this star. This star is very helpful to me and all of you, right?"

Kat being the book nerd while growing up, was the first to reply and said, "It depends on who you ask these days, but yes, there are nine planets, including yourself. And you're also correct, the star you revolve around, and the life living on it wouldn't survive without it. If the sun was hotter, the water and the oceans and any life on you would evaporate and die. You would become one lifeless rocky planet. If the sun were cooler, then all of the water and oceans on the planet would freeze and not be able to support life."

"Do the other planets within this solar system support life on them?"

Arwen replied and said, "None of the other planets in this solar system have life on them. Life is rare and very special in the galaxy. Are you able to feel or sense the other nine planets?"

"Sense? I'm not really familiar with this term and the meaning of it. I know they are other large bodies like me, but I'm not exactly sure of how I know this stuff. Maybe it's because we all share the same sun and the same radiation? Maybe?"

Alder added, "Yes! My goodness, you're so smart. This is exactly how it works. You're able to sense or detect the various forms of radiation from the many different stars in the galaxy. This is how you can contact Ghia. These stones are from Ghia, and they share the same radiation Ghia has. The stones radiation isn't exactly the same as this sun, but it's slightly different. Is this something you would be able to search for? I have an idea of where we come from in the galaxy. It may not be exact, but I'm pretty sure I can get you to look in the approximate location. There is an area of stones placed in a circle which we call Stonehenge. This was the original place where Ghia contacted you so long ago. Ghia knows about this place. This is the place where all the colonists first arrived on Earth. We built this stone circle soon after we got here."

The Earth asked, "I know the other planets exist, and I tried to talk to them in the way I'm talking to you right now. None of them answer or really do anything except spin and revolve around the sun. Are any of them sentient, like me?"

"No, I'm pretty sure none of the other planets are able to reach this level of being sentient. The galaxy is so large and vast, but there are very few planets who are like you. This is the reason the Quantum Guild came into existence. Its purpose is to help other planets like you, to share knowledge, and give assistance when needed, to help it obtain the most beneficial symbiotic relationship between the planet and the life contained on it," Alder said.

"Are you sure Ghia won't try to hurt me? I'm a little afraid to contact it."

Surprisingly, Pat answered this, and said, "Hey, big guy, we got you covered. It's like going to a new school. At first, it's always awkward and weird. I should know 'cause I had to go to a lot of new schools. The cool thing is they get to know you, and you get to know them. If their cool, great! Then *hang* with them. If they aren't decent or are giving you attitude, then screw'em! You get to choose which ones are your friends or not. It sounds like there are loads of other planets who are part of this Guild. From what Alder and Arwen have told us about Ghia, it sounds like a decent planet to get to know. If you don't like what they have to offer, then you don't have to be part of it. It's always your choice. The thing is, if you don't at least try it, you won't know if what Alder, Arwen and Mordag are saying about this Quantum Guild is true or not. If what they are saying is correct, then it might help you a lot. I haven't known them for very long, but I do trust them. Just my two cents on this. If it were me, I would at least try it. You have nothing to lose."

Kat looked at her brother fondly, and said, "Nicely said, Pat."

"I need some time to think about this. Can I contact you tomorrow at this place you call Stonehenge? Alder you will need to help me to look in the correct area of the sky to search for Ghia."

"Certainly. I think the best time is early morning around 4:30 AM. This is when you can usually see the constellation where Ghia is."

"I've also given back to you the original quantum stones you gave to me. You can find then outside in the grass near the rear of this building," Earth said.

Stonehenge

Salisbury Plain, Wiltshire, England

Friday 4:30 AM

The sun had not risen yet, so the area was still shrouded in darkness. Alder using the orange stone took the whole group to Stonehenge and they appeared just outside the circle of stones. He also brought a small lantern to give additional light to the whole circle of stones. Alder walked into the center of Stonehenge. He looked up at the sky to look for the constellation where Ghia was located.

While he was doing this, Arwen and Mordag walked around to different sarsen stone pillars and placed a particular color quantum stone at the base of each stone pillar. When they returned to the center of the circle, they placed the lilac, yellow, white, and black stones on the ground.

Alder said, "I think I have the constellation where our home world is located. Everyone needs to stand over by the different stones where each quantum stone is located."

Arwen and Mordag helped to direct them to where each of them needed to stand. Arwen and Mordag came back to the center with Alder.

Alder spoke to the Earth in his mind, and when he did this, the Earth spoke to them all at the same time. Alder asked, "Earth, can you see the constellation I'm looking at? This should be in the general direction of our home world. Try to sense the other planet and the radiation it's emitting which is similar to the quantum stones. It's a little bit like when you can sense the other planets in this solar system, you can sense planet Ghia in a similar way. We will use these stone pillars to help give you additional power to cast your search. I'm sure you will be able to sense other planets which are emitting differing radiation patterns from the suns they orbit. Keep searching for Planet Ghia and you will find it. I'm sure of it."

"Yes, I'll try."

Alder said to everyone around the stone circle, "Think of the Earth and how each of you try to interact with it when you're becoming in tune with the quantum stones. Just try to feel those small particles and how they are vibrating or spinning. Don't worry about making them go faster or slower. Just sense them.

The Earth will use this to give it power to reach out very far into the vastness of space."

As Alder said this, the lilac stone started to glow brighter and brighter. All around Stonehenge, a large dome of purplish shimmering haze could be seen covering the whole circular area around Stonehenge. Next, the yellow stone also started to glow brightly. A beam of yellow light shot out from the yellow stone, straight up to the sky. It passed through the purple shield with no problem. The white and black stone also started to glow.

As the white and black stones started to glow, the other quantum stones all started to glow in a myriad of colors matching each stone's color. The base of the stone pillars also started to glow brightly in a myriad of different colors. In the center of the circle, Arwen, Alder and Mordag stood holding hands.

The air was electrified in color and power. Everything felt palpable and solid. Alder could be heard saying to everyone in the mind link, "Stay focused everyone. Everything you're doing is working great. Keep your minds open and let the Earth guide us."

Everyone standing around Stonehenge, could feel the power and electricity in the air. Harriet started to hum. At first softly, then louder. After a second or two, Pat started to hum also. Everyone was infected with this, and they started to hum the same song of the Earth. It was a song with no words, just humming. Pretty soon it was everyone's voice. After a short time, everyone in the circle could hear the Earth say, "Contact! Hello Ghia. My name is Earth."

There was no response from the planet the Earth reached out to. All the stones continued to glow brightly.

Everyone heard in their mind, the Earth say, "I don't know why it doesn't respond. Did I do something wrong and make it angry at me? What can I do, Alder?"

"No, you did everything correctly. I wonder if my planet Ghia is hurt or sick and this is the reason why it isn't responding. Let's try again later tonight. Maybe around midnight. Is that OK with you?"

Petulantly the Earth said, "OK, we can try again later. It hurts my feelings that Ghia won't answer me. I'm sure I sent a message to the right planet."

Mordag said, "I'm sure Ghia would respond if it could. It's always looking for new planets to talk to it. Don't be discouraged, we will try later."

All of the glowing stones started to slowly diminish and soon became their normal color. Now, the only light was from Alder's lamp in the center of the stone circle. Arwen and Mordag went around and collected all of the stones. When they returned to the center, everyone joined hands and Alder used the orange stone to teleport everyone back to Slane castle.

It was still very early in the morning. As a group, everyone felt disappointed they were not able to contact Ghia. Kat voiced her disappointment about this, and she said, "I really wish we could have contacted Ghia today. Do you know why we weren't able to speak to Ghia? Was there something we did wrong? It felt like everyone was able to tune into the stones, right?"

In a way, it was good Kat brought this up. Alder said, "Actually, I think we were doing everything correctly. I was really hoping this would work for us today, also." He looked at Arwen and asked, "I have never heard of anything like this before. Have you?"

"No. This is very unusual," she said.

Alder said to everyone, "Let's rest and try again tonight."

They all agreed and headed off to go to bed for a few hours.

Harriet's bedroom

3:00 PM

"Harriet! Harriet! Harriet! Wake up my friend, Harriet."

Out of a deep sleep, Harriet rolled over in her bed and slowly started to wake up. Who was it trying to wake me up? It sounded like the Earth.

"Harriet, I need to talk to you, please answer me."

Now wide awake and cognizant of the Earth talking to her in her mind, she responded, "Hi Earth. What do you need to talk to me about?"

"I spoke to Ghia. I spoke to Ghia. And Ghia responded!"

"Great! I'm so glad it did, what did it say?"

"First, Ghia is so nice and friendly. I don't know why I was afraid earlier. It's my first time talking with a planet. It was so wonderful. Even better than the belly rub when I was a dog. Ghia is so smart but is also so nice. You would love going there. It has two moons called Dru-..."

"Earth! What did Ghia say?" Harriet interrupted the stream of thoughts being sent to her in a rush of excited statements.

"Yes, yes you're right. Ghia is in trouble. There is an alien race controlling Ghia and all the planets of the Quantum Guild. It monitors all communications with Ghia and other planets. The aliens don't know me, so I can talk to Ghia. These aliens also watch any communication of the people who live on Ghia or are natively from Ghia. The alien recognizes Alder and Arwen, so it prohibits Ghia talking to them."

"We need to talk to Alder about this. We should get everyone together to hear this."

"Harriet. Harriet. My Harriet! There is no time. I woke you up because you know my song and can talk to Ghia. Will you do this?"

Harriet was surprised by this question. Fundamentally she's a social scientist, so her answer was a yes without hesitation. "Yes! Of course. Tell me what you need me to do."

"I'll guide you to Ghia. When I talk to Ghia, the alien race doesn't notice me, for some reason. Then you will hear Ghia talking to you. OK?"

"OK. Do I need to go somewhere?"

"No, just try to listen to Ghia. Relax the way you usually do when you're gardening."

Harriet relaxed and tried to clear everything out of her mind. She started to think of her grandma and when she would help her tend to her plants and vegetables. Slowly Harriet could hear a far off sound of music. It got a little louder as it got closer.

The music encompassed her. She felt like the music was all around her and was wrapping her in a blanket of sound. The music changed. Or did it? It was still music in her mind but behind the music at the same time was a voice and it was addressing her. She focused on the voice, like when she would be in a crowd with a lot of people and trying to focus on just one voice. She heard, "Harriet can you hear me? I'm Ghia and it's nice to meet you."

Harriet quickly said, "Hello Ghia, it's an honor to talk to you. The Earth says you need my help. What can I do for you?"

"Earth told me some of my children are still surviving from when they first arrived there so long ago. I need to talk to speak with them. I cannot do this unless they have a special tool. The alien race won't allow anyone who was born on Ghia to come back to me. I would like you to come to Ghia and let me give you a tool which will allow them to come back to Ghia unnoticed. The Earth and I'll work together to make it possible to travel to Ghia for a few hours of your time. Once we give you these special stones for my children, we will send you back to Earth. These stones are the way I can communicate with my children. Can you help us with this?"

Harriet's mind was in overdrive right now. Ghia wants her to travel to a foreign planet. Is it safe for her to do this? How long does it take? It sounds like it would be like traveling to Stonehenge this morning. Is this all I need to do or is there something else here she isn't noticing? Can she bring a friend? Yes, she's terrified but extremely excited at the same time. Yes, if she must travel, she needs to ask someone to go with her.

"Ghia, I'll gladly do this, but would it be possible to bring a friend with me? I'm very excited, but I'm also a little afraid. Having a friend would help me a lot?"

She heard back, "I suspected you would ask this, and the answer is yes. We must do this quickly. The Earth and I will meet you in the back where you tried to make the pumpkin seed grow in one hour."

"I will be there with my friend. Thank you."

In a few seconds she could feel she was alone, and no one was talking to her in her mind. She would need to hurry. The obvious choice of who to bring with her was Pat. She also thought Kat would also be a good person to bring with her, because she's very smart. However, Pat would also be very excited to do this, and it would be a lot of fun. Brian also was a good choice, but he has a wife and child. This would put him in a difficult position. No, Pat was the person she wanted to go with.

She got up and went to find Pat and asked him to meet her outside in an hour.

Chapter 23 – The Proposal

"My mistakes are usually so enjoyable that I tend to repeat them."

- Lisa Kleypas

Brian Keefe

Slane Castle Slane Ireland

Friday 4:00 PM

Brian was tossing and turning in his sleep. It was the same dream he would typically have about the day when Brian was showing his brother Jerry how he could use fire to toast his marshmallow. It was also the same day when he received the 3rd degree burns to his left arm and shoulder. This time the dream was different. Instead of his finger carrying a small flame to the stick holding the marshmallow, a thin yellow light came out from his finger, and he ignited the marshmallow the way he did in the past.

The next part was different. Usually when he did this, Jerry would egg him on to make it burn brighter and burn hotter. This time, Brian reached up to the marshmallow and cupped his hand around the marshmallow, and his hand glowed a bright yellow light. When he took his hand away from the marshmallow, there was no flame anymore. The marshmallow was perfectly toasted. The whole marshmallow was that perfect caramel brown color on the outside of the marshmallow you strive so hard for. Sometimes you get it perfect, but more often or not it is a blackened bubbly mess. When he looked at his hand, it wasn't glowing and just looked the way it normally did.

Oddly, his parents came out into the backyard like they have many times in this dream. This time it was different. He father patted Brian on the back and complimented him on what a nice job he had done on toasting Jerry's marshmallow. Brian smiled at his father, but as he did this, he felt it wasn't real at all.

Brian woke up and sat up in his bed. What an odd dream. It never ended like this. As he thought about it, it started to make a little bit of sense. The thing Alder mentioned about lasers and power charges not getting depleted. Without realizing it, as he thought about his dream, he felt something had changed in him.

His ability to change the fire and making it burn brighter or burn lower, was always something he knew he could do by pushing the particles to go faster or slower. When he did this, he always focused on a single spot and then the fire would burn higher or lower depending on how he pushed it, but it was always just a single directed push to a single spot. His dream was showing him a different way of doing this. If he focused on pushing in many different directions, he figured this would be like toasting the marshmallow perfectly. Treat objects like they are being put into an oven or a kiln. Heat and force are coming from all sides and all directions.

Brian wanted to try this, but he definitely didn't want to do this inside the castle. If he was going to do this, then he would have to find a good secure place, where he couldn't cause any problems or danger. Slowly, he got out of his bed and walked over to the window to look outside in the back part of the castle. He saw Harriet and Pat were standing in the same place where they had tried to make the pumpkin seed grow. They were holding hands and facing each other. Bashfully, he thought it best to move away from the window and not intrude on them.

He was about to turn away from the window, and head downstairs to get something to eat. Before he turned away, both Harriet and Pat disappeared. He thought he was seeing something different, but he looked again, and they were not there.

Were they practicing using one of the stones? He couldn't see any stones in their hands. Did they just disappear, or did they teleport somewhere? Should he tell Alder or Arwen about this? It was probably nothing, but he felt reasonably sure this was something he should tell someone about. Maybe Kat would be the right person? He thought, yes, he should go tell Kat.

Brian left the room in search of Kat. He didn't want to wake her up if she was still asleep. Her room was a couple of doors down from his. Thankfully, her door was open, and she wasn't in her room. He went downstairs to the big drawing room with all the books and shelves they were in the other day. He saw Kat sitting in one of the leather chairs reading a book about celestial navigation. She looked up as Brian came in and sat in a chair near her.

"Hi, did you get some sleep after this morning being a bust?" Kat asked.

"Yes, I did. Hey, I just saw something strange happen. I wanted to tell Alder or Arwen about it, but first I wanted to run it by you, if that's OK?"

"Sure. Is it about Pat? It's almost always about my brother Pat when conversations start like this."

"Yes, as a matter of fact it is. I'm not trying to interfere with anything, but I just thought it was something important and I should let someone know."

"Nothing you can tell me about my brother would surprise me. Trust me."

"OK, well I woke up about 10 or 15 minutes ago and I had a weird dream which I have had many times before. Today, it was different. Alder told me something about my ability with fire, and how it was more than just making a fire grow stronger or weaker. I wanted to go outside and try something and possibly take a different approach to this weird ability of mine. I was looking out the back window for a safe place to go where I wouldn't burn anything up, just in case something went wrong. I saw Pat and Harriet standing in the same spot we were in, when we were trying to make the pumpkin seed grow yesterday. They were both facing each other and holding hands. Then all of a sudden, they both disappeared. It looked exactly like the way Alder and Pat had disappeared in the conference room in Boston. The strange thing about this was neither one of them were holding any of the stones. Is this even possible?"

"I have been meaning to ask Alder about this. He keeps saying we are the first people to be able to use these stones in the way he's teaching us. He mentioned a couple of times we could be able to manipulate these quantum properties without the stones. In some ways, I think he's right. I can tune into animals really easily, but when I held the red stone, it was so much larger than just tuning into another life form. It was feeling the actual life force of a living thing. It's a little hard to describe, but the actual life force of anything is so incredibly powerful. It's like being next to a nuclear reactor. I have to be careful I don't get overpowered by it. So, yeah, I think all of us have an ability to tap into these quantum properties and be able to manipulate them without the stones."

Brian added, "I agree with you on this. I can do the fire manipulation without any help from the stones. Alder said, my ability is much more powerful than just starting a fire. He alluded to it like being able to create a laser beam of light and cut through stuff. This was what I was going to go outside and try to practice, when I saw Pat and Harriet together and they just disappeared. Do you think Pat or Harriet are able to do this? Maybe they have to work together to accomplish this?" Brian asked.

Kat answered, "I know Pat has used the orange stone before, so he has more practice using it. This might be how smoothly he seems to be able to do this without one of the stones. I think Harriet has a way to tap into the Earth like none of us have the ability to do. It might be they have to work together to accomplish disappearing or teleporting. Also, not to put too fine of a point on this, I think Pat is a little smitten by Harriet. He has acted a little strangely around her. I have only seen him act this way just a few times before. I care about my brother, and I don't want him to get hurt. I think Harriet is a good person, and she doesn't strike me as being someone who would deliberately try to hurt Pat.

"Yeah, I agree with you. I think she's a sincere person, but I think she's also a little shy. From what I have seen with Pat over the last couple of days, I wouldn't consider Pat to be a shy person at all, right?" Brian asked.

Kat exclaimed, "You're preaching to the choir now. Try being around someone who is almost 99% of the time, very loud, obnoxious, rude, and downright selfish! As his sister, I can tell you, he's a lot of work to be around. Once in a while, Pat shows you something really nice, but it's a long time inbetween those moments."

Kat quickly added, "Can I go with you if you're going outside to practice your ability with fire? I'm curious about it. That's if you don't mind?"

Brian laughed a little and said, "It's funny. I think the only people who have ever seen me do this, was my wife and my brother. I'm really careful around the other firefighters I work with. If any of them saw me do this, it would freak them out in a really bad way. Even though, I have used it many times to lessen a fire or even make it burn hotter, if the other guys at the firehouse knew about this, then they wouldn't trust me. It's like a death sentence to a firefighter. Trust is the most important thing you have with them. But yeah sure, you can come with me and watch the firebug starting fires."

"Great! Do I need to bring a bucket of water with me, or do you think we're good?"

"Well, it's actually kind of a good idea. I don't want to damage anything. I was thinking I could try with a small stick or something. In my dream, I'm showing my brother how I can toast a marshmallow, like we used to do when we went camping as kids. I doubt Kayleigh has any marshmallows handy."

"Let's start small. I'll bring my bottle of water if we need to douse something."

The both of them headed out of to the field near the back of the castle where they had tried to make the pumpkin seed grow. When they got to a certain spot, there was only grass around them, so it seemed like a safe place to try Brian's experiment.

In a way, having the dream helped him to visualize a narrow beam of light coming out of this index finger. They both sat down on the ground cross-legged. Brian put the stick on the ground in front of them. He put his finger over the stick and tried to imagine a yellow light coming out of his finger and pointing it at the thick part of the stick. At first, nothing seemed to happen. Then slowly his fingertip started to glow in a yellow light. It wasn't hot, and he was trying to imagine a narrow beam of light coming from his finger. He was thinking it would act like the way a flashlight worked. The yellow glow from his finger turned into a beam of light similar to how a flashlight would light something up with a beam of light.

Quantum Mind

Surprisingly, his finger didn't feel hot or any different. Nothing happened with the stick. He focused on making the light stronger. In his mind, he imagined the light from his finger, was controlled by a dimmer switch. A dimmer switch is normally a common thing you would find in your house for adjusting the brightness of some overhead lights. He turned the dimmer switch to a higher setting. As he watched it, the beam of light coming from his finger did become brighter, and he started to see a little smoke starting to come off the bark of the stick.

Brian pushed the light up even higher and stronger, and it cut cleanly through the stick. Slowly, he moved his finger to another part of the stick, and he cut off another slice of the stick. This was really a strange sensation. There was heat coming from his finger, but it didn't feel painful or uncomfortable. Sensing Kat was next to him, she was ready with her water bottle, ready to extinguish any fire needing to be put out. He stopped the light beam coming from his finger and he decided to try something totally different.

Why didn't he think of this earlier? He reached into his pocket and found some of the Euro coins he picked up when they arrived at the airport in Dublin. He thought Malcolm would love to have some of the euro currency and coins when he got back home. Brian's father used to always bring him some of the foreign currency or little mementoes of his many trips abroad for his company. He took out a €1 and a €2 coin. If his finger was spewing out a laser beam, then cutting or melting a copper and nickel coin should be possible. At least this was his thinking at first.

Kat seemed to tense up a little when she saw where he was going with this. She didn't say anything, but Brian could sense she was excited to see if this was possible. He suspected she didn't realize it herself, but Brian was positive she was holding her breath, in anticipation of this next test.

Brian put the €1 coin on the ground. He put his finger over the coin, so it was pointed at the center of the coin. He repeated the same process he attempted with the stick. Once Brian got the beam of light going, he imagined being able to turn the dimmer switch even higher than before. For one split second, the coin threw off a spark and reflected the beam of light. Thankfully, it wasn't pointed at Kat or himself. The spark lasted for only a second before the beam of light went straight through the metal leaving a clean raisin sized hole in the center of the coin.

His dream showed him how he could cup his hands around the marshmallow like it was an oven and heat would be coming from all directions. He placed the €2 coin in his left palm and cupped his right hand over it.

"This time I'm going to try to melt it. Keep your water bottle handy if this goes badly," Brian grinned.

He was pretty sure he could melt the coin into a different shape, but he wasn't exactly sure how his left hand was going to feel holding onto a very hot coin in his palm. No way to know unless you try it.

With his right hand cupped over his left he imagined all the light and heat coming at all directions exactly the same way he did this in his dream with Jerry's marshmallow. After about 10 seconds of the intense heat being forced onto the copper and nickel coin, he removed his right hand. The coin indeed melted. The bottom of the coin wasn't hot to his hand. He asked Kat to pour the water over the coin in his hand. As soon as the water hit the coin a plume of steam arose from the coin. His left hand still didn't feel hot.

Once the coin was cool enough to touch the top of it, he picked it up with his right hand. The front face of the coin was perfectly smooth and was a swirling mixture of copper and nickel. The entire top and the stamping of the coin was removed and perfectly smooth. This makes sense if you were to reheat a coin with a stamp on it, then this is what it would most likely look like.

Both Kat and Brian heard Alder calling to them. He told them Kayleigh had prepared some food for everyone if they wanted to come inside for dinner.

Brian winked at Kat and said, "We will have to try and do this some more maybe later. I wonder if Pat or Harriet are back from wherever it is, they went."

Large Drawing Room

Friday 8:00 PM

Brian and Kat met everyone in the same dining room they had eaten the fantastic dinner Kayleigh had prepared for them the other night. They were joined by Alder, Arwen, Kayleigh, Cathal, Callum and Mordag. It was obvious that Pat and Harriet were not in attendance tonight. Arwen asked if Kat had seen Pat or Harriet earlier.

Before Kat could answer, Brian said, "I saw Harriet and Pat earlier today about maybe 4:00 PM. They were in the same part of the field where Kat and I were just at. I saw Pat and Harriet disappear like Alder and Pat had done the other day. I didn't know whether they were trying to practice something or not. I didn't see them holding any stones though."

Arwen looked at Alder and he reached in his pocket for the orange pouch to check whether the orange stone was missing or not. He reached in and took out the orange stone.

Alder asked, "You said Harriet also disappeared with him?"

"Yes, I'm sorry I didn't tell you earlier. I wasn't sure if they were just trying to practice without using the quantum stones."

Alder said, "Well, I'm sure they must have a good reason for where they are now. There's plenty of food here so we can save a plate for them when they get back. As for me, Kayleigh, you have outdone yourself again tonight. They don't know what they are missing."

As usual, Alder had the unique gift of turning an awkward tension in the air into a much more palatable, pleasant tone. Everyone took a plate and served themselves the different dishes Kayleigh had made. It really was a great meal. Toward the end of the meal, Kayleigh got up to start taking care of cleaning up the dishes and plates. Arwen and Mordag both commanded her very sharply, but in a sweet way, for Kayleigh to sit and relax. They were going to clean up and do the dishes. Kat also jumped up and insisted she also help clean up.

Brian was about to get up and offer to help, but he caught Alder giving him a quick look and grin. This was a clear signal from Alder telling him to not get into the middle of this. Brian nodded in agreement.

Changing topics, he showed Alder the modified coins he changed earlier before dinner. Both Alder and Cathal were impressed. Cathal mentioned there was a blacksmith many years ago, who had a really interesting talent for forging and molding different metals. He didn't think he had the same skill Brian had, but it was rumored, he was the only one who could make the fires hot enough to mold different ores he was able to forge. In fact, there was a sword of his craftsmanship in one of the other rooms on this wing of the castle.

They all went into the other room to take a look at it. Cathal also told him of how this sword was first brought forth. It was used in the infamous battle between the Catholic King James II who ruled over England, Scotland, and Ireland and his nephew and son-in-law, the Protestant King William III or as he was called in the day, "William of Orange". This battle was extraordinarily bloody and there was a great loss of life. It was a very impressive sword.

From outside the room, there was a noise of anxious animals wanting to be the first to reach the front doors of the castle. When Alder, Brian, Cathal, Callum, and Kayleigh caught up to them, the 3 dogs were sitting patiently at attention, focused on the large oversized front set of doors in the grand foyer entrance to the castle. Kat, Mordag, and Arwen also came out from the kitchen area to see who was at the front door.

The grand set of doors opened, Patrick and Harriet came into the castle. They didn't seem to be surprised at everyone meeting them at the door. The both of them were just radiating incredible excitement. Pat as usual, was the first to speak, "Hey guys! You're not going to believe where Harriet and I just came from."

Arwen gasped, "Alder do you smell that? Oh, I haven't smelled this in so long." Her brilliant eyes were now tearing up and joyously crying. Taking deep breaths of the subtle and unmistakable smell she sensed as soon as the doors opened, and Patrick and Harriet came inside. She went over to both of them and grabbed them into a big hug, savoring in the smell of their clothes and any other little pheromones which they were excreting into the air.

Alder just exclaimed, "Ghia!"

Both Arwen and Alder were being overcome with such an emotional response, they were trembling. Mordag who was also caught up in the rush of intense emotions. She quickly realized how intensely this was affecting them and herself. She quickly said to Callum and Cathal, "Boys, help Arwen and Alder to a place we can sit down, or they are going to collapse."

Kayleigh also understood this immediately. She grabbed onto Mordag while both Cathal and Callum and guided Alder and Arwen to the drawing room to sit down. Harriet and Pat understood why they were so excited, but it was smart of Mordag to get them into another room. This wasn't the only information they would need to hear this evening. They had very big news and they wanted to make sure they didn't overwhelm them.

Brian and Kat were still not sure of what just took place, but it seemed like Pat and Harriet had gone to planet Ghia. They were also anxious to hear the story they were about to tell everyone.

Once everyone sat down, all eyes were on Harriet and Pat. Harriet started to tell them of all the events which happened today.

"Earlier today, the Earth woke me up. It told me it had a long talk with Ghia after we tried to contact Ghia this morning. There is an alien race which is against any planets who are trying to attain sentience. It's prohibiting Ghia from talking to other member planets or member symbiotic races of the Quantum Guild. Ghia heard the Earth this morning when we went to Stonehenge. Ghia wanted to respond but it could not because Alder, Arwen and Mordag were involved in this initial reaching out to Ghia. This alien race can determine if someone tries to communicate with Ghia, and if they are a native of Ghia. Since Alder, Arwen, and Mordag are natively from Ghia the enemy prohibited Ghia from establishing any communication with them."

Harriet paused for a second and Alder asked, "Can it determine the race of anyone else who was part of this initial contact with Ghia? I mean, will it start prohibiting anyone from Earth contacting Ghia in the future?"

Harriet continued, "From what Ghia told us, the answer is no. This alien race has the knowledge of everyone who is part of the Quantum Guild. Since, Alder, Arwen and Mordag are recorded as colonists for the Guild they prohibit communication with you. The rest of us are not recorded with the Guild, so we are invisible to them. This also means, Cathal, Kayleigh, and Callum are also not prohibited. Ghia contacted the Earth after we made the attempt earlier today. Ghia asked the Earth for some assistance with something. It wanted to know if the Earth could find someone from Earth to come to Ghia and bring back a special stone. This special stone will mask the information which the aliens use to determine if it was part of the Guild. Ghia and the Earth asked if I would go to Ghia. I also asked if Pat could go since I was a little afraid to go alone."

Harriet reached into her pocket and retrieved 3 stones and handed one to Arwen, Alder and Mordag. The stone was crystal clear, looking like a large clear quartz or glass.

Harriet continued, "These stones are the only way to talk to Ghia or to travel to Ghia. The Earth was instructed in how to make these stones also so if more of them are needed it can make them."

Pat who had been silent during this, said, "Your planet is losing a war at the moment. Harriet and I only saw a tiny bit of the planet, but its moons are being destroyed. Alder, I think you mentioned one of your moons was a large provider of resources to your planet and other member planets. It's being bombarded everyday with drilling for those resources and stripping it off them. The people on Ghia are having a really tough time also.

Many of the population are being locked up for trying to foster symbiosis with the planet or planets. Anyone who was associated in any way with the Guild is in jail or dead. I hate to say this, but the situation is very dire. I went to Ghia, because I thought it would be cool, but it has really shaken me up a bunch. Thousands of other planets are all systematically being destroyed. Whether it's being stripped for resources, experimentation, or terra forming dramatically. Ghia said there were tens of thousands of planets who were part of the Guild. The number is only about less than 100. It's only keeping those few planets because it enslaves the people of a planet or there are some resources which it needs to continue to strip it of. To be honest with you, it makes me sick. I was so excited to come back home, because I knew the Earth wasn't being used this way. At least it isn't right now at this moment."

Kat had never heard her brother say anything like this before. This wasn't the smartass or sarcastic comedian. She could see he was acting with a purpose for something other than himself. Seeing her brother saying this gave her a little bit of clarity. She looked at Pat and said before she realized she had said it out loud, "No!"

All eyes turned to Kat, and she realized she had vocalized her thought. She couldn't back out now and firmly said, "No! This cannot and will not happen. I have never been to Ghia before, but I'll be damned if this is allowed to continue. We have to do something! Please someone tell me there is something we can do here to help put a stop to it. This is so wrong. We have these quantum stones, why can't we use them against this alien race? Blast them out of existence. Use the time stone to prevent this from happening. There must be something we can do?"

Pat and Harriet both said at once, "Yes, I agree."

Everyone turned to Alder. He knew they wanted an answer from him. Alder took a deep breath and said, "It saddens me to hear this about Ghia and the other member worlds. There is more information we need here before we can make any choice of action. I appreciate your solidarity with us, but we cannot ask you to put yourself at any risk. First things first, Arwen and Mordag and I need to talk to Ghia to get all the information about this we can."

Pat said, "Mordag, your brother Imadin spoke with Harriet and me. He sends his love and is anxious to speak to you."

Mordag's eyes lit up and she smiled as new tears came down her face.

Cathal said to everyone, "I hope you all know in whatever action you decide to take, you must include us in this. We were not born on Ghia so we must surely be invisible to this alien force taking over Ghia. We are always here to help you in anyway we can."

Brian was excited but he needed to be cautious here. He would do anything he could to help out with this, but he also needed to make sure his wife and his son were a part of any decision on this. Brian said, "I'll help out in anyway, I can, but I have my wife and son I must also include in this endeavor."

Alder quickly looked at him and said, "Brian, and the rest of everyone here, we are not going to include anyone into this if there is a risk or danger. Thank you all for your support, but I think we need more information about this before we can do anything. I suggest we go to Stonehenge, later tonight as we planned, and get more information on this."

Stonehenge, England

Friday, Midnight

Everyone met together in the castle at midnight. The entire group consisted of Pat, Kat, Harriet, Brian, Mordag, Alder, Arwen, Callum, Cathal, and Kayleigh. The 3 dogs also met them in the room where they were about to depart from. It was touching to see the dogs watching them prepare to leave. Kayleigh had made sure one of the other staff at the castle would be able to keep the dogs and the rest of the castle running while they were away for an unknown amount of time. Kat could sense the excitement in the dogs, and she knew they wanted to go with them to help out. She touched each of them, and said they would be back soon, but she was grateful for their support.

Once everyone was ready, they all grabbed hands with each other, and Alder teleported them to Stonehenge in the same place they had arrived at this morning. The sky was incredibly clear tonight and the moon was full and gave everything an ethereal quality of greenish moonlight. The Earth spoke to them when they arrived. Alder gave the blue stone to Cathal, Kayleigh, and Callum and the Earth spoke to each of them in order to get their individual signature which the Earth could use to communicate with them.

The Earth also created 3 additional clear stones for Kayleigh, Cathal and Callum to use so it will mask their identity as a child of someone from Ghia. It wasn't clear if they would need these additional stones, but if they were not needed then they might be useful to allow someone else in the Guild to escape these aliens.

After all the stones were placed correctly, the purple stone glowed, and a purple balloon rose from the stone to encompass all of Stonehenge with a protective purple dome around the circle of stones. The Earth was present and spoke to them, "I'll contact Ghia now."

In a few moments, they could all hear a new voice in their minds. It spoke to all of them, surprisingly in English, "Greetings my children and greetings to Earth's children. I'm so happy to finally be able to meet you all. I wish it had been under different circumstances. Our planet and several other planets are imperiled by this new alien force which has overtaken our world and many other worlds similar to me."

Everyone said "Hello Ghia. We are very glad to meet you also. Please, let us know how we can help you."

Ghia continued, "The Sentient Guild of Quantum Symbiosis started thousands and thousands of years ago. The Earth was still forming into a planet at this time. We were starting to find other planets in the universe who were also sentient like myself and we started to help each planet go through a process of working with the dominant species residing on each planet, we showed them how to form a relationship with those people and to help each other in the relationship to thrive and grow. The Quantum Guild grew to have over 45,000 worlds which were part of our growing and thriving member planets and races.

The Earth interrupted Ghia and said, "Can you believe it? There are 45,000 other planets like me out there. I can't wait to meet all of them. Sorry, Ghia. I didn't mean to interrupt but I'm just so excited I can't stand it."

"That's ok, child. We are very excited to meet you today also. It was about 3000 years ago, when we came across a planet which was on the verge of gaining sentience, but it was a ruse and a trap for the Quantum Guild. This planet contained an alien race called the Egran. The Egrans detest any planet who is sentient. They especially hate any planet which joins in a mutualistic symbiotic relationship with its dominant species living on the planet. It goes around the known universe and tries to break these symbiotic relationships. The Egran's only strive for power and knowledge. Sadly, many of our planets have been left in a state where they have receded into a kind of comatose state. It's a self-protection mode a planet sometimes goes into, in order to protect itself. They came for Ghia after we sent our colonists to work with the Earth to help it gain sentience and work with the humans helping both to thrive and grow."

"Have you been able to communicate with any of the other worlds? Maybe this is where Arwen and Mordag can help Ghia. If we can wake up these other planets, is there a way we could get enough of them to usurp the Egrans?" Alder asked.

"Unfortunately, we haven't been able to reach out to the Earth since then. The Egrans prohibit us from talking to any of the other member worlds. We have been able to secretly talk to some of the stronger members of the Guild and help each other in a very limited way. The Egrans enslave, arrest or kill anyone who fights them. They are a very highly advanced race and have weapons with tremendous power. They want all the planets in the Guild because it's a wealth of resources for it. It's also a large workforce for them to use in whatever way they want to. It's quite dire back here on Ghia. Ghia's moon is valuable to them but for some reason they haven't done anything to us."

Arwen said, "Maybe this is where we could be helpful. If we went to other worlds and tried to shore up the symbiotic relationship between the planet and the life living on its surface, would this help?"

Ghia replied, "This fracturing and splintering the symbiotic relationship has been a devastating consequence for the races of people who live on these planets. Life is very difficult and surviving from day to day is a tremendous struggle. Imagine if the Earth gave up on its magnetic poles and there was no electromagnetic shield surrounding your planet, all life would cease to exist on your planet. This is essentially what is happening all around the galaxy. Many worlds who have worked together for eons and eons, almost since the universe was first born, they have known sentience and strived to create life in a never ending cycle of life and death. This alien race has a mastery over this life and death cycle and vehemently uses this against all the planets. It threatens to kill all life on a planet unless it does its bidding to mine resources, or it just kills them to get them out of the way. It's a barbaric race we have encountered. We are at a loss of how we can overcome this entity."

Mordag added, "Ghia, I know we can help in this effort. Please let's come to you and we can figure this out."

"The Earth has told me about some of its children are able to manipulate the quantum stones in a marvelous way. From what I have heard from the Earth, is that some of you are even more advanced in skill with the stones, than some of our greatest champions who have used the stones in the past. Mordag, your brother Imadin has a plan he would like to execute to battle against this foe. He would need your help in doing this. He would like to know if you would come back to Ghia to help him work on this plan. The same is also true for Alder and Arwen. Even if you decide to come to Ghia for a short time, you can always return to Earth anytime you want to."

Everyone listening to the Ghia, all said at once. "Yes, we want to go to Ghia and help free Ghia and the other planets."

Everyone except Pat and Harriet agreed in unison. Alder noticed this and smiled. Without Pat or Harriet saying anything, Alder knew they had already given their answer to Ghia.

Arwen looked at Brian and said, "Brian, we can't ask this of you. The sacrifice is too great."

A wave of frustration came over Brian's face. "This isn't fair. Can I talk to Julie and Malcolm first? I want to help with this, and I know I can help. Alder, I have a secret weapon which you said no one on your planet has ever seen someone do before. Kat just saw me drill a hole in a metal coin with a laser from my finger. You called them light spears. I need some guidance on this, but I'm positive I can surprise the heck out of these idiots holding Ghia hostage. If no one on your planet can do this, then they won't be suspecting this. We should use this to our advantage."

Pat could be heard saying, "Shit, lasers are so cool! I would love to see these bastards fight against my buddy Brian with his light spears. He would totally *pwn* them!"

Brian looked up at the purplish colored sky and said out loud, "Ghia, let me get my wife and child to come with me to Ghia. We can find a way to fight this alien race and send them all back to whatever hell they came from."

Harriet who had been quiet during this whole time, looked at Pat and said, "Pat let's take Brian to get his wife and son to come to Stonehenge."

"Abso-freakin-lutely! Come on Brian lets go."

Pat, Harriet and Brian broke contact with everyone and walked outside of the purple dome. The strength of the dome and the connection stayed intact without them adding to the collective power to maintain contact. Everyone else was still focused on the conversation happening inside the circle, so no one saw Brian, Harriet and Pat silently disappear.

In a few minutes Pat, Harriet and Brian returned to Stonehenge with Julie and Malcolm. Harriet gave one of the blue stones to Julie and Malcolm so they would be able to communicate with the Earth and Ghia. They all joined the rest of the people in the circle under the purple shield.

Ghia was now addressing Julie and Malcom, "Hello my children. Your planet Earth is happy for you to come and meet it. My name is Ghia, and I am a planet located in a galaxy a very long way from your planet Earth. Malcolm your father, Brian, has a unique ability to bend and transform light into a powerful energy. This may be able to help us defeat an alien race called the Egran, who is occupying my planet and several thousands of planets around the universe. Brian wanted you to come and meet both the Earth and also me. We are very glad to meet you."

Julie was speechless. Malcolm said, "Hello Planet Ghia. It's very nice to meet you. My dad is very special, and he can do a ton of things with fire that are so cool. If he says he can help you then you better believe that he can!"

Brian looked quizzically at Julie and then at Malcolm. Julie looked totally flabbergasted. How did Malcolm know how he could manipulate fire? Malcolm saw the confused look on his face and said, "Dad, seriously did you think I didn't know? Of course, I know. Uncle Jerry told me one night when I asked him how you got the burns on your arm and shoulder. He feels horrible about it, and he thinks it's his fault. I told him you never thought it was his fault."

Malcolm directed this to everyone in the circle watching this exchange and said, "Come on daylights burning, well OK, not daylight, but moonlight is burning here. Let go to Ghia and kick some Egrans ass!"

It started with Harriet, but a giggle is very contagious. She was laughing and giggling at what Malcolm just said. Then they Earth started to giggle, and pretty soon everyone was in tears from laughter. Malcolms statement was so simple, but it was just so pure and honest. Even Ghia was laughing. When Julie started laughing, Brian could tell she was behind going to Ghia to help.

It took a minute or two, but everyone settled down and became more serious. Ghia and Earth said as one voice, "Julie and Brian, we have no right to ask you to go to Ghia. We realize your first responsibility is to Malcolm, even though his boldness and courage is refreshing, we can't ask you to do this."

Brian looked at Julie. He didn't want to put her on the spot with this decision. He said, "Thank you for understanding this. I really do want to help you and the rest of the people here who I have gotten attached to. I'm sorry everyone, but I really have to go back to Pl-."

Julie interrupted Brian, "Hold your horses their honey. Ghia, if we went to your world, is this a one way trip or is it something we could easily come back to Earth if we needed to?"

"Coming and going would be very easy for you to do. You're natives of the Earth so your signature is like a bright star in the sky for the Earth to see. We could send you back as easily as it is to come to us. Why?"

Julie looked at Brian and said, "Brian, Mal's right if you can help in this, you should help. If Malcolm and I went with you, there might be a way we could help also. Who knows, maybe Malcolm has a surprising ability using these stones the way everyone else does?"

Alder said something in his native Ghian language to Earth and Ghia. Ghia replied back to him also in the Ghian language.

The Earth said in English, "Yes. Yes, I can do this. Give me one minute and I'll have it ready."

They all waited for something to happen. Everyone felt like something had passed between Earth and Ghia and wouldn't be spoken about until the Earth finished whatever it was working on. The ground in front of Malcolm rumbled a little bit like something was trying to push its way up through the ground to come to the surface. After a few of the rumblings, two stones pushed their way up and became visible. Each was a round oval stone but instead of being one specific color like the other quantum stones, it contained all the colors in a myriad of beautiful blending of colors.

The Earth said, "Malcolm and Julie, this stone I have just created is a special stone and is something you must carry with you at all times. You must promise me you will carry this with you always. It's a stone which is made from me, and it's programmed to take you from anywhere you're in the universe and it will bring you back to Earth. All you have to say is 'TAKE ME HOME' and it will transport you back here to Stonehenge. It will also take you and anyone else you're connected to back here. Promise me you will do this?"

"I promise, Earth," Malcom said in his most serious voice.

Julie also said she promised to do this.

Ghia asked everyone, "When do you want to come to Ghia?"

Alder looked at everyone and he knew what there answer was. He said, "Ghia, I think everyone is ready. Please take us home."

Everyone in the circle, including all the quantum stones, all became invisible and were transported 490 light years away to planet Ghia.

The End

Book 2 – Quantum Mind

Epilogue

It felt a little blinding to be in darkness with a full moon and then to be almost immediately appearing in a room with very bright sunshine. Everyone was squinting a little from the effect of the bright sun. It wasn't as yellowy, or as intensely white in brightness as the sun of Earth, but a little more of a yellow and orangish kind of light. Still, it was very bright, and took a couple of seconds for their eyes to adjust.

Their senses were trying to assimilate all the input they were receiving. There was a smell of the ocean. The room they were in was rolling as if it was on water. The ceiling of the room was mostly made of a type of clear glass and in the center was a large skylight open to the air. The temperature was comfortable but warmer than the midnight air of Stonehenge. The floor was light grey and the walls were white.

Everyone was sitting in a padded high backed chair firmly built into the floor of the room. Each chair had a set of shoulder and body restraints which were firmly secured around each of them. They were snug but not too tight. The restraints it appeared were purely for safety.

At one end of the rectangular room, a similar chair contained a man with short black hair sitting in it. He smiled and a wave of emotion overcame his face. Before he was about to say anything Mordag said, "Imadin!"

"Sister! I have missed seeing you for so long. Does everyone feel OK? Is anyone in pain or hurt?"

Alder looked around at everyone, and they all said no.

Imadin continued, "There will be a time later for a reunion, but time is short. We must move our craft away from Ghia now. Please hold on, we are about to travel to our moon Druna. If you feel sick or in pain, please push the white button on your left hand rest. It will calm your stomach or relieve pain."

The skylight in the ceiling closed and the clear glass became opaque and smoky grey. Internal lighting on the floor appeared. Imadin's chair, revolved 180 degrees to face the front wall. He pushed a couple of buttons, and the wall turned into a full floor to ceiling display of information. One side of the screen had a picture of the planet and the trajectory they were about to take to go to the second moon of Ghia. Another part of the screen told them all kinds of information about the craft, and the trajectory they were about to embark upon.

Once everything was in motion and the craft was away from the planet, everyone could feel a subtle shift of gravity in their bodies. It was clear, at least from the monitor Imadin was looking at, they were now officially in space. Why didn't they feel weightless?

Alder overheard Malcolm asking his mother this question. Alder turned to Malcolm and told him this ship has a gravity drive to create an artificial gravity on the ship.

Imadin turned, and said, "Yes, this is correct. We have a way of changing our inertia from outside this ship to an opposite force inside this ship. It might feel like we are not moving at all, but we are moving very fast right now. We should arrive there in a few moments. Once we arrive, we will be transported to our sanctuary, and we can talk and catch up on what has been happening to Ghia over these many years. There are also no

Egrans watching, so we will be free to talk. It's so great to see all of you again. We have missed you so much. It is now when we need your help the most."

This next book, called Quantum Entanglement, will continue the story of Ghia's struggle against the Egrans and the fight for the Quantum Guild.

Thank you!

MD Hanley

Also, by MD Hanley

Bit By Bit

Carbon Copy

Humility: A Spiritual Way of Life

Watch for more at my website

http://www.mdhanley.com/

or

https://www.hanleyadamspublishing.com

Thank you for reading Quantum Mind! I hope you enjoyed it as much as I enjoyed writing it. If you did, I would be grateful if you could take a moment to leave a review on the site where you bought this book, or if you want to go to https://www.goodreads.com and share any thoughts or information you would care to leave about this book. Reviews are incredibly helpful for authors and also help other readers discover new books.

Thank you for your support and happy reading!

MD Hanley

Did you love *Quantum Mind*? Then you should read

Bit By Bit

Here is a sample of his book,

Chapter 1 - Gary McKeown

As witnesses later recalled two small dogs waltzed into the dance studio, grabbed the cat and waltzed out

- The Far Side by Gary Larson

200 miles east of the Australian coast.

It's 6:30 AM in the South Pacific Ocean about 200 miles from the east coast of Australia. This early in the morning, there's a breath-taking view of the South Pacific Ocean with the sun climbing ever higher and becoming warmer. The surface of the ocean had what looked like dozens of tiny little mirrors reflecting back to the sun. A familiar tug of war between the sun and the South Pacific Ocean that's been going on since the earth was first formed. The sun continuously beats down on the ocean surface and the response of the ocean is to reflect back to the sun. At the end of each day the ocean and the sun call a truce until the next day. The salty smell of the ocean is strong and pungent. This salty smell is not unpleasant, but it hints there is nothing between the boat and Australian coast.

The triple decker diving boat rocks gently on the water, anchored to a point in the ocean above the S.S. Yongala shipwreck site. Among most scuba divers, the Yongala is one of the premier dive sites around the world. The SS Yongala was a passenger ship out of Melbourne heading towards Cairns, Queensland in 1911. On the way up the coast they ran into a severe cyclone and sank. All passengers and cargo were lost. Over the years, the Yongala has become an artificial reef and the home of many species of fish and beautiful coral formations. The wreck sits in an area of sandy shoal about 120 feet underwater at about 4 miles west of the Flinders reef.

The warm sun feels great compared to two days earlier in Boston where a cold winter had a 'Kung-Fu' grip on New England. Gary McKeown is 48 and physically in good shape. Gary was never the type to go to the gym religiously every morning and lifting huge weights to attain huge muscles. Gary had always liked working out but his attitude toward physical strength was very pragmatic. If he was hanging on the edge of a huge building, would he have the strength to lift his body to the roof or safety without having a huge issue? Could he also do the same if someone was injured and he needed to carry them on his back? Yeah, he figures he could do that but that's it. People at the gym he belongs to are the 'gym rats' getting their bodies ready for the apocalypse and would need the strength to carry eight people on his or her back to get to safety. To each his own, I guess.

Gary starts to think about the events that got him here. He had almost cancelled the whole diving trip when he got a call about 3 hours before his flight out of Boston. His friend Ben Costello, who was supposed to come on this scuba diving trip, told Gary that he was in the Emergency Department. He was on a ladder doing some of the last-minute things that his wife had asked to do when he had fallen and broke his leg.

With the prospect of canceling all his plans and staying home over the Christmas Holiday, Gary's business partner, Roger Tillson, mentioned that he might be able to help Gary. Roger still stayed in touch with a mutual friend, Barry Parker, who they both knew from their Northeastern College fraternity. Roger said that Barry had been pestering him to go scuba diving with him so Gary agreed to let Roger see if Barry was available.

In fifteen minutes, Roger walked into Gary's office and announced that he was the great miracle worker. Roger said he had to call in huge favors. Use some of his contacts with the airlines, use favors owed him. He had to use his amazing negotiating skills to be able to miraculously pull this off. Roger had bought an American /Qantas Airline round trip airline ticket for tonight's flight out of Boston, got all the Visas that were needed, booked a cabin on the Spoil Sport diving boat Gary and Ben were going to take. Unfortunately for Barry he had to fly coach and share a cabin with one of the crew.

Gary smelled something wrong here. How could all this be done in 20 minutes? Even if it wasn't last minute, it still took a while to book all of these things. At the last-minute Roger was able to book an American Airline/ Qantas Airline coach ticket to Brisbane Australia and then a 3-hour flight north to Cairns, Queensland? And even more surprising was to get a spot on the seven-day scuba diving boat, Spoil Sport. Obtaining all the tickets and visas for this was done in the space of about 20 minutes'?

At first Gary thought something was not quite right here. If feels as if Barry already had airplane tickets, visas, and a reservation on Spoil Sport. Even though he was suspicious of this, he was really looking forward to this trip. Reluctantly, he agreed and packed up any papers he was currently working on. He would look at these when he came back. The next 10 days was going to be a great way to just relax and unplug for a while.

Gary went out to the dive deck to see the sun rising. He loved this time of day. Peaceful and calm. The quiet and calming factor of the dive deck is like a house of cards. Undisturbed. No one has broken the silence yet.

Pretty soon, there's a buzz of people going in every direction on the lower diving deck. Some of these are the Spoil Sport diving boat crew. The rest of the people on the deck are the passengers who were there for one thing and only one thing, scuba diving. All sizes of people were here, big, small, tall, or short. The amount of neoprene was obviously abundant!

Almost everyone on board is going on this dive, except Barry. He has not shown up on the diving deck yet. Most people are sitting on one of the three rows of benches. Underneath the bench is a bin that holds all their scuba gear, snorkel, masks, diving fins, weight belts and diving computers. Behind each person is one scuba tank attached to their BCD (Buoyancy

Compensator Device). Each tank had been filled earlier that morning with Oxygen, or an Oxygen Nitrogen mix.

On the left and right of the dive deck are a short set of stairs leading to a flat platform, only about a foot above the surface of the ocean. This is where they can put their fins on and jump into the ocean. At the back of the dive deck is a chalkboard that displays the information for their dive. On it is written various depths of the different parts of the dive sight. One of the dive crew starts to get everyone's attention and proceeds with the diving brief.

Whether it was an Oxygen, or a Nitrox mix, it was very important that they be certified to use the right mix. Each carried its own life-threatening ramifications from Nitrogen narcosis or Oxygen toxicity. Incorrectly using the wrong mix can have dire consequences.

Like most scuba diving boats, they have two hard fast rules. Initial when you leave the boat and then initial it when you come back on board. The other rule they have is what they call, 'Peace on the Reef'. This means look all you want, but don't touch. The Great Barrier Reef is one of the world's most beautiful treasures and some of the reef formations take decades and decades to grow that way. Humans can ruin this wonder of the world very quickly and it needs us to respect it and not destroy it.

Since Gary has never dived with Barry before, it was really important to be reading from the same page when they are diving. Over the years Gary has learned the hard way that some people are very safe to dive with and others are not. Gary and his friend, Ben, always approached diving with safety in mind. Gary had not dived with Barry before, so he wanted to make sure they were using the same hand signals. He stressed how important it was to dive as a team. Don't wander off 50 yards away from your dive buddy. What if you have a problem with the tank etc.? If someone gives you thumbs up that doesn't mean 'Ok' but means to ascend. Checking your tanks air supply and communicating when it's half empty and when it is a quarter tank left.

Keep checking your dive computer for how long it is safe to stay at a certain depth. Always, always do safety stops. Stop at 60 feet for 3 to 5 minutes, stop at 30 feet for 3 to 5 minutes and finally stop at fifteen feet for 3 to 5 minutes. If you don't follow these safety stops then you are not allowing your body to release the nitrogen from the various parts of your body and muscles. Gary would rather abort a dive for safety rather than push the envelope just to see something interesting.

This is the first dive which Gary and Barry are scuba diving together. Immediately, Gary could tell that Barry's diving experience was little to none. If you took a vacation to the Caribbean, there were many hotels that would give you a quickie 3-hour scuba dive class and you would mistakenly believe that you had your official scuba diving license. What you received from the hotel was not a PADI Scuba Certification but was a recreational diving certificate. It was only valid at their hotel, and it only allowed you to go to a depth of 30 feet with a certified diver.

It was still light out and the visibility was good. They swam out to the guideline that was about 20 yards from the boat. They slowly released air in the BCD to allow for a gradual descent. Going down slowly helps to equalize the pressure that builds up in the sinus passages. As soon as they descended about 5 feet, Barry just dropped like a rock and let out all of the air from his BCD to help him descend quickly. When Gary reached the same depth and swam over to Barry, he could tell that Barry had a lot of pressure pulsing into his temples and sinus's tissues. When this occurs, you can do one of two things, stop descending or pinch your nose and try to blow air out of your nasal passages. This is called the Valsalva technique. This will help to equalize your eustachian tubes in your inner ears and releases the pressure that builds up. Depending on a person's physiology, some people have a great deal of trouble while others do not.

Gary thought Barry's behavior was a total rookie mistake. He got Barry's attention and asked him if he was ok. He asked him by putting his hand to his nose, as if he was going to equalize the pressure, and then gave an OK signal as a question to see where Barry was. Barry shook his head to say 'no'. Gary said in hand signals, stay for 3 minutes and if the pressure equalizes then they would continue the dive. If not any better, we would ascend to 60 feet and again wait a couple of minutes to see if it corrected the pressure he was feeling. Barry decided that he would just do what he wanted and grabbed the guideline and pulled himself quickly up the guideline.

On his way back to the surface he pushed a girl who was descending, out of his way. As he pushed her aside, he ended up getting his hand under her regulator hose, that connects to the air tank, and yanked it out of her mouth, as he moved his left arm up the guideline. She was a seasoned diver, so she recovered quickly. As Gary ascended to follow Barry, he reached the diver that Barry just bumped into. He tried to pantomime an apology to her. She nodded and accepted his apology.

Later in the morning Gary, and most everyone on the boat, is hoping to do a dive before lunch. Gary is starting to get annoyed that Barry has not come out to get ready for this dive. If Barry didn't show up soon, Gary was going to ask one of the other divers if he could tag along with them on their dive. Gary is partly hoping that Barry doesn't show up for the dive, which would be a blessing. As soon as he was thinking this, Barry stumbled down the stairs to the diving deck.

Shortly after the dive brief, everyone started putting their scuba gear on and trying to get in the water as fast as possible, maximizing their dive time. One thing about scuba diving trips, they follow a consistent pattern of dive, eat, and then dive some more. Generally, you can get anywhere from four or five dives a day. Most conversations people had with each other on the boat were generally about the type of fish or coral that they saw on the last dive, or a hope that they would see it on an upcoming dive.

"Hey, are you up to doing this dive?" Barry asks.

Gary replied, "Yes I am. You're going to love seeing the Yongala site. Now we are doing a regular air tank dive so hopefully we can stay down on the Yongala wreck for at least 45 or 60 minutes. Also, let's just take our time descending to about 110 feet."

Gary had all his gear on and waited for Barry to put on his equipment. Once he had all his gear on Gary asked, "Ok Barry can you do a scuba gear check for me?"

Barry looks confused asking what Gary wants him to check?

"Never mind I'm pretty sure that my gear is on correctly. Let me do a gear check for you." Gary starts to go through the gear checklist on Barry's gear. This checklist is something that you learn at the very beginning of your lessons for scuba diving. Gary checks for any tangles in his primary regulator and also his secondary regulator. He also checks that Barry's air tank is turned on and open. Gary checks Barry's dive computer and checks that his BCD vest is on correctly and that his weight belt has the proper amount of weights.

Now they are all set and wait patiently to get into the water. When it is their time, they go down the stairs to the flat platform which will allow them to put on their fins. There is a crew member on the platform with a clipboard that each diver needs to initial at the beginning and end of their dives. The crew member also checks that their air tank is fully on. Gary initials the clipboard and hands it to Barry. Barry was hoping for this to happen, it didn't happen earlier. Now that Gary put his initials down, Barry crossed out Gary's initials and initials in the space next to his own name. By doing this he effectively makes it seem as if Gary did not go on this dive.

"Barry let's just take our time on this. We need to stay together and not wander off. We also need to be clear on the hand signals."

Barry says sarcastically, "Ok Gary, I get it. Come on let's go down there".

Barry and Gary swam over to the guideline that they will use to descend. They both started to slowly descend down to the ocean bottom. As they descend, pressure builds up in their sinuses and they must clear this using the 'Valsalva' technique.

Barry was dropping like a rock and not equalizing. Eventually Gary caught up with him and Gary could tell he had a problem with the pressure build up in his ears again. Gary mimicked Barry to pinch his nose and blow out. After doing this about 4 times, Barry gave him a thumbs up. Wrong hand signal. Thumbs up means go to the surface. Gary mimicked the ok hand symbol which is where you make a circle with your thumb and index finger. Once again, Barry did a thumbs up signal. Gary shrugged his shoulders to indicate that he did not understand. Barry did the 'Ok' symbol realizing why Gary was confused. They continued diving and exploring the reef.

The SS Yongala ship is just amazing. There is every type and size of fish and coral outcroppings. Everywhere you look there is something interesting to see. The boat is tilted to the left and you can see all the compartments and rooms on the ship. The rule that we were told by the crew was not to go inside the ship or to touch any of the fish or coral outcropping.

Gary was looking at a fantastic coral formation at the bow of the ship. Barry swims toward Gary and does not stop his momentum so he bumps right into Gary. Now, Barry is stepping on the coral formations and breaking them off. At one point, he is stepping on parts of the boat and breaks it off.

Gary is mortified and pissed off. Enough of this guy. Now Barry is chasing a grey reef shark swimming away from the boat, Gary is able to catch up to him and motions him to go back to the Yongala. Barry shakes his head 'no'. Barry reaches over to

Gary and pulls his mask off. Gary is surprised and pissed. Once Gary exhales and replaces the water that was in his mask, he again looks for Barry. Barry is now another 50 feet away

Gary thinks why the hell would Roger go diving with guy? Gary catches up with Barry. It's only sand here. Gary looks for the ship, but the visibility is not great, but he is pretty sure if he back tracks, he will be able to find the ship. Barry points even further away from the ship. Gary says no and points behind where he believes the ship is. Barry looks at Gary with a big grin and then pulls his mask off again. As Gary is trying to clear his mask, Barry reaches over and turns Gary's air off. While Gary is dealing with his mask, Barry takes off his weight belt of 45 lbs. of lead, and puts it on Gary with the release clip in the back so it will be difficult to get off. And then Barry swims back to the ship.

Gary looks at his dive computer and it says that he has been down at 110 feet for too long. He was down here at this depth for an hour and twenty minutes which is 20 minutes longer than he should. Gary starts to have problems getting oxygen and realizes that his tank has been turned off. Gary tries his safety respirator, and it is still bad. Worry starts to creep in from the sides. Gary can't reach the knob to turn the air tank on. Ok well this is what you train for when you get certified. First you need to take off the BCD vest. Gary can't get the weight belt off because it is hooked around his BCD vest and the release clip is in the center of his back.

Nitrogen Narcosis is starting to envelop his body and brain. Gary has felt this before and knows that if he doesn't fix this soon and ascend that he will die. Slowly Gary can feel the different parts of his body start to shut down. As unconsciousness comes marching toward him, he stops struggling and uses whatever air is left. I guess Barry didn't totally turn off the air; Gary takes little sips of air. Unconsciousness wins and Gary stops struggling. Gary is trying to not go unconscious, but it starts to win. Just before Gary goes under, he sees a hand turning him over and taking off that bloody weight belt. His last thought was why did Barry do this? Was this Roger's plan from the beginning?

One of the divers on board the SpoilSport is looking for Gary to show him some the pictures he had taken on the latest dive. He asked one of the crew members, if Gary had finished his dive or was still under? He says, "No, Gary never left the boat."

The diver that was looking for Gary said he absolutely went diving. He saw him under water by the bow of the Yongala ship. This is worrying for the crew member. He looks at his sheet again and doesn't see Gary's initials. But maybe he forgot. Better safe than sorry. He tells the captain that there is another diver down there and all the other divers have signed in, except Gary McKeown.

Four divers from the crew check in all directions. The crewman, Steve, finds Gary and immediately puts his second respirator for Gary to buddy breathe. He turns Gary's unconscious body so he can remove the weight belts from Gary's gear. He takes Gary and makes a rapid ascent to the surface.

Next, Gary is being carried up on the boat and placed on the top part of the boat. The captain radios the EMT's and they are sending a medical helicopter. The captain asks the crew to clear all the sunbathing chairs and block the steps up to this part of the boat from other divers.

In about 30 minutes there is a medical helicopter landing on the top floor of the boat which is usually used for sunbathing. The medical team carries Gary from where he was laid down, on a stretcher, and then onto the helicopter.

Barry runs up to the helicopter and starts to get in. The first aid people said no way. Barry said that Gary was his brother and he needed to go with them. The guy in the helicopter grimaces and then nods his head for him to get on board. Barry is happy to be done with scuba diving. It bore him to tears. So tired of pretending to be really interested in the fish or the slimy coral. The only thing that Barry was thinking when looking at those fish was wishing he had a spear gun to shoot at them. The whole time he was underwater he kept thinking about what each fish would taste like.

They are about 25 minutes from Mater Hospital in Brisbane. After they land on the roof of the hospital, Barry follows them to the elevator to take Gary to the emergency department. Barry acts like he is following them there but stops at the intake desk to give the clerk Gary's name and insurance information. He also gives a contact number of Roger's cell phone. Barry asks her if there is a bathroom. She points to the right of the automatic doors to exit; Barry says he will be back in a moment. As he walks towards the men's room, he goes out of the emergency door as another couple is walking through the doors. Barry never makes it to the restroom.

Barry flags a taxi down and asks him to get him to the airport. Roger is going to be pissed that I haven't finished the job. The little bits he heard in the helicopter was that he was showing signs of an acute nitrogen narcosis coma. This new event may make Roger happy.

Chapter 2 - Lucy McKeown

"Watch out world

I am wearing my sassy pants today!!"

- Lucille Ball

Lucy McKeown, who is 49 years old, has always been in good shape and has a lean body to show for it. Her figure is highlighted with a head of fiery, red curly hair. She has dealt and worked with men who look at her and think that she can be easily swayed or intimidated. Make no mistake on that! Men have tried to act all superior making sure the little women will do what they want. She doesn't mind playing along if it gets her to achieve her goal. However, if you poke the bull then be ready to get the horns!

Growing up with her younger brother, Gary, there were some real knockout fights. He always knew how to get under her skin and push the right buttons. Gary has a special gift in which he has a nearly perfect, total recall of anything that he sees or reads. When they were younger, this could be infuriating. He would correct her about any of the slightest details, that she was describing to him or to someone else. Lucy remembers slamming many doors when she was a teenager.

Conversely, she knew the way to get him to *toe the line*. Maybe it was a maternal thing, but at times she knew that if she offered any comment toward the quality of their daily chores, he would just short-circuit.

She was almost nineteen and Gary was seventeen, when they both learned about the death of their parents. This was devastating. Every part of their lives turned upside down. This was a turning point for them. An unspoken truce developed. They were both hurt, as anyone would be. It became apparent that if one tried to hurt the other, then they were indirectly hurting themselves.

Lucy is usually a calm person and rarely gets very annoyed or angry. Today was not that day. She is feeling extra angry today! It's not that she's in a rush, or there was heavy traffic, she just felt mad at everyone and everything. Lucy turned on the radio and a popular song came on. She liked this song but turning it up really wasn't doing anything to improve her mood.

Lucy navigates her blue Subaru though the winding path to get to Ashwood, a long-term care facility. This is where her younger brother, Gary, was being treated as a patient. Gary had returned from Australia in a type of coma called an "anoxic" coma. This type is largely due to oxygen deprivation. Gary had been in this coma state for the last 2 years.

Lucy pulls into the Ashwood facility and the same thought keeps bouncing into her head. Why do they call it a *long-term care facility*? It's a nursing home. This is a familiar conversation that she has with herself every time she drives the 45 minutes to visit her brother.

Walking through the front entrance, she goes to the set of elevators on her right. On the ride up to the third floor, the feelings of anger and annoyance turn into a feeling of sadness and longing. She misses her brother.

When the elevator door opens, she walks over to the nurse's station. One of the nurses sees Lucy and pushes her chair away from the computer to face her. She can see the monitor the nurse was looking at and it was no surprise that it was her Facebook page. This nurse, Milly, was someone Lucy usually saw when she came here every couple of weeks.

As usual, Milly is wearing light green hospital scrubs and white tennis shoes. One her chest she has a solid blue patch with a white tree in the middle and below the tree it says "Milly Howards, RN".

"Hi Milly. Have there been any changes on Gary's care that I should know about?", Lucy asks.

Milly pulled out Gary's chart, attached are several papers that show all of the blood tests, brain tests, and various care items like feeding, or changing his different linens etc.

"Nope. No changes since last time.", Milly said with a strong emphasis of "last time".

"Has the financial department contacted you? Betsy Richter came by earlier today and said that she needs to talk to you", Milly adds.

Lucy says, "*Nope*" trying to mimic Milly's last response to her. Why does anyone say "nope"? Saying just 'No' is a smaller word and conveys the same thing.

Bit By Bit

"You can give Betsy my cell phone number if you want."

As Lucy was walking toward Gary's room, she could hear each room's combinations of noise makers. Whir, hum, buzz, or beep. Each room added to the concerto that was being played for the long spotless white hall. It's kind of funny but also not funny. These monitors and machines helped each person's health in some unique way.

Even though it was only about 1:00 everyone seemed to be sleeping. From Lucy's point of view if someone died, Milly wouldn't probably detect that until the next shift came on for the evening.

This was frustrating that the staff didn't see the obvious minimum care they should be giving to patients. She doesn't need to get into the politics of the Ashwood facility, because she keeps on top of Gary's care. She must do this because if *she gave them an inch, they would take a mile.*

As Lucy rounds the corner and enters room 33C, she sees Gary in his bed, hooked up to several machines. Some to check blood pressure, another to give fluids, and others to administer various nutrients to his body. Lucy is not startled or shocked to see her brother like this. She visits Gary often, so she is used to this. However, it does make her feel very sad. She misses talking with Gary. She misses both the laughing and fun that they had always shared and also some of the arguments they would get into. But now is not the time for sadness or self-pity.

Lucy has a routine that she follows every time she comes to visit. She reaches into her pocketbook and brings out a notepad.

She lists the things needed to be attended to by Ashwood staff. They have not given him a shave since the last time she visited. He should get a haircut. She walks to the end of his bed and looks at his chart. It's supposed to list anything that the staff has done for his care. She's not surprised to see several days with blank entries.

It annoys her when she sees this. It just highlights that Ashwood is not doing a great job taking care of him. She makes several entries in her notebook.

Lucy pulls out a bottle of skin conditioner and begins to cover Gary's feet, legs, and arms with this. She washes his face; pulls out a razor, bottle of shaving cream and a small hand towel and proceeds to shave the growing beard and mustache on Gary's face. Ashwood really doesn't like it when she does this. They are concerned with liability rather than personal care. The staff here only does as little as they can get away with. Next, Lucy takes hold of Gary's limbs and moves them all around and does little stretching exercises for his tendons and muscles.

After she had finished shaving Gary, and was satisfied with his clean-cut face, she reached into her voluminous pocketbook and pulled out the Stephen King book "Dead Zone". This was a book that Gary had read several times. Lucy never understood why he would reread a book since he has an almost perfect recall or eidetic memory. He said he just likes to go through the process of reading the story. The smells, the colors, the tastes, and the feelings conveyed by the author are a little different each time he rereads a book. She found it ironic that this book was one of Gary's favorites. The story is about a guy that's in an accident and ends up in a coma. The character wakes up after several years and discovers he has a new psychic power of precognition. Maybe Gary ironically had a precognition that he would be in a coma many years later after reading this book.

Lucy finishes the chapter she was reading and collects the things that she brought in with her and heads out to her car. When she passes the nurse's station, she talks to Milly about seeing if she could have someone give Gary a haircut and also to make sure that he was being attended to on a regular basis.

Milly says "Yup."

Lucy walks over to the elevator and starts to make her way out to her car. She was just opening the door to the parking lot when someone from behind her called out her name. She turned to face the person with the screechy voice echoing and reverberating in the large atrium.

"Ms. Hamilton, ah Ms. Hamilton? May I please speak to you?" That voice is Betsy Richter from the financial office. She always addresses Lucy with her married name. She had changed her last name back to her maiden name because it was a constant reminder of her husband, David, who died from cancer 12 years ago.

Betsy asks if she had time, could she come to her office to discuss the financial arrangements for Gary's care. Betsy has one of those super sweet fake personalities that was far from being sweet and far from being real.

Betsy said, "Ms. Hamilton, I have tried several times to reach you regarding the cost of your brother's care. I wanted to alert you that the cost for your brother's care has gone up substantially. Four months ago, the cost for your brother's care increased by five thousand dollars. The money that was being sent to Ashwood for Gary's care wasn't the full amount to cover his care.

Lucy was speechless. Since the day that Roger Tillson called her to inform her about Gary's scuba diving accident, he has been true to his word. She remembers it as if it was yesterday. Roger made a solemn promise to her that the cost for Gary's care would be paid, no matter what the cost.

"Did you speak to Mr. Tillson about this? He's the one who has been paying the cost for Gary to be here. I'm sure that he would be able to take care of this."

Betsy looked a little baffled. "Tillson? I am not aware of a Mr. Tillson being involved in the financial responsibility for your brother's care. I always assumed it was paid by you, or that Gary had set up a trust account to provide for his care. Let me pull up the account and let's take a little *looksy*", Betsy said as she plopped into her chair.

After a minute or two, Betsy said "When your brother was first brought here, we received a letter from a company called Trinity Trust Holdings in Boston. They asked that all financial bills and statements be sent to an account at Trinity Trust Holdings. For the last two years every bill sent to this account has been paid for within one business day. For the past four months the bills were sent but the payment was only enough to cover the cost of his care before it was increased."

Betsy continued, "I am sorry about this, but we really need to find a solution. The current total for Gary is $22,575. At least half of it needs to be paid by the end of the month, which is in two weeks. If payment cannot be made, then I'm sorry to tell you that Gary will need to be moved to a different care facility. For the last several years all, patients that are unable to pay for the full amount of their care are sent to the state-run UMass hospital in Worcester."

Lucy knew the UMass Hospital very well. It's not a place where you would want to be a patient. There have been many stories about different doctors being sued and a high rate of patient deaths over the years. Many have given it a nickname as the *Death Hospital*. People go in, but they do not come out. It sent shivers up and down Lucy's back.

Betsy continued her rambling on about the cost of her brother's care. She said they could accept a credit card, a cashier's check; or if Lucy had a saving's account with enough money to cover at least half of this bill today.

Lucy is only half hearing Betsy. It was taking an enormous amount of energy to get control of the tornado of thoughts and emotions going around in her head. She just kept repeating in her head "that bastard! that son of bitch!" I knew I should not have given Roger any control over Gary's care. Who or what is this Trinity Trust Holdings company?'

She said to herself, stay focused. How can I possibly pay this off? And then it hit her all at once. First things first. Get my brother out of this place. She can take care of him better than they can. Why does Gary need to be here, really?

She and her husband were very good at saving money. Nothing extraordinary. A little bit here and a little bit there started to add up after a while. When David died, he left a lump sum of money for Lucy and the kids. This helped to cover bills for tuition and also to help pay down the mortgage. She felt the cruel irony of his love when anyone called her by her married name.

Why didn't she think of this earlier? She paid off the mortgage several years ago, so paying the money for this hospital was not something that she couldn't have. That's exactly what I am going to do. Busy with the paperwork, Betsy didn't really notice that she wasn't paying attention to her.

Then, Lucy interrupted Betsy in mid-sentence and said, "Betsy I do not want Gary to be moved to the UMass hospital. I will be going to the bank tomorrow, to get a cashier's check for the balance that is due. Please let me know the total amount that is due by 10:00 AM. I will have an ambulance take my brother from Ashwood at 2:00 PM. I would appreciate it if you could have all the paperwork ready for me when the ambulance is here. I will also need to know the address and phone number for the company that has been sending payments for Gary."

Now it was Betsy's turn to be speechless. "Ok, if you want any of the medical records for Gary then please let me know the name of the long-term facility that will be handling your brother's care."

Lucy looked at Betsy with a firm commanding face and said, "Betsy, I will be taking my brother home to live in my house. Honestly, it's just easier for me to give my brother the care that he needs. I am quite sure I can do as well if not even better than Ashwood have done."

Betsy made one last attempt with Lucy, "How are you going to be able to take care of Gary? How are you going to do that? You won't have any of the medical supplies or medical equipment that is needed. How will you transport him to your house? I have already called the UMass hospital and they said they would hold a bed for him at the end of the month. Ms. Hamilton. I really think you are making a big mistake. Also, I do not think that moving your brother is legal!"

That was a big mistake for Betsy. She assumed that this would be fine without Lucy's input. Betsy thought that tossing the veiled threat to Lucy about this not being legal would make Lucy comply. Nope, that is not going to happen. If Betsy wants to play this game Lucy thought, then I can also play with her.

"Betsy it is unfortunate that you did not include me into your plans for Gary to move to the UMass Hospital. If you had consulted with me on this, I would not have agreed to it. So legally you are not allowed to move Gary unless I approve it. I am my brother's health care proxy and his legal guardian. This means that all medical decisions for Gary are with me. I plan to bring him home to my house, I can take care of him just as well, if not better than Ashwood has. I have a large room on the first floor of my house that will be perfectly sufficient for Gary's care. These are my brother's wishes when he asked me to be his health care proxy. So, if you could have all the paperwork done by 2:00, that would be perfect" Lucy said assertively.

Betsy was still speechless, it appeared she was having a hard time wrapping her head around this. Finally, she said, "Ok I will get the paperwork ready for tomorrow, but it will be tough to complete on such short notice. Do you want me to see if one of the Ashwood staff will be able to continue his care? They could stop by to help you on a regular basis."

It was difficult to contain her pleasure when Betsy said it would be difficult to get the paperwork done. Ha! Betsy had no problem cornering her and asking her for $22 thousand dollars payable in two weeks. Lucy responded, "No Betsy, I have been in contact with several different hospice organizations that are closer to me. When I spoke to them one woman came out and looked at where I would have Gary and felt that it was not a problem at all. In fact, she said that she would be able to provide a comfortable bed, like the ones used in hospitals, and provide any medical supplies or equipment that Gary would need. I think this will be a better situation for Gary". Lucy hated to tell lies but everything she just said to Betsy was a total lie. The look on Betsy's face was all that Lucy wanted. The cash stream that Lucy brought into this facility was now shut off.

As Lucy walked out to her car she was smiling. Why didn't I do this earlier? On the drive home she thought, now where the hell will I find a hospital bed for Gary? Her favorite song came on the radio, and she turned the volume up as loud as she could. Lucy was very happy, indeed.

Chapter 3 - Freddie

"Anyone who does anything to help a child in his or her life is a hero to me."

— Fred Rogers

One year later

The late July sun was overhead and felt great. To Lucy, the air and the warmth felt like being wrapped in her most comfortable robe and slippers. The smell of pine trees and pinecones filled the air. The squirrels at the border of Lucy's property were just running back and forth dancing to their own tune. Chasing each other and then running up a tree and then immediately running down. Lucy never really figured that one out, but it made her smile and laugh each time she saw them.

Lucy was in a zone right now. Wearing her ear buds and listening to an eclectic playlist of songs booming from her old iPod. Lucy is wearing a big white and red poker dotted hat. Apparently, it's the new 'La Rive Gauche' to make yourself look like a red and white beetle. She doesn't care because the music is turned all the way up, and she is wiggling her butt to the beat of the music as she's tending to her garden.

The smells from her rows of tomatoes, zucchini, and cucumber plants are unique and distinct. The garden has a very musky and intoxicating smell. The soil is a strange color of deep dark brown. Almost black but not quite. The soil looks moist but not necessarily with water. It contains a rich amount of nitrogen, phosphorus, and potassium. Only the best for my garden Lucy thought.

Lucy is so content with her gardening that she doesn't notice the big white and black shadow coming up behind her. When Lucy turns, she sees Gary's 4year-old Great Dane, Freddie. He has dirt all over his nose and several bits of roses, sunflowers, begonia stems and flowers either in his mouth or on his black and white fur. Lucy can't decide to be angry at him for destroying her flowers or laughing at how cute he is. Freddie realizes that she likes the flowers he brought her so now she's going to give him a treat or play rip up flowers game with him. Lucy can't contain it and bursts out laughing. Lucy feigns with her right hand that she is going pat him and give him some affection. And then the left hand comes down quickly and starts scratching Freddie's belly and long neck. He falls for this every time. But that's ok, he likes it, and he gives Lucy a big, sloppy lick all over her face. Freddie likes this game.

Looking at her watch, Lucy realizes that she needs to go to the grocery store before her two boys come over for dinner tonight. She rushes inside the house and changes her clothes; grabs her wallet, keys, and phone; puts Freddie's water dish outside; and gets in her car.

As Lucy is driving to the grocery store, she thinks about what has happened with her brother since his trip to Australia. When Gary traveled, she always got a message from Gary of where he was. Gary had been looking forward to this diving trip for a while, so it would not be unusual for Gary to extend this trip for a few days or a week. Christmas and New Year in Australia occurred in the warmest months of the southern hemisphere. Lucy thought maybe he would stay longer because it was so far away.

After two weeks of not hearing anything, she started calling some of the people that might provide more information on where Gary might be. The first call was to Gary's friend and diving partner, Ben Costello. When she called his cell number it rang for a long time before someone picked up.

"Hi, is this Ben Costello?" Lucy asks.

"Yes, it is. Who is this?"

"This is Lucy McKeown, Gary McKeown's sister. I was wondering if you knew where Gary is. I haven't heard anything from him since before his trip to Australia."

Ben responds after several seconds and with a little hesitation, "Sorry Lucy, but I don't know where he is. I broke my leg on the day we were supposed to fly out of Logan. I had to cancel my trip, but I thought he was still going anyways."

"Ok thanks Ben. If you hear anything, please let me know."

There was a slight pause when Ben answered her question. Most times that hesitation, even if it is a slight one, tells a lot. Generally, it means that a person is hunting or searching for words. Lucy doesn't buy it.

She went to his hi-rise apartment in the city and could not find him. The man at the front desk knew Gary and said that he had not seen him at all for several weeks. Lucy called Gary's work number and still no one answered. Lucy started to worry.

His absence and not checking in with her was very peculiar. He usually calls to let me, and others know that he's ok.

Maybe his assistant, Rose, knows where he is. Lucy met Rose several times since Gary hired her. She liked her and thought she was the perfect *anti-Gary*. She's one of those people that's incredibly meticulous and detailed. She also has no problem speaking her mind about anyone or anything. One night, Rose and her husband had gone to dinner to celebrate Gary's birthday. Rose said jokingly that the four years she had worked for him were such a chore, but she really loved it. He contradicted her claim that he hired her four years ago, Gary said it was five years ago.

Rose just looked at him like he was a little boy, like a foreigner and who didn't know how to speak English.

She raised her voice thinking that talking louder in English would translate the meaning of what she was saying.

She said "You really are a lost cause. No, you are wrong. I still have the offer letter that you gave to me, and it has been four years and three months that I have worked with you. You really are very forgetful, where would you be if you didn't have me keeping all this straight for you?"

Gary looked at Lucy and winked. Lucy knew that he was giving Rose a "win". Gary has a very uncommon type of memory. This rare gift, an eidetic memory, allows him to have a nearly perfect memory recall of anything that he hears or reads. She knew that he was letting Rose win this one.

Since Rose was always plugged in, she knew where everybody was. Lucy called Rose's cell number. She picked it up on the first ring. Lucy told her that she had not heard from Gary, and he was missing. Lucy asked Rose if she had heard from Gary or if she knew where he is currently. Rose said that she had not heard anything. In fact, she had tried to contact him and just got his voice mail. Rose said that she would look into this and if she finds out anything she will call. She also gave Lucy Roger Tillson's contact number and said that he might have some more information about Gary's whereabouts.

The next day after talking to Rose, Lucy called Roger. When she dialed the number, the phone rang for a long time. She was just about to hang up when a woman answered.

Lucy asked, "May I speak to Roger Tillson?"

The female voice on the other end said quickly, "Wrong number." And hung up the phone. Lucy redialed but this time the line was busy.

Ironically, Roger called her a couple of days after she attempted to talk to him. He told Lucy that Gary was in a scuba diving accident. He continued by saying that he brought Gary home to Boston two weeks earlier and had him checked into the Ashwood Long-term Facility. Roger also mentioned how much money he had spent to have Gary flown home. This was Roger's classic sound bite that he likes to play. Implying, all would be lost if Roger had not been there and saved the day.

She had only interacted with him on three different occasions. The first time was at a company sponsored event to celebrate reaching a certain sales target. The event was a huge "dog and pony" show for potential venture capital investors. Lucy was a master at detecting "bullshit". Right from the start she could see through Roger's s smarmy salesman-like demeanor. It was very phony and disingenuous.

Roger asked Lucy to meet him at the Ashwood facility. She agreed to meet the next day. She met Roger at the Ashwood facility and he wanted her to sign several documents concerning Gary's care. She confronted Roger with why he had not called her almost a month ago when this happened. Roger stammered a little bit, but he told Lucy that immigration was difficult because Gary did not have his passport. Lucy half heard Roger because she knew that she would never find out the real truth about this.

Of all the documents that Roger wanted her to sign, two of the documents she would not sign. The first was a form that named Roger as the power of attorney. Gary already had a signed a document that made Lucy his power of attorney. Another document was to make Roger his Healthcare Proxy. Again, Gary already had a signed document that named Lucy and her son, Peter, as his Healthcare Proxy. The last document named the person who would be responsible for the financial charges. Lucy said that she should be the named person on the contracts. Roger looked at Lucy and made a solemn vow to her that he would take care of all the finances. He just wished for Gary to get better.

Lucy was not going to give Roger any type of power with respect to Gary's health. Once again, people thought that her good looks and pleasant personality were a sign of being ditzy or just a dumb woman who would just sign whatever was put in from of her. Nope, that will never happen.

Lucy remembered that meeting with Roger from time to time, but today she had errands to do, and Gary needed to be cared for.

Later that day....4:00 PM

When Lucy got home and unloaded all the groceries, she had time to go through her normal routine daily care for Gary. As usual, Freddie follows Lucy into the former office where Gary is staying. Several machines and IV tubes are connected to him. She starts to wash his face and arms. She puts a couple of towels under his head and does her best to wash his hair. Usually, she did this when either the kids were here to help her, or with the help of the strong hospice nurse, who stopped by twice a week. She checks that all the fluids are properly connected; and checks his blood pressure, temperature, and oxygen levels. Everything looks good.

Freddie can't stand it any longer, he wants to see his friend Gary. Freddie stands up on his hind legs and sees that Gary is sleeping. He takes two big licks of Gary's face thinking that Gary will wake up and play. He goes back down on four legs and looks at Lucy and nudges Gary's hand. Nothing happens. Freddie doesn't understand. If he does that with Lucy or her sons and if he is persistent enough, he will get a belly scratch or a treat. He likes both of those options and sometimes he gets both a treat and a belly scratch. What a life.

Lucy rewashes Gary's face and hands. And then goes to the kitchen to make dinner. Freddie usually would follow because he would always get scraps. But today he decides he's going to stay here in his dog bed until his friend wakes up. Freddie's dog bed was actually a full-size couch that Freddie had claimed as his bed. Within 15 minutes, Freddie is asleep and has dog dreams of running though fields trying to catch rabbits or something.

After Dinner

"Mom, that was great, thanks. I wish the cafeteria at school had something like this. The food there doesn't even come close to this" says Patrick McKeown as he gets up and helps his brother Peter clear the table.

"Don't worry Patrick, I made two extra pans of lasagna. One for you and one for your brother."

Patrick looked at Peter with a little grin on his face. He was hoping that she would make extra "left overs" to bring back with him to college.

After dinner was cleaned up, Lucy asked her boys if they wanted some desert.

Peter said, "I can't right now, I'm too full." Patrick nodded in agreement.

"Ok, let's sit down and catch up. Tell me what's going on with you two. How's the new job working out, Peter?" Lucy said. Peter McKeown was 22 years old and had recently graduated from Northeastern University in Boston. He had just started working at a software company in Cambridge, MA. Usually, he stayed at his girlfriend's apartment, but occasionally he would come back home, even if Lucy had to bribe him with Lasagna.

"This company is awesome. People are super friendly. They assigned another developer to shadow me and show me the ropes. We get along great. He's an older guy, like 35, and he's a wicked gamer", Peter answered.

"That's great, I'm really happy for you. My credit card is also very happy that you're working", she said and gave Patrick a wink.

Peter started to say something, but Freddie started barking and whimpering. Freddie comes rushing around the corner forgetting that he's a really big dog and that his momentum does not stop his forward motion. Freddie slams into the wall but is unfazed and keeps running at full tilt toward the couch that Lucy and Patrick were sitting on. The whole time, Freddie was barking and whimpering.

Immediately, Lucy thought Freddie had to go outside. Peter was ahead of her and opened the door to let Freddie out. Freddie didn't make a move to the door. Freddie's barking was getting more insistent. Freddie looked at Lucy and gave a big growl bark. Ok, something is up. Freddie races out of the room and down the hall to the room where Gary was staying. Lucy is now worried. Freddie never acts like this.

Patrick, Peter, and Lucy ran into Gary's room. The lights are off but most of the machines throw out a green glow and make tiny noises. Lucy turns on the lights and looks at Gary's bed. Some of the noises that the machines are making are actually alarms to signify that it was not receiving any of a dozen vital signs. Lucy looks at the bed and Gary's eyes are wide open, and he is sitting up in the bed. Lucy is too stunned to say anything. Patrick doesn't hesitate and blurts out, "Holy SHIT!" Gary looks at Patrick, Peter and Lucy and says, "Hi guys!" Freddie sticks his nose in between everyone and looks at Gary.

Gary gave a little pat on Freddie's head. "Hey buddy, WOW you have grown."

About the Author

For the last 30 years, I have been working and consulting in the software engineering field. The only rule that you have to follow in this type of career is that you will never know it all. Once you realize that you are a master at some part of technology, you can guarantee that it will change and evolve. Whether it was being an individual contributor or a managing director of teams around the globe, there was always a unique new and exciting challenge. An adventurer at heart, some of my hobbies are scuba diving, flying, and hang gliding. Debuting my first novel has been a great experience and a lot of fun.

www.ingramcontent.com/pod-product-compliance
Lightning Source LLC
Chambersburg PA
CBHW072037190726
48294CB00005B/1302